CRYSTALLINE AURA

CIL GREGOIRE

CRYSTALLINE AURA

CIL GREGOIRE

PO Box 221974 Anchorage, Alaska 99522-1974
books@publicationconsultants.com—www.publicationconsultants.com

ISBN 978-1-59433-137-4
ebook 978-1-59433-169-5
Library of Congress Catalog Card Number: 2010929468

Manufactured in the United States of America.

Dedication

To my grandson
Samual
Who loves magic
As much as I.

Contents

Acknowledgments

I express special thanks to my reader mentors, Renamary Rauchenstein, Herman Thompson, John Connolly, and Becky Smith, who read through the first draft. Their comments and suggestions were invaluable.

Also thanks to Joe Gregoire, Lisa Caldwell, and John Connolly, once again, for reading over the manuscript as I worked through the rewrite.

Chapter 1
A New Beginning

Anthya appeared on the swirling blue and white planet standing in shoulder-high, golden-green prairie grass undulating in a gentle ripple of warm breeze under a flawless blue sky. Her creamy white smooth skin and long pale gold hair blended into the landscape, the dark cloak she wore a deep shadow immersed in the wave of grain. But the tranquil emptiness surrounding her contrasted sharply with the tense urgency of her mission. She had to find a safe hiding place for the crystal.

Theon approaches, the Oracle warned her in a telepathed message.

And then Theon was there, strong and fearsome...in the sea of grass...swimming toward her.

"Surrender the Oracle!" Theon demanded holding up a golden medallion in his powerful right hand...as a threat?...for protection? The rune etched upon it glowed as he slowly advanced. "I don't want to hurt you."

"Droclum must be destroyed!" Anthya shouted back with unwavering focus and determination. Drawing on the abundant molecular force around her, she hurled a bolt of energy in Theon's direction, then disappeared...but not before the satisfaction of hearing Theon bellow in pain.

From the vast prairie, Anthya teleported around the planet zigzagging back and forth from one hemisphere to another, erratically changing course, direction, and latitude, until the wispy trails of magic left behind became an intricately tangled web too confusing to untangle.

Hopefully this would give her the window of opportunity she needed to complete the mission. Failure was not an option.

Anthya clutched her long, flowing cloak around her, even though the crystal's aura protected her from the frigid wind blowing across the snow-covered glacier on which she stood. The sprawling glacier filled the steep-sloped mountain amphitheater and spilled over down the mountainside. Barren, brutally beautiful mountain peaks protruded from convoluted rivers of ice under a darkly foreboding blue and purple sky. *This is the place; I will hide it here.*

Anthya knew her stay would have to be brief to avoid detection. Tearing her mind from the immense surroundings, she reached into her cloak and pulled out a small, roughly cylindrical crystal glowing softly from within in ever-changing colors. The crystal floated between her thumb and forefinger.

"You will be safe here," Anthya spoke softly to the crystal.

Theon is near, the Oracle warned again.

"Then there isn't much time…sleep." And with a graceful, decisive flick of her arm, Anthya released the crystal…and then she was gone.

The crystal arched out over the surface of the glacier, rolled a short distance on the wind-hardened snow, and dropped into a crevasse, where it came to rest on an ice shelf far below. No longer glowing colorfully, it lay there seemingly lifeless, barely distinguishable from the ice and snow. Then the crevasse slammed shut with crushing power… but the crystal was not vulnerable to the glacier's formidable mountain-crunching force.

As night fell, it started to snow, and by morning, three feet of fresh snow blanketed the landscape. The snow continued to fall, off and on, throughout the long dark winter, adding to the glacier's mass. The cool, short summer that followed hardly melted a dent in the glacier's surface. With summer's inability to counteract the greater forces of winter, the glacier continued to grow.

Year after year the crystal became buried deeper and deeper into the expanding glacier, the sheer weight of the ice forcing it to flow continuously, imperceptibly forward. Year after year, decade after decade, century after century, millennium after millennium, the glacier inched forward carrying the crystal along with it. The ice groaned and moaned as it scoured out a broad valley. Crevasses opened and closed like the vast undulations of a crawling monster, pulverizing the mountain into gravel all along its path. Still for millennia the glacier continued to move forward carrying the crystal further down the mountainside.

Then gradually the earth became warmer and the glacier more fluid. Ice-melt cruised through cracks and fissures. As the earth continued to warm, the leading face of the glacier began to retreat, the melt run-off creating rivulets through the detritus left behind. The rivulets converged and became a stream, and as the glacier continued to calve, melt, and retreat, the stream joined by other streams became a mighty river.

The river took over where the glacier left off, carving a deeper, narrower valley through the glacial till. Slowly grasses and the hardiest of plant life encroached on the barren landscape, along with insects and birds. Soon small mammals appeared.

As a thin layer of topsoil developed, alders, willows, and berry bushes took hold. Over time, spruce trees found anchor for their roots in the primitive soil and dotted the landscape, followed by stands of birch, and the boreal forest became the home of even larger mammals; snowshoe hares, ground squirrels, coyotes, foxes, wolves, moose, and bear.

Then man appeared in the valley and gave the valley and river a name, Susitna. They called the land Alyeska and the mountain Denali. Later they called the land Alaska and the mountain McKinley. Man came for various reasons: to live off the land, to look for gold, to look for furs, or just to look. Eventually, man came with machinery and laid down railroad track through the remote valley roughly following the course of the river, providing accessibility to the beautiful, but rugged wilderness.

Still far from the fruiting valley, the crystal continued to sleep in its icy tomb. Once a tiny ice worm inadvertently touched the crystal, arousing it briefly from its slumber, but sensing no sentient life, it quickly slept again.

Then one day a massive chunk of ice calved off the glacier's leading edge. The mammoth boulder of ice crashed onto the rocks and ice below, and tumbled into the shallow braided stream.

Deeply embedded in the newly formed ice island slept the crystal. Throughout the short, cool summer; wind, water, and sun ate away at the ice, but by the coming of winter, though somewhat diminished in size, the grounded iceberg still remained. The winter freeze settled in, and snow blanketed the ice.

Seasons passed; summer came, and went, and came again. The ice chunk containing the crystal, now only a remnant of its former grandeur, could no longer endure the increasing warmth. The sun beat down on the crystal, now partially exposed, and melted away the ice chunk's last tenuous grasp.

Plop, the crystal dropped out of the ice, tumbling into the silky glacial stream…bobbing away in freedom.

The crystal's voyage downstream was slow at first, gradually picking up speed, careening over rocks and plunging through white water as it descended toward the broader valley below. But its progress was not totally free of obstacles or hindrances. Log jams and boulder jams blocked its way for periods of time, imprisoning the crystal until the river's seasonal rhythms and fluctuating water levels freed it once again.

As the valley leveled out, the crystal floated along serenely in the whispering silt-laden river. Eventually, an eddy in the current caused by submerged boulders sent the crystal drifting toward the shore. It floated out of the main current and into quieter water wobbling slowly toward the sandy riverbank.

Rahlys, slender but solid, wobbled down the aisle to the rocking motion of the little northbound flag-stop train hurling her toward her new home, her own remote log cabin in the woods. Spectacular views of golden yellow birch forest shimmering in the September sunlight, and dark green spruce spires standing out in stark relief against the surrounding gold, flashed by the rows of windows as the creaking, clacking train pushed onward. Continuing to wobble forward, Rahlys picked her way, stepping around kids and dogs, as she headed for the baggage car. Her stop was coming up and she wanted to be certain all her boxes, packed with food for survival and her art supplies, could be accounted for.

Lively conversation fell to silence as she pushed her way into the baggage car among similarly clad men in plaid cotton flannel shirts, jeans, hiking boots, and Carhartts, along with the cheery, rotund, busybody conductor who greeted her, breaking the ice.

"Ms. Rahlys!"

Rahlys nodded in acknowledgement. Four local men, ranging from strong and robust to grizzled and gray, turned to appraise her thin, almost middle-aged body, her pale blue eyes, and the hint of gray in her long, straw-brown hair. A flame of self-consciousness lit her face under the men's studious glances. She spotted her boxes stacked neatly together and went over to count them as the train slowed down.

"So you are the new owner of Trapper Bean's place," said a robust middle-aged man with brown hair that matched his eyes and a lean and muscular frame earned from rugged living. "I'm Vince, your neighbor to the north, by the way…how long are you up for?" he asked, eyeing her stack of boxes.

"All winter, and you?" Later the men will probably take bets on how long I will last, she thought disconcertingly, and braced herself for the gentle lurch of the train as it came to a stop.

One of the men, gray and grizzled, in his late fifties, flung his rifle over his shoulder, grabbed the hand rail along the outside of the door, and nimbly climbed out of the baggage car down to the rail bed below.

"And that's Grumpy George."

"I'm not grumpy," grumbled George from down below.

"George is your neighbor to the south."

Rahlys watched as Vince and the conductor handed George's boxes down to him. "Is that all of it?" the conductor asked as he counted his boxes.

"That's it," George shouted up, and stepped a little further back from the tracks.

The conductor radioed to the engineer. "All clear!" And the train pulled forward. "Next stop, Trapper Bean's trail."

Trapper Bean's trail…of course, it had been Trapper Bean's trail for thirty years. She couldn't help but wonder how long it would take before they called it Rahlys' trail. Ignoring the silent stares, she stacked her boxes, empty water jug, small hand-carry ice chest, backpack, and rifle closer to the baggage car door. Vince stepped up to help.

Rahlys counted her pieces again, then picked up her rifle as the train slowed down and came to a stop. Placing the rifle over her shoulder she started for the handrail as she had seen George do…but Vince scrambled down ahead of her.

"Wait!" the conductor halted her when she tried to follow. "I'll open the passenger door and put the steps down." The remaining silent men handed her supplies down to Vince while the conductor led her out the baggage car to the passenger door, setting an extra portable step down on the gravel rail bed. Standing near the bottom of the steps he guided her down, as though ready to catch her if she should stumble and fall.

"Thank you," she smiled up at him. By the time she joined her stuff on the side of the tracks, Vince was already back in the baggage car. "Thanks," she called up to him and waved.

"Sure." He smiled and nodded as the train pulled away and picked up speed, clacking on up the tracks. Rahlys watched the train go until it disappeared around a curve. And soon all was silent except for the murmur of the river as she stood alone, immersed in a vast wilderness, her cabin still a half-mile hike away.

The air felt cool after the warmth of the train. Rahlys zipped up her red fleece jacket, then loaded the rifle with four shells from her pocket, and put it on safety. The rifle was just an accessory she felt, for she seriously doubted she could get a shot off fast enough to stop a charging bear…even with the safety off.

"First task," she said out loud to no one, "move boxes into the edge of the woods and cover them with a tarp," which she had the foresight to bring. It will take quite a few trips to carry it all in she realized after hauling her precious supplies just a few feet into the woods and stashing them between two birch trees along the trail. By the time she was done, sweat covered her forehead and she had to unzip her jacket to let in some air.

After cooling down a bit, Rahlys was ready to start walking. With her pack on her back and the rifle slung over her shoulder, she picked up the small ice chest filled with perishables and an empty water jug, and stepped under the golden canopy of the forest. The fruity smell of ripe high bush cranberries permeated the air, and the trail squished soft and wet from recent rains under the soles of her hiking boots. To her relief, she saw no bears lurking in the bushes.

Warm sunshine chased away the earlier morning chill and a gentle breeze dabbed off the lingering dew as she hiked the well-worn, golden, leaf-strewn trail. The underbrush, so tall and lush and green just a few weeks before when she and Maggie first came to look at the cabin for sale, was thinning out as it withered into reds, browns, and yellows.

Rahlys felt the stress and bustle of the outside world drain from her mind and the exertion of the hike warm her body as she reached the crest of the first incline. With corporate restraints and deadline stress now abandoned, she breathed in deeply the clean, cranberry scented air, exhilarated by her new-found freedom.

Growing up on her parents' homestead, Rahlys had always enjoyed the woods, but in the heat of youth and ambition, she had left the isolation to seek the offerings of a greater world, starting with Anchorage, and then on to Seattle. After art school, she landed a job that turned into a career with an advertising firm right there in Seattle. She thought she could never be happier; she was doing what she truly loved.

Of course, one's perspective of happiness and success becomes redefined over time, and Rahlys became increasingly disillusioned with urban and corporate life, and increasingly yearned for the a return to a simpler, freer way of life. Now she was returning to a rustic lifestyle to paint, and to recapture the feel of living in the mythical woods of her youth.

A light breeze rattled the golden leaves of the birch trees. They tinkled and shimmered in the sunlight, many losing their grasp in a shower of leaves. By the time she reached the top of the second rise, she was so warm she had to stop. Dropping her load, she took off her jacket and tied it by the sleeves around her waist. She lifted her long hair momentarily from the back of her neck to cool off as another playful, passing breeze produced another shower of golden leaves. Then Rahlys picked up her burdens once more and moved on.

The trail leveled out from here with only minor ups and downs making it possible to maintain a steady pace. "Yoo-hoo!" she sang out periodically to alert any bear of her presence. "I'm suppose to make noise so I don't startle you, Bear!" she called out into the silent woods. But the hike was pleasantly uneventful, and after some time she was at her spring, the cabin in sight on the next rise.

Stopping at the spring, she reached for the tin cup conveniently hanging from a broken tree branch. Filling it with spring water that spouted out of the end of a pipe, she drank her fill. The water was refreshingly cold. Leaving the larger water container for later, Rahlys took a smaller water bottle from her pack, emptying out the tap water from town, and re-filled it. A mere scratch of a trail branched off from the spring to a small plywood sauna painted red. "Alright, almost there." She flung her pack on her back, picked up the rifle and ice chest, and climbed the final rise.

In a sunny, overgrown clearing overlooking a creek stood a tightly-constructed, two-story log cabin with dovetail corner notching and gable windows shining golden in the autumn sun. A long sunny porch graced the front of the house, while a smaller utility porch serviced the back. There were also several out buildings. A wood shed, a generator shed, a storage shed, and an outhouse graced the back edge of the clearing. To Rahlys it was a palace; finally she was home.

"Araaak!"

The raven's sudden loud squawk in the immense silence startled Rahlys. Then she spotted him perched on the woodshed, his radiant black feathers gleaming in the sunshine. Probably looking for whatever he can scavenge, she thought. There had been a raven around when she and Maggie came to look at the place. Pickings must have been good when Trapper Bean was around…but Rahlys had little to offer.

The raven's visit a few weeks ago had inspired her to start a painting using the raven as a subject. She wanted to do some more sketches, but there wasn't time for that now; she needed to hike in more of her supplies before nightfall. But to insure future visits, Rahlys dropped her pack on the back porch and reached into it for the remains of a muffin, which she tossed in his direction. The raven hesitated, wary of her intentions, but as soon as she turned her attention away, he closed in on the muffin, and taking a couple of hops to achieve take-off, flew away. *Hopefully he will return.* Then Rahlys stepped up onto the back porch, and unlocked the door to her new home.

It was cool inside the cabin. She left the door open to let in the warmer outside air. The first floor was one great room with windows all around that let in light and offered vistas of the surrounding woods. A built-in counter divided the kitchen from the living room, and stairs led to a bedroom above. The cabin was sparsely furnished with sturdy, rustic furniture built by Jack Bean. There was a large table with four chairs in one corner, and a massive armchair and a daybed by the large living room window offering a view of the mountain.

Rahlys unloaded her pack, putting the food items away in the pantry and dropped the ice chest down into the root cellar under the kitchen floor. Then she went out the front door to sit in the sun where it was warmer. What a beautiful day…but an underlying nip in the air promised a cold night. After a brief rest, she shut the cabin doors, and taking her rifle and empty pack, she headed back down the trail for another load.

Raven flew westward along the creek searching its banks, hoping to find a half-eaten salmon carcass left behind by an obliging bear. A broad shallow section of the creek was one of the bears' favorite fishing spots, and with a little luck, he would find a salmon head with some lingering tidbits of flesh still dangling from it. There! Just what he was looking for, and not a bear in sight!

Raven landed near the salmon carcass, and just to be on the safe side, dragged the delicacy a little further from the creek edge, under cover, before indulging. Then, with his hunger momentarily defused, Raven decided to visit the river, since it was so conveniently close.

Raven took off toward the river, but the thermals were so seductively perfect, he could not resist taking a joy-riding detour, soaring on the air currents high above the forested hills and river below. Finally, he spiraled down and landed on a gnarled, weathered log marooned on the sandy beach near the mouth of the creek…and sat peacefully attentive as he listened respectfully to the murmuring of the river, when something caught his eye.

Perched on the log, Raven watched sunlight glint rhythmically off the surface of something floating in the water as it wobbled to shore. He hopped off his perch and stepped up to investigate as the light-reflecting object hesitantly touched the sandy beach. After cocking his head sideways to get a better look at the unfamiliar object, Raven decided to give it the old beak test. With an air of investigative importance, he gave the mystery object a good, hard peck.

The crystal woke up, glowed brightly,…and then dimmed.

Raven, still not sure what to make of it, gave the object another resounding peck. The crystal brightened and dimmed again. Running out of options, he picked up the crystal in his powerful beak, and gave it a jaw-breaking squeeze. Crystal and raven lit up, glowing softly in ever-changing colors, the crystal in pretty pastels, while Raven's shiny black feathers flashed iridescent. Startled, he opened his beak and dropped the crystal onto the sand.

"Araaak!" he cried with profound astonishment. The raven paced around in utter confusion as he tried to sort it all out. Then, as though compelled, he picked up the crystal with his beak, and taking off with ease, flew away from the river eastward following the creek.

Rahlys had packed in the last load for the day; the rest could wait. All the food boxes and her art supplies were safely in the cabin and a warm fire crackled in the woodstove. She unpacked her small table easel, paints and brushes, and the unfinished raven painting, placing it on the easel. "I better bring the water jug up from the spring before I settle down to paint," she said out loud. Then she heard the raven's piercing cry.

"Araaak! Araaak!"

Grabbing a sketch pad and her red fleece jacket, Rahlys hurried out the back door. The raven was prancing up and down cackling loudly.

"Kla-wock! Kla-wock!" he chortled as he flexed his wings and puffed out his hackle. Rahlys sat on the porch step and hastily sketched, capturing in quick, fluid strokes the raven's large chunky body, his ample beak, and the beautiful long black feathers of his flexing wings. She overlapped sketches as the raven changed positions; it was a study in motion.

"What are you so excited about?" Rahlys finally asked, putting her sketching down.

"Araaak!" the raven answered. Then with his beak, he picked up something glowing off the ground. Rahlys couldn't make out what the raven held and approached the agitated bird to get a closer look.

"What do you have there?" she asked with curiosity. The raven took a couple of steps closer, seemingly no longer as wary of her presence, and dropped the glowing crystal on the ground in front of her. Then he flew up and landed in a nearby tree where he watched as Rahlys stooped for a closer look at the object the raven had brought. She reached out to touch it, but hesitated with uncertainty. It looked like a crystal of some sort. Odd how it reflected light, almost as though the light came from within.

"Araaak," the raven called encouragingly.

Rahlys reached down and cautiously touched the stone. As soon as her fingers made contact, the crystal burst into brightness. Quickly she drew her hand back, and the brightness dimmed. Should she attempt to pick it up? After a couple of uneventful minutes, Rahlys reached for the crystal again, carefully picking it up. The crystal burst into light, and Rahlys felt a strange quivering surge of energy rush through her. Startled, she dropped the crystal, but to her astonishment, instead of it succumbing to gravity and falling to the ground, the crystal flew up and hovered, shining softly in the air before her.

"Where did you find this?" She glanced at the raven and then back at the crystal, feeling silly addressing the bird, but there was no one around to pass judgment.

"Araaak! Araaak!" the raven answered. Then to her surprise there was the faintest tingling in her head as images of the crystal floating to the bank of the river, flittered across her brain.

Totally baffled, Rahlys stared at the crystal in awe. She backed away from it, and it followed her. Gathering her courage, she moved toward it, after all the raven didn't seem hurt from contact, plucked the crystal out of the air and shoved it into her jacket pocket, quickly zipping it shut. The crystal did not try to escape. She felt with her fingers through the fabric of her jacket reassuring herself it was there.

The crystal dimmed, but remained alert. Satisfied, the raven flew off.

Rahlys headed down to the spring. The sun was setting behind the distant, forested, western ridge. As the jug filled, she took in the radiant sunset of lavender, orange, and pink spilling across the sky. The colors spread out and intensified into a magical brilliance, then slowly, as the sun sank further down below the horizon, the gorgeous colors began to fade. With the disappearance of the sun, the air rapidly began to chill. It's going to get cold tonight, Rahlys realized as she screwed the cap back on the nearly full jug, as full as she could comfortably carry, and headed back up to the cabin.

There is an intruder.

What? The trail to the cabin passed right by the spring, and no one had passed by. Where did the idea that there was an intruder come from, anyway? She dismissed the thought. But as she crested the rise, she could see the back door to the cabin was wide open. Had she failed to push the door close all the way? Perhaps so; or the wind could have blown the door open…although there wasn't much wind. As a precaution, Rahlys set the water jug down and peered inside through a window.

To her surprise, there in the middle of the living room was a large black bear. He sniffed the air as he headed for the kitchen and her freshly stocked pantry. Her easel lay smashed on the floor, the unfinished painting trampled on by a muddy bear paw. Rahlys' heart pounded as she watched the scene unfold. What should she do? She couldn't just let the bear trash her cabin. And the rifle she had so faithfully carried up and down the trail was now inside the cabin, unloaded.

The bear lumbered to the pantry and ripped the door off its hinges, sending it crashing to the floor. She needed to act fast. In desperation she formulated a plan. Since the back door was still wide open, she ran around to the front shouting and banging on the cabin in the hopes the bear would obligingly leave. Reaching the front door, she opened it and banged it shut hard several times. The disturbance caused the bear to pause and look in her direction, but it wasn't distracted for long. Almost immediately he turned back to the pantry sniffing its contents, knocking boxes, cans, and jars to the floor. The food supply that she had worked so hard to bring in was in jeopardy. She would have to take more drastic measures. With her heart pumping fit to burst, Rahlys raced into the cabin waving her arms and shouting at the top of her lungs, "Out! Get out of here!"

This time the bear decided to respond! Instantly, it turned, dashed across the cabin floor, took a running leap over the daybed, and crashed through the large living room window on his way to the woods.

"No! Not through the window!" Rahlys cried in despair as bear and shattered glass exited, leaving an empty hole framed in jagged fragments, open to the encroaching night. Frantically, Rahlys ran outside. Hundreds, perhaps thousands of shards of broken glass littered the ground. "My window!" she cried frenziedly, waving her arms from the shattered glass on the ground to the gaping hole…willing the window back together again. How would she ever get it replaced?

And then…unbelievably…inexplicably…the myriad shards of glass sprang up from the ground, coalesced together in mid-air, and landed back into place…unscratched and unmarred in any way, exactly as it had been before. The window was whole once again.

What? Rahlys mouthed speechlessly. Her heart pounded in her ears with mounting fear, her mind stunned with disbelief as she stretched her brain to the limit trying to understand. She stood there for a while unable to move, or to speak, or to think. *Had it really happened?* She was questioning her own senses.

She looked at the ground; it was clear of any broken glass. She looked at the window the bear had jumped through, no longer shattered, there in the cabin wall. Repeatedly, the scenes replayed in her head; the bear in the cabin, the shattered window, and then the image of the window springing back whole again. *Am I losing my mind?* Darkness was setting in and she began to shiver from the chill air. In a daze she headed for the warmth of the cabin.

Upon entering, she made sure the doors were firmly shut. It was already dark inside, so she lit a lamp. There was the pantry door on the kitchen floor with spilled food all around it, and the easel on the floor in the living room, tangible proof the bear had been there. She picked up her easel, setting it back upright. It was undamaged; the bear had only knocked it over. Moving the pantry door out of the way, she cleaned up the mess, and then she spotted her unfinished watercolor still attached to its art board backing. The bear's huge, muddy paw print nearly covered the paper. With the paw print still in hand, she walked over to the large west window and touched it, reassuring herself it was real. Her fingers met firm, solid resistance.

"The crystal!" Rahlys unzipped her jacket pocket and out flew the crystal, spinning slowly as it made its way around the room, then came to a stop, hovering in front of her. "You are the source of this madness!"

The crystal did not respond.

"What are you? Where did you come from?"

But whether it couldn't or wouldn't, the crystal did not respond. It was crazy for her to expect it to. The inexplicable phenomenon made her feel ill at ease. Could the crystal really be responsible for what had happened?

With an effort to return to normalcy, Rahlys refilled the wood stove, and moved the kettle over to the hot spot for tea. While the tea water heated, she took out cheese from the root cellar, and crackers from the door-less cupboard. The crystal followed her every move.

She needed to find a place to keep it while she figured things out.

For now, she returned the crystal to the pocket of her jacket, hanging it on a peg by the door.

The water boiled, she made tea, and barely ate. It had been a highly eventful day. Unanswerable questions filled her head until exhaustion finally won out, and with her last reserve of energy, Rahlys climbed the stairs to her bed.

Rahlys fell asleep instantly. At first she just slept…but then she started to dream of crystalline mountains, of blue-green and orange valleys, and of golden seas. She traveled through the vast void of space between galaxies, and for millennia she slept deep in a glacier as it moaned and groaned down the mountainside. Then after a while the dreams faded…and she just slept.

Chapter 2
Discovery

Rahlys slept late into the next morning, waking up groggy from over-sleeping. To her pleasant surprise, the cabin was still warm. She sat up in bed, the events of the day before flashing through her mind. The raven. The crystal. The bear. And a new life in a new home. For years Rahlys had thrived on pressure, schedules, and deadlines. But today she would establish a new routine of simple living.

Upon coming downstairs, she checked the wood stove first, opening the damper to let in more air, then easing open the door. Inside, the last charred chunk of wood coal glowed from the additional oxygen. The airtight stove did a great job holding a fire overnight. Rahlys stirred the coals and fed the stove split rounds of birch. She would have to replenish her firewood supply on the porch, she noted. Fortunately, Trapper Bean believed in stocking up on firewood;…the wood shed was full. Rahlys put on a pot of coffee, then stepped out to greet the day, grabbing her jacket as she went out the door.

The cloudy, cool, fall day that greeted her made her shiver. She remembered the crystal was in her pocket as she hugged the jacket to her on her way to the outhouse. "Magic crystal, keep me warm." And then…was it her imagination, or was she suddenly warmer?

"Araaak! Araaak!"

The raven. Rahlys stepped out of the outhouse. The wind had picked up, and the sun was barely peaking through the clouds. Golden leaves poured down all around her carpeting the ground. The trees looked bare compared to the day before. She felt the contour of the crystal through her jacket pocket with her fingers as she searched the edge of the forest for the raven. *Where are you?*

"Araaak!" the raven called again as he glided down into the sunny clearing and landed several feet away from her in another drizzle of golden birch leaves.

"Good, morning, Raven! What mischief are you up to today?"

"Araaak!" An image of a muffin, like the one she had fed him, flittered across her mind.

Rahlys smiled over the pictorial message, "I'm all out of muffins, but I have an apple in the root cellar, if you like...," but before she could finish her sentence, the raven flew off. "I can't help it if you're so impatient."

The aroma of coffee perking assailed her senses as she entered the cabin. She hung up her jacket, and gratefully poured herself a cup, sipping on it immediately. Then setting the cup on the table, she sat in front of the unfinished, bear-trampled painting of the raven, reliving the event in her mind.

Thus occupied, Rahlys reached blindly for her coffee cup a short distance away. The cup met her half way. Sooner than she had expected the cup was in her hand. She looked at the cup curiously. *It must have been closer to me than I thought.* But in light of recent events, she decided to experiment. Setting the cup back down, a little further away this time, she placed her hand in readiness on the table, and willed the cup to her. Instantly, the cup appeared in her hand.

Rahlys rushed to her jacket hanging on the wall, and unzipped the pocket containing the crystal. The crystal floated out and spiraled around slowly, glowing softly in ever-changing colors. Examining the crystal in the light of a new day, she stared at it with wonder...and fear. "What are you?" she asked mystified.

The crystal did not respond.

Plucking the crystal out of the air she held it up, staring into it... the crystal brightened in her hand. There were so many questions she needed answered. Was it possible to communicate with the crystal somehow? Concentrating, Rahlys focused her thoughts on it. *Where did you come from? How did you get here? What do you want from me?*

The glow intensified but the crystal did not 'speak.' When she ceased at her effort, easing her hold, it flew out her hand.

Had the crystal warned her about the bear? It felt like someone or something had spoken in her mind. And had she really received visual messages from the raven? Those images had been accompanied by tingling, flexing sensations in her brain. She could still feel a faint soreness in her head, like the ache of a muscle that has been forced into strenuous activity it is not conditioned for.

Rahlys laid out a fresh sheet of watercolor paper on the table with her sketches of the raven all around her, along with her paints. The crystal hovered above, adding light to the area. *Brighter*, she requested lightly, and the crystal brightened, providing more light. She was set, but before starting, she conjured an apple from the root cellar for breakfast, and despite the soreness in her head, sliced it into wedges with intense mental concentration.

Holding an apple slice in one hand and a paint brush in the other, Rahlys turned to her work, sketching freely. Quickly the raven took form in overlapping motion, fragmented, strutting around on the page, the crystal in his beak emitting its strange, colorful, hexagonal light.

Letting the first layer of pigment dry, Rahlys stood up and stretched. The crystal dimmed and followed her as she paced about the room. She knew she needed to find a safer place to keep the crystal than in her jacket pocket. Where should she keep it? Then suddenly Rahlys noticed, hanging on a peg on the wall, a small leather pouch that blended in so well with the log wall, it had gone unnoticed until now. She took down the pouch, caressing the supple leather, and examined the excellent workmanship. "It looks like one of those little talisman pouches that early humans wore around their necks," she said out loud, then turned to the crystal. "Here is your new home." Directing her thoughts, she conjured the crystal into the pouch, and pulled the little leather drawstrings, closing it tightly. A long leather thong, woven into the sides of the pouch, formed a loop large enough to go over her head. Putting it on, she tucked the pouch inside her shirt where it settled between her breasts.

Then her eyes fell on the severed pantry door. Could it be repaired in the same manner as the window? Pointing from the severed cabinet door to the open pantry, she imagined it fixed, willing it back together. To her astonishment still, the pantry door flew up and landed in place. Rahlys examined it, opening the door and closing it again; it was perfect in every way.

What else might she be capable of doing? The thought was as exciting as it was frightening. Across the room Rahlys spotted a book she had found on the floor behind the daybed. She conjured it to her; instantly, it appeared in her hand. Then she sent it back to the daybed.

Since she could teleport objects, could she teleport herself? Rahlys closed her eyes and concentrated, breathing deeply as she mentally placed herself outside in front of the cabin. And then she was there. She felt the cool, fresh air on her face even before she opened her eyes… wide! There, just a few feet in front of her, stood an angry bull moose with ears raised in alarm over Rahlys' sudden close appearance. *Oops! I should have looked out the window and checked the clearing before teleporting out into it.*

*Back in the cabin! Back in the cabin…*she willed with all her might, and then, to her immense relief, she was back inside. Rahlys ran to the window, her heart pumping hard in her breast as she watched the moose charge the spot where she had stood only moments before. It had been a close call; she would have to learn to use caution.

Struggling to regain calmness, Rahlys grabbed her sketchpad and sketched the confused animal in several poses as it puzzled over her sudden disappearance. After a while, the moose ambled over to some brush at the edge of the clearing, the incident apparently quickly forgotten, and munched briefly on leafless alder branches. Then it moved on, disappearing into the forest.

Rahlys set down her sketchpad. It was time to do some chores, and there were still boxes of supplies to haul in. With pack and gun in hand, she stepped out ready to head down to the tracks for the first load, when she was struck with an idea. Perhaps she could just conjure the boxes to her…right here on the porch would be fine. It was a long distance, but it certainly was worth a try.

Rahlys could picture the last three boxes of clothing and household items wrapped in a blue tarp, wedged between two birch trees. She visualized the boxes and blue tarp on the porch beside her, willing them there…and then there they were. The crystal's magic had saved her a lot of time and effort.

Joyfully, she unpacked the last boxes, putting the items away. The time she had captured, she used to add another layer of pigment to the raven painting, giving it more depth and detail. Pleased with the results of her work, she stepped back. It would have to dry before she could do more.

Rahlys headed for the woodshed to replenish her kindling supply. She had become skilled with an axe as a young woman, and remembered the important principles. Bring the axe blade straight down perpendicular to the wood, not in a swinging arc that brings the axe blade toward your legs. Men have strong shoulder muscles; therefore, take short, hard swings with a axe. But a woman has stronger back muscles than shoulder muscles, so must lift the axe over her head, putting her back into it to obtain sufficient force.

Choosing a dry spruce round from the stack, Rahlys placed it on end on the chopping block and whacked it hard in the center with the splitting maul. The wood cracked loudly, but remained whole. She swung at it hard a couple of more times before it split into. Putting the maul aside and picking up the axe, Rahlys split each half-round into several thin wedges, then sliced up the wedges into a pile of gleaming white kindling. With a quick mental thought, she tried transporting the loose pile of kindling at her feet to the porch. But instead of the pile appearing in the box by the back door as anticipated, it fantailed out in an arch, landing strewn across the ground from the wood shed to the porch, the leading piece falling far short of its destination. A lack of cohesion in the bundle had defeated her effort. As she walked to the porch, Rahlys mentally lifted each stick of kindling into her arm, marched up the steps with the bundle, and deposited the kindling in the wooden box by the door.

She needed to replenish her firewood supply, too. Giving her fledgling mental powers a rest, Rahlys grabbed the orange plastic sled Trapper Bean had left behind, and returned to the woodshed. Even without snow, it was easier pulling the sled over the grass, still moist from the morning dew, than carrying the heavy chunks of wood across the yard in her arms. Several trips later, her convenient firewood stack on the porch was replenished.

With the chores done, Rahlys was ready to return to her painting. But by now the sun had come out in full force and a warm, sunny, autumn day beckoned. Instead of settling down to work, Rahlys lingered outdoors to enjoy perhaps the last warm day of the season. She wandered over to the edge of the forest and walked a short distance beneath the nearly bare trees. Turning to look back in the direction of the cabin, she saw it still in sight through the thinning foliage. At her feet, golden leaves filled the slight depression of a game trail, creating a denser golden ribbon through the mottled gold-leaf strewn forest floor. She followed the trail deeper into the woods. Unexpectedly, a ground squirrel suddenly dashed up a nearby spruce tree, chattering angrily over being disturbed.

The sudden explosion of sound in such immense quiet startled her, causing her to jump, but the narrow rut of a trail could not accommodate the move, and she landed on a cushiony throne of lichen covering a decaying log. Her seat was so comfortable and the forest setting so charming, she remained seated despite the seeping dampness on her bottom. The squirrel, deciding to ignore her, resumed its task of running along the spruce branches, detaching an abundant crop of spruce cones by gnawing the cones loose with its teeth, then letting them drop to the ground. Later he would certainly collect the harvest and store it for the winter. Wishing she had her sketch pad with her, she made some mental sketches nevertheless.

Over the next few days, the warm days of autumn turned cold and drizzly. When the clouds finally parted, temperatures dropped well below freezing overnight, revealing sun-glittering frost the next morning. Rahlys stared out the window as she sipped her morning coffee. Most of the trees were already bare of leaves, but some still sported a thin golden crown. The last remaining leaves continued to drop, a few at a time. The ground's golden carpet turned brown.

Nibbling on an apple wedge, Rahlys studied the painting on the table of the squirrel in the frenzy of harvest. Vividly displayed on the easel was the finished painting of the raven with the crystal.

"Araaak! Araaak!" The raven's cries pierced the walls of the cabin.

Grabbing a hand full of apple wedges, Rahlys rushed out the door as aerial views of her cabin and yard flittered across her mind. The images had to be coming from the raven! The raven spiraled down for a landing just a few feet away from her.

Rahlys tossed him an apple wedge. The raven took the necessary step up to it and started eating. She was pleased that he seemed to trust her now and didn't back away with the treat before digging in. She watched intently as he consumed the apple with obvious relish. There was something special about the raven. The crystal must have enhanced him with magic. She threw him another slice of apple as the sun warmed the cold earth and melted the frost.

A visitor is approaching.

What? She looked around warily. Was the bear returning? Rahlys eyed the cabin longingly as a source of relative safety.

"Hello! Anyone home?" A human voice called out, not from the trail as one would expect, but from the woods. Rahlys turned toward the direction of the call, throwing down the last couple of pieces of apple. Grabbing the opportunity, the raven scooped up one of the slices in his beak and flew off toward the creek as Vince entered the clearing wearing a small pack and carrying a rifle. "Hello," he said again as he spotted her near the cabin.

"Hi! You came through the woods?"

He approached, removing his cap. "Yes, there's a game trail that runs along the ridge overlooking the big swamp. It's a fairly nice hike in the spring and fall, and half the distance of taking the people trails via the railroad tracks. I often visited Bean this way when the season was right."

To Rahlys's surprise, thoughts and images of Bean brushed her mind. "Would you like some water?" she offered.

"I have some in my pack. Thanks. The place hasn't changed much." His eyes roamed around, then settled back on her. "I brought you a house-warming present." Propping his rifle up against the cabin, Vince took off his pack and set it on the porch. "I'm not much of a cook, but I bake a mean loaf of bread." From his pack, he handed her a bag containing the most perfect loaf of bread she had ever seen.

"Why thank-you!" She could not help but be impressed. "Won't you come in?"

Vince followed her inside. There was little to see in the nearly bare cabin. His eyes landed on the painting of the raven boldly displayed on the easel. "Nice painting!"

"Thanks!"

"The cabin looks a bit empty."

"Empty, what do you mean?"

"Well, Jack spent most of his spare time making leather goods for the local tourist trade, pouches and bags, some vests and moccasins, things like that. There were always piles of stuff stacked on the floor, and hanging from pegs on the wall."

Rahlys picked up drifting threads of thought and fleeting images of the cabin as it had looked when Bean lived here. She had to admit the walls were bare. Eventually she hoped to cover them with her work, but it would take time, and most of her matting and framing supplies were in town.

Vince examined the painting in progress of the squirrel clinging to a spruce branch, chewing off spruce cones that fell to a pile on the ground below. "Interesting point of view. So you are an artist." It was as much a question as it was a statement.

"I worked as a commercial artist for a company in Seattle for many years. Now I'm working freelance. Have a seat."

Vince sat at the familiar table, remembering his visits with Jack. Rahlys cleared the table, moving her work to the daybed.

"What brought you to Alaska?" he asked.

"I was born here actually, grew up in a remote log cabin in the Matanuska Valley." Rahlys was pleased by the surprised look on Vince's face. It was not the answer he had expected. She sensed he had come over to check on her, expecting to find an inexperienced woman in distress in the woods. "My parents passed away several years ago, and the cabin is long gone. Now there's a subdivision where the old homestead used to be."

Avoiding his gaze she stooped down, opened the root cellar door, and from the suspended shelf within, brought up a pitcher of tea, and a jar of homemade blueberry jam to go with the bread. She placed the items on the table. "How long have you lived up here?"

"Seven years. After retiring from the Marines, I wanted to be as far away from humanity as possible."

"Wife? Children?"

"No…unfortunately…I've probably missed out on an important part of life."

"And what do you do with all your time so far from humanity?"

"I write action/adventure novels."

"About your life?"

"No, well, yes…but not directly."

"So, how many novels have you written?"

"I've published two, and I'm working on a third."

Rahlys sliced the bread and poured tea, and they ate quietly enjoying each others company. Then Vince broke the silence.

"I'm going into town on the train tomorrow and coming back Saturday if you need anything," he offered.

"Actually, my friend Maggie is coming up for the week-end on Saturday's train and she's bringing some things up. But there is something you could do for me."

"Oh, what's that?"

"I need a lesson on handling and maintaining a generator," she said as they ate.

"Sure. Bean's generator won't start for you?"

"I haven't tried to start it yet, I wanted to know more about it first. It's getting dark earlier every day, and the oil lamps really aren't bright enough to paint by." There were light fixtures, switches, and receptacles wired in throughout the cabin. "By the way, your bread is excellent. I could use a lesson in baking bread, too."

"And the blueberry jam is superb. Did you make it?"

"No, Maggie did. She came up with me from Seattle, and thinks picking berries and making jam is mandatory if you live in Alaska."

After lunch they walked out to the generator shed together. Rahlys carried a notebook with her.

"You're going to take notes?"

"Yes." She smiled up at him.

Vince instructed Rahlys on how to check the oil, and had her add some from the stockpile Bean had left behind. Then they checked the fuel tank. Rahlys took note of her fuel supply. Eventually she would have to have a drum freighted up by rail. He showed her how to choke the engine; then he flipped the start button to 'On' and pulled the rope. The generator sputtered and died. Vince pulled the rope again, and the generator spitted angrily until he turned off the choke, then the engine picked up speed, smoothing out into a steady noise. Once the engine was running smoothly, Rahlys flipped on the breaker to the house.

Back at the cabin with the doors shut, the generator was barely audible. Rahlys went about turning on switches, delighted with the prospect of cheerful, bright light for the upcoming long, dark nights, Vince enjoying her delight.

"I usually leave one light on when I go to turn the power off," he said, "so that when I turn it on again, I can see right away if the electricity is on in the house. When shutting down, it's all in reverse. Turn the breaker off first to take the load off, then shut off the motor. Always check the oil. That's the most important thing. If you don't let it run out of oil, you will be alright."

Leaving a light on, they went back to the generator shed and Rahlys shut off the power. "Thank you so much."

"It was my pleasure." His smile was reassuring. "Well, I better get moving. I still have chores to do before nightfall." He picked up his pack from the porch, and his rifle leaning against the house, and headed off into the forest. Rahlys watched him go. It was a bit reassuring to have a neighbor close by, only a mile away, in case she ever needed help.

As soon as Vince disappeared from sight, the raven swooped down out of nowhere, picked up the last apple wedge off the ground, and took off again, continuing on his way. She was alone.

Rahlys went back into the cabin and conjured the book she had found behind the daybed to her hand. She read the cover. *Cold Fire and Hot Ice* by Vince Bradley. There was an inscription inside, *To Jack, my friend and mentor, thanks for all your help*. It was signed simply, Vince. With curious interest, Rahlys sat down and began to read.

When darkness approached, she started the generator, and flooded the cabin with light. In jubilant celebration she cooked a dinner for one of brown rice and sautéed vegetables on the wood stove, and opened a bottle of wine she had been saving for a special occasion. Then she painted into the night.

Much later, when she made her way to the generator shed, the northern lights shimmered in wavering bands of green, red, and white across the cold night sky. She shut off the generator and gazed with wonder at the brilliant display of swirling light. Here was magic on a grander canvas than she could ever paint.

Anthya and Zayla walked barefooted across golden sands under a sparkling yellow sky. Their footprints disappeared behind them as they walked. The blue-green and orange foliage of the jungle covered the hills that rose from the sandy plain and looked out toward the golden sea. Beautifully colored shells, all shapes and sizes, and several crystals, reflecting light, defined the high tide mark. A warm sea breeze blew their light sleeveless dresses against their legs. "I chose this isolated beach for our walk for its beauty as well as its remoteness," Zayla said, obviously enjoying the warm sand between her toes, for a smile graced her aged, worry-worn face. Her long black hair was streaked with gray, but her deep, dark eyes sparkled, reflecting infinite wisdom.

Anthya was as light in feature as Zayla was dark, her long, straight hair, the palest yellow, her complexion creamy white, her eyes the lightest shade of bluish gray. "It is also a favorite spot of mine," Anthya said...for it was true. She and Zayla had conferred here often, and it was from an outcrop in the cliff straight ahead that she had collected the crystal that had become the Oracle of Light.

"So, you have news for me?" Zayla asked looking deeply into Anthya's eyes, to the depths of her soul.

"Yes, the Oracle of Light has found a Guardian." She paused. "But I have been unsuccessful in finding the Dark Orb...and destroying it."

"Don't be so hard on yourself, Anthya, it was not meant to be. And anyway, it is too late now. The Orb of Darkness has also found a Guardian. Fate is now in their hands. All we can do is try and help the Guardian of Light in any way that we can."

Chapter 3
Fear and Adversity

Small, puny Franklin walked through the warm humid night alone. He turned into a dark alley, unafraid. That had not always been the case. Usually he was plenty afraid, but now he could kick butt. A feral cat, one of many that roamed post-Katrina New Orleans, jumped out from the darker shadows, startling him out of his thoughts. Franklin, his eyes adjusting to the darkness, extended his arm, aimed at the cat with his finger, and pulled the trigger of an imaginary gun. The cat screeched, stiffened, and fell over dead. A satisfied smile glimmered across Franklin's solemn face. Not so long ago, he would have salivated over the dead cat, but now he could feed his dark, scrawny body anything he desired.

Leaving the alley, he turned onto the sidewalk of a brightly lit street, with the smell of fried oysters in the air, and came upon a bistro that opened out onto the sidewalk. The server behind the counter placed a freshly constructed, paper-wrapped po'boy sandwich on the counter and turned to get the drink order while the customer continued to browse over the offerings. Franklin walked by, hands in pocket, and teleported the sandwich and the soft drink to his secret hiding place, then circled the block back to the dark alley.

When he was sure no one was looking, he slipped behind a dumpster and pushed against the masonry at ground level. A slab moved with a dull grating sound, revealing an opening barely large enough for even Franklin's undernourished body to slither through. Once through, he sat up maneuvering his body carefully in the narrow space, and conjured the stone slab back into place. The aroma of the fried oyster po'boy permeated the long, narrow crevice between two windowless walls little more than a foot apart. The ends of this narrow space had been sealed off forming a continuous facade on the outside, concealing a long, thin rectangle of forgotten real estate. Above, two roofs sloped down coming within inches of each other, leaving only a thin line of sky above. It would not be the place to hold up during a rainstorm. In the center of the strip of slightly muddy ground with a bit of straggly grass growing, was an old, rusty drainage grate over a trough that led who knows where. Franklin reached into his pocket and pulled out a smooth, round orb about the size of a large marble. A tiny red and orange flame flickered softly through smoky gray swirls within the orb.

Light. The orb brightened at his mental command. Placing the shining orb suspended in air, Franklin grabbed the sandwich, unwrapped it, and bit into it hungrily.

Franklin had found this place accidentally when running from the police. He had hidden behind the dumpster, squeezing into an impossibly small space between the dumpster and the wall when the wall gave a little from the pressure of his body against it. Franklin turned around to investigate, and with some effort, he managed to move a small slab of masonry revealing the empty space. By the time the cops had arrived, Franklin was securely hidden on the other side.

To pass the time, Franklin had traversed the whole length of the long, narrow space, inspecting it carefully, then he squeezed his way down to sit and wait out the threat. As he sat in boredom, his finger toyed with the smooth surface of a marble buried in the hard, dark, delta mud. He looked down at it without real interest at first, but to his surprise the marble appeared to be glowing under his caressing finger. With cracked, dirty fingernails, slowly, he chiseled the orb out of the hard-packed ground. Since then, things had changed.

Halfway through his sandwich, Franklin reached over, opened the soda, and guzzled a third of it down, after which he devoured the rest of the po'boy. Soon he would no longer fit in this tight space, especially eating like this. When he finished his dinner, he plucked the orb out of the air and sent it a mental command, *Off.* The orb extinguished to its usual dark glow. Placing the orb back in his pocket, he moved the slab concealing the entrance, and listened. All was quiet in the alleyway. Franklin teleported himself back out into the alley, then with a wave of his hand, set the masonry back in place.

A waning moon had risen high in the night sky, throwing some light into the alley. Then as luck would have it, just as Franklin was heading out, three punks he recognized, and had had encounters with before, always ending in pain and misery for him, entered the alley.

"Well, look who we have here," the hard-faced, heavyset youth he knew was called Jake taunted as the gang slowly approached. Franklin stood his ground, concentrated, and sent a powerful mental punch to Jake's left jaw. Jake's head swung sharply as though he had received a hard right in a boxing ring.

"Aw, shit!" Jake hollered grabbing his jaw, dancing in pain. "What kind of voodoo is that?" he cried. The other two paused with uncertainty at the sight and sound of Jake's mishap. "Get him!" Jake rallied, recovering.

The three of them started to close in on Franklin again. Franklin focused his mental concentration, and projected a powerful force that sent Jake crashing into a brick wall, breaking his neck and cracking his skull. The other two went flying in the air, tumbling backward. Jake's body landed limp and lifeless at the base of the wall. As soon as the other two managed to get to their feet, they ran from the alleyway, leaving Jake behind.

Franklin felt no remorse or twinge of conscience over Jake, he didn't spare him a glance. *It is time to begin my new life*, he thought, and walked out of the alley…never to return.

———

Maggie was coming up for the weekend! For the next couple of days, brimming with excitement over the prospect of Maggie's visit, Rahlys made preparations; cooking, cleaning, and stocking up on wood and water so there would be little to do in the way of chores while Maggie was here. Outside, a cold drizzle herded the landscape into winter, but inside it was invitingly cozy and warm. She finished reading Vince's novel, and finished the painting of the squirrel's harvest. But the crystal she kept stashed away, wary of its intent and purpose, for despite cheerful productive days, her nights had become troubled by tormenting dreams.

The dreams were strangely surreal, even alien, and deep within them lurked the presence of great evil...seemingly searching for her...but miraculously, never finding her...as she struggled to repel detection, eventually waking in a sweat from the strain of the effort. *Why is the evil seeking me out? Is it the source of the crystal's power? Is the crystal truly evil? If it is, I must destroy it.* Rahlys tried to imagine how she could destroy a crystal that glowed and was capable of flying around.

She restlessly paced around the room trying to think. *Does using the crystal's magic consequently commit me to something unknown? Could it irretrievably possess me...corrupting me? Has it done so already? Could I escape from the crystal's power even if I wanted to?*

Rahlys stopped wearing the crystal upon her person, and hid the pouch in a drawer upstairs. She wouldn't be using magic during Maggie's visit, and she was thinking it may be best to stop using magic altogether, for the unknown source of the crystal's power was beginning to scare her. She thought about telling Maggie about the crystal, but if it was truly evil, she didn't want her involved.

Finally, it was time to meet the northbound train coming from town. She grabbed her rifle and pack, and headed down to the railroad tracks. The air had turned decidedly colder, forcing Rahlys to wear a warm hat, gloves, and a heavier jacket. All the trees, except for the evergreens, were bare, the brilliant autumn colors had turned to brown, and the cold drizzle of the days before had transformed the nearby mountains into snow-dusted, white peaks that gleamed cleanly, heralding the approach of winter.

Successive frosts had withered away the underbrush, giving her a clear view through the trees. The walking was easy, mostly downhill. It was comfortable on the trail, but once out of the woods, the wind along the tracks nibbled away at her warmth as she stood there waiting for Maggie's arrival.

Born and raised in Seattle, Maggie had been Rahlys' roommate when she first arrived at art school, a country bumpkin from the Alaska woods, and despite having very little in common, she and Maggie had bonded, becoming lifelong friends. Maggie had opted to live in the dorms because her parents could afford it, and she wanted out of the house. Delighted with Rahlys' innocence, street-smart Maggie took the woodswoman under her wing and showed her the ropes to city living. For Rahlys, Maggie added new excitement to her life that she had never experienced before.

Rahlys and Maggie were dorm mates for only a short time. Before the second semester rolled around, Maggie took off on a cross-country motorbike tour with a dashing 'bad boy.' The tour ended tragically several months later, when the young man and his motorcycle were crushed under a bus. Returning to Seattle, her heart broken, Maggie looked to Rahlys for solace. It was then that they decided to rent an old, but spacious apartment with character, located close to work, school, and the park.

To make ends meet, Maggie found a full-time job as a bartender, making it on tips, and Rahlys worked as a waitress part time at the local diner to supplement her art scholarship. For the next couple of years, they lived there contentedly, Maggie there sometimes, and sometimes not, depending on what relationship she was in…but she always paid her half of the rent so she always had her own room to go to when she needed it.

When Rahlys finished school and landed an incredible job with a prosperous advertising firm, Maggie was already happily settled with a plumber from Arkansas. So they let the apartment go, and Rahlys bought into a new condo. For the next eight years, their lives took separate paths, but they stayed in contact, even after Maggie and Bob eventually moved down to Arkansas. Rahlys met Aaron, and soon he moved in with her. Then Maggie's life came crashing down again when Bob died suddenly of a heart attack at the young age of 37. Maggie, widowed and childless, returned to Seattle and moved in with her aging mother.

So when Rahlys kicked Aaron out the door and decided she needed a drastic life change to be happy, Maggie, being in a life slump of her own, was willing to follow her to the ends of the earth…well, at least to the end of the road. For when Rahlys announced she was buying a remote cabin and moving into the wilderness…Maggie came to a halt.

Finally, Rahlys spotted the train's light coming up the long straight stretch of track from the south, its approach building anticipation. The engine passed her by pulling ahead, aligning the baggage car door with her trail. She hadn't expected Maggie to have much in the line of baggage. And there was Maggie, standing next to Vince, waving excitedly from the baggage car as the train came to a stop.

"Why hello, Ms. Rahlys!" the conductor greeted her heartily, "I've brought you some company." Maggie's face was all smiles as Vince and the conductor handed down two large cardboard boxes and a pack, then the conductor escorted Maggie around to the passenger door.

Vince called down to Rahlys over the hum of the diesel locomotive. "My four-wheeler is parked in the woods at the foot of my trail. I'll take a load up to my cabin first and light a fire, then I'll come back down and bring up your boxes with the four-wheeler."

"Alright, thanks," Rahlys said. Maggie was coming down the steps, so she hurried over to her.

"Hi," Maggie gave Rahlys a quick hug as soon as her feet hit the gravel rail bed. Then they stepped back from the train as it pulled away. "Wow, this sure looks different from this summer!"

"What's in the boxes?" Rahlys asked. They sure were heavy.

"Food. I don't want you to go hungry out here in the woods. I figured you would be out of fresh stuff by now. And your mail is in here." She held up the small cloth bag she was carrying.

"Maggie, you're an angel."

"Not yet, but I'm working on it." Maggie's auburn red hair poking out of a purple knitted hat added vivid color to the nearly colorless October landscape. Her flashing green eyes complimented her animated spirit.

Rahlys put the mailbag in her pack. "We can't leave the boxes here. We need to move them away from the railroad tracks. Vince said he'll bring them up with the bike."

"Bike?"

"Well, the four-wheeler."

Maggie donned her pack, and they each grabbed a box and headed into the woods. "You have a very nice neighbor."

"I see you've met."

"He came over and introduced himself. The train was late, so we talked for quite a while. Vince said he was impressed by how well you were doing out here."

Rahlys couldn't help but smile. "He said that?" It felt great to have someone to chatter with again for a couple of days. She had enjoyed the solitude she had so craved, but now welcomed the distraction of companionship.

"Yes, and he complimented my blueberry jam." Leaving the boxes just inside the woods, they started up the trail. "Town has really quieted down now that most of the snowbirds and tourist are gone." 'Snowbird' was the local term for someone who left in winter for warmer climes. "How have things been going out here?"

"It's been wonderful. I've been warm, and comfortable, and I've had time to paint." Rahlys wanted to tell Maggie how her life had been impacted by a strange crystal, but still she decided against it. If the crystal proved to be dangerous, it was best not to place Maggie in harm's way. The crystal was an element of uncertainty, and Rahlys did not like uncertainty.

They hiked for a while in silence through the empty fall woods, then stopped for a breather after a particularly steep part of the trail. "So, what do you think of Vince?" Maggie asked.

Maggie's question caught Rahlys by surprise. "Oh...he seems nice enough. Sort of the strong, self-reliant type."

"Are you interested in him?"

"What? No...I'm not interested in a relationship right now. I've made one gross mistake already."

They spoke little during the rest of the walk, saving their energy for hiking, and reached the cabin before they heard Vince's four-wheeler approaching. Maggie and Rahlys stood by the porch listening and waiting in the almost warm sun burning through thin clouds until Vince pulled up beside them with the boxes.

"Why, thank you, kind sir!" Maggie greeted him. "That was certainly quicker and easier than carrying them."

Vince smiled warmly, but with a little shyness at Maggie's boisterous nature. He unloaded the boxes onto the porch, but didn't linger, refusing their offer to stay a while. "Well, you ladies have a good day. I need to get back and tend to my stove so my cabin will be warm tonight." Then he turned toward Maggie. "Tomorrow, before you take the train back to town, I'll bring you the book I was telling you about."

"Oh good, thanks!"

Then without further ado, Vince started up the four-wheeler and headed back down the trail.

"So what book is that?" Rahlys asked curiously as they carried the boxes inside.

"It's a book on living off the land in Alaska. He says it covers everything from picking berries and gardening, to smoking fish and canning salmon. It even shows how to dress a moose in the field." Rahlys was taken by surprise. This was a new side of Maggie she had never seen before.

Upon entering, Maggie's glance swept over the two matted watercolors prominently displayed on the counter. Rahlys had had the foresight to pack in two precut mats in anticipation of this moment. "Oh! Your paintings are beautiful!"

Rahlys put away the groceries while Maggie gazed at her work. Pulling a canning jar out of one of the boxes, she held it up. "What's this? Canned salmon?"

"Yes, I had a chance to go salmon fishing with Spit Fire and Hound Dog. Spit is a bush pilot and Hound Dog a musher. They're not much to look at, but they sure are loads of fun. I'll introduce you to them when you come into town."

"I can hardly wait."

Maggie turned back to looking at the paintings. "They're so full of life and movement," she said, picking up the one of the raven with the crystal in his beak. She moved it about as though changing the reflection of the light off the crystal, "Does that raven still come around here looking for something to eat?"

"Yes, he was the model for the sketches."

"Nice crystal! It almost looks magical! Wouldn't it be great to have a raven bring you a magic stone," Maggie said wishfully, as she propped the painting back up on the counter.

Rahlys almost dropped the cup she was taking out the cupboard. Quickly she composed herself, "Nothing comes that easily."

"You're right about that!"

Rahlys longed to tell Maggie about the crystal, but couldn't bring herself to do so. What if the crystal really was evil? She didn't want to expose Maggie to any danger. She needed to find out more first, but how?

Soon they were settled at the table sipping tea. "Do you know Vince is a writer?" Rahlys reached over and handed Maggie the paperback she had ready on the table.

"What is this? *Cold Fire and Hot Ice* by Vince Bradley. Our Vince Bradley?"

"Yes, and its good, too."

Maggie flipped through it, then read from the back page. "A retired marine decorated for bravery and a confirmed bachelor, Mr. Bradley lives alone in a remote cabin in Alaska's northern Susitna Valley. Well, how about that! I can't wait to read it."

"You can take it with you; I finished it. It was so compelling, I could hardly put it down."

The afternoon and evening passed quickly with much laughter and cheer. There were boisterous moments, and of course quiet reflective ones. Rahlys was torn between wanting Maggie to stay longer and wanting to get back to her work…and of course there was the crystal hidden upstairs in a drawer. After a particularly long pause, Maggie brought Rahlys out of her musings.

"Do you think about Aaron a lot?"

"No." In fact, Rahlys was shocked by the realization that she barely thought about Aaron at all. Her new home and setting, the crystal's magic, even the dramatic changing of the seasons had so filled her thoughts and senses, an unfaithful ex-boyfriend had been the furthest thing from her mind.

"Mama said Aaron's been by looking for you."

Rahlys' stomach tightened at the news. If she were still in Seattle, Maggie's information would have been disquieting, but there was little concern that Aaron would find her here. "He need not waste his time." Rahlys shuddered away her memories of Aaron. Thankfully, he was out of her life forever.

"Are you where you thought you would be twenty years ago?"

"I'm where I want to be." Rahlys answered without hesitation. "It's so peaceful out here in the woods…and so challenging…and beautiful… and real." She tried to put how she felt in words. "It's hard to explain, but you have a more intimate relationship with nature when you have to go outside to use the bathroom."

"But winter is coming, fast! It's going to get colder and darker."

"It will be hard, I know, but still, this is where I want to be."

"What about a man in your life?"

Over the years, Rahlys had dated intermittently, but mostly she had found dating to be a waste of time. Love, she was certain, would be happenstance, not the result of systematically trying on men like shoes in a shoe store. Instead, she had poured her heart and soul into her career, hence most of her time had been taken up with work. As a result, her career had taken the fast track to success. But eventually, she had become more and more disillusioned by the anonymous sale of her talent for the sake of commercialism, not to mention the stress and strain of an urban lifestyle. For years Rahlys had dreamed of returning to Alaska, to a life of her own in a cabin in the woods, and had saved a respectable portion of her respectable income toward that goal. As for having a man in her life, a year ago, Rahlys had succumbed to the pursuit of tall, dark, dashingly all-the-women-had-their-eyes-on-him handsome Aaron, and Aaron knew how to play the role of a knight in shining armor…at least until he got what he wanted. It didn't take long for him to show his true colors, and after kicking Aaron to the curb, Rahlys decided to make the move she had been planning on for so long.

"I do not want a man in my life right now," Rahlys said emphatically. "I just want to get to know myself. What about you? Are you where you want to be?"

"I wanted to be married with six kids." Maggie and Rahlys broke into laughter. How little they had known about life when they first met! Twice Maggie had been in love and death had taken love from her, and not once had she been blessed with a child. "Life sure doesn't turn out like you expect it to."

The next morning a dusting of snow covered the landscape under heavily laden gray clouds reluctant to relinquish the rest of their load. "It certainly is beautiful and peaceful out here! But I wouldn't want to do it alone," Maggie said, as she stared out the window at the transformation. "So when are you coming into town?"

"Eventually. Thanks to you, I can hold out for a little longer." Rahlys dreaded leaving the woods and making an excursion to the city. "When I have a few more watercolors needing framing, I will come out and we can go shopping, and I'll do some matting and framing. Then I'll take my paintings over to the local gallery and see if I can drum up some interest in them."

They heard Vince's four-wheeler approaching, and jumped up, stepping out to meet him. "Good day, ladies!" He looked up at the ominous sky, "It sure is passing up a good opportunity to dump on us." Then Vince pulled a book out of his pack, and handed it to Maggie. "Here is the book I promised you."

"Thanks! I'll make sure to get it back to you."

"There's no hurry."

"Well, come on in and stay a while. It's not train time yet." Vince followed the ladies into the toasty warm cabin.

"It's warm in here!" He unzipped his coat, putting it on the back of a chair, and sat at the table across from Maggie. Rahlys took the tea kettle off its metal trivet and placed it directly on the hot stove. The water started sizzling almost immediately. Then she laid out some of the foods she had prepared for Maggie's visit. Vince noticed the copy of his book on the table.

"Oh I need to take that, too." Maggie jumped up and stuffed the empty mail bag, the book on Alaska survival, and Vince's novel into her pack.

"I read your book." Rahlys said as she poured hot water into tea cups.

"And?"

"I'm impressed. I couldn't put it down."

"I see you matted the raven painting. Now, what are you going to do with it?"

"Hopefully I will sell it, why?"

"Let me know when you put a price on it. I'd like to own it. That raven has been around here a long time. He was Jack Bean's most constant companion when Jack was living here."

"So where is Jack Bean now?" Maggie asked.

"He's living with his daughter down in Oregon. Jack is getting up in years; she's taking care of him now."

All too soon Maggie's visit was coming to an end. "I could give you a ride down to the tracks," Vince offered. Rahlys saw the opportunity for some time alone.

"Go ahead. I'll catch up. I don't mind walking."

With much excitement, Maggie gathered her things together and jumped on the four-wheeler behind Vince. A few isolated snowflakes drifted down as they took off and Rahlys followed them down the trail. Finally, she was alone again. She wanted to think about the crystal, but fear clutched at her heart. A magpie with its black and white wing feathers splayed out like paper fans, flew across the trail, its long iridescent tail steering his flight. "Cheee, cheee!" a chickadee chirped, in a nearby spruce tree. She thought of the raven and wondered what his reaction was to the snow.

By the time Rahlys caught up with Vince and Maggie, they heard the train whistle in the near distance. Soon it was right along side them and Rahlys hugged Maggie good-by. All too quickly, Maggie was onboard, and the train chugged on down the tracks.

Vince started up his four-wheeler, and waving so long, he took off up the trail that ran north through the woods paralleling the railroad tracks, connecting his trail to hers. Rahlys was alone. Alone with her thoughts and fears. The heavy dark bluish-gray clouds sank even lower over the landscape, and it began to snow in earnest. Beautiful, big, fluffy white snowflakes drifted down silently through the sleeping trees.

It was nearly dark by the time she made it back to the cabin. She started up the generator to brighten things up, then sat at the table trying to decide what to do next. The crystal haunted her thoughts. Deep inside she felt she was capable of wondrous abilities, but she was fearful of confronting the crystal again, having become wary of its power. The strange dreams had not returned during Maggie's visit. Perhaps she was being overly cautious. With brave determination and some trepidation, Rahlys went up to her bedroom. She removed the pouch from the drawer, and stalling for time, took it back downstairs. Trembling with apprehension, she emptied the crystal out onto the table. The crystal floated up glowing softly. Rahlys stared at it with renewed wonderment. *What are you?* Reaching for it, she gently took it in her hand. The crystal brightened to her touch.

———

Inebriated and exhausted, Aaron staggered drunkenly down the hallway of a rundown apartment building in Seattle. He could hear a television and a crying baby through the thin walls to his left, and a couple fighting down the hall to the right. At the end of the hall a boom box echoed the latest rap beat. Aaron was having a hard time focusing enough to find his door, all the behind-wall sounds were confusing his polluted brain. Finally he stumbled to a door with peeling gray paint he thought might be his, and tried the key he managed to retrieve from his pocket after considerable fishing and swaying in place. With surprising ease, considering his state, Aaron turned the key, and the door opened. He nearly fell into the room, wobbled himself back into balance, and shut the door.

The room smelled of cigarettes and stale beer. Rahlys hadn't allowed him to smoke in the upscale home they had shared. Of course, it was her condo, but he had been gracious enough to move in…and they had lived there together for seven months…wasn't that sharing? Then just like that, the bitch ditched him.

Sure, he had made a few mistakes, but why did she have to be so cold and unforgiving. He made it to the sagging sofa and crashed into it. Without another thought, Aaron fell into a deep sleep.

The sun was streaming in through tattered holes in the shade as Aaron opened his dark, brooding eyes, which under better conditions, softened beautifully when he smiled. Now they were heavy, and slightly out of focus as he lifted his cloudy head off the sofa. His usually immaculate medium short black hair stuck out in twisted tufts, and the dark shadow of a beard masked the hard lines of his face. Grabbing his throbbing head, he lowered his feet to the chipped tile floor, heaved his long, thin body into a standing position, and staggered to the bathroom. A few moments later he was back on the sofa.

With his head pounding and his stomach churning, Aaron brooded about his life as he laid miserably awake on the sofa. A few months ago he had been on top of the world with a decent job, a fine place to live, and a financially successful girlfriend. His job as a receptionist at the advertising firm had been the best job he ever had, and a great opportunity to meet beautiful women. Some even went out with him.

But in his heart, none compared to Rahlys. He could not believe his luck when she finally agreed to have dinner with him. Over the next few months, he charmed her off her feet, and soon he moved out of his shabby apartment, and into the lap of luxury.

Life with Rahlys opened up new opportunities…both good and bad. Being a man of opportunity, Aaron took the opportunity to help Rahlys spend some of her money, and ran up a gambling debt. There was no reason for her to be so upset, he was going to pay her back. Then he started sampling the irresistibly beautiful women who frequented the parties Rahlys was sometimes obliged to attend. When Rahlys came home unexpectedly early one evening and discovered him in bed with a cocktail hostess from the last party, she kicked him out the door, literally, with his pants in his hands.

Rahlys was so powerfully mad, Aaron decided to give her a cooling off period before putting on the charm to win her back. Meanwhile, with nowhere to go, he met up with some old buddies, stayed with them for a time, and went on a drinking binge that cost him his job. But what irked him the most was when he went to see Rahlys to humble himself, Rahlys had already quit her job, leased out her condo, and moved back to Alaska!

Figuring that Maggie would be in the know, Aaron looked for her at her mother's, only to find out that Maggie had taken off too. Now all he had left was a hangover.

Aaron sat up and his stomach growled angrily. Searching the kitchenette for food, he found a beer in the refrigerator and saltine crackers in the cupboard. He brought his finds back to the sofa. Unable to endure the quiet, Aaron turned on the television for company, but his thoughts returned to Rahlys. Maybe I should go to Alaska! Some have struck it rich there in gold, and oil, and fish. What is Rahlys doing back in Alaska anyway? Maybe its time I found out. Alaska may be just the place for a smart fellow like myself.

Chapter 4
A Visit From Afar

It was a clean and well-rested Franklin who strolled past the Cafe Du Monde carrying an empty white paper bag with white cord handles. He breathed in deeply, relishing the rich aromas of strong coffee and sweet fried dough. The chattering crowd amidst clanking white cups and plates, gave no notice to the faddishly dressed youth in new Levis, Nikes, and a black t-shirt that read *Laissez les bon temps rouler* (Let the good times roll), as they sipped coffee and inhaled powdered sugar covered beignets.

From the cafe Franklin headed toward the river, the white paper shopping bag no longer empty, and settled on a bench along the river walkway. Opening the bag, he pulled out a warm, fluffy beignet and devoured it hungrily. Then with more patience, he reached into the bag again, bringing out a little metal shaker canister filled with powdered sugar. He sprinkled the next deliciously hollow, golden brown beignet snowy white, and dived into sugary ecstasy.

With stealth by magic, Franklin had learned to acquire the necessities of life, and more, but he still roamed the streets, a homeless loner. Franklin had always been a loner. He could barely remember his flighty mother and had no recollection of a father. He did remember his grandmother though, simple, soft-hearted, legally blind, and a bit senile. When his mother left him behind as excess baggage at the age of seven, Franklin was supposed to be in his grandmother's custody. But when his mother left without telling her mother goodbye,

Franklin staged a farewell visit with Granny, and effectively slipped through the cracks.

For the first few weeks on his own, he lived in the little dilapidated shotgun house that he knew as home in the lower ninth ward, just two blocks from Granny. There was still some food left in the house to eat, he slept in his own sagging bed, and spent most of his time watching TV. It wasn't until the utilities and rent went unpaid, that strangers came snooping around, so under cover of darkness Franklin moved bedding and a few personal belongings to a ramshackle shed behind Granny's house, and moved in.

He lived in that shed for the next five years, even interacting with his grandmother, not as Franklin, but as a neighborhood boy named Ben. Unable to see him, and in her state of mind, it was easy enough to disguise his true identify from her. Franklin did odd jobs for her around the house for food, or change, and told her vivid stories about the sights around her that she could not see. Sometimes she told him of her grandson Franklin, who had moved away.

Then one day he found his grandmother dead, sitting in her rocker. Franklin bowed his head for a moment in quiet respect to her spirit, then walked through the house picking up what little money he could find, mostly loose change, and without notifying anyone of his grandmother's death, walked away, leaving her body to be discovered by a welfare worker the next day.

The next few years were mean and lean. Franklin ate out of garbage cans and slept in alley ways, hiding from cops and gang members alike. Then he found the fiery orb. He touched the smooth round glass in his pocket reassuringly. Now gang members avoided him and cops had no reason to give chase.

His hunger satiated, Franklin ambled away from the river through the narrow streets of the French Quarter to the rhythm of Jazz, Blues, and Rock n' Roll, even this early in the day, drifting out of the numerous bars. He spied a pretty, young woman in a flowing red dress. As Franklin concentrated, the skirt of the dress flew up in a non-existent wind, revealing white, lacy panties. The girl shrieked as she struggled to pull her skirt back down. Franklin walked on unhindered, no one connecting him to the incident.

He turned the corner onto Bourbon Street to the cacophony of honking traffic. Why, he could add to that! As he walked down the sidewalk, he sent every car's horn blaring, creating a din that sent resident pigeons into flight. Like a skeet shooter, Franklin shot as many pigeons as he could out of the air, mentally firing deadly bolts of force at the targets. Dead pigeons dropped on to pedestrians and traffic, adding human shrieks, and the crunch of fender benders to the din and confusion. Franklin laughed fiendishly at his canvas of chaos.

When his merriment was spent, he entered a video arcade. Able to activate any game with a thought, he spent hours in virtual combat with multitudes of enemies...but he had no patience with defeat. When a game didn't go as he wished, he would fix it to his satisfaction.

Franklin didn't mind being a loner, or not having friends, not really. What did he need friends for? He could find plenty to do for entertainment. What he needed was his own headquarters, a place he could call his very own.

Franklin's wandering through the city went on well into the night, and when he was finally exhausted and ready to sleep, he teleported himself nightly into a furniture store he had found, and climbed into his bed. Well, it wasn't his bed exactly, but it was the most magnificent bed he had ever seen, and he returned to it night after night. It was so massive, there was a stool to help you climb into it. From the bed frame four huge mahogany posts rose majestically at the corners, reaching for the ceiling. The great bed looked sad and trapped in the crowded store, begging to be freed. Franklin climbed up into it, consoling it, and went to sleep.

Restful sleep turned into restless dreams. He was hot molten lava, flowing through jagged crystal mountains. Violent eruptions shook the mountains, shattering crystals and spewing him across the galaxies. For millennia he lay buried under river silt until a great flood washed the silt away. Then it was morning and someone was unlocking the doors to the store.

Franklin woke with a start. Daylight illuminated the front store windows. He reached into his pocket for the orb, as he did every morning, to assure himself it was still there. Then pulling it out, he squeezed it tightly in his hands. *Find me*...Franklin paused...*Find me and my bed a safe, comfortable place to live. A place where no one will ever find us*, he half pleaded, half demanded.

There was a gentle tug and a soft flutter of energy in his brain…and then Franklin and his bed were plunged into darkness.

———

Dirty snow splattered up from the tires of traffic honking at jaywalkers trying to cross busy Fourth Avenue in downtown Anchorage. To Aaron, the city didn't look like much. Old buildings and new ones were all jumbled together, the city's horizon line nearly insignificant by Lower-48 standards. But the city was redeemed from total drabness by the Chugach Mountains that encircled it to the east, and to the west, Cook Inlet, a mighty arm of the Pacific Ocean reached far inland to Anchorage's port just a few blocks away. A warm wind from the Gulf of Alaska was bringing in unseasonably warm temperatures, turning the snow on the city sidewalks to slush. The sky overhead hung low, dark, and gray.

Aaron, not acclimated to winter, shivered in the damp wind. His shoes were soaked through, his toes numb with cold. He had begged, borrowed and stolen to make it to Alaska, and had little money left to buy winter boots. Then he came upon an Army Navy Surplus Store and walked in; at least he could warm up a bit. The shelves and racks were piled high with coats, hats, boots, socks, packs, sleeping bags, canteens, knives…and just about anything else you could need for survival in a brutally cold environment. Aaron looked in his wallet, and considered. He could either have warm feet, or eat tonight. Which would it be? He stepped outside to think on it, then came to a pawn shop with a pair of used boots displayed in the window. They looked like they would fit.

Aaron was feeling like his ill luck might be changing for the better as he strolled down the sloppy sidewalk carrying his newly purchased boots and socks in a shopping bag with enough money left over for a little something to eat. When he stumbled on the Brother Francis Shelter with room for the night, he began to feel downright lucky. Tomorrow morning he would hitchhike out of town. Rahlys and Maggie were in some little end-of-the-road hick town far north of Anchorage. This much he had found out in little devious ways from their friends.

He hoped Rahlys appreciated all he had been through to get here, he was starting to wonder if she was worth it.

Aaron fluffed up the hard, flat pillow he had been provided and stretched out on his cot, covering himself with a thin, wool blanket. An old man in another cot coughed from time to time to clear his throat. Occasionally, the peace was disturbed by a distant siren or the screech of brakes from the city that carried on beyond the walls of the room, otherwise it was quiet. Warm, dry, and fed, Aaron soon fell into dreamless sleep.

Rahlys lifted sleep-heavy eyelids to gray morning light, her body pressed into the mattress, weighted with grogginess. The residue of dreams, unlike any she had experienced before, drugged her mind. But now, all she could recall was a name…Anthya. Who's Anthya, she wondered, her eyes focusing on the log beams overhead, each as unique as the tree from which it was hewn. Then she turned her head toward the dull light seeping in from the window, and spotted the crystal suspended stationary over the birch night stand beside her bed, its soft light competing with the emerging dawn.

After much soul searching, Rahlys had decided that she would not confine the crystal to its pouch for a time. Perhaps this way, she could learn more, and it was unlikely anyone would be coming around to see it. Why had the crystal allowed her to tuck it away like a common object not currently in use? Because the crystal is an object, she reminded herself.

Rahlys sat up and stretched. "Anthya," she said out loud, committing to memory the name from her dream. In an unexpected response to her utterance, the crystal brightened sharply, circled around…then hovered in place and dimmed back down again.

"You know Anthya, don't you?"

The crystal pulsated light, spinning on its axis in seeming confirmation.

Slipping out of bed, Rahlys gasped in awe as she glanced out her bedroom window at the clearing, forest, and creek below. Deep fresh snow had transformed the landscape overnight into a winter wonderland. Snow draped heavily from tree branches and blanketed the underbrush in soft fluffiness. Down below, the creek ran darkly through the pristinely white landscape.

And it was still snowing.

With the excitement of a child eager to try out her new sled, Rahlys rushed to get dressed. The crystal followed her downstairs, patiently waited for her to don boots, hat, and coat, then rushed out the door behind her. Rahlys stomped out a trail across the backyard making her way to the outhouse. Except for its light, the crystal was nearly invisible in the falling snow, whispering ever so softly in the still air, as it sifted down through the trees.

Returning from the outhouse, Rahlys paused in her tracks, taking in the beauty and wonder of it all. Again she stomped the snow with her feet, packing the trail more on her way back to the steps. Then with a burst of magic, Rahlys brushed the snow off the steps. Reaching the porch, she knocked snow off her boots, grabbed an armload of firewood from the stacked row, and entered the warm, cozy cabin. When the door closed behind her, leaving the crystal outside, almost immediately it appeared again beside her, unmindful of any door.

After loading the stove, Rahlys donned her snowsuit, and grabbing the empty five-gallon water container and the plastic sled from the porch, she headed down to the spring, the crystal following her. There was a better way to break trail then stomping through it. Dropping the sled at the edge of the hill, she settled into it with the water container between her knees, and wiggled the sled forward. Snow drifted into the sled with her and collected on her as it continued to fall. With the aid of gravity, the sled moved slowly down the unpacked slope and stopped as the trail leveled out by the spring access.

The crystal explored around the immediate area while Rahlys stomped down snow, kicked away the hollow icicle that had formed around the stream of water coming out of the pipe, and placed the container under the spout. The water flow was slow and the container large, so she had time for more sledding while it filled.

Teleporting herself back up the hill, she dropped the sled to the ground and plopped down into it. Her second run was faster and took her further down the trail. By her third run, the sled had enough momentum to reach a second decline in the trail, helping her go even further. Carrying the sled, she walked the short distance back up to the spring and loaded the full water container into the sled. Then with focused concentration Rahlys teleported herself, the sled, and the water container to the back porch.

Rahlys made quick work of the chores after that, using magic to haul water and restock the firewood on the porch. But how she was going to eventually restock her wood shed was a dilemma she had yet to resolve.

Determined to maintain a schedule of sorts, Rahlys set herself up to paint. Then with a cup of hot cocoa cradled in her hands, she stared out into the snowfall, mesmerized, longing to depict it on paper. Placing the cup aside, she reached for a thin soft brush, dipped the tip in even thinner color washes, and gingerly, minimally defined the underlying structure of the forest, softening the infusion of subtle hues with a damp cotton swab. Between strokes, she glanced out at the white landscape, then back down at the white paper in front of her. The crystal hovered placidly nearby, lighting her work.

Then suddenly the crystal flew out of position and spun in the air around her. Questioningly Rahlys looked up from her work.

Anthya approaches.

Startled by the unexpected message, Rahlys stood abruptly nearly upsetting her work, her stomach wrenching tightly as fear stabbed at her heart. *But how…?* She recognized the name from the dreams and staggered under the possible portent of such a visitation. *What should I do?*

Then there in the room standing just a few feet from her appeared a slender, wispy woman, her features so light she looked more like an apparition than a living being. A dark blue cloak draped over Anthya's shoulders partially concealed a gown of shimmering silver. Before Rahlys could decide how to react, Anthya spoke softly, moving slowly toward her.

"Please do not fear me, Rahlys, Guardian of the Oracle of Light, I mean you no harm. I am Anthya, Councilor of the Crystal Table."

Rahlys' heart beat in her throat. She was unable to think as she struggled to comprehend the presence before her. Immediately, the crystal flew to Anthya and hovered over her outstretched hand. Rahlys fought a sharp pang of jealousy over the crystal's lack of loyalty, then panic… was it being taken away? She felt a tremendous urge to summon it back. Then as though sensing her stress, the crystal flew up from Anthya's hand and returned to hover near Rahlys.

Quickly Rahlys reached up and grabbed the crystal while she had a chance. Enclosed in her fist, she held it close to her body as she struggled to release enough tension in her throat to enable her to speak. "Where did you come from? And why are you here?"

"I am from a world far away across the galaxies. I have come to unveil to you the history of the Oracle of Light…and your destiny." Images of a distant planet with crystalline mountains and golden seas brushed Rahlys' mind. How could her destiny be linked with this alien world? The heavily ominous words, spoken with such gentle wisdom were foreboding. Rahlys stood speechless as Anthya continued her tale.

"When I was young, not yet a millennium of your Earth-years old, there lived on our world a very evil sorcerer named Droclum who nearly destroyed our planet through his insatiable greed and lust for power. His most prevailing opponent was the great sorceress Anthya, for whom I am named." Mental images of Sorceress Anthya and the Sorcerer Droclum provided Rahlys visual references as Councilor Anthya related the history.

"Anthya and her followers learned that Droclum had produced a spell of horrendous darkness, a spell that opened the gate to immortality, with repercussions that could threaten our world. Only the darkest evil is powerful enough to achieve such a feat. In the final battle, Anthya dealt Droclum a fatal blow, but it was too late. The evil spell had already been wrought, and the body of her fallen foe, dissipating into smoke before her, was sucked into the boiling cauldron of Mt. Vatre. The mountain, and the ground beneath it, shook and heaved violently in an effort to rid itself of the abomination. For many planetary rotations, the cauldron boiled and the planet shook, until finally Mt. Vatre exploded cataclysmically, blowing a part of our world asunder."

The images Rahlys saw were terrifying as well as spectacular. A planet erupted, sending a fountain of molten glass and rock exploding into an interstellar shower of shattered crystal, ash, and rock.

"In this eruption, Droclum's formidable powers and evil being were forged into a fiery smoky orb and spewed out into space. Anthya and her followers traced the voyage of the Dark Orb across the galaxies through folds of space and time, until it was swallowed up and lost on this world that you now call Earth."

"Why are you telling me all this?" Rahlys shuddered.

"Because one day you will face Droclum and the powers of the Dark Orb."

For a fleeting moment Rahlys felt a touch of the unspeakable evil and unbearable darkness that was Droclum. It was the same evil that searched for her in her dreams.

"Why is he looking for me?"

"Because you are the Guardian of the Oracle of Light!"

"The Oracle of Light," Rahlys said softly, and the crystal became warmer in her tightly clenched hand.

"All of Anthya's efforts over time to find the Dark Orb and destroy it failed. She blamed herself for the scourge placed on your world and ours, for not defeating Droclum in time." Again Councilor Anthya paused, but Rahlys refrained from speaking, waiting quietly for her to continue.

"When Sorceress Anthya was near the end of her longevity she called me to her. In her hand she held a small cylindrical crystal I had given to her as a child, a crystal untainted by Mt. Vatre's cataclysmic eruption." The crystal fluttered in Rahlys' tightly closed palm.

"She asked me to accompany her to her private chambers, and there with quiet, solemn ceremony, Anthya laid down on her divan. She asked that I stand beside her, and holding my hand for added strength, she squeezed the crystal in her other fist while she worked her last spell. The great sorceress seemed to age before my eyes. In the end, her body was tired and drained and her magic was gone, for her wondrous magical powers had been siphoned out of her and into the crystal. Then she took her last breath."

Rahlys was stunned by the incredible story she was hearing. "But why, why did she do it?"

"To give Earth a fair chance. It was I who was given the mission to transport the crystal containing the Oracle of Light to this world and hide it until it was time for a Guardian to possess its powers. Fate chose you as the Guardian of the Oracle, and Anthya's powers are now within you. When Droclum emerges, only you will have the ability to destroy him."

Rahlys' heart almost stopped beating. She shuddered recalling Droclum's essence from her dreams. "Me, destroy Droclum! But how?"

"You are a powerful sorceress. You and your warriors will find a way."

"My warriors?" Images of Vince, Maggie, and the raven appeared in her mind.

"Explore your powers, use your imagination, but heed one warning. If you use your power for evil intent, you will surely die."

Icy cold fear crept through Rahlys' spine. "What if I don't want these magical powers?"

"It is your destiny. You have been chosen."

The crystal would be contained no longer, and fluttered insistently in Rahlys' closed fist. In response, she opened her hand. Finally freed, the crystal flew out, zinging madly about the room, then came to a stop next to her, spinning slowly like a gyroscope.

"The crystal is a highly useful tool; it can help you in many ways. But remember, Sorceress Rahlys, Guardian of the Light, the power of the Oracle is already within you."

And with that, she was gone.

"Wait!" Rahlys cried out to the emptiness where Anthya had stood, but Anthya did not return. Rahlys paced the floor, too tense to sit, as she tried to absorb all she had been told. "I am a powerful sorceress," she said out loud as she continued to pace in agitation, the crystal following behind her like a tamed hummingbird. Out of habit, she stopped at the woodstove, opened it to check the wood supply, but didn't even look inside before shutting the door again. She was too distracted to think. "I am a powerful sorceress, and with my friends and a bird, I am to save the world." Well, that sounded about right. The crystal, from a world so far away, followed her as she continued to pace the painted plywood floors. "I must destroy the malevolent magician Droclum," she said aloud, and cold fear beaded down her spine as once again she recalled the feel of Droclum's evil. Droclum must be destroyed! But how? Fear tied her insides into knots at the thought of such a powerful adversary. And her warriors…were they entangled by association? Maggie, Vince, and the raven encompassed her entire social life since moving into the woods. Was involvement with the crystal part of their destiny too?

When Rahlys had finally paced herself out, she sat and stared into nowhere. With a feeling of cold dread, she recalled Anthya's dire warning. *If you use your power for evil intent, you will surely die.* Rahlys shuddered involuntarily. What exactly might be construed as evil intent? Glancing out the window Rahlys shook her head; there was too much to think about. It had stopped snowing and the sun was peeking timidly through tattered clouds revealing patches of blue sky.

"I need to go outside and get some fresh air." Rahlys bundled up warmly, conjured the crystal back to its pouch, and placed the loop around her neck letting the pouch fall between her breasts. As she stepped out, a breeze was already knocking some snow out of the trees. The enlarging hole of blue sky overhead promised a clear, cold night.

Rahlys hiked aimlessly around the cabin through the mid-calf deep snow and then down the gentle slope to the creek. The water in the creek babbled unhurriedly around rocks and boulders ringed in ice. Little disks of ice formed on the surface of the stream where snow-laden branches and brush, bent over by the snow load, touched the water.

Where did Anthya come from, Rahlys wondered, and how did she get here? She said she was Councilor of the Crystal Table and had been named after the great sorceress Anthya, whose powers she now possessed. She had been present when the crystal was infused with Sorceress Anthya's powers. How long ago was that? Anthya claimed she was still young at the time, only a thousand Earth-years old.

On a barely protruding ice-coated rock mid-stream in the creek, a dipper, short tailed and slate gray, bobbed up and down on fragile legs just inches above the cold, gurgling water. Rahlys gingerly stepped her way over snow-covered rocks to the water's edge. Suddenly she slipped, her right foot going out from under her, her body twisting down while her left foot remained wedged tightly between two rocks. Sharp pain shot up from her left ankle overriding the additional pain at impact points on her arm and hip even though snow helped cushion the fall. Through clenched teeth she writhed and moaned. As some of the pain eased, she tried to extricate her left foot, but the slightest effort to move it brought renewed agony. Slowly shifting position she managed to free her foot from the rock crevice. Then sitting back on the snow-covered rocks, she pulled off her left boot, opening the laces wide to minimize the pain, and gritted her teeth as she examined the ankle. It was extremely sensitive to the touch, but she could move it, and her fingers did not feel any misplaced bone. She tried to stand, but could barely put weight on it, and the rocks were slippery with ice and snow. Since she couldn't walk, she would have to teleport herself back to the cabin.

Rahlys closed her eyes and relaxed, drawing on the force within her, and envisioned the warm interior of her cabin, willing herself there.

Opening her eyes, Rahlys breathed a sigh of relief as she found herself in the comfort and security of her living room. Now at least she wouldn't die of exposure. She had been foolish to go out on the slippery rocks. What if she would have had to crawl all the way through the snow to get back to the cabin? She wiggled out of her coat and removed her boots, then managing to stand, limped over to the chair and sat down. Removing the sock on her left foot, her ankle loomed swollen and bruised. But even as she stared at it, the discoloration began to fade and the swelling to recede. She could touch it now without wincing in pain. Finally she tried standing on it again, then strolled around the room. She didn't even limp. Incredibly, her ankle was healed!

Chapter 5
A Trip to Town

The next day dawned still, clear, and cold, the sky painted brilliantly blue. When the sun came up, the trees cast long, thin, blue shadows across sparkling white snow. Dressed comfortably in her winter gear, the crystal snug in its pouch against her breast, Rahlys strolled across the sunny clearing gazing upon the glittering white forest. Movement caught Rahlys' eye as two squirrels scampering from tree to tree, triggered tiny, cascading avalanches of snow from branches they set in motion.

Where's the raven she wondered, and looked up as though expecting to see him. She could envision him flying in such a perfect sky. *Raven, where are you, my warrior?* she called out mentally. Then she saw in her mind the expanse of the snow-covered valley far below. Her vision soared above the trees and hills and river, floating on air. She knew she was seeing through the eyes of the raven. Her perspective lowered, as the raven descended and followed the creek eastward. Then the images in her head dissolved, as she saw the raven approaching.

"Aaaark," he called when he spotted her. In a flutter of black feathers, the raven landed on the snow beside her, looking up at her expectantly.

"Kaw! Kaw!" The raven's claws sank deeply in the snow causing him to waddle around a bit to pack down a place to stand. Rahlys didn't have any treats on her, but there were a few apple wedges left on the table in the cabin. She conjured them to her hand.

"Aaaark," the raven said with approval. Had the crystal really endowed the raven with special powers, like the ability to telepath images? She dropped the apple wedges down on the snow between them and the raven indulged. By Vince's testimony, he was just a raven, a raven that had grown accustomed to being fed. She sensed his enjoyment of the treat, and his ease with her, as well as his inquiry for more.

"That's it for now," she told him. Why did this wild bird answer her summons? Had the crystal somehow formed a bond between them? How could he possibly help her to defeat Droclum?

With nothing left to eat, the raven hopped into take-off, barely clearing the ground, one talon drawing a line in the snow for several inches before he banked into height over the forest. Soon, he was out of sight.

Rahlys made her way to the generator shed. The railroad local freight was due in a couple of days, and she needed to take an empty fuel drum down to the tracks, so it could be picked up and taken into town to be filled. Rahlys herself was going out for a week, on Sunday's train. She would make sure the fuel drum was taken to the fuel station, and then delivered back to the railroad freight depot.

Rahlys entered the generator shed. She checked the oil, and opened the last bottle of motor oil left behind by Trapper Bean. A case of motor oil needed to be added to her list. Then she filled the fuel tank. The generator was ready to go for tonight.

Closing the generator shed behind her, she made her way to the fifty-five gallon fuel drum covered with a tarp, and using a hand-operated fuel pump, pumped out all the remaining fuel, filling two five-gallon plastic containers. Then balancing the nearly empty drum on an up-ended round of firewood, she drained the drum into an empty coffee can to make sure it didn't have water from condensation or particles of trash left in it. Rahlys then screwed the bung cap back on, closing the drum; it was ready to take down to the railroad tracks.

The trail leading out to the railroad corridor lay undisturbed since the last snow. She could teleport the drum down to the tracks easily enough, but the presence of a drum without human or mechanical prints leading up to it would be inexplicable to railroad workers riding the rail, or Vince, if he should come around. She could pull the drum on a sled, but although the snow had settled and compacted some, walking all the way through the unpacked snow would be tiring. But what if she just made it look like she had broken trail pulling the sled?

Rahlys conjured the sled to her, placed the empty drum in it, then dragged the sled to the head of her trail, studying the track left on the snow. Formulating a spell, she drew on her strength and the energy she could feel around her, pressing into the snow the imprint she wanted to replicate. Rahlys teleported herself and the sled with the drum in it to a spot just a few hundred feet from the edge of the woods and the railroad tracks. The magically imprinted sled tracks ran the entire length of the trail.

Leaving the drum standing several feet from the railroad tracks, Rahlys decided to hike part of the way back up the trail. She breathed in calm and contentment as she hiked through snowy woods enjoying the quiet beauty and solitude…and the exercise. Early darkness was already creeping in by the time she teleported herself the rest of the way back to the cabin.

That night Rahlys started her next painting. In it, a strong, independent woman with long, light brown hair and pale blue eyes communed with a noble raven in a glittering snow forest with deep blue shadows. As she painted, she recalled the raven's eye view of the forested snow-covered valley she had seen, rising away from the river into the foothills of the distant mountains. Had she really summoned the raven, a wild and free creature of the forest? Did the crystal's magic extend that far? Anthya's sudden appearance and disappearance had not allowed for asking questions. And where is Droclum? The thought of him sent cold shivers down her spine. There had been no more dreams wringing her out through the night. She had uprooted her life, discarding comfortable success, in search of freedom, solitude, and time to paint. Now she was fulfilling that dream, but the life she had chosen was haunted by the looming threat of Droclum, who sought her as his prey.

Rahlys kept her focus on painting as the days passed without incident. An encounter with Droclum began to seem less and less imminent, and she allowed herself to relax her worries a little. Rahlys removed the pouch from around her neck and released the crystal. *I am going to paint your portrait.* The crystal hovered around her as she set up. Taking out a fresh sheet of watercolor paper, she clamped it to her art board, then dampened the paper with a sponge. Finally, reaching for the crystal, she grasped it gently between her thumb and forefinger, positioning it in front of her.

Rahlys gazed deeply into the crystal, entering it, looking at it from the inside out, seeking its essence…and started to paint. The crystal, suspended in air before her, began to revolve slowly in place, emitting a soft kaleidoscope of color-changing light. Rahlys tingled with creative energy, becoming totally absorbed in her work. As though by magic, the crystal took shape on a snow-covered spruce branch in the night forest, the snow sparkling in the colorful, multi-faceted light. Rahlys worked intently, possessed, late into the night, pacing impatiently while letting a layer of paint dry. Not until the painting was complete did she allow herself to fall out exhausted on the daybed downstairs.

As Sunday approached, Rahlys prepared to leave the woods with both anticipation and dread. It was going to be hard leaving for a whole week. The mere thought of leaving for so long was disquieting. There wasn't much to pack, she still had clothes left at Maggie's, but she packed some laundry to wash in town, and her paintings, fashioning a portfolio out of cardboard and duck tape to carry them in. Her paintings were an expression of the intimate nature of life in the woods, and it was a lifestyle she was learning to cherish.

Rahlys felt a growing separation from society, the powers of the Oracle intensifying the dilemma. The crystal and its magic must be kept secret she realized, for the consequences to her life if the media, and therefore the world, learned about the crystal were too staggering to contemplate.

Train day dawned clear and cold. Rahlys stood waiting patiently by the railroad tracks, her pack, laundry duffel, and portfolio beside her, as she listened for the approach of the south bound train that would take her to town. Reluctantly, she had allowed the fire in the stove to burn itself out, adding just enough wood when she woke up this morning to keep the cabin somewhat warm until departure. Upon leaving, she locked the cabin doors, lamenting the days until her return.

Finally she heard the train's distant whistle. It was running late. As the train inched closer, she could hear the pull of the locomotive's slow approach, the sound fading in and out as the tracks followed the meandering contour of the hills and river. Then finally lights appeared coming around the bend.

Standing beside the tracks, Rahlys waved her arms, and the engineer blew the whistle in acknowledgement. The train pulled up to a stop with the open baggage compartment door directly in front of her.

"Hello there," Vince greeted her as he reached down for her pack.

"Hi!" So Vince was going in too! She handed her pack up to him, followed by the duffel and her portfolio. Warm air embraced her chilled body as she boarded the train through the passenger door. Finding an empty seat, she eased into it, basking in the warmth.

Rahlys stared out the window at the scenery rolling by, an immense full moon wobbled orange and bloated on the darkening horizon, and night descended over the cabin in the woods as the last glowing ember in the wood stove died out. Slowly the logs of the cabin walls released their stored warmth to the encroaching frost. All was quiet. Neither wind nor shrew or vole stirred. The deserted cabin grew colder and darker.

Rahlys pulled her thoughts away from home, and psyched herself up for town. It will be fun hanging out with Maggie again, refreshing to see new sights. The break from established routine would be like a holiday, she convinced herself. The door that led to the baggage compartment opened and Vince walked down the aisle of the passenger car, locating Rahlys. "How have you been?"

"I've been great. Thanks again for the generator lesson. You were helpful."

"My pleasure, any time. Have you sent in a fuel drum yet?"

"Yes, I sent a drum in Thursday. I should have plenty enough fuel to last until the next freight."

"Will you be in town for a while?"

"A week. I need to do some matting and framing, and Maggie and I are going shopping."

"That's right. Maggie said something last week-end about you coming into town." Before Rahlys could ponder on Vince's comment, the train blew its whistle announcing their arrival.

When the train pulled into the station, Maggie was there to eagerly greet them. She gave them big hugs and chattered excitedly. "It's going to be a fun week having you two around."

There was less snow here than up in the woods, and the parking lot was slippery with ice. "Be careful! It's slippery!" Maggie warned. Rahlys skated on the ice as she loaded her pack in the bed of Maggie's pickup truck and carefully stashed her portfolio behind the seats in the cab. "Can you give me a ride to my truck?" Vince asked.

"Yes, of course. It's a mess around town too! All that warm weather caused a meltdown. It even rained instead of snowed one day. Then when it turned cold again, there was ice everywhere! Walkways and driveways are slicker than snot." They loaded Maggie's truck with Vince's pack and duffel bags, stepping gingerly to avoid slipping and falling on the ice. It was already dark when the three of them jammed into the truck's cab. Maggie drove over to where Vince was parked, her studded tires gripping the ice. When she came to a stop next to Vince's ice-encrusted truck, he jumped out of the passenger seat, and lifted his pack and duffle bags out the back. "Are you ladies going out later?" he asked Maggie.

"Yes, we'll meet you at the bar in a couple of hours."

"I'll see you then," and he turned toward the task of thawing out his truck. Maggie and Rahlys headed out of the tiny, downtown area of the little community boasting a post office, school, fire hall, library, hockey rink, two stores, two restaurants, a bar, and numerous gift shops.

"Guess who's in town," Maggie said as soon as they passed the stop sign and turned onto the unpaved road leading out toward Maggie's place. Rahlys gasped. There was no need to guess, she could read Maggie's thought clearly.

"No!" she cried with dismay. "What is Aaron doing here? Are you sure? Have you seen him?"

"No, but Spit said he was at the bar asking if anyone knew us. Spit didn't like something about him, so he and Hound Dog just sat there, and didn't say anything."

Just the thought of Aaron being here put a blight on the holiday spirit she had started to embrace. "What is he doing here? Why?"

"I'm not sure, but sooner or later he is going to find us." The pick-up rattled down the snow-packed gravel road, "I think Aaron fancies himself still in love with you."

Soon they pulled up to the well-cared-for, reddish-brown, wood-sided house surrounded by woods. Maggie had worked endless hours at two jobs during the lucrative summer tourist season, and had put a down payment on the small two bedroom house a short ways out of town even before Rahlys found Trapper Bean's place.

"It looks like I'm going to be here for a while," she said at the time. Rahlys ended up renting a room out of Maggie's house to have a place to stay, and work, when in town. The house was on the grid, so there was no need for a generator, and it had its own well offering all the amenities of town living such as running hot and cold water, flush toilet, bathtub, even a clothes washer and dryer. And there was a road to it.…It was town.

Rahlys followed Maggie in, carrying her pack and portfolio. The changes to the place in the nearly two months she had been gone truly amazed her. The house had been in need of some tender loving care. "You have been having work done on the house. It looks great!"

"I did it myself." Maggie's spirited nature glowed with pride.

"What?" Setting down her pack and portfolio, Rahlys strolled about admiring the transformation. "You did the work yourself?"

"Sure. I can hammer and paint. Bob and I did lots of remodeling in our home in Arkansas. Now that I'm only working twenty hours a week instead of sixty, I've been spending time fixing up the place."

"I love the decorative shelves in the living room…and look at the new cabinets and counter top in the kitchen!"

"Hound and Spit helped me put those in. It was easy. Everything was ready-made. All we had to do was screw things in place."

Rahlys opened the door to her room to let in some heat. Cold air rushed out. Carrying her things into her room she took a quick survey of its contents. Her room was unchanged. A twin bed covered with a brightly colored quilt, a little tattered in places, but still warm and serviceable, filled one side of the room. Next to it stood an improvised night stand made from a wooden spool that once held electrical wire. A battered veneer chest of drawers bought at a garage sale held her unused clothing. On top of that laid a stack of mat boards, covered with a dust cloth. A collection of empty picture frames leaned against the wall. There were enough materials on hand to at least mat and frame the work she brought out with her. Depositing her things on the bed, Rahlys left the chilly room to join Maggie in the kitchen where she was preparing tea. Passing by the fuel oil heater, its built-in fan blasting out heat in an effort to compensate for the cold infiltrating from her bed room, Rahlys paused momentarily to absorb the warmth.

"Of course, I didn't do anything to your room yet," Maggie assured her as she entered the kitchen. "You should decide on what colors you would like…but take a look at my room!"

After completing the tour of home improvements, Maggie poured cups of rosehip tea. She had harvested and dried the rosehips herself from the abundance of wild rose bushes that grew around her property. Since moving to Alaska, Maggie had been consumed by a growing interest in nature's bounty.

"So how have things been going in the woods?"

Rahlys didn't know how to answer. She promised herself repeatedly that she would tell Maggie about the crystal…and Anthya…and Droclum. She didn't know what to say. She didn't know how to begin. It no longer seemed real, here, away from the cabin and woods. She touched her chest to reassure herself the crystal was still there.

"Are you alright?"

"Yes, yes, why?"

"Well, you didn't answer, and then you touched your chest."

"Oh, I was just thinking." Rahlys had shared secrets with Maggie before. What should she tell her now? "Mostly, I've been doing chores and painting. Instead of ice, we have over a foot of snow up there. You should come up and see it."

"I will. Has Vince been by to check on you lately?"

"No, the last time I saw Vince, until today, was the weekend you came up to visit."

"He seems to feel you would rather not be disturbed."

"When did you see Vince? He said you mentioned to him, I was coming into town."

"Vince was in town a week ago, and gave me a call. So I invited him over for dinner and we went out for a few drinks."

"Really!"

"You don't mind, do you? I know you found him first."

"No, I'm glad to hear it."

After enjoying the light dinner with wine that Maggie had prepared ahead of time, Maggie was raring to go. "Come on, let's go out for a bit," she urged. "I'll introduce you to some colorful characters."

Rahlys wasn't really enthused about going to a smoky, noisy bar, but she smiled and agreed. "Alright. We might as well."

The din and odors that assailed their senses as they entered the aging bar were comprised of a pounding beat from an electric bass amplified to deafening decibels, the chatter and laughter of a packed house trying to talk over the music, human sweat, stale beer, and ancient cigarette smoke. Spotting someone, Maggie dragged her deeper into the melee toward one corner of the bar. "That is Hound Dog and Spitfire sitting on the end," Maggie said near her ear so she could hear over the music. "Hound Dog is the musher I told you about. Mostly he mushes tourist around, but he's run the Iditarod a couple of times, too. And Spit is a pilot. In the summer he does scenic flights to the glacier and drop-offs to remote locations. He's been everywhere, and knows a lot about Alaska." The number the band was playing came to an end and the gyrating, thrashing, sweating throng came to a swaying stop.

"Hi, guys!" Maggie greeted as they approached.

"Maggie! Hey, what's happening?" said Hound Dog. Then the music and gyrating and thrashing started up again. Rahlys surveyed the crowd while Maggie negotiated drinks and chatted with Hound and Spit.

"You want to dance?" The unkempt, inebriated inquirer nearly fell as he leaned toward her, his breath, reeking of alcohol, brushed her cheeks.

"No, thank you. I don't dance." She backed away as well as she could in the crowded space. Maggie turned toward her and pressed a glass of wine into her hand. Vince, having spotted them in the crowd, wove his way toward them through the sea of motion.

"Hi, I'm glad you made it." His rugged outdoorsman's face was a little flush, his usually serious brown eyes twinkling. He certainly looked like he was having a good time.

"Where do you stay when you're in town?" Rahlys asked with genuine interest.

"I have a place close to downtown, across the tracks. Great for a bachelor." She could read his hopes of Maggie spending some time with him there this week. "Did you finish any more paintings?"

"A few. I plan on matting and framing what I have, and looking into displaying them at the local arts and crafts gallery. *The Crystalline Raven* will be ready for you to pick up by the end of the week."

"Good, I plan on taking it back into the woods to hang in the cabin. Would either of you ladies like to dance?"

"You, go ahead," Rahlys offered Maggie to Vince, and they pushed their way deeper into the pulsating mass leaving Rahlys to visit with Hound and Spit.

"So, Rahlys, you are Maggie's friend, the one who bought Jack Bean's place?" Spit shouted to her over the music, his thin gray hair sticking out in several directions.

Rahlys nodded confirmation.

"That's a pretty nice cabin."

"It's a beautiful spot. And Jack Bean left everything in perfect order. It has been wonderfully comfortable. Did you know Bean well?"

"Well enough. Jack lived up there for thirty years."

Rahlys sipped her wine and surveyed the crowd that included no one she really knew. Then Spit leaned toward her again.

"There's a guy hanging out in town looking for you, going by the name of Aaron...hard, dark, brooding eyes...not the kind to be trusted." Rahlys admired Spit's perceptiveness. If only she could have had his insight a couple of years ago. Her stomach clutched in distaste at the certainty of eventually having to confront Aaron. What if he came in here tonight? She squeezed herself deeper into the corner, feeling a sudden urge to leave. Confrontation was not her strong point. Don't be a coward, Rahlys told herself. You can handle Aaron; he is powerless. You must be courageous. There will eventually be a far greater adversary to face.

The music stopped again, and Vince and Maggie pushed their way back through the crowd.

"Phew, I'm hot!" Maggie tried to fan herself with her hand.

When the next number started, the crowd whooped and hollered into swinging, bouncing motion again. A couple of band numbers later, Rahlys and Maggie finished their drink and stepped out into the cold, dark night.

"I was so afraid Aaron was going to walk in the whole time we were there," Rahlys admitted to Maggie. "I don't know what to say to him when I see him. I wish he would just go away." Snowflakes streaked toward them in the headlight beams of the truck as they drove home.

"What do you mean you don't know what to say to him? You tell him to leave you alone and get a life."

The next day, Rahlys had the house to herself. The mat cutter and a choice of different color mats covered the kitchen table. She spread her paintings out on the counter, looking then over. Choosing *The Crystalline Raven* to mat and frame first, she took it to the table. The fragmented depiction of the raven with the crystal in his beak was specked with the soft colors of the crystal's light against the faceted blue-black darkness of the raven's feathers.

To determine the best mat color combination for the painting, she placed the different color mats, one at a time, next to it and observed the effect. Finally she chose a three-color combination of gold, white, and black. The mat cutter did a swift job of cutting the mats. Then she mounted the painting between the matting and an art board backing and held it away from her to observe the effect. The result was stunning.

Aaron approaches.

Rahlys froze, incapacitated by indecision. Soon there was a sharp knock at the door. It was particularly startling because she had not heard anyone drive up.

Aaron knocked again. She thought of not answering, but the door wasn't lock, and surely he would try the doorknob if no one answered. Reluctantly she went to the door and opened it.

"Why, hi, Rahlys! You are certainly a beautiful sight!"

Rahlys fumed. "Go away, Aaron. I don't want to see you. I don't love you! Hell, I don't even like you. You're just a weasel, that's what you are," and Rahlys slammed the door shut in his face and locked it.

"Now, Rahlys, Honey, don't be like that. I've came a long way to see you," he shouted from the other side of the door. "I've changed, honest. There's no one but you. Please, let me in."

"No, I just want you to go away and leave me alone," she shouted back. Rahlys felt for the crystal through her shirt. Could she compel him to go away with magic?

"Aw, come on, Baby, it's cold out here. I don't have a car, someone gave me a ride and dropped me off."

"Then you better start walking." Rahlys resolutely refused to let him in. If she were to make that mistake, it would become even harder to get rid of him. Invariably he would be in need of something, beginning with a place to stay. Rahlys focused her thoughts, directing them toward him. She searched for his personal essence, focusing on the life signature that was his alone, willing him to go, mentally pressing the message into his brain.

You want to go. Go away. Leave from here now.

She felt his reluctance, but she pushed harder. To her relief, after a hesitant pause, he turned away and headed off toward the road.

Aaron didn't know what possessed him to forgo his attempt to persuade Rahlys to open the door and let him in. He felt compelled to leave, and turned away without looking back. At the end of the short driveway, he strolled toward town, the cold air nipping at his unprotected hands and head. After going nearly a mile down the frozen, deserted road, rapidly losing body heat from his unprotected extremities, Aaron began to wonder why he had left. He thought about turning around and marching right back, when a car stealthily approached him from behind. Hoping for a ride, Aaron put his thumb out, and a pale, bluish green Subaru came to a stop beside him. The passenger car window rolled down, and warm air rushed out at Aaron as he looked in the window to address the driver.

"Could you give me a lift into town?"

"Sure. Get in."

The window rolled back up as Aaron climbed into the passenger seat. "Thanks." He rubbed his hands and blew on them to bring back the circulation as they headed toward town.

"I'm Half Ear," the driver introduced himself.

Aaron looked at his stout, weathered benefactor with puzzlement, an ancient looking pouch slung over his shoulder, "Yeah, I'm Aaron…Half Ear?"

Half Ear removed his stretched-out gray stocking cap, and showed Aaron his misshapen right ear. The top of his ear was a jagged edge instead of a smooth curve. "Bitten off by a bear, it was. A mean old grizzly, too. But me…know what I did…I just bit that old grizzly bear's ear right back."

When Aaron asked to be dropped off at the downtown bar, Half Ear parked the Subaru in the back, and they entered together, taking stools next to each other at the bar. Aaron and Half Ear occupied those stools till well into the evening, with Half Ear buying the beer. When Aaron could no longer stand without wobbling, Half Ear led him out of the bar, and across the street to his own unassuming bachelor pad where Aaron fell out on the sofa.

It was well after dark by the time Maggie and Rahlys were driving home a couple of days later from their long and exhausting shopping trip to Wasilla. "Watch for moose," Maggie reminded Rahlys, her eyes glued to the road as she drove them homeward along the pitch black Parks Highway. Thick clouds blanketed the night sky, sealing it off, preventing any moonlight or starlight from shining through. All that could be seen was the slice of road in the headlights.

For Rahlys it had been a long week. Thankfully, it was nearly over. The local arts and crafts gallery now had her work on display, and she looked forward to doing some more painting. With a pickup truck load of food and supplies, Rahlys was anxious for the evening to pass, and the next day to arrive, so she could take the train back into the woods.

A collision is imminent.

The message roused Rahlys out of her musing. "Maggie, stop the truck!"

"What?" Slowing down, Maggie strained to see what she assumed Rahlys had seen, but saw nothing.

"Stop the truck! Now!" Rahlys screamed. Maggie responded to the urgency in her voice by slowing to a near stop as she continued to search for something, anything, in the beam of her headlights. They had the road to themselves. There was not another headlight in sight.

Then they saw it. A moose was standing in the middle of the road staring them down as they approached. Maggie came to a stop, a safe distance away, and waited for the animal to make a decision.

"How did you know it was there? Have you become psychic?"

"I'm not sure," she answered truthfully. Rahlys had not yet found the time or place to tell Maggie about the crystal. After some time, the moose turned and ambled across the road and into the darkness.

A half hour later they pulled into Maggie's driveway weary from the long day, and unloaded the truck. Rahlys packed up the cardboard boxes Maggie had collected for her from work, separating items by priority. She left her pack empty for the perishables like eggs, milk, and cheese that would spend the night in the refrigerator. These she would pack in the morning. There was a box of frozen stuff she packed up and carried out to the truck to stay frozen. She had also bought more frames, mat board, watercolor paper, and paints which she also packed to take. "How are you going to get all this up to the cabin?" Maggie asked. "There's enough food here for one person for a month."

"That's the idea, I don't want to have to come out again for a while. It may take a few days, but I will get it up there." Of course Rahlys knew she could just teleport it all home at once. In fact, she secretly teleported a couple of boxes to the cabin that night to cut down on the load, knowing they would never be missed.

A few isolated snowflakes sputtered down as Maggie and Rahlys pulled into the train station the next morning. People huddled in several groups around piles of packs, boxes, and duffle bags, chattering patiently as they waited for the train. Soon Rahlys had a neat stack of her own as they unloaded the truck into a pile on the platform in line with the others. Looking around, Maggie spotted Vince walking back from the parking lot. Vince was also going back into the woods. Then they heard the train whistle in the near distance.

"Is that your stack?" he asked as he approached, indicating the pile they were standing next to.

"Yes," Rahlys confirmed; the train was already in sight.

"I can give you a hand getting things up to the cabin with the snow-machine," Vince offered. The train pulled into the station, and came to a stop. Vince rushed up to the baggage car to help. Ever so quickly people and baggage were unloaded and loaded.

"Bye, sweetie," Maggie gave Rahlys a quick hug.

"I can't wait until you come up to visit." Rahlys said, hugging Maggie goodbye. By the time Rahlys turned to grab a box, helping hands had already eliminated her stack. Then Vince rushed over and gave Maggie a hug. As they boarded the train, Maggie headed back to her truck, but not without turning and waving.

Rahlys sat back in her seat letting the stress of the past week drain from her body. She was on her way home. Finally, the interrupting trip to town was over, and she could get back to work. As the snow-covered landscape slipped by her window, she thought about her frozen cabin waiting for warmth, her empty easel waiting to display her next work. She could hardly wait to be settled back into her routine.

Then sooner than she expected, the train was stopping at the foot of her trail, and Vince and the conductor were helping her unload her boxes. When all her pieces were accounted for, she waved farewell, and the train pulled away, quickly disappearing around the bend...severing her link with the rest of the world...leaving her standing alone in a frozen wilderness. Rahlys released a deep sigh of relief as she soaked in the quiet stillness of the deep snowy woods all around her.

She was home.

Chapter 6
Revelation

Franklin waited cautiously for his eyes to adjust to the darkness that engulfed him. But there didn't seem to be any perceivable light for his eyes to adjust to. Not wanting to reveal his unexpected arrival to whatever may be lurking in this unknown darkness, Franklin didn't move or make a sound. He was still on his bed. Wherever he was, the bed was with him. He could hear water gurgling softly not far away, and considered climbing down in the dark to investigate, but the fear of dropping into a void held him back. After considerable time, during which nothing had stirred, Franklin reached into his pocket and pulled out the orb.

Light.

The orb floated up out of his hand, brightening as it ascended up, and up, lighting the stone walls and great emptiness of a grand cavern. His enormous bed was dwarfed by the massive natural stone dais on which it rested. At the other end of the chamber the floor dropped down in rough steps to a trickling underground creek that flowed through the cavern's lower end. The little stream entered the cavern through a narrow gap in the moist dripping stone wall, and flowed out through another.

Only in pictures had Franklin seen anything like this before. Rocks and boulders generally weren't found in the Mississippi River delta. He teleported himself off the bed and stood there in the immense cave gazing about in amazement. The bed looked small in the vast space, the four corner posts reaching for but not coming anywhere close to touching the high curve of the vaulted stone ceiling overhead. The sound of the flowing water begged for his attention, and he made his way down to the level of the stream.

Clear water, so clear the rocks of the streambed could be seen through it, flowed continuously into the cavern and quickly left again through openings in the stone. Franklin looked around. There was no sign of anything living, neither plant nor animal. He stooped, putting his fingers in the water, and drew them out quickly. The water was cold to the touch. In fact, his whole body was becoming chilled and he started to shiver as the cold, damp air sucked away at his body heat.

Warmth, Franklin commanded. And the orb emitted an aura of warmth around him. Then, directed by an inner voice, Franklin focused mentally, drawing energy from around him and within, concentrating that energy on a focal point on the wall of the cavern. A spot on the stone started to glow, growing increasingly larger and hotter and brighter. Pivoting a quarter turn in each direction, Franklin invoked more areas of heat and light, until the stones' warmth and eerie orange glow filled the cavern, taking the chill and dampness out of the air.

Franklin summoned the orb back to his hand, and directed his attention once again to the stream. The mysterious stream that flowed so secretly through its dark, rocky world was especially fascinating to Franklin. He stooped to peer into the low, dark crevice to see where the water was coming from, but the serpentine tunnel, lost in darkness, did not reveal its secrets. Franklin opened his hand releasing the orb and commanded telepathically, *Show me the path the water is taking.*

The orb dived down into the opening, lighting the way as it sped upstream, projecting images back to Franklin as it ducked and swerved around the protrusions and irregularities of the narrow, low, snaking rock tunnel just inches above the flowing water. From time to time the passage through stone opened up into small caves and connecting tunnels, only to quickly narrow down again. In places, the opening became so small, the orb had to dip into the water to squeeze through. Mile after mile, the orb cruised through the stone labyrinth, until finally Franklin conjured it back to his hand.

Then Franklin made his way over and around rocks and boulders to the other end of the stream's flow where it disappeared through another hole in the rock. After a thoughtful pause, Franklin commanded the orb again.

Slower this time...show me the path the water is taking out.

The glowing orb floated down and into the broad thin crevice in the rock, sending back images as it drifted over the stream that nearly filled the low passageway. It was some time before the course finally widened out into a small, low cave with a narrow rock shelf just inches above the level on the water.

Halt! Franklin commanded the orb, and it came to a stop. Franklin sat on the floor of the cavern by the stream with quiet concentration. He ducked his head down as a precaution, and conjured himself to the stone ledge in the little cave where the orb glowed and hovered in place.

Gingerly, Franklin lifted his head feeling for the ceiling with his hand. The cave proved to be just barely big enough for him sit up. *Continue,* he directed the orb, and the orb slipped through the opening in the stone, following the flow of the water, leaving him in darkness. Franklin sat in the cramped, chilly cave as the lighted images of the orb's passage unrolled in his mind. The course curved steeply downward, the water cascading over rock as it hurried along its way. Then the little stream plunged into a larger one, also hurrying along. The opening in the stone became greater as the volume of water increased, the rushing water careening madly about the passageway shifting direction frequently in its downward spiral. Then suddenly it broke forth into emptiness, the orb hovering in an enormous cavern over a waterfall that dropped into a large underground lake. Franklin gasped in awe as the orb flew out over the lake, its distant shore lost in darkness.

Find the shore, he instructed filled with excitement.

The lake proved to be immense as the orb attempted to cross it. When it discovered a narrow strip of rocky beach sandwiched against the water's edge and the stone wall of the cavern Franklin ordered it to halt.

Focusing on the strip of beach, Franklin teleported himself to it, appearing suddenly on the shore of the lake with the low roar of the waterfall in his ear. Who could have ever imagined such a place? He looked up, but the high ceiling of the cavern was lost in darkness. The surface of the water, undisturbed by tempestuous storms and changing tides, lay smooth and inky black before him.

Gingerly, Franklin hiked the narrow rocky shore, guided by the light of the orb. The sound of the waterfall diminished over time with distance. Sometimes he had to climb over boulders or teleport around obstacles to make progress. But it was the grumble of Franklin's stomach that finally brought the expedition to a halt. Since the prospect of finding food here seemed unlikely, he summoned the orb to his hand and teleported himself back to his cavern with its welcoming warmth and orangey glow, his home, furnished with his own great bed. But there was nothing to eat here either. He still needed to find food.

Take me to the surface, he commanded the orb.

Almost instantly, Franklin was in freezing cold and blinding sunlight, floundering in deep snow on a steeply sloping mountainside. His frantic movements shuddered through the snow shelf, breaking it loose. The severed snow pack began to move, sending Franklin tumbling, amongst chunks of snow, down the mountainside.

"Ahhhh......" he screamed as he went into free fall over the edge. Franklin strained with all his might to teleport himself to safety before being crushed on the snow and protruding pinnacles of rock far below. He was screaming still when he landed in the cavern on his warm soft bed.

Franklin didn't move for a while, but just lay there trying to catch his breath, assuring himself he was still alive, as the snow he brought with him turned to water. He would teleport himself back to the city to graze he decided. But as recent experience showed, it was necessary to be cautious when suddenly placing oneself somewhere without knowing what is about. Recovering sufficiently from his ordeal, Franklin pondered over a location he could safely focus on as a portal, and ended up concentrating on the ramshackle shed he remembered behind his grandmother's house. He hadn't been there in years, but surely no one would be there. It did not occur to Franklin that things may have changed since his grandmother's death, and the onslaught of hurricane Katrina.

Franklin concentrated on the dilapidated little shed, drawing it from his memory, and teleported himself to the location. Warm, humid, free-flowing air with the smell of the river a short distance away touched his face as he suddenly appeared on a vacant lot in the lower ninth ward. The shed, as well as the house, and all the other houses on the block, had been bulldozed and cleared away, grass and weeds already growing again in the muddy soil. It was dusk here, which struck Franklin as strange. It had been bright daylight up on the mountain. Fortunately there was no one around to notice his sudden appearance out of nowhere.

His stomach still growling, Franklin went in search of food, teleporting short distances when the coast looked clear to speed up his progress. The first source of food he came to was a hot dog vendor on a street corner sitting in a lawn chair next to her cart. The vendor, gray and plump, viewed Franklin suspiciously as he approached. Franklin met the woman's gaze head on, mentally taking control. A pained expression contorted her features, then the vendor went into automated action. Without saying a word, Franklin directed the woman in the construction of a chili cheese dog with everything on it. Unfalteringly, the vendor executed the task. When it was complete, she handed the creation over to him. Taking it, Franklin gave the woman a mental nudge, pushing her back into her chair. Her heart came to a stop as he walked off, indulging in his first bite.

His hunger satiated, for a while, Franklin located a Winn-Dixie supermarket. Now that he had a place of his own, it was time to do some serious grocery shopping. Pushing a shopping cart, Franklin toured the isles filling the cart with anything and everything he wanted. The cart was already overflowing when he came to a bin of watermelons in the produce section. Cautiously, he surveyed his surroundings, patiently waiting for a mother and her young daughter to turn the corner before teleporting two thumping-ripe watermelons to his bed in the cavern.

A soft gasp drew his attention. Turning around, Franklin spied the young girl who had taken another peek at the strange boy with the overfull cart, just as the watermelons had vanished into thin air.

Franklin stared at her forebodingly, and she stared back, mesmerized, paralyzed by mounting fear. He relished the horrifying fear the child projected back, her terror exciting him. Then suddenly the girl turned and fled, running to catch up with her mother. Immediately, Franklin teleported himself and the full shopping cart to the security of his cavern, where no one would ever be able to find him.

After her excursion to town, Rahlys fell back into her daily routine. She did chores and sketched subjects for paintings during the short daylight hours, getting fresh air and exercise in the bargain, and pondered over the Oracle's magic, and the threat of Droclum as she painted late into the night. Then she slept hard in undisturbed sleep until the late morning sunrise.

Rahlys stepped out under dull gray clouds. Somewhat aimlessly, she walked over to the combination shed/workshop, looking around. Since ownership, she spent little time browsing through its contents. Basic hand tools hung on the wall, or rested on a work bench; a plane, a hammer, a couple of saws, some rope, a cable come-a-long, a chainsaw, and an old pair of snowshoes. Garden tools stood in one corner. Rahlys looked at the chainsaw with uncertainty. Although she had watched her father handle a chainsaw growing up, she had never used one herself, and her supply of firewood would not last forever. Eventually she would have to think of cutting firewood for next winter. Maybe Vince would give her a lesson on the use and maintenance of a chainsaw. Finding nothing of interest for the moment, she went back outside, latching the shed door.

This was the day for local freight; her full fuel drum may already be down by the railroad tracks. How could she find out without actually going down to look? Clearing her mind, she tried summoning the raven. Rahlys had no way of knowing if the raven was anywhere near by. So far there had been seemingly no limitations on distance, but if he was too far away, he wouldn't be of help.

Where are you, Raven? she called silently.

Then Rahlys saw a view of the river from a perch high in a cottonwood tree. To communicate her need, she sent a mental image to the raven of the foot of her trail near the railroad tracks.

Raven, receiving the summons, took off from his perch flying south. As he approached, she saw the cliffs come in close to the tracks, then back away again as the river meandered in and out of view. Then the railroad tracks crossed a creek. There were more hills, and finally the terrain flattened out a bit, and Rahlys saw her own trail and a blue, fifty-five-gallon drum sitting there…with no one in sight. Her fuel drum had arrived. Rahlys conjured an apple from the root cellar, and teleported herself down to the tracks to join the raven waiting for her, perched on the drum.

"Ka ka-kaw!"

"And ka ka-kaw to you too!" Rahlys held the apple in the palm of her hand and severed it into four perfectly formed wedges. "What do you think of that?" she asked, placing one wedge in the raven's beak. The raven devoured it quickly.

Rahlys needed to move the drum away from the tracks, but if she pushed it over and rolled it into the woods, surely she would be unable to stand it up again, and she didn't want to leave a full drum on its side. But wasn't her magical strength far greater than her physical strength? Rahlys fed the raven the rest of the apple while building up her confidence. She was becoming increasingly aware of the invisible molecular energy around her, and slowly learning how to draw on it. Could she really teleport this much weight? It was time to find out. She focused her thoughts on the drum, concentrating on its density and structure. Then with some uncertainty, pinpointing in her mind a spot in the yard not far from the generator shed, she placed her arms around the drum, drawing heavily on the energy around her. She felt a wrenching sensation, and the burden of weight, followed by a thump, and she was there, standing in unpacked snow beside the generator shed, her arms still embracing the drum with the raven still perched on top.

"Aaaaaark!" Raven cried in mild protest, and flew off into the woods. Rahlys smiled with pleasant satisfaction as she watched him go.

Maggie was coming up for the weekend, and Rahlys was resolved to confide in her about the crystal. She needed someone to talk to. The enormity of her powers and Droclum's looming threat were becoming more than she could bear alone. Anthya had implied that Maggie was one of her warriors, and Rahlys intended on making it so.

Sunlight gleamed through the trees erasing the memory of cloudy, gloomy days, as Rahlys hiked down to the tracks to meet the train. Just a few puffy, white clouds drifted lazily across the bright, blue sky. The trail was packed down now, making for easy walking. Numerous small tracks made by squirrels, shrews, and voles could be seen crossing the snow in various directions.

As she neared the foot of her trail, she could hear a snowmachine approaching from the north through the woods. Then she saw its light as it wove through the trees toward her. Vince pulled up and cut the engine just as the distant train whistle from the south caught their attention.

"It's going to be almost on time," Vince said looking at his watch. Rahlys realized that Vince was also excited over Maggie's weekend visit.

But as Maggie got off the train, it was obvious that she was the most excited of all. "Oh, it is beautiful! Look at all the snow!" She hugged Rahlys and Vince exuberantly.

"I can take one box, the pack, and one of you on the first trip." It was just like Vince to get right to business.

Rahlys knew Maggie was eager to ride the snowmachine. "You go up on the first trip," she offered. "The cabin is warm. I'll be there before too long." Vince placed a box in the luggage rack behind the seat of the snowmachine, and then the pack on top of it, strapping them down.

"A snowmachine ride! This is so exciting! Are you sure you want me to go first?" Maggie asked, barely able to contain her desire.

"Yes, I'm sure." Rahlys smiled, enjoying Maggie's excitement.

Vince started up the snowmachine and got on, scooting forward some so Maggie could sit behind him. "Go ahead and start walking. I'll pick you up when I come back for the other box," he told Rahlys. And off they went, Maggie holding on to Vince for dear life. Gradually the sound of the snowmachine faded in the distance, as she followed its track toward the cabin. She had already climbed the first rise and was in sight of the second, when she heard the snowmachine approaching again. Then there it was, coming at her. Rahlys stepped off the trail into the unpacked snow, and Vince came to a halt beside her, engine running.

"You want to ride?" Vince asked over the engine noise.

"On the way back."

He nodded and continued down the trail to pick up the last box. She thought of teleporting herself the rest of the way so he would marvel at her progress, but decided not to draw that kind of attention. By the time Vince pulled up to her again with the last box strapped on, she had made it up the second rise, and was on the home stretch. He scooted forward so she could get on while the machine purred contentedly.

"Ready?" he called back to her once she was settled.

"Yes!" They took off and Rahlys threw her arms around Vince's waist to hold on. She read his amusement and relaxing some, held on to the sides of his coat instead. When they reached the last rise, Vince leaned forward off his seat gunning the machine up the hill. Rahlys leaned forward as best she could, and soon they were level again and in the yard.

"Alright!" Maggie greeted from the porch and Vince killed the engine. After they dismounted, Vince undid the strap and lifted the box onto the porch.

"Thanks," Rahlys smiled warmly. "Do you want to come in for a cup of coffee?"

Vince wanted to stay, but knew he shouldn't. He needed to do some work on a novel that had a pressing deadline, and Maggie had already invited him over for dinner later.

"I'll give you girls a chance to catch up. What time is dinner tonight?"

"Six o'clock?" Maggie threw out, and everyone agreed.

"Then I'll see you ladies at six." He started up the snowmachine, and took off down the trail.

Rahlys reached for one of the boxes. "Oh, everything in that box is already frozen," Maggie explained, "except the chicken for dinner tonight, so it can stay outside." Rahlys opened the box; there was chicken, frozen meat, frozen vegetables, fruit juices, even ice cream. It was a good thing that colder temperatures had settled in.

"And this is fresh stuff." Maggie moved toward the other box, but before she could reach it Rahlys teleported it inside.

Maggie stared at the vacant spot where the box had been in disbelief. "What happened to it? It was right there!" She looked for it all around her.

"I took it inside. It's on the counter in the kitchen."

"You couldn't have…it was right here…" Maggie mumbled under her breath in confusion as she marched into the cabin. There sat the box of produce on the counter. "But…how?" she finally got out.

"I teleported the box from the porch to the counter using magic." Maggie looked at Rahlys with concern. She had to explain before Maggie believed she had gone insane. "Remember the painting of the raven with the crystal that Vince took up to his cabin?"

"Yes, *The Crystalline Raven*. It's a great painting."

"Well, the crystal in the painting is real."

"So?"

"I mean the crystal is…really magic."

Confused as to what response Rahlys expected, Maggie laughed a little, politely. Rahlys took a deep breath; it was obvious Maggie didn't believe her, but she had to convince her, so she forged on.

"When I moved here in September, the very day I moved in, the raven brought me a crystal. It is like no crystal I have ever seen before; it glows from its own light! When I picked it up, I felt a surge of energy rush through me. Then one thing happened after another. I received a mysterious message in my head, followed by a bear in my cabin. The bear exited the cabin through that window." Rahlys pointed to the window, whole and intact, offering a view of the mountain glowing in the light, with dark blue shadows. "The window shattered into a thousand pieces. Distraught, I ran outside hollering and screaming, waving my arms and crying. Then before my eyes, thousands of shards of broken glass coalesced back into place as a window. I couldn't believe it! I was terrified! I thought I had lost my mind." Maggie looked at her as though she had indeed. To Maggie, Rahlys was not making a lot of sense. Rahlys was near tears, her heart pounding, as she relived the experience.

"Where is this magic crystal you're talking about?"

Rahlys stretched out her hand and conjured the crystal from its pouch. Immediately it appeared hovering above her open hand. She moved her hand away, and the crystal remained suspended in air revolving ever so slowly.

"Oh my gosh!" Maggie gasped. Maggie looked incredulously from the hovering crystal to her friend begging to be believed. "Why, it's beautiful!" She stepped closer, inspecting the crystal without touching it, feeling the air around it, looking for suspension wires, or something. Then without warning, Maggie reached for it with her hand. The crystal brightened to Maggie's touch. Rahlys froze in anticipation of what might happen, her heart racing as she watched. If the raven had been effected by the crystal, would Maggie be too?

"I've never seen anything like this before," Maggie said turning the crystal around, looking at it from all angles. "This is incredible. It glows and changes color, I can see why you say it's magic."

"I don't think you do." Rahlys said, conjuring the crystal to her. The crystal disappeared from Maggie's hand, and reappeared hovering between Rahlys' thumb and index finger, then she released it again. "The crystal is from another world in a distant galaxy. It was brought to Earth many years ago, and now I possess its magic."

"What magic?" Maggie still feared Rahlys was becoming delusional from living alone in the woods.

Calmly, Rahlys picked up a glass from the table and hurled it hard against the floor. The glass shattered into numerous pieces that scattered across the room. Maggie was shocked by Rahlys' behavior. Then with intense concentration, Rahlys snapped her fingers and the glass coalesced back whole in her hand again. Now Maggie was speechless. She placed the glass down on the table and waited, giving Maggie time to absorb the inconceivable...giving her time to process the unbelievable.

"So that is how you knew there was a moose on the road when we were coming back from town?" To her relief, Rahlys knew she now had Maggie's confidence on her side.

"I had received a message from the Oracle saying a collision was imminent." The crystal continued to hover near her. "Not only can I teleport objects, but I can also teleport myself." But Maggie just shook her head in disbelief. Of course she could not expect Maggie to just accept such a claim, and she didn't blame her. "I'm going to the back porch to get an armload of firewood," she told Maggie, and then placing herself on the back porch in her mind she was there. The crystal disappeared with her. As she loaded her arms with kindling to start a fire in the cook stove, Maggie dashed out onto the porch, flinging the door wide.

"Rahlys!" she cried, relief surging into her face upon seeing her. "How did you do that? It's like you just disappeared!"

"Basically, I place myself somewhere in my mind and will myself there, and then I'm there." She walked through the door Maggie held open and dropped the armload of kindling on the floor near the wood cook stove. Maggie continued to stare in amazement as the crystal followed her around.

"There's more. We can talk while we make a pie for dinner," she said softly, and handed Maggie apples, a bowl, and a knife. Maggie peeled and sliced apples while Rahlys built a fire in the cook stove and related the details of Anthya's visit. Maggie was a captive audience and for quite a while very little peeling and slicing actually got done.

"And you've felt this Droclum searching for you in your dreams?"

"Yes, and I'm afraid. Anthya said the day would come when I would have to face him." Rahlys reloaded the firebox, and adjusted the baffle to direct the heat to the oven.

"What are you going to do if Droclum shows up?"

"I don't know."

"Why would someone with a life span of thousands of years need immortality?" Maggie wondered. And then on a different track, "Do you think the crystal might actually be evil?"

"I've wondered that myself."

"Has it tried to make you to do things you don't want to? Something you know is wrong?" Rahlys thought carefully, but couldn't think of anything.

"No, in fact Anthya offered a dire warning, 'If you use your power for evil intent, you will surely die.'"

"Now, that's scary!"

After constructing a prize-winning apple pie, they sipped coffee while waiting for the oven to reach temperature. Operating a wood stove was a mastered art for Rahlys. All the years of her youth she had cooked and baked along side her mother, tending the firebox. Once the desired temperature was reached, Rahlys dampened the draft to hold it. Then she put the pie in the oven.

"Does Vince know about the crystal?"

"No, and he doesn't need to know. At least not yet. You are the only one who knows…you and the raven."

"The raven? You mean the raven that brought you the crystal?"

"Yes. I think the raven has powers too."

"What?"

"One day when I wondered where the raven was, it came as though I had summoned it. And as he flew toward me, I could see the hills and the creek from high above the trees as though I was seeing them through his eyes." She could read Maggie's doubt, but there was no magic trick she could perform to convince her…or was there? "Let's go outside for a while," Rahlys suggested, and conjured the crystal back to its pouch as they put on coats, boots, and hats against the cold. Then Rahlys grabbed the bowl of apple cores she had saved.

"What's that for?"

"The raven," she said, and led Maggie out the cabin. Cold air hit them as they walked out the front door. The sun, already low on the horizon, offered no warmth. All was still and quiet as they walked out onto the circular drive Vince had packed around the cabin with the snowmachine. Even the few wispy white clouds that dotted the iridescent sky seemed suspended in time.

Rahlys sought the raven in her mind, while Maggie stood quietly, expectantly still. There was no sound or movement, until the rat tat tat of a woodpecker boring a hole in a nearby tree broke the silence.

Not far away, the raven felt an irresistible urge tug at his brain. He took off from his perch atop a dead tree with a broken top near the bears' favorite fishing hole. The salmon run was long over...the urge to spawn spent...and the death and decay after sexual relief had been carefully cleaned up by scavengers, the sacrificial site buried now under snow. The raven was hungry, and the summons promised food. But as he approached the clearing, it was clear She was not alone. Taking precautions, he landed on top of the woodshed where he could survey the situation from a safe distance.

"You did it," Maggie cried in amazement. "You summoned a raven!"

"Aaaark!"

Rahlys dropped the apple cores down on the trail. "It's okay, you can come down. No one is going to hurt you," she said telepathing a sense of reassurance to the raven. Rahlys and Maggie walked further along the circular path, giving the raven some space, and after some deliberation, he flew down to the offering.

As the women completed the circuit to the front porch, the distant sound of an approaching snowmachine caught their ears. It was probably Vince. The crystal was already safely tucked away in its pouch. They stood in front of the cabin, their bodies now comfortably acclimated to outdoors, and listened to the sound grow nearer. Then they spotted the light blinking through breaks between the trees. As the snowmachine approached, they noticed he was dragging something behind it. With the apple cores consumed, the raven took off as Vince crested the rise into the clearing and the last glimmer of sun slipped below the horizon.

Vince made a wide circle around the cabin, and stopped in the front yard, shutting off the engine. Rahlys walked up to greet him.

"Hi, neighbor!"

"Hi, there! I thought since I was coming anyway, I would drag your trail for you."

"So, this is a trail groomer?" Rahlys inspected it closely. "Looks like an antique bed spring to me."

"That's what it is. Best trail groomer there is." Vince's face was red from snowmachining.

"Come in and warm up. I have coffee made," and without debate, Vince followed them into the house. The aroma of apple pie baking filled the room.

"How's your book coming?" she asked once they were seated over steaming cups. "Can you tell us anything about it, or is it a secret?"

"I can tell you about it at least as far as I've gotten. It's a spy story that takes place in the 1990s after Czechoslovakia divided into The Czech Republic and Slovakia. There are top secret files that belonged to the former Czechoslovakian government and are wanted by the new Czech government. But the documents ended up in the hands of the Slovakians who don't even realize they have them. My spy is after those files. I have about a third of the novel written, and I've been proofing another novel that is about to go into print."

"Have you been to the Czech Republic?" Maggie asked.

"No, I've been to the former Czechoslovakia." Vince described a country of cobblestone streets, ancient buildings, and tiny villages with few luxuries. Rahlys picked up even more detail from his memories as he told of his travels. Soon apple pie came out the oven, chicken and vegetables were roasting, and coffee was replaced with wine. Rahlys couldn't remember the last time she had had so much fun. Solitude was wonderful, but everyone needs a little socialization once in a while. It was delightful having company.

The next morning, Maggie and Rahlys huddled over steaming cups of coffee staring out the cabin windows mesmerized by thick, fluffy snow flakes falling in the dawning light. They reflected over moments of last night's dinner party, the refuse of which was still around them. All the food had been excellent. Vince had brought a loaf of his knock-out bread and had supplied a second bottle of wine. The cabin had filled with laughter as the three of them relaxed and released in comfortable friendship. Rahlys noticed that Vince put a twinkle in Maggie's eye that hadn't been there before, and her impact on him was equally obvious.

"Let's have another look at that crystal," Maggie said bouncing alive after just one cup. Rahlys conjured the crystal from its pouch and it hovered around them, glowing softly. When it came close to Maggie, it stopped. She reached up and grasped it, and the crystal brightened. "Oh, it just sends tingles down your spine."

Did Maggie now have magical powers, Rahlys wondered. "Let's try something," she said, and Maggie released the crystal.

"Try what?"

"Give me your coffee cup." Rahlys placed Maggie's cup a short distance away from her on the table. "I want you to place your hand on the table and beckon your cup to it. Like this." Putting her own cup down, she focused on it. The cup disappeared from its former position on the table, and reappeared instantly in her hand.

"You think I can do that?" Maggie exclaimed. "But how?"

"Just relax and focus. Place the cup in your hand in your mind, and it will follow through."

Not thoroughly convinced, Maggie readied her hand on the table a short distance from her cup, and concentrated as Rahlys had done. At first, nothing seemed to happen, but then, to Maggie's amazement, the cup began to wobble slightly.

"Wow! Did you see that?"

"Yes. Try again." Maggie obliged and concentrated with all her might, but again the cup only jiggled hesitantly in place. Repeated attempts yielded the same result. "I don't seem to have your talent."

"But moving the cup at all means you have somehow been affected by the crystal."

Maggie pondered that, then got up and refilled her cup with coffee. She looked out the window, then sat back down. "Vince is supposed to come by today to take me snowmachining. Do you think he will still come, if it's snowing?"

"I don't think he would miss it for the world. Besides, snow and snowmachining go together."

When Vince arrived, they had already cleared away brunch and Maggie was pacing the floor. She had purchased all new winter gear on their shopping trip, fluorescent green, from snow pants to mitts. Quickly she was suitably attired for the excursion and rushed out to meet him. The sky had lightened up a bit, but it was still snowing.

"I brought an extra pair of goggles for you to use," Vince said handing her a pair of bright red goggles. "Without them the snow would sting your eyes on impact. They protect your eyes from branches, too."

"How much longer before train time?" she asked, adjusting the goggles to rest comfortably on her face.

"We have four hours left. Plenty enough time to make it to my place and back." Vince started up the snowmachine, and Maggie waved and whooped with glee as they headed down the hill. Rahlys was glad to see them off. It gave her some time to do chores and putter around the cabin. Rahlys loved Maggie's company, but she also enjoyed her solitude.

The snowfall continued to subside as the snowmachine seemingly floated down the trail, cushioned with fresh snow. Maggie threw her arms around Vince as they leaned into the curves. Soon they were at the intersection to Vince's trail. They could see the railroad tracks a couple hundred feet away as they made a hard right heading north. Then Vince came to a stop, engine still running, and turned around to check on her. "Are you okay?"

"Yes, this is great!"

"Alright then." He squeezed the throttle, and they were off again. The trail paralleled the tracks for about a mile and then turned east and climbed into the hills again. Maggie was loving the ride, and the scenery was magnificent.

Then Vince took what looked like a detour off the main trail weaving through a stand of stunted black spruce, entering into a large expanse of white. The snow started coming down harder. With all obstacles out the way, Vince really let it rip. They zoomed full bore across the level field of snow, forming figure eights an ice skater would have been proud of. Maggie felt like they were flying, it was so fast and smooth. The heavily laden ceiling pressed down, and the snowfall thickened around them. Vince came to a stop in the middle of the expanse of white.

"You want to drive?"

"Me, drive? Are you sure?"

"Sure! There's nothing to hit out here." They switched places, and Vince gave her a couple of quick instructions. Maggie made a hesitating start. "You need to keep some speed up to stay afloat…but not too fast." Maggie pressed her thumb harder on the throttle and the machine surged forward. Quickly she got the feel of it, and they were sailing across the snow with ease. When she came to a stop, Vince reached over and hit the kill switch.

The heavy snowfall curtained them off from the rest of the world. Not even the closest trees could be seen through the all encompassing white, the only sounds their breathing and the soft whispering of falling snow. They took off their goggles and soaked in the beauty and magic of the snowfall…and the magic of being alone together, in a lingering kiss.

When the train was nearly due and Vince and Maggie still hadn't returned, Rahlys became concerned. *Maggie where are you? Are you alright?* she reached out telepathically.

Maggie and Vince were just about to leave for the train stop when Maggie grabbed her head as she walked from Vince's back porch to the snowmachine. "Are you alright?" Vince asked seeing the pained, confused look on her face.

"Yes," she said, dismissing the thought and smiled. Vince started the snowmobile, and she took her place behind him on the seat. Then it happened again. Maggie was sure she was hearing Rahlys calling her in her head? It made her brain itch.

We are leaving Vince's cabin now, headed for the train stop, she tried to telepath to Rahlys, and laughed at herself for trying.

Good! I was worried about you. I will meet you there. Maggie jolted with shock at the reply. Feeling her sudden movement, Vince slowed down enough to glance back at her.

"Okay!" she reassured him smiling again. He turned around and resumed speed. They glided easily down the trail. It had stopped snowing, and pale blue shadows crossed the trail as the setting sun peeked through the forest. The snowmachine twisted and glided up and down the contours of the trail, and in short time they arrived at the train stop where Rahlys greeted them warmly.

"How was the snowmachine ride?" She could read the excitement in both of them, the interest they had in each other, as well as the friend-ship they felt toward her.

"It was great! I drove, too!" Maggie described being at the throttle with great enthusiasm. When Vince wasn't looking, they exchanged confirm-ing nods with one another. "I got your message," Maggie whispered.

"I know." She had communicated telepathically with Maggie! It was similar to the connection she had with the raven. Maggie and the raven did have something in common. They had both been in contact with the crystal.

The train was late as usual, and they paced around packing the snow down to help relieve boredom and fatigue from standing in one place. To pass the time, they talked about what they planned to do that eve-ning and rehashed memories of things they did long ago. Then a train whistle blew in the distance. It was about time; they were getting cold standing around, and it was starting to get dark. Finally, the light on the locomotive came into view around the curve, and the engineer blew the whistle to acknowledge their stop.

Things happened rather quickly after that. Maggie gave them both hugs and stole a hasty kiss from Vince. Then all too swiftly she boarded the train, and it carried her away.

Vince offered Rahlys a ride back to her cabin, but she insisted on walking instead, and after friendly goodbyes, they went their separate ways. Starting up the trail, Rahlys listened to the hum of the snowma-chine fade in the distance. Then placing herself mentally in her warm, cozy cabin, she was there.

Chapter 7
Other Worlds

Day and night became meaningless in Franklin's subterranean world. Most of his time he spent spelunking, or exploring around the great underground lake. He teleported in a pirogue, paddles, and a long pole and set out across the satiny dark water, the orb lighting the way. Probing with the pole, Franklin discovered that the lake was shallow for several boat lengths out from the beach. He could see the rocky bottom as he glided over it, and then suddenly the bottom disappeared, the sounding pole finding only water. He conjured a stone from the beach, and let it drop down into the water, watching its descent. The rock went down, down, down disappearing into the dark depths before ever hitting bottom. Taking up the paddles, he attempted to traverse the lake, paddling and drifting for hours without finding a distant shore. Sometimes he would extinguish the light of the orb, stashing it away in his pocket, and listened in the dark to the mute rumbling of inner Earth, his eyes searching for some hint of natural light, his existence lost in the vast void of darkness.

When ready for rest, Franklin slept fitfully in his magnificent bed, and dreamed, or so it seemed, of another consciousness, frighteningly evil and powerful. His body, sweating profusely, trembled, as the earth…if the strange world in his visions could be called Earth…shook violently, and magma and steam pushed upwards into a shattering eruption that tortured Franklin's body again and again. Then the spasms would subside, and memories of dark intrigue, illicit satisfaction, and shrewd cunning were followed by strange, meaningless messages.

She is here, or at least her powers are. I can sense them. We must find the receptacle of Anthya's magic and destroy it before it destroys us.

Over time, the nagging voice became clearer and haunted his consciousness during his wakeful hours as well. What did the messages mean? Who was Anthya? The voice in his head said she was here. Where? And what was the receptacle of her magic that he was to find and destroy before it destroyed *us*? Who did *us* refer to? Did *us* include himself? These thoughts tormented him incessantly as he crawled on hands and knees, slithering on his belly through the cracks and crevices in the mountain.

You must fortify, the dark spirit warned him. *Cast a spell to prevent a surprise attack. The energy is all around you. Draw on it. I will teach you how.*

Franklin knew his underground chamber was unreachable...unless someone had powers similar to his own. But he learned to draw on the molecular energy around him and cast a protective shield over his domain that prevented anyone with power from entering.

Anthya's Oracle has found a guardian, I can sense the release of her magic, you must find her and destroy her, before she destroys us, the message threatened over and over in his tortured brain.

But how can I find such a person, Franklin wondered.

By detecting the use of magic, the voice answered.

Working off his mental anxiety, Franklin crawled for hours through a tunnel offshoot the orb had found for him. There was no water flowing through the tunnel, although there must have been at some time. He contorted his way upwards through a short spiral that opened out into a space large enough to stand in. As he gained his feet, a ray of natural daylight streamed in through a pea size hole in the cave wall, the ray of light striking him on the chest.

Franklin flinched from the tiny beam, as though the ray were a laser cutting through to his heart. Then he realized the beam of light meant a window to the outside world. He approached the aperture, fantasizing over what may be on the other side. As he placed his hand beside the hole to peer out, the jumbled rock wall, tenuously held together by roots, soil, and gravel, gave way, crumbling into its components, leaving a basketball size breach in the wall of the cave. Daylight and cold fresh air that smelled of the sea poured in. He pushed on the wall around the opening, at first with his hands, and then with magic, sending rocks and debris bouncing down the mountainside, tearing away at the loosely held cave wall until most of it had crumbled away, exposing a terrain so strangely steep and precarious looking to a flat-lander, he dared not set foot outside for fear of plunging to his death. Evergreen forested mountains, partially obscured in mist, squeezed up against one another like the ridges of an accordion. Between two peaks, a tiny glimpse of the ocean glistened in feeble sunlight shining through a hole in the clouds.

The cave itself was perched up the side of a mountain slope on the edge of a rocky ravine over which a trickle of snowmelt gurgled its way downhill. There was snow on the ground between the dark, coniferous trees above him, but starting several yards below the cave, the ground was bare, sloping into a deep, narrow valley steeped in damp, dark mystery. Hemlock-spruce forest uniformly covered the steep slopes, putting him eye level with the tops of some trees. Nestled in the boughs of a towering hemlock, he could look down into what looked like a giant bird's nest made of small branches and pine needles. There was no sign of human civilization anywhere in sight.

Then casting a glance back to the interior of the cave, yet another surprise was revealed in the light. Franklin went to investigate. An array of bones, very old looking bones, roughly outlined the skeleton of a large animal. He walked reverently around the skeletal remains, pondering on its origin. An animal of such size could never have entered the cave from the direction Franklin had. That meant it must have entered from the outside.

Franklin speculated over what might have happened. The crumbling cave wall was of a different make up from the solid rock structure of the rest of the cave. It must had been open at one time. Perhaps the animal, whose fossilized bones marked its grave, had been taking shelter here when a rock slide blocked off the entrance, trapping the beast inside… and dooming it to certain death. The macabre scenario excited him, and he repeated it over and over in his mind. Centuries of rain, wind, snow, and ice, with the help of earthquakes and gravity, must have eroded away at the rock slide, wearing away and breaking down the blockage to the entrance, until finally a tiny ray of light could shine through.

Franklin picked up the fragile, massive skull with reverence, holding it up with both hands. Strange, sightless eye sockets stared back at him. What a magnificent find! Gently, Franklin cradled the skull in one arm, then scooping up the rest of the skeleton with a wave of his hand, he returned to the warmth and orange glow of his subterranean haven.

Arriving at the cavern, Franklin placed the skull next to the rest of the skeleton on the massive stone table he had constructed himself by magically shaping the stones and moving them into position. The enormous thick stone slab that served as the tabletop, rested solidly on a stone base twice as thick and nearly as wide. Franklin sorted out the skeleton, now a jumble of bones on the table, examining each one closely as he laid them in neat rows according to size and shape. What kind of animal could it have been, he wondered. Some of the bones were large like clubs, others thin and curved. There were round bones and flat bones, and smaller ones that clattered when they touched each other. Could these have been fingers or toes? He picked up one of the smaller bones and placed it alongside his own finger. If it were indeed a finger bone, it would have been part of an awfully large hand.

Franklin's attention went back to the skull. Picking it up, he caressed it in gentle admiration. Holding it in front of his face, he stared into the eye cavities, then turning it in his hands, he examined it from all angles. The top part of the skull, including the eye sockets, looked eerily human. Carefully, he set the skull back down.

In due course, Franklin teleported back to the cave where he had found the skeleton…and daylight. Looking out from his perch, he spotted an eagle taking shelter in the boughs of a fir tree, not far from the empty nest of twigs. He gazed out over the coastal forest, dripping under misty rain, the mountain peaks shredding the low clouds into slivers of mist that filled the valley crevices.

Franklin wanted to explore the world beyond the cave. He wasn't afraid of rain, but the sloped terrain looked awfully slippery. Still, he was determined. He focused on a spot of ground he could see beneath the trees, and teleported himself there. Instantly loosing footing, he landed butt first on the wet, decaying hemlock and spruce needles that cushioned the sloping forest floor. Slowly, Franklin got back on his feet, adjusting the angle of his body to the sloping ground to remain upright.

The woods were a jumbled tangle of dead and broken trees lying across, against, and between dripping, wet, living trees, all so covered with moss and lichen, it was hard to tell where the dead trees ended and the living ones began. Franklin soon learned that navigating the steep forest meant controlling his downward plunge between spots of less slope. Soon he was near the base of the mountain which leveled off some into a dense, narrow valley.

Franklin teleported himself down to the gentler slope of ground, breathing a sigh of relief. Taking the orb from his pants pocket and rolling it between his fingers, he commanded, *Keep me warm and dry.* Franklin could feel the chill leave his body, and his clothes dry next to his skin, despite the misty rain. Then returning the orb to his pocket, he pressed on.

The leafless winter underbrush became increasingly dense as he neared the stream that cut through the gap between mountains. Franklin climbed through a long stretch of sturdy alder, the towering branches, twining and twisting into living monkey bars. Spotting a clearing not far away, he teleported himself to it, and found himself on a narrow beach at the edge of the forest.

The beach was nearly as steep as the mountains, its pebbly, dark slope, slipping sharply into the silvery gray water shimmering dully under gray clouds. Steep peaks surrounded the bay in a tight embrace. In the near distance, fog obscured a narrow, watery break that opened to the ocean.

Franklin explored the mountainous world above ground with the same zeal he had explored the subterranean world deep within the mountains. He roamed the hills and valleys startling foxes and deer, and was startled in turn by a black bear. Bald eagles soared high overhead, and red foxes repeatedly crossed his path. He mentally choked off the life of a deer that crossed his path, teleporting a haunch back to the open cave, roasting it over an open fire. The rest of the carcass, he left in the woods, and the next day, eagles and ravens were taking turns cleaning the meat off the bones.

Along the shoreline, Franklin hiked the steep curving beach from point to point and beyond, discovering more steep forested mountains and more curving beaches rising out of the sea. The sea itself rose and fell with the tides, sometimes nearly covering the beach all together, and other times exposing more beach than he had imagined.

But when Franklin wearily climbed into his great bed, he slept fitfully, his dreams and his mind possessed.

We must find the possessor of Anthya's powers, before she becomes too strong, the voice within repeatedly warned.

"But how, how can I find her?" he silently screamed in feverish nightmares.

You must seek and follow the use of magic.

Dark, gloomy days dissolved into bright, moonlit nights. By day, the bashful December sun, fearful of being seen, hid behind clouds low on the horizon, not daring to climb above the stark, bare birch, and dark spruce spires of the forest, creating gloomy, sun-lacking days. But at night, the moon, full and robust, had no such qualms about showing off, and rose high, gloating over its brilliance, illuminating the snow-covered forest and dispelling the gloom of day.

In the light of the full moon, Rahlys thrashed about in her bed. She strained to wake up, struggled to breathe, but the nightmare refused to relinquish its hold. She was in an underground cavern that glowed eerily orange. She could see no one, but she felt Droclum's presence smoldering around her, the reek of evil was smothering her.

Rahlys sat up suddenly, her night clothes damp from sweat. Moonlight streamed in through the window. She was safe…for now. But for how long?

Giving up on sleep, Rahlys crept downstairs, lost in thought. She sat at the table, staring at the full moon shining brightly through a large break in the clouds. The hole opened to the heavens, the clouds' tattered edges aglow with heavenly light. Below, the snow-covered landscape, bathed in moonlight, loomed mysteriously inviting, beckoning the adventurous to sally forth. With art paper before her, and paintbrush in hand, Rahlys immersed herself in the moonlit night. Using soft washes and subtle accents, she stroked the luminous night onto her paper.

Then night turned to day, and the clouds slowly dispersed offering soft blue shadows and pale rays of sunlight filtering through trees. Clearer skies brought colder temperatures. Each day the sun made briefer appearances, and the thermometer dropped below zero.

Rahlys felt as though her body was in slow mode. As winter solstice loomed, the short, low-light days increasingly drained away her energy and drive. Unmotivated, waiting for daylight, she sat listlessly sipping her midmorning coffee. When day finally dawned crisp and clear, the sun, distant and cold, lightened the sky, twinkling thru snow-flocked trees. But Rahlys' sun deprived sensors wanted more. She needed to find a better vantage point with a clear view to the south so she could soak up some unfiltered sunlight. She wanted to see the sun.

Successive snowfalls had added up and an accumulation of over two feet covered the ground. Walking off a packed trail meant sinking to one's knees every step of the way so Rahlys retrieved the snowshoes that hung in the storage shed.

The snowshoes were of the traditional wood and webbing type, a long oblong tapering to a point in the back, but they boasted of modern, lightweight, neoprene bindings with Velcro fastenings. Rahlys placed the snowshoes down on the packed trail, and slipping her feet in place, strapped them on around her boots. The snowshoes felt heavy and clunky walking on the packed trail, but when she stepped off into unpacked snow, it was a totally different sensation...sort of like walking on marshmallows. The snowshoes sank only a few inches under her newly distributed weight, making a soft snow-packing crunch with each step, and leaving behind a beautiful snowshoe print trail.

Navigating without falling though took a little practice. It was necessary to lift the front of the snowshoes high enough to clear the snow when stepping forward, and keep the foot level, packing the snow evenly underfoot. She had to walk slightly bowlegged to accommodate the width of the shoes and avoid stepping across the other snowshoe, for to do so with any momentum guaranteed a face dive into the snow. Then there were the hidden land mines, woody stems of dormant underbrush hidden beneath the snow, poised to pierce the webbing of snowshoes and trip its wearer. After untangling herself a couple of times, Rahlys got the hang of it, and soon had a rhythm going, as she headed for a spot not far away where she was sure she would have an unobstructed view of the sun.

It was so cold, even the physical exertion barely warmed her body, and moisture from her breath frosted her hair and eyelashes. Staying on her ridge, she followed the creek, the sunlight filtered by the forested ridge on the other side. Eventually, the opposite ridge dropped down into muskeg, leaving a clear view to the south.

And there it was, the elusive, shining, yellow orb, burning cold and bright above the southern horizon. Joyfully, Rahlys stepped out into full sunlight. "YOO HOO!" she cried out jubilantly in smoky breath, spreading her arms to embrace the light.

Her cry echoed off the surrounding hills, arousing a bald eagle perched in a nearby tree. The eagle took off, gracefully spreading its magnificent wings to an astounding breadth, then slowly, definitively, the powerful wings stroked the air, and the eagle glided out over the snow-covered muskeg, wings extended. Each time it pumped its wings, the eagle gained height spiraling up in an ever widening circle over the expansive drainage basin.

With wonder, Rahlys stood in the cold sunlight, staring out across the great emptiness to the distant mountains, then up again, to watch the eagle soar high overhead. Where was Droclum in all this immensity? Was he near or far? Rahlys' body, damp from perspiration, quickly became chilled.

Warmth, Rahlys directed mentally to the crystal, and an aura of warmth formed around her, driving back the chill. Soon the sun was heading home, dipping into the south southwest, but even after the sun sank below the horizon, it glowed on in her mind's eye as she reluctantly turned westward toward home.

Darkness descended as she reached her clearing. Rahlys started up the generator. Then teleporting in an armload of wood for the stove, she entered the welcoming warmth of the cabin.

After tea and a light supper, Rahlys laid out watercolor paper and paints. She lightly sketched in pencil the outline of the composition she had in mind. As she added blues and grays, yellows and lavenders, the scene began to materialize. From the vantage point of a forested ridge, a bald eagle glided high over snow-covered muskeg, the cold, distant sun, low on the southern horizon, struggling to warm a frozen world, with snowshoe tracks leading up to the view in the foreground. The hike had invigorated her, dispelling her gloomy-light blues. She felt so much better, she made a mental promise to herself to get out and exercise some every day.

That night as Rahlys slept soundly, the troposphere above her boiled in turmoil. A front of warmer, moist air moved in from the south and collided with the heavy band of arctic cold that hung over the valley. Both air masses stubbornly refused to give way, pushing and shoving, thrashing it out into a snowstorm, the snow piling high on the valley below.

By morning, two feet of fresh snow muffled the landscape. The heavily laden trees leaned over, bent in morning prayer as the dark sky still brooded overhead. The snow was so deep Rahlys teleported herself to the outhouse and back. Then after a hearty breakfast, she grabbed the snowshoes stuck in the snow close to the back steps, and keeping her resolve to get out more, she headed down the trail toward the railroad tracks.

The snowshoes sank deeply into the fluffy, barely settled snow as Rahlys tunneled under snow-laden trees and branches. She paused under a young birch hanging low over the trail, its top overburdened with heavy snow. Stepping aside, she grabbed the tip of a branch, shook it, and quickly let it go. Snow showered down, and the tree top, relieved of its burden, sprang back out of reach. To her surprise, she heard the Raven's familiar squawk, and looking up, saw him fly across the trail just above the trees.

"Araaak!" The raven circled overhead and landed in a nearby tree, sending down a cascade of snow. "Kaww!"

Well, hi there. What have you been up to? Rahlys asked, conversing with him for her own amusement.

"Araaak!"

Yes, that's how I feel too. Have you seen Vince lately? He says you're a pest, but I'm sure he means it in a loving way.

As though in response, the raven flew off. Then Rahlys received mental pictures of Vince's still unbroken trail. Soon he was flying low over Vince's cabin, and Rahlys spotted Vince in the yard. He gave the raven a cursory glance, then started up the snowmachine. After circling his cabin a few times to pack down the snow in the yard, Vince headed down the trail. Flying high overhead, the raven followed him briefly, then veered off. The images ceased, but Rahlys could hear the snowmachine in the distance. She continued on. The railroad tracks were in sight when Vince turned onto her trail. Seeing her, he came to a stop, and shut off the engine.

"Good job!" he praised her as she approached. "It's a lot easier breaking trail uphill, if someone snowshoes it first."

"How have you been?" she asked when she reached him.

"Great! And you?"

"Dragging with these short low-light days, otherwise, fine." With the heavy, dark cloud cover, dusk would follow dawn with little day in between.

"So you are doing some snowshoeing, I see."

"Yes, trying to stay in shape and beat the gloomy-day blues. I was starting to zombie out."

"I wanted to let you know I'm going out on the train Sunday, for the week. If you need anything, I'd be glad to pick it up for you." Vince paused, "I'm also going to try and convince Maggie to come back with me for the holidays."

Rahlys was fairly certain he would succeed. "How about, I give you a list to give to Maggie?"

"That would work. I'll drag your trail tomorrow, since you've already broken it, and pick up that list." He put on his headphones and goggles, and started up the snowmachine, but he needed a turnaround. Looking around, planning his route, Vince stood on the running boards, straddling the seat. After acquiring some speed, he forced the snowmachine off the trail, into the unpacked snow, breaking a loop through the trees...and headed back up his trail.

Dressed in her silver council robe trimmed in green, her long, dark, graying hair bound with jewels to match the jewels on her sandals, Zayla paced the smooth stone paths of the garden atrium that adjoined her rooms, impatiently waiting for Anthya. She took a deep breath to calm herself, then rehearsed the foundation of her support for Anthya's proposal in her head. Anthya had impressed upon her the urgent need. Now, could they convince the Runes of the Crystal Table?

Anthya, similarly dressed, and looking as fresh as the flowers bathing in the golden sunlight, entered through the lavender stone arch at the end of the lush garden. "Shall we go? The Council will be meeting momentarily."

"Yes," she said with ease, and followed Anthya through the arch to the Way, a long, wide paved avenue sheltered under crystal skylights that fractured the golden sunlight into mosaics of gold, green, rose, and lavender. Stone archways lead out to public gardens, pools, athletic fields, and fountains. Beyond, carved into the mountains, private living quarters opened out onto these public arenas.

At one end of the Way stood the Academy, at the other, the Council Hall. A few other council members could be seen rushing toward the great chamber. Anthya and Zayla teleported themselves forward, and reverently followed the other councilors into the crystal-domed hall. They quietly took their seats in high-backed crystal armchairs, elegantly carved, the seats and armrests softened with cushions of embroidered silver. Eight chairs encircled a large, oval, crystal table. Before each chair, a symbol was etched into the table, representing one of the eight Runes of Power. At one end of the table, a ninth chair, still empty, sat on a crystal dais a short distance away. The council members waited expectantly for the High Councilor to arrive and engage the assembly.

Clova, the High Councilor, with dark velvety smooth skin, and long jet-black hair restrained in jeweled ribbons, entered the chamber and stood before the assembly. Without delay, she began with the traditional preamble, "I welcome you here today, Councilors, that we may seek together, purpose and direction, for the greater good of all." The skylight above them darkened and the eight Runes of potent power: crystal, water, fire, air, soil, sun, moon, and void began to glow. "The power of the Runes will indicate who will speak, and in what order. When the symbol before you hovers over the table, you are recognized. No one else, besides myself, is allowed to speak while your Rune is in place. When it dissolves, your say has ended, and you are to say no more. Speak falsely, and you will be banished from the Council." Anthya noted that she was 'crystal,' and Zayla was 'fire.' "If everyone will focus their thoughts, we will begin."

The first speaker chosen by the Runes was Councilor Brakalar, head master of the Academy. A glittering replica of the ancient symbol for water floated up from the etching in front of him, and took position hovering above the center of the crystal table. "Councilor Brakalar, you are recognized," the High Councilor said, and took her seat on the crystal dais overlooking the proceedings.

Brakalar rose. Strong and solemn, eyes full of wisdom, he began to speak. "As you all know, I have been working with a team of talented magicians to create a counter-spell capable of overturning the corruption of Droclum's evil that taints the wastelands and ruins around Mt. Vatre. I feel the time has come to decontaminate and reclaim the area. There is a candidate from the Academy ready for assignment who has been working very closely with me on the project. His name is Sarus. He is very dedicated, a gifted sorcerer, and offers high hopes of success. I propose assigning Sarus leadership of a mission to the wastelands to explore and reclaim the lost part of our world." It was clear from the silent nods around the table, that the councilors were in agreement.

Zayla wrung her hands in a nervous twitch as she recalled the first mission into the wastelands...long ago, with similar goals. She and Brakalar had been on that mission...and there had been discoveries... secrets which they still held.

The Rune remained in place, so Brakalar continued, "The other two candidates for assignment are Kaydra, a cunning sorceress, yet sensitive mentor, and Quaylyn." Brakalar paused, choosing his words carefully. "Quaylyn is an extraordinary sorcerer, the most gifted we have seen in a long time; but sadly, he lacks...restraint."

Zayla almost gasped at the mention of Quaylyn's name. Would the Runes compel Brakalar to confess what he knew? But the watery Rune dissipated, and the sun symbol floated out from in front of Councilor Renna, and hovered over the table.

Renna, their chosen representative to the Worlds' League, had wild, reddish-brown hair barely contained by jeweled ties. She smiled fleetingly at the councilors. "A healing for our ruined lands has been long overdue, and Sarus is indeed a promising candidate for such a mission. Regarding the remaining candidates for assignment, I would like to bring to the Council's attention the Worlds' League's need for a talented sensitive to serve as mentor to Twaka, our newest member in the Worlds' League. I believe that Kaydra's strengths would be ideal for the troubled planet." Again, general consent was felt around the table.

Then Anthya was taken by surprise when the sun Rune suddenly dropped back into place before Renna, and the glowing crystal Rune rose from in front of her to take its place. Zayla felt Anthya's confusion over how to begin; the councilors waited patiently for her to speak.

"The Power of the Runes clearly wants us to hear what you have to say," Clova, the High Councilor, coaxed her.

Slowly Anthya began, "When I carried Sorceress Anthya's Oracle to Earth, I hid it deep in a glacier in the northern latitudes of the planet for safekeeping until Anthya's powers were needed to confront Droclum. But recently, Earth's global climate has experienced accelerated warming which has melted back the glacier and released the Oracle. As fate would have it, the same global warming generated a devastating storm in another region of the planet that unearthed the Dark Orb... which is Droclum. Both Anthya's Oracle and the Dark Orb now have Guardians." Anthya paused to collect her thoughts. She could feel Zayla's moral support. The crystal Rune remained in place above the table, waiting for Anthya to continue.

"The humans of Earth have evolved brains which are capable of tapping the natural elemental forces that abound, but these abilities remain unknown, unused, and generally not trusted, hence undeveloped. Rahlys, the guardian of Anthya's Oracle, shows great potential for development. But she is overwhelmed with the power that flows within her, and there is no one to guide her. We can be certain that Droclum will see to the training of the embodiment of his new life. I feel that in all fairness, Rahlys and her warriors should also receive help in developing their abilities." Anthya had reached the critical point where she intended to volunteer her service, but to her surprise, the Rune returned to its place before she could do so.

The Rune for soil hovered over the crystal table reflecting its light. Jarlon, master of sorcery and defense, a dark and brooding man, began to speak, "I agree with Anthya, that we should do whatever we can to help Rahlys defeat Droclum; we certainly do not want Droclum to gain enough strength to return here, or threaten another world. Droclum must be stopped on Earth, and as quickly as possible, before he builds up too much strength. I sensed Councilor Anthya's willingness to volunteer for this mission, but while Councilor Anthya is a great mentor, she is not a warrior. I suggest we send Quaylyn instead. I have worked with Quaylyn at the Academy, and I believe he is ready for the challenge of a mission to Earth. He's bright, talented, and trained as a warrior. What Brakalar calls lack of restraint is actually high-spiritedness. The soil Rune returned to its place before Jarlon.

Zayla nearly gasped audibly. She was deeply disturbed by Jarlon's proposal, but no one else seemed to be. That was because they didn't know what she knew…except for Brakalar. Zayla could not read Brakalar's tightly closed thoughts.

No additional speakers were indicated. The skylight overhead lightened, and the Runes, etched on the crystal table, darkened. The High Councilor stood and spoke with unflinching authority, "Councilor Brakalar will prepare Sarus for his mission to Mt. Vatre. Councilor Renna will prepare Kaydra for her mission to Twaka. And Councilor Anthya will ready Quaylyn for his mission to Earth. I bid you peace." And with that, the High Councilor walked out the Council Hall.

Zayla and Anthya walked out together. It was done. Quaylyn would be sent to Earth to instruct Rahlys on the use of her powers. Zayla hoped the decision was the right one. At least Anthya seemed at peace with the choice. "I will leave you to your task," she said, calmly, and smiled.

Anthya watched her go, then sending out a mental search, she located Quaylyn's signature at the outdoor athletic arena outside his living quarters, and teleported herself there. An elaborate Traw playing field laid before her. The grueling sport of wit, speed, and dexterity had been a passion of hers when she had been a student at the Academy. She spotted Quaylyn on the court, immersed in a heated game, with Sarus and Kaydra teamed against him…and Quaylyn was obviously winning. The three Traw players stopped as she approached, their expectations of the news she may convey after Council taking precedence over the game.

"Quaylyn, I would like to speak with you," Anthya said with quiet authority, her poise serene.

Sarus made a move, his golden eyes flashing, "Brakalar is calling me," he announced, "Good day, Councilor Anthya." And he vanished from their sight.

"I'm being called, too," Kaydra said, her dark animated eyes betraying the excitement she was trying to control. With wavering composure, she handed Quaylyn the playing wand she had borrowed, then she too, disappeared.

Dark orange rain clouds could be seen on the horizon, promising much needed rain. Anthya could feel the increase in humidity, as a warm, moist breeze stirred the air, lifting escaped strands of her long, pale hair off her neck and shoulders.

"I challenge you to a game of Traw," Anthya said after the others had gone. Her challenge took Quaylyn by surprise, but he quickly recovered.

"Your challenge is accepted, my lady." With tousled golden brown hair and twinkling dark blue eyes, he gave Anthya a princely bow and handed her Kaydra's Traw wand. Anthya had always enjoyed Quaylyn's boyish streak, but she could see how Brakalar would find him undisciplined. The rainstorm was moving in, the sky turning darker, as the breeze yawned into wind. They would be soaked before the game was over.

Anthya hadn't played Traw for untold time, but she would try to be a worthy opponent. A person's true character was often revealed in competition; she would see what Quaylyn had to offer.

A Traw playing field is composed of a large diamond, divided into nine equal smaller diamonds, three of sand, four of stone, and two of sod. A center line divides the playing field into two triangular courts. Each court consists of three inner triangles of golden sand along the center line, two diamonds of lavender stone in the center, and an outer diamond of blue-green sod at the back of the court. While the areas of sand and sod are level, the areas of stone rise irregularly out of the ground, creating obstacles to be clamored over during play.

Anthya and Quaylyn took their positions on the diamonds of blue-green sod at the back of their courts, facing each other across the playing field. The first big drops of golden rain splattered down on court and players.

"Is the challenge still on, or are you afraid of getting wet?" Quaylyn called out a little roguishly.

Anthya raised her Traw wand over her head to indicate she was ready, and Quaylyn did the same. It began to rain in earnest. A flash of light connected the two wands momentarily, and the game began.

As the rain beat down harder, both players flicked their wands sending glowing spheres zooming into their opponent's court. The rules of the game were simple. Draw into your Traw wand all the spheres launched by your opponent that you possibly can, and make it as difficult as possible for your opponent to draw in the spheres that you launch.

Anthya quickly released a second sphere to the opposite end of Quaylyn's court, while scrambling over a stone monolith to get into position to score. The areas of rock didn't rise over knee high from the ground, but trying to traverse its rugged contours while keeping one's eye on an incoming sphere was challenging. A wand had to be within a hand's breadth of the spheres to draw them in, so players had to move rapidly over the varying terrain of the court. During the course of a game, each wand would release twenty-seven spheres, one at a time, and the speed and trajectory of the glowing orbs was determined by the wand action.

Anthya drew in the first sphere and rapidly launched two more while leaping across the court toward the next incoming. The rain came down in golden sheets, but the wind had already moved on. Anthya's sandaled foot slipped off the wet surface of the stone as she reached for an incoming sphere, and she fell hard on her side. Quaylyn successfully drew in all the spheres she had sent, then gasped in concern when he spotted her fall. Anxiously, he started toward her court, but Anthya sent out three more spheres in scattered directions, keeping him busy while she got back to her feet, and yet another before he finished dealing with those; and then another, and another. She wasn't giving up so easily.

Quaylyn, leaping and diving, an athlete in graceful motion, recovered them all while sending off a couple of volleys of his own. Steady rain drenched the world around them, but the intent Traw players barely noticed. Finally all spheres were launched, drawn-in or lost, and the two players, bruised and scraped and utterly exhausted bowed respectfully toward each other. The final score: twenty-seven to twenty-four, with Quaylyn the victor.

"You have played most honorably, my lady." And that she had.

Quaylyn could hardly believe how close she had come to matching his score.

"Thank you." Anthya collected herself. "I have an assignment for you from the Council. I am to prepare you for a mission to Earth."

Chapter 8
An Unwanted Guest

Aaron sat across from Half Ear, the ever-present ancient pouch slung over Half Ear's shoulder as they rode the northbound train up to Half Ear's cabin. "That's Jack Bean's trail right there, where that snowmachiner is grooming trail," Half Ear said pointing out the window in response to Aaron's earlier inquiry. It was the first evidence of human habitation they'd seen from the train for quite a while. "But he ain't there anymore." Half Ear's thin, reddish brown, unkempt hair barely concealed the remaining stub of his right ear, bitten off by a bear...or so he claimed. Aaron got the mile post number from the conductor. He would need it tomorrow, on his way back.

"Heard Jack sold his place to a woman,"...Half Ear continued, "and she's living up there all alone." Aaron settled back into his seat and let him talk. "A woman oughtn't to be living out in the woods alone. It ain't safe. Why a woman comes into her time of the month, a bull moose or bear can smell it a mile away. And there ain't anything more ornery than an aroused moose or grizzly."

Aaron glanced at his crude, tough companion seated across from him. Some of the things Half Ear came out with simply took him by surprise. Not wanting to reveal to Half Ear that he knew the woman who had bought Jack's place...and he had been shamefully shunned by her...Aaron turned back toward the window saying nothing.

Aaron and Half Ear had become good friends since the ride back into town. The two had hit it off quite well, and after a few drinks, or rather, quite a few drinks at the bar, Half Ear had let him crash at his downtown pad. Aaron felt it was his biggest stroke of luck so far. Living off a pension, Half Ear had money for cigarettes and beer…and shared generously.

Half Ear was planning a three-week stay at his cabin up the tracks, which he did periodically to dry out, but Aaron was only going up for the weekend and would be taking the train back out the next day to watch over Half Ear's place in town while he was gone. Secretively, Aaron formulated his plans. He would be making a stop on the way back to town. The frozen white landscape glided by as the little train clattered on. Silently brooding, Aaron gazed out at snow-covered, forested ridges that dropped down into snow-covered, rocky ravines that rose into snow-covered, rolling hills. Why would anyone want to live in this frozen wasteland?

"We're almost there," Half Ear announced, and stood up heading for the baggage car. Aaron followed him.

"Are you going up for a while?" the conductor asked Half Ear.

"At least until after the stinking holidays are over. But he's going back tomorrow," Half Ear said, indicating Aaron. They piled packs, boxes and snowshoes in readiness by the baggage door. Then the train came to a stop in front of a low ridge bordering a small creek that ran under a layer of snow and ice. With more finesse that Aaron thought him capable of, Half Ear climbed down to the frozen, white, wind-blown rail bed. Aaron handed their things down to him, then climbed down himself, shivering in the cold.

"You fellows stay warm!" the conductor called to them. Aaron watched the train continue on without him, until it disappeared from sight. He was stuck here now with no way out until tomorrow.

With packs on their backs and snowshoes on their feet, Half Ear led the way up the ridge. Aaron quickly learned that breaking trail uphill on snowshoes through deep snow with a heavy pack on your back was no easy task. Fortunately, the distance was not great. Soon the winter landscape leveled out and the cabin was in sight. Huffing and puffing for air, Aaron dumped his pack on the porch. Half Ear stepped deftly out of his snowshoes and onto the porch unlocking the front door while Aaron lit a cigarette, as soon as he could catch his breath, and surveyed his surroundings.

The large one-room cabin, with a sleeping loft, was built on a ridge overlooking the railroad tracks, the Susitna River, and the Alaska Range to the west. It certainly was a spectacular view Aaron had to admit. Behind the cabin, snow-draped forest stretched up the next hill. By the time Aaron finished his cigarette, Half Ear had a fire roaring in the woodstove and was hauling in the packs to unload them.

Aaron got out of his snowshoes and went in. It was still freezing cold inside of the cabin despite the roaring fire in the stove, but his attention was drawn away from the cold. In utter amazement, Aaron gazed around at cabin walls covered with guns, stuffed animal heads, traps, and furs. The man often surprised him. He didn't know what to make of Half Ear most of the time. Unexpected wisdom and adeptness seemed to lurk behind the imbecile facade.

"Did you hunt and trap all these trophies yourself?" Aaron asked.

Half Ear answered in shy modesty, "Why…yes,…that I did."

By the time the men had finished hauling in the rest of the food and supplies, the trail was fairly well packed, and the inside of the cabin was starting to feel warm. Half Ear reloaded the stove, and rolled a cigarette.

"What kind of guns do you have here?" Aaron asked. He knew little about guns, and had practically no experience handling one.

"Well, there's a 30-06 rifle over the window, and a 12 gauge shotgun over the door. I keep them loaded and in easy reach. A man never knows when he might have to defend himself out here in the woods." Aaron silently agreed and wished he had some protection himself. "But my valuable guns I keep locked up in here."

Half Ear removed a thick foam rubber cushion from a large window seat that concealed a securely locked gun locker. He unlocked it, and pulled out an arsenal of pistols and rifles, some in cases and holsters of their own. Aaron could hardly believe what he was seeing as Half Ear showed him the weapons, relating all he knew about each one, as he handled them with ease.

"Would you like to do some shooting?"

"Would I?"

Half Ear pulled out a couple of sturdy cardboard targets and handed Aaron a .357 magnum pistol. Then he chose a Colt .45 for himself. They loaded their guns from a cabinet next to the gun locker filled with reloading equipment and ammunition, and stuffed their coat pockets with ammo. Half Ear grabbed a hammer and some nails and a couple of pairs of cellophane-wrapped ear plugs from the kitchen drawer on the way out.

"I get a supply of these from the railroad workers from time to time," Half Ear said handing Aaron a pack of ear plugs.

On snowshoes, Half Ear marched toward the hill, pacing off the distance, and nailed a target on the trunk of a birch tree at the edge of the clearing. He attached a second target on another tree standing next to it. These obviously were not the first trees to be sacrificed in this matter, for telltale ragged tree stumps, capped with snow, dotted the area.

"Which target do you want?" he asked Aaron when he was done.

"I'll take the one on the left."

"Very well. You're up first. Let's see what you can do."

Aaron raised the heavy pistol in his right hand, searching for the target. His hand wobbled so much he couldn't take aim, so he placed his left hand over his right to steady it enough to line up his arm with the target. Then bracing himself for the recoil, he squeezed the trigger. The shot shattered the silence, reverberating into infinity, the bullet missing the target altogether.

"You shoot like a girl," Half Ear chided.

Without hesitation, Half Ear lifted the Colt pistol in his hand with familiar confidence, aimed at the target on the right, and fired, splintering the quiet into a thousand echoes, hitting the bull's eye.

By the end of the first round, Aaron had hit the edge of his target twice, while all six of Half Ear's shots clustered on and around the bull's eye. Despite his poor marksmanship, Aaron felt empowered by the gun in his hand and longed to own one.

Darkness was creeping in by the time they shot up all the ammo in their pockets. They retrieved their targets for inspection. A gaping hole yawned through the center of Half Ear's target, while only six easy to count holes pierced Aaron's, the closest, half the distance to the bull's eye.

The next morning Aaron woke up coughing, his throat scratchy. He stretched out wrapped in his sleeping bag on the cushioned bench that concealed the gun chest serving as his bed. It was still dark, and he could hear Half Ear snoring softly in the loft overhead. Aaron coughed again, suppressing it as much as he could so as not to wake up Half Ear. Drinking some water would help, Aaron decided. He got up, and finding the cup he had left on the table the night before, he made his way in the dark to the water bucket, feeling his way. The drink soothed his throat, and he shivered back to bed.

When he opened his eyes again, it was getting light out, which meant that it was already mid-day. The cabin was toasty warm, but quiet. Slipping out of the sleeping bag, Aaron felt a bit dizzy as he sat up. He waited for the dizziness to pass, then stood up and walked over to the stove. Through the window, he saw Half Ear approaching the cabin with an armload of wood.

"Good, you're up," Half Ear said jovially upon entering, and dropped the load of wood on the floor by the stove. "Ready for some more target practice?"

"Sure," Aaron said with more enthusiasm than he felt. He wanted to shoot, but the cold air that entered the cabin with Half Ear chilled him, and he hugged even closer to the stove. Soon he started feeling weak and dizzy again and needed to sit down.

"You okay?" Half Ear asked as Aaron sat, pale and trembling, in the nearest chair.

"I must be coming down with something; I feel a bit chilled." Aaron sneezed twice in rapid succession, and Half Ear tossed him a roll of toilet paper.

"There's been a flu bug going around in town. I'll fix you some breakfast that will mend you right up." Half Ear became a whirl of activity as he whipped up eggs and patted sausage meat into patties. Soon unappealing odors wafted through the room.

The worst of his chill having passed, Aaron stepped into his boots, slipped on his warm coat, throwing the hood over his head, and stepped outdoors into the chilled air. His head felt light as he made his way to the outhouse. It would be good to get back to plumbing. A raven flew over, squawking loudly overhead, as Aaron returned to the cabin shivering. The odor of Half Ear's cooking assaulted his nostrils.

"Breakfast is nearly ready. Here's some water to wash up with." Half Ear added hot water from a steaming kettle to the basin of fresh water on the stove, and handed Aaron a washcloth.

Breakfast was a heap of scrambled eggs with a generous serving of a dark sausage that had a rather strong taste. "What kind of meat is this?" Aaron asked after swallowing the first mouth full.

"Bear sausage. I shot the bear last spring. "Good, huh?" Aaron didn't really think so, but decided not to disagree, eating what he could force down, while Half Ear wolfed it down with obvious relish.

After a hearty breakfast and a couple of cups of strong coffee, Aaron felt somewhat better, and the two men stepped out to target shoot. Aaron shivered in the sterile cold air, huddled deeply in his heavy coat seeking warmth. Soon the temporary adrenaline rush Aaron got from shooting, helped to override his bodily discomforts. Half Ear holed out the center of his target again, but the tree behind it, though tattered, remained standing. Aaron was also satisfied with his results as he compared today's target with yesterday's. Twice as many shots had hit the target, and one hole was only an inch from the bull's eye.

As they prepared to go down to the tracks and wait for the train, Half Ear surprised Aaron with a gift, the .357 magnum pistol he had been target practicing with, loaded and ready, complete with holster. Genuinely touched, Aaron accepted the gun with hearty thanks. It was indeed a valuable gift. At last he felt he had a true friend.

A few breaks in the clouds added color to the sky as they hiked down to wait for the train. Soon the color would fade into night. The trail was now packed enough to manage without snowshoes. Aaron had felt okay for most of the day, but with the waning daylight and dropping temperatures, his chills returned. Fortunately, they didn't have long to wait. A train whistle blew in the near distance. Then Aaron was bidding his friend farewell as he boarded the train with his pack, welcoming the warm comfort inside.

"Where to?" the conductor asked and Aaron gave him the milepost number and handed him a ticket Half Ear had provided.

"Are you going to visit a friend?" the conductor asked, noting the mile post.

"Yes." Aaron didn't offer any further friendly conversation, so the conductor continued down the aisle, swaying gently to the rollicking clatter of the train.

Aaron stared out the window at the frigid landscape. The snow-covered rocky ravines, rolling hills, beaver ponds, and forested ridges flashed by in reverse order, until the train slowed once again, and the conductor jostled back down the aisle toward him. "It's your stop," the conductor informed him. Grabbing his pack with the pistol inside, he followed the conductor out the passenger car to the stairs, and disembarked into the cold. To his surprise, he was not alone. A man lifted up a large duffle bag into the baggage car, then headed toward him. Aaron tried to step aside and avoid interaction, but the man purposely extended his hand and quickly introduced himself, "Vince. Vince Bradley. And you are?"

"Aaron," he answered reluctantly. Recognizing the name of Rahlys' ex-boyfriend, for Maggie had filled him in on the history, Vince hesitated boarding the train.

"Ready to go, Vince?" the conductor called, fidgeting over the delay. Still Vince hesitated, eying Aaron suspiciously;…would Rahlys be alright alone with this guy? Maggie had said he was harmless.

"Yes," Vince said, deciding it was none of his business, and bordered the train.

Aaron watched the train pull away…its warmth and light glowing through the windows in the twilight. With a sinking feeling, he stood alone in the growing cold and darkness, weak and chilled, not sure he had made the right decision as he watched the train dwindle out of sight.

Aaron turned away from the tracks toward the woods. The groomed trail was easy to follow. He hardly noticed a second trail connecting to it from the north, and continued straight in the direction the snowmachiner had been facing when Half Ear had pointed out Trapper Bean's trail from the train the day before. Perhaps it was the snowmachiner who got on the train. Who was this Vince Bradley, Aaron wondered. Did Rahlys have a new boyfriend?

The trail climbed, then leveled off, then climbed and leveled off again…and still there was no cabin in sight. The cold air seeped in to his skin, chilling him through, despite his exertion and the warm clothing he wore. He shivered, feeling weaker with each step he took. The beckoning path glimmered in the soft, early moonlight filtering through shredded clouds in a darkening sky. A trail of such perfection had to lead to somewhere, he reasoned, and continued on.

Aaron went from freezing to steaming hot, and broke out into a profuse sweat. Weakness slowed his progress as energy drained from his body. Peeling open his outer layers of clothing, he exposed his feverish body to the cold air, and pressed onward, forcing one foot in front of the other. In a state of feverish delirium he continued forward, envisioning Rahlys, so meticulous and wholesome, administering to him with tender care. All he had to do was make it to her. Then the heat subsided, bringing on the worst of chills. Shivering uncontrollably, he came to the third rise, and detected the muffled sound of a generator. Relief flooded through him...someone was here, if not Rahlys, then someone else. Surely even the worst recluse would not just let him die on the trail. The steepness of the rise brought Aaron to his knees. Slowly he crawled up the final uphill climb, to behold golden light streaming out of cabin windows and wispy smoke rising from the chimney... before collapsing in the snow.

Aaron slept, barely stirring. Warned by the Oracle of Aaron's approach, Rahlys had seethed with fury. How dare he come and shatter my sphere of tranquility and purpose! Reluctantly, she had come to terms with the crushing fact that she would have an unwanted guest for a whole week, while waiting for another train out. But rage had turned to humane compassion as she felt his struggle, his thoughts so feverishly distorted they were impossible to read.

Nearly dragging him indoors, she helped him out of his pack, and some of his clothing, and settled him into the daybed downstairs. He was as compliant as a lamb and went down with hardly a word. Covering him warmly, she thought he was already asleep when he opened shining, dark, feverish eyes and whispered, "Thanks, Baby," before falling into a deep slumber. The showdown would have to wait.

Rahlys stared at his ruthlessly handsome face as she checked on him from hour to hour to make sure he was still breathing. Watching him, her heart constricted in renewed pain as she relived the discovery of Aaron's infidelities. How could she have fallen for him? Why was it so hard to get it right when making such an important decision? But of course thinking is least rational when in the throes of making choices of the heart.

Hours later, Aaron's undershirt was soaked with sweat. She thought about waking him up to change it, and reached for his pack to look for a dry one. But when Rahlys unzipped the pack and looked inside, there were no clothes…just a gun in a holster. A cold shiver ran down her spine. Carefully she checked to see if it was loaded…and it was! Had he come to kill her? She hadn't read that thought when he arrived, but his thoughts had been distorted by fever.

She knew that Aaron wasn't the most endearing of people, but he wasn't violent. So why was he carrying a gun? Rahlys unloaded the pistol, teleporting the bullets into the woods for safe keeping, and returned the empty pistol to Aaron's pack. Then she conjured down an oversized t-shirt from upstairs that she used as a nightshirt, but when she tried to wake him to change, his eyes barely fluttered open, so she let him rest, and went to bed.

Upstairs, the crystal glowed alertly in its snug leather pouch. The moonlight streamed into the bedroom window as the moon ascended the night sky, splashing light across the rug on the floor. Rahlys meant to sleep lightly in case Aaron woke during the night and needed her, but it was morning before she opened her eyes again. She jumped out of bed, dressed quickly, and hurried downstairs to check on him. On the daybed Aaron continued to sleep, his forehead now cool to the touch. By the time he finally stirred, the cabin was toasty warm, and she had drunk a whole pot of coffee by herself, while rehearsing what she would say to him.

"Good morning, how are you feeling?"

"Better."

Relieved to see him finally awake, Rahlys brought over the t-shirt she had laid out for him and a fresh, cold glass of water. "You need to drink some liquids. You sweated like crazy last night." She knew her words sounded forced, but she was calm.

Aaron sat up weakly, and touched the crusty undershirt, now dry from body heat, sticking to his body.

"Here." She handed him the glass. Obediently, he drank half the glass of water, then laid down again as though the effort had exhausted him. "Thank you."

"Let's change your shirt."

Aaron sat up again, and she helped him into the clean shirt.

"I need to step out on the porch," he said, bringing his feet to the floor and reaching for his pants. When he was dressed and on his feet, she helped him into his coat, and he stepped outside into the cold, crisp air. Soon he wobbled back in feeling dizzy, light-headed, and weak. Letting his coat drop to the floor, he headed back to the daybed and lay down again, slipping under the covers without removing his pants. Soon he was back asleep.

While Aaron slept, Rahlys headed out to do chores. She wanted to be outdoors breathing fresh air. The rips in the clouds had once again closed tightly shut, creating yet another gloomy, low-light day. In just a few more days, winter solstice would finally be reached, then the sun would start its slow ascent. The daily gain of daylight will be miniscule at first, only seconds a day, but gradually that lengthening will grow to minutes and over time dissolve darkness into the endless daylight of summer. Eventually.

Rahlys made her way to the woodshed and teleported a supply of firewood to the porch. She also needed kindling. Choosing a dry spruce round, she set it on end on the chopping block. But instead of lifting an axe, she concentrated intently, drawing in energy from the elemental forces around her, and focused that energy on severing the molecular bonds in the wood. The spruce round cracked sharply as it splintered apart into sticks of kindling that clattered to the frozen ground, forming a ring around the chopping block.

Firewood done, Rahlys sauntered down to the spring with empty water containers and a sled, dilly dallying along the trail while the containers filled. A flock of grosbeaks passed through the forest around her, flittering from tree to tree, feasting on energy-packed leaf buds awaiting spring. Two eye-catching rosy red males escorted three harder to spot drab olive green females on their relentless mission to consume and expend energy.

As the grosbeaks moved beyond her viewing, she cast a fleeting eye on the sauna a short ways down the hillside. Of course…a sauna, that was the solution, she realized with sudden delight. Until now, Rahlys had felt that readying a sauna just for herself didn't justify the accelerated consumption of her valuable firewood supply so she had been opting for a daily pan bath by the stove instead. But there was not enough privacy to pan bathe now that Aaron was here, so a sauna was the perfect solution.

Rahlys had grown up taking steam baths on her parent's homestead. Every other day, her father would split wood for the sauna, building a hot fire in the barrel stove that heated the little log building so hot it made you gasp for air as you entered. Water poured over hot rocks encircling a glowing red stove, sent out blistering hot waves of steam. At the end, they would douse their bodies with cold water, or throw themselves in the snow.

Rahlys mentally pressed a trail into the snow leading to the bathhouse, and teleported herself there. Brushing the snow off the steps with her feet, she stepped into the building. A slit of a window looking out toward the creek let in the gloomy light of day. Since it would be getting dark soon, Rahlys decided to let the trail set up overnight and get an earlier start on the sauna tomorrow. She could survive one more night without a bath.

Aaron turned over and opened his eyes when Rahlys walked into the cabin with the containers of water. "It's about time you wake up again. Are you ready to try and eat something?"

"Maybe. Where have you been?"

"Out doing chores. I broke the trail to the sauna. Tomorrow we can fire it up. How are you feeling?"

"I'm not sure. I'll be able to tell after I've been up for a while."

"Well, I have some chicken noodle soup I can heat up." Tension was growing in her voice despite her resolve to remain calm.

"That sounds great."

Rahlys emptied the soup in a pan, added water and put it on the woodstove to heat. "How is it that you arrived by a southbound train?" she asked. She could feel her resolve spiraling out of control.

"I've been staying with Half Ear in town. He has a cabin up the tracks a few miles north of here and invited me up to see it." Rahlys knew that Half Ear was another colorful local character and received a mental picture of him from Aaron's fleeting reflections as he spoke. So that was where he got the gun! "Half Ear pointed out your trail from the train. He's staying up there at his cabin for a while, and I'll be house-sitting his place in town."

"So why didn't you stay on the train and go back to town?"

Aaron didn't speak, but she could read his thoughts. He resented her refusal to have him, to be with him. There was no doubt that he even loved her in a way, but more as a comforter and provider than as a soul mate. And he was jealous of Vince.

"Vince...," she said out loud without meaning to.

"Is this Vince fellow your new boyfriend?" he asked, evading her other question.

"No, why are you here?"

This time he answered. "Well, I thought if we were maybe stuck out in a log cabin in the woods, where we would be forced to spend some time together, maybe things would work out for us again. Sounds sort of romantic, don't you think?"

"Aaron, we will never be a couple again. I don't love you. When you learn to accept that, maybe, just maybe, we can be friends...distant friends."

"Why can't you forgive me?"

"I don't want to forgive you. I want you to go away and leave me alone. I've moved on. You need to do the same!"

"Why have you done this? Why did you leave your successful career, and swank apartment, all the parties, and your friends, to move to the middle of nowhere?"

Rahlys knew that Aaron wouldn't place value on the things she cherished, but she outlined it for him as best she could. "My career was a boiling cauldron of stress. I lived from one deadline to the next, applying my talent to artfully duping the public into consumerism. The apartment was sterile, and the parties...ugh! For you the parties were a fabulous arena for picking up beautiful women, but for me they were excruciatingly meaningless. And my only true friend came with me."

A long quiet of hurtful resentment filled the space between them. Then Aaron broke the silence. "You don't even have a bathroom," he said getting up, preparing to go outside.

"I have time and freedom to live and paint."

Aaron left the cabin without answering. By the time he returned, weak and shivering from the excursion, Rahlys was calm.

"I need to lie down again," he said shedding some clothes, and snuggled under the covers. Soon he was fast asleep, the uneaten soup boiling away on the stove.

Yet another cloudy, gloomy day dawned. It was becoming doubtful to Rahlys that the sun would ever shine again. On the bright side, clouds blanketing the earth kept temperatures from going subzero, which would make the sauna easier to heat.

When she came downstairs, Aaron was sitting up, studying her most recent paintings, and looking more alert than he had in days. He had little to no interest in art, but found himself drawn into the work before him. He barely glanced at the painting resting on the easel, its colors subtle, but vibrant with motion, of a snowmobiler breaking trail under snow-laden trees after a heavy snowfall, but he could hardly tear his gaze away from the unfinished painting of a log cabin at dusk beckoning invitingly with warm light streaming from its windows, and wood smoke drifting lazily from the chimney. "You do nice work," he said looking up as she came down the stairs. With hostilities now defused, they spoke to one another with cool civility.

"Thanks, I'm glad you like it."

While Aaron went down for a mid-morning nap, Rahlys headed out with newspaper and a lighter to fire up the sauna. A powdered sugar dusting of snow fell as she conjured over kindling and firewood from the woodshed to the bathhouse. When she opened the stove, ash fell from the ash-filled fire box, so she conjured over the metal bucket and scoop she used to shovel out the stoves from the woodshed. Being careful not to remove the layer of sand at the bottom of the stove that protected it from burn out, she shoveled out the ash and carried the bucket of ash out of the bathhouse. It was still snowing as she stepped off the trail into the deep snow and broadcasted the entire contents of her bucket with one broad sweep of her arms. The ashes flew up and out, landing shockingly black on the pure white snow.

Rahlys stared in horror at her desecration of such purity, but even as she watched, the fine snow coming down transformed the black streak into a dark shade of gray. As more snow fell, the dark gray turned into increasingly lighter shades of gray, creating a virtual study of shades that unfolded before her eyes. Mesmerized, Rahlys continued to watch until the lightest gray turned to cleansing white.

When she had a roaring fire in a clean stove, she conjured full water containers from the spring, pouring their contents into large tubs, then teleported the empties back to the spring. After filling the tubs, she brought over more wood to add to the fire later. When all was done, Rahlys sat on one of the benches and listened to the pleasant, soft roar of the fire, the tiny room already comfortably warm. It felt good to have a warm space to herself away from Aaron. She waited and loaded the stove again, before heading back up to the cabin.

Aaron stirred, waking from his nap. He thought maybe he was doing better, and might even be able to handle a sauna. Getting up, he dressed and walked around. Then he sat at the kitchen table and ate a little. They spoke, but only on the most mundane of topics, and after several minutes of strained conversation, Rahlys went back down to the bathhouse to reload the stove.

Hot air rushed out as she opened the door to the sauna and stepped in, shutting the door quickly behind her to hold the heat. The tub of water on the stove was starting to sizzle. She loaded the stove once again and stepped out into the cool snowfall.

Aaron was still sitting up staring out the window when she reentered the cabin, but it was evident as he turned toward her with glassy eyes and headed back to his bed, that he was not yet recovered enough for a sauna. Promising to fire up the bathhouse again in a couple of days when he was stronger, Rahlys set him up with wash water, soap, and towels. Then grabbing towels for herself, and her robe, she rushed down to the waiting solitude of the bathhouse.

Rahlys hung her robe in the cold dressing room, undressed to bare skin, and slipped quickly into the sauna room seeking warmth. Exquisite heat, and a flood of memories, engulfed her cold body. Parched, dry air filled her lungs.

She reached for the metal dipper in the pan on the bench and quickly drew back her hand, the handle too hot to touch. Grabbing it with her washcloth, she submersed it into the tub of cold water on the floor. Now cool to the touch, Rahlys used the dipper to dribble hot water from the tub on top of the stove onto the heated rocks around it, sending up billowing waves of hot steam. Then she stretched out on a bench, allowing herself to relax. Sweat and tension oozed through her pores, as her mind expanded into thought.

In just three more days Vince will be back on the northbound passenger train, and Maggie will be here too, she hoped. Then on the following day Aaron will finally be able to leave on the train going south. She just had to get through the rest of the week, she told herself as sweat beaded on her breasts and abdomen and trickled down her sides.

It hadn't been bad really. Since Aaron slept most of the time, she still had had time to paint, and he'd been too sick to be threatening. Sweat poured from her body as she gasped from the heat. She sat up and poured cold water over her hot skin, dousing her body heat. Then she dribbled more water onto the hot rocks, vaporizing it into steam before settling down again to sweat some more. Lulled by heat and relaxation, the Oracle's sudden message came as a shock.

Aaron has found the crystal.

While Rahlys steamed, Aaron washed up with the water she had set up for him. When he was finished, he slipped on his pants, and put on the undershirt Rahlys had washed and dried for him. Then he washed his underwear and the loaned t-shirt in the warm soapy water left over from his bath, and after rinsing them out, hung them up by the stove to dry. With nothing else to do, Aaron sat down and watched the fading daylight. Why would Rahlys choose to live this way, hauling wood and water and using an outhouse? She didn't even have a television!

Bored, Aaron got up and walked around inspecting the living room and kitchen. The furnishings were sparse. There was a table and some chairs by a window overlooking the yard. A massive armchair and the daybed, both made of logs, served as living room furniture. Even the cupboards and drawers contained only bare essentials. Not finding anything of interest downstairs, Aaron wandered upstairs to the bedroom.

The bed was made, of course; even in the woods Rahlys would not fail to make her bed in the morning. He looked at the darkening view from the window. There was still no sign of Rahlys returning from the bathhouse. Out of curiosity, he opened the top drawer of the chest next to her bed, and found a small, soft, leather pouch, buried under socks. What is this? Picking it up, he opened it, and emptied the contents into his hand. To his astonishment, a softly glowing cylindrical crystal fell out, brightening as it touched his hand…and then vanished into thin air.

Chapter 9
Detecting Magic

When Maggie and Vince finally arrived on Saturday, Rahlys and Aaron were there to meet the train. Rahlys mentally begged Maggie for relief from Aaron's company while they were loading the snowmachine sled with supplies. It was Vince, bless his heart, who gallantly came to her rescue.

"Ah…Aaron, why don't you come stay with me at my cabin tonight, and give these girls a chance to catch up. I have some fine sipping gin," Vince offered. Rahlys felt more gratitude for Vince's valiant offer than she could possibly express.

"Alright…thanks." Aaron was just as relieved to get away from Rahlys' sullen disposition, though he was surprised by the invitation. Surely Maggie would have painted an unfavorable portrait of him.

Aaron had said nothing about the crystal when Rahlys returned from the bathhouse, but it was uppermost in his mind. She saw the scene of the crystal laying in his hand and disappearing in a flash of light, as it played out in his thoughts over and over again. He couldn't ask her about it. He shouldn't have been digging in her drawer to begin with. And if she were to accuse him of taking it, he had no idea where it was. So he had said nothing. But she noticed he watched her with a new, cunning alertness. She kept an eye on him too, searching for signs that contact with the crystal had affected him in some way.

Rahlys kept the crystal on her person at all times after that. She thought it best not to replace the crystal in the pouch or to remove the pouch from the drawer, so when Aaron went back looking for it again…which he did…he would think she still didn't know it was missing.

Maggie was less concerned over Aaron seeing the crystal than Rahlys. "What do you expect him to do? If he goes off blabbing about a magic crystal, people are going to think he's a lunatic. It's not like he has any evidence."

The next day, Maggie, Vince, and Rahlys watched, thankfully, as the southbound train rolled away with Aaron aboard. A flood of relief lifted their spirits as they watched the red light of the caboose fade in the distance.

"We'll see you tomorrow then," Vince said, moving toward the snow-machine with Maggie in tow.

"I bet you're looking forward to some time alone." Maggie broke away from Vince to give Rahlys a little hug while Vince started up the snowmachine.

"You have no idea. A week in the woods with Aaron is an experience I never want to repeat."

Maggie sat on the snowmachine behind Vince, and cracked an imaginary whip. "Get a move on there!" she called out merrily. Vince gunned the throttle, banking the turn onto his trail, while Maggie whooped in delight.

Rahlys smiled as she watched them go, then headed up her own trail on foot. She could teleport herself home instantly, but she felt like walking. The twilight forest beckoned softly, offering peace and solitude. It felt comforting to be alone in the quiet woods. Slowly, the tightly wound spring within her slackened its tension.

Aaron, absorbed in thought, stared out the window into the growing darkness as the little train sped back to town. His gut ached with long-ing to gaze upon the crystal…the crystal he had held for one minis-cule moment, before it vanished from his grasp. While Aaron brooded angrily, the train clattered single-mindedly southward, the snow-bur-dened forest rolling by unseen in the dark.

When Vince invited him to stay at his cabin, Aaron had found an-other clue, a fragmented, somewhat abstract painting of a raven and a crystal. A glance at the artist's signature confirmed his suspicion. The glowing cubist crystal in the painting was the crystal he coveted. But how did the raven fit in, and what did Vince know about the crystal?

Once back in town, on a hunch, Aaron walked into the local gallery. His effort was greatly rewarded; it was almost like finding the real thing. There hanging on the gallery wall was a perfectly rendered portrait of the crystal hovering in snowy spruce branches, lighting the night. Finally, he could gaze upon it to his heart's content. Here was tangible proof the crystal did exist, and it was not just a figment of his imagination. He had to have that painting!

A professionally dressed young woman with mossy brown hair and dull dark gray eyes approached Aaron after noticing his long intent stare at one work in particular.

"It is simply a magical painting, isn't it? We have a couple more works by this particular artist on display."

Aaron turned toward the woman as though pleasantly surprised by the unexpected presence of great feminine beauty, "Why, yes indeed, it is certainly beautiful…just like you. Call me Aaron," he said, and extended a hand to her.

Startled, the woman hesitated, then smiled demurely, and rewarded him with a weak handshake. "I'm Ilene."

"And would that be Miss Ilene?" Vince asked still holding her hand.

"Yes." She smiled again, the smile almost bringing a little life to her eyes. He let her hand go.

"Well, Miss Ilene, I would like to purchase this painting. What do you say we negotiate the transaction over dinner?"

"There is nothing to negotiate, Mr. uh…Aaron. The price is on the painting."

Aaron needed to come up with the money somehow, but meanwhile, he had to be certain that no one else walked away with the painting, not that there was much chance of that at this time of year. Business would be deathly slow at the gallery until spring when tourists started arriving in droves. Still, he had to be sure.

"And do you work here regularly?" he asked. If not, she wouldn't be worth the effort.

"Sometimes. Mama is down in Oregon visiting her sister, so for now, I'm in charge."

Perfect, Aaron thought. "I would like for you to do me a little favor. I don't have the money on me right now, I'll need just a little time to get it. Could you put the painting on the side somewhere for a while, and I'll purchase it just as soon as I can."

"How long?"

"Well, now we have something to negotiate over dinner, don't we. Let's say 7:00?" He gazed into her eyes, hopefully.

"Okay, I live above the gallery."

Excellent. "I'm visiting from out of town, staying at a friend's place down the street."

"Oh, who's your friend?"

"Half Ear."

Ilene's face lit up. "You know Half Ear? Are you related?"

"He's a family friend."

"I've never known Half Ear to have any family…or friends. I heard he's up at his cabin."

"He is. I'm watching over his place."

"You know, people say Half Ear is simple, but if you ask me, he is no fool," Ilene said. "He goes about his business doing his own thing, with no regard for what people think, but if you need help, he is the best friend you could have." Aaron could only agree.

Aaron took Ilene out that night for burgers and a few drinks. The drinks added sparkle to her eyes and softened her shy restraint, but he had been unable to break through her defenses. Nor did she remove the painting from the exhibit. But Aaron soon discovered there was a seasonal need for strong backs to shovel roofs threatened by heavy snow. He put up 'for hire' notices on community billboards. Soon he was shoveling one roof after another, and had more than enough money for the painting.

While working for the money, under the pretext of visiting Ilene, Aaron visited the painting every day to assure himself it was still there. Finally, the painting was his, paid for in full, and he took it with him to Half Ear's flat. That night Aaron sat in front of the crystal's portrait, gazing into its depths, drinking to its well being…till early morning. Maybe if he stared at it long enough, the painting would offer some insight into how he could gain possession of the real thing. Perhaps it was just his eyes playing tricks on him, but after enough beers, Aaron thought he could actually see the crystal spinning off its soft glow as it hovered in place.

When Aaron finally crashed into restless sleep, he dreamed he had possession of the real crystal, and it had endowed him with wondrous magical powers. Wielding great magic, Aaron acquired riches, and power, and beautiful women galore. The world became his for the taking.

Upon waking, Aaron was convinced his brief contact with the crystal at Rahlys' cabin had given him magical abilities. With great excitement, he grabbed a wooden spoon from a kitchen drawer and waved it around like a wand. Spotting an empty beer can on the table, he flicked the spoon wand toward it. The can didn't move. After a few attempts, with nothing happening, he began to feel silly, and gave up the notion.

Maggie reveled over the power of the snowmachine under her control as she zoomed along through the sun-brightened forest and cold fresh air on her way to visit with Rahlys. In preparation for wood harvest, and to accommodate the women, Vince put in new trails through the mile of woods that separated Rahlys' cabin from his. The woodlot trails connected to Rahlys' trail at a point closer to her cabin, creating a shortcut. The ride was going smoothly until Maggie came across a large spruce tree across the trail, blocking the way. Without loosing speed, she turned the snowmachine hard to the right to make a detour as Vince had taught her. The snowmachine sank deeply in the unpacked snow. Instinctively, Maggie added pressure to the throttle, increasing the speed to stay afloat. With her heart pumping wildly, she struggled to maneuver around dense forest and brush sticking up out of the snow, seeking to regain the packed trail. But instead of finding the opening she needed, she became boxed in altogether in a tangle of alders and fallen trees. With nowhere to go, the snowmachine dug down to a stop, buried to the seat in snow.

In dismay, Maggie shut off the engine. This was going to take a while. What rotten luck! It was the first time Vince had let her take the snowmachine out by herself, and she didn't want to abandon it in defeat. Maggie stomped down the snow around the snowmachine, then tried lifting its back end and moving it over in an effort to turn it around.

Heaving with all her might, the rear of the machine shifted to the side a couple of inches. She went to the front of the snowmachine and pulled on the skis to turn them in the direction she wanted to go, but the skis were so entangled in alder buried in snow, she couldn't move them. When she tried pulling the machine backward, it wouldn't budge. Maggie sat on the snowmachine seat in frustration, unzipped her snowsuit a little to let out some worked-up heat, and focused her mind on Rahlys, seeking contact.

Rahlys, I need your help, Maggie called, continuing to concentrate until she felt Rahlys' thought.

What's wrong? Are you hurt?

I'm alright, but I'm on the snowmachine, and I could use some help. A tree fell across the trail, and I took a detour to nowhere. Now the snowmachine is stuck.

Where are you?

I'm in the woodlot, somewhere off the south side of the second loop.

I'll find you. Rahlys summoned Raven to solicit his help in locating Maggie. Responding to the summons, Raven took off from his favorite perch, and in moments, was flying over the area. It didn't take the raven long to locate Maggie and the snowmachine. Soon Maggie saw the raven circling overhead, and jumped up when Rahlys appeared suddenly.

"How did you get yourself in such a fix?" Rahlys chuckled over the half buried machine.

"Aaaark!" The raven, now perched overhead, seemed to be asking the same question.

"I think it's a trap," Maggie declared with conviction. "I expect Vince to jump out from behind a tree anytime now and scare us within an inch of our lives, if he can."

"Now calm down! Trees fall across trails all the time." Rahlys sat on the snowmachine seat. "Get on."

"What are you going to do?" Maggie asked.

"I'm taking us out of here."

An instant later, Maggie, Rahlys, and the snowmachine arrived in Rahlys' front yard. "Wow! That was incredible! You are truly amazing."

"Aaaaark!" the raven called, arriving moments later to remind them of his help.

"Now go see what Vince is doing," Maggie playfully directed the raven after Rahlys gave him a treat.

"Kawock, Kawock!" the raven gurgled and took off once again.

Vince listened to the diminishing sound of the snowmachine as Maggie drove through the woodlot. Her progress was easy to follow; sound traveled long distances on such a clear, cold day. Then strangely, the drone of the engine came to an abrupt stop. Maggie was on her way to see Rahlys; there was no reason for her to stop so far from her destination. More curious than concerned, Vince took off walking down the trail toward the woodlot.

When Vince reached the fallen spruce tree, he could tell that Maggie had taken a detour. The track marks of her hard right turn were clear to see. Had she made it back to the packed trail? To find out, Vince climbed over the tree and walked on, looking for her tracks rejoining the trail...but found none.

"Maggie!" Vince called, and waited for an answer, but no answer came.

Locating Vince on the trail, Raven flew in closer and telepathed images back to Maggie and Rahlys. Through the eyes of the raven, they saw Vince walking the trail. "See, he was planning on scaring me!" They watched as Vince climbed over the fallen tree.

"He's looking for you," Rahlys said. It was the furthest she had ever reached for a thought. Then strangely, a large birch tree directly in front of Vince began to shake violently. Vince looked around bewildered. There was no wind and all the other trees remained still. "That's strange," Rahlys said half to herself.

Then a second tree began whipping around beside him. Vince sought to move out the way, but when he tried to distance himself from the mad trees, he ran into an invisible wall blocking the trail. There was nothing to be seen, but reaching out in front of him, his fingers met resistance.

"What's happening to him?" Maggie asked with growing concern. A third nearby tree began swaying erratically. Surrounded now by fiendish trees, Vince tried desperately to escape through an alder thicket on the side of the trail, but the alder branches took on new life, preventing his passage.

"Droclum," Rahlys whispered, as she watched Vince try to get away.

Then the light of the bright forest began to fade as a peculiar dark cloud formed above him. The darkness rumbled ominously, the threatening turbulence swirling faster as the darkness dropped ever lower, filling the sky. "I can feel his presence," Rahlys said shuddering, for even from where she stood, the residue of evil magic electrified the air, overwhelming her senses with repugnance. She struggled against the revulsion and forced herself into action. She had to save Vince. She was the only one who could.

"Rahlys, do something!" Maggie cried out, but Rahlys was no longer standing beside her. Through the raven's eyes she watched in horror as a dark funnel of black vapors descended from the swirling mist, drawing down around Vince, enclosing him. Vince screamed in mounting terror, the cloying evil presence clogging his consciousness.

Then in an instant, Vince and the cloud were gone. The trees stood still once again...undisturbed, in a peaceful, sunny forest.

Maggie froze in stunned disbelief. She still hadn't moved when Rahlys and Vince appeared suddenly beside her. "Vince!" Maggie cried joyfully, but the initial flow of relief was quickly staunched as Rahlys crumpled down onto the snow.

"Rahlys...oh no...Rahlys!" Maggie dropped to her side.

"What's going on?" Vince asked frantically, striving to regain control.

"She's breathing," Maggie whispered. "We need to get her warm."

"Aaaark! Aaaark!" the raven landed on the snow near them.

Hardly noticing the raven, Vince lifted Rahlys and carried her inside, laying her on the daybed. Rahlys moaned and stirred as Maggie ran upstairs for pillows and blankets. Gently, she tucked the covers in around her when Rahlys opened her eyes.

"Can I get you anything?" Maggie asked.

Water, Rahlys telepathed to Maggie, her mouth too dry to speak.

Maggie dashed off to comply, rushing back with a full glass, and Vince helped her sit up enough to drink, then eased her back down. "Can you explain...at all...what just happened!" Vince's eyes were wild with the need for answers.

"Maybe," Rahlys whispered. "More water please."

Vince made a move to help her up, but with a sigh, she sat up on her own. Parched from the taxing use of such magical force, she drank the rest of the water. Though weakened by the power drain on her system, her head still throbbing from the mental exertion, Rahlys attempted to explain.

"I think Droclum detected my use of magic and set out to capture me, but found you instead. He probably didn't know he had the wrong person. I'm just thankful I managed to wrestle you from his grasp."

"What? Who's Droclum?"

Rahlys could follow his brain's effort to try and rationalize what had happened. She knew it was time to fill him in. While Maggie listened with the quiet intensity of a child enjoying a favorite story being retold, Rahlys told him about the crystal and her feats of magic. She related what little she knew about the great sorceress Anthya and the evil sorcerer Droclum and their world, and described the strange visit from Councilor Anthya, the great sorceress' namesake, who told her one day she would face the Dark Orb.

Vince listened, staring at her incredulously.

Franklin pondered on the whisperings that steeped in his brain. *Journey with the orb to seek and follow the use of magic*, an inner consciousness urged. Lying on his bed, Franklin reached into his pocket and pulled out the smoky orb. Gazing into it momentarily, he gave the command.

Seek and follow the use of magic.

The orb, without leaving Franklin's hand, issued forth from its solid matter as invisible energy. It sped through the mountain to the surface, pulling Franklin's consciousness along for the ride. Franklin journeyed with the crystal over ocean, mountains, and valleys. The presence in Franklin's mind had detected magic being used from this direction before. And then Franklin felt it…the use of magic. It was ever so faint, a mere flutter of energy, a distant tremble, as subtle as the pull of the moon on the tides. *Find the spot!* Franklin commanded the orb.

The spot proved to be a dense thicket of trees and brush in a cold, bright forest of spruce, birch, and alder. A man paced about, seemingly confused, or agitated, about something. Surely this was not the guardian of Anthya's Oracle. Franklin probed his mind, but could pick up no awareness of the Oracle. He was simply looking for a woman who had disappeared somewhere in the forest. Could the woman he was looking for be the possessor of Anthya's powers? He had to find out.

Franklin watched with delight as he trapped the man cringing in terror under menacing trees and an even meaner black cloud. He started sucking up his victim, control over his captive certain, until unexpectedly, a powerful opposing force latched on to his prey. He had found the Guardian of Anthya's Oracle after all! The brightness and strength of her magic stunned him.

A mental tug-of-war ensued. Franklin strained with all his might to hold on to the victim his opponent hoped to save, the effort draining his strength. Still the challenger held on, pulling the prize mightily from his mental grasp. In defeat, Franklin returned to his limp, still body on the bed in the cavern, weak and spent. He had not expected to encounter such power, such strength of will. The Guardian of the Oracle had whipped him, kicking him aside with his face in the sand.

———

The reality of the crystal and its magic was hard for Vince to readily digest. Even with the crystal in his hand, or spinning in the air around him, he found it hard to accept. "And you really believe the crystal has somehow enhanced the raven!" Vaguely, Vince remembered the raven landing on the snow near them after Rahlys had pulled him free from Droclum's clutches. Maggie and Rahlys had described to him how they had watched the whole episode with Droclum through the eyes of the raven.

"Can you summon that bird anytime you want?"

"So far."

"What do you say we go outside for a while and see if we can bring in the other member of our team?" And with that, they all got up, put on coats, and stepped out into cold sunshine filtering through bare trees. A clear, blue sky glowed overhead. The crystal, following Rahlys outdoors, glinted in the sunlight.

Rahlys gazed up at the brilliant blue sky as she focused on Raven. It was easy to imagine him in such a gorgeous sky, and soon she was seeing frozen muskeg far below. Rahlys telepathed the raven's projected image to Maggie and Vince.

"This is incredible!" they exclaimed together.

The raven flew over a cabin on a forested ridge. A drift of wood smoke indicated someone was there. "That's George's place, your neighbor to the south," Vince informed them. Snowmachine trails were seen looping around through the forest below them, and then a lone snowmobiler came into view through the trees. "There's George. Looks like he's putting in some trails to cut firewood too."

Then Maggie spotted the raven. "There he is," she pointed. The mind meld dissolved away as the raven flew across the creek toward them.

"Aaaark!" Raven called as he flew over. Spotting Vince, he came in for a landing on the wood shed roof.

Rahlys conjured an apple from the root cellar. Holding it in her hand in front of her, she concentrated on the apple's structure, drawing the energy needed, directing it with precision. With the grace of butterfly wings unfolding, the apple split apart into six perfect wedges.

Rahlys mentally reassured the raven, coaxing him to join the group on the hard packed snow of the yard, and handed apple wedges to Maggie and Vince. Raven took a hop and glided off the wood shed roof landing a few feet away from them.

"Good, Raven!" Rahlys said, and dropped an apple wedge down to him. *Don't be afraid*, she telepathed, *no one here will hurt you.* She could sense the raven's trust as he indulged in the apple, then she stepped aside so Maggie and Vince could feed him.

What a fine, handsome fellow of a bird you are, Maggie telepathed to the raven, and Rahlys and Vince alike, and dropped him some more apple.

"Aaaark!" the raven responded to the praise, and gobbled up the treat without hesitancy.

Vince scratched his head in puzzlement, then stepped in closer. The raven took off, returning to the roof of the woodshed. "Look, I'm sorry for all the times I called you a nuisance," Vince called up to him.

"Aaaark! Aaaark!" the raven cried in protest. Rahlys and Maggie doubled over with laughter.

"Try communicating with him mentally," Maggie suggested.

"Communicate mentally?" Vince asked with uncertainty.

Yes, just think your thoughts and feelings to him, Maggie explained to Vince in a telepathed message.

"Ouch!" Vince grabbed his head.

Like Maggie, the raven, and myself, it seems you have the power of telepathic communication. Vince winced from the ache in his brain as Rahlys' message registered.

"It doesn't ache anymore once you get used to it," Maggie reassured him.

Unconvinced, Vince gathered his thoughts, and projected them to the raven. *I have to hand it to you, you are one hell of an air reconnaissance unit.*

"Aaaark!" the raven replied and Rahlys and Maggie laughed all the harder.

To Vince's surprise, he could feel the mental connection to the raven. *So, what do you say? Can we be friends? You have given me new insight in regards to your worth.* He held out the tantalizing fruit. *Apple?* and with that, the raven flew back down, landing close to Vince, who tossed the apple pieces to him. "We are indeed a team of four."

"I hardly see the four of us as a threat to Droclum," Rahlys said, looking over her companions.

But Vince was ready for action. "We'll see about that. Droclum has been beaten before; he will be defeated again. This time we'll make sure he stays down. We must prepare. We need to explore the extent of the Oracle's powers, and lay out some plans. We don't know when Droclum will strike again. And we should include the raven in our training as much as possible."

"But surely we aren't going to go looking for trouble?" Rahlys asked. "Where would we look anyway?"

"Well, there is plenty enough evil around, but I have a feeling we won't have to go looking. One day Droclum will return."

So Vince called a meeting to assess the situation and plan some strategy, his years as an officer in the Marines kicking in. Vince's last active tour of duty had been during the first war against Iraq, to liberate Kuwait. Since then, all the action he had seen was written in his novels. The crystal's existence and what it meant to their safety was starting to sink in. The encounter in the woods had clarified one thing, the threat of an opposing magical force was real.

"But how did he find us?" Vince put the question before them, inviting speculation. "Judging from Rahlys' abilities, there may be no limit to where Droclum can go in an instant."

"Perhaps Droclum lives close by and he has detected Rahlys using magic. He knows she's here, because he has been watching her," Maggie offered.

"I think Maggie is on the right track. I believe Droclum's powers may include the ability to locate me from a distance, by detecting the use of magic," Rahlys said. "Think about it. Why do you suppose the encounter happened where it did? Because that spot was magically active long enough to allow detection…if someone was actually searching." Rahlys laid it out for them.

"Maggie telepathed me when she got the snowmachine stuck, and I teleported myself to her. Then I teleported the snowmachine with us on it away from there. But then Vince walked up on the trail just on the other side of the alders to nearly the same spot. There was no one else around, so Droclum latched on to Vince."

Maggie and Vince found Rahlys' theory plausible. "If that were the case, then you would have the power to do the same," Vince said.

"I don't really want to locate Droclum, I want to prevent Droclum from locating us."

"But you said yourself, one day you will have to face Droclum and destroy him," Vince reminded her. Fear gripped Rahlys upon hearing his words. Couldn't her magic also hide her from Droclum?

"Perhaps with the help of the crystal, I could cast a spell of protection over our region, concealing our presence," she said. It was worth a try. As Vince and Maggie looked on, Rahlys seemed to go into a trance as she focused mentally, drawing on the source of power within her. Rahlys could feel the magical charge build as she wove her spell. Then the charge ignited into visible energy as she invoked the crystal…*Spread a protective shield over the land, obscuring it from Droclum's detection.*

Vince and Maggie saw a glowing gossamer thread loop and swirl above Rahlys, and start to rise. As Rahlys remained fixed in place, the wispy, ethereal filament of light continued to rise, wraithlike above the clearing, and formed into a shimmering ring, expanding over the forest as it rose high above them. When it reached its ultimate height filling the sky, the glimmering loop dropped down like a curtain, forming a luminous transparent dome to the horizons before vanishing from sight.

"Hopefully that will help keep us safe for a while," Rahlys said.

"So where do you think Droclum is now?" Maggie ventured to ask. No one answered.

It was a worthy question, but Rahlys didn't want to find Droclum just yet. Hopefully, he hadn't been caught under the protective magic shield, assuming there really was an enchanted dome concealing them from Droclum's detection.

———

Aaron rode the northbound train on his way to see Half Ear. If anyone could figure out the truth about the crystal, he figured Half Ear could, for Half Ear, he had decided, had a certain mystic quality about him. Drawn out of his thoughts as the train began to slow down, Aaron slowly realized it was arriving at his stop. Jumping up, he grabbed his pack containing the pistol and holster, some more ammo,...that bitch had taken his,...and fresh food for Half Ear. The train lurched to a stop, tumbling Aaron toward the exit.

Half Ear was standing on the trail by the tracks waiting for him. Aaron had sent him a bush message over the local, public radio station, telling him he was coming.

"Good to see you so robust again," Half Ear greeted him. "I told you that bear sausage would do the trick."

"Yes, you did." Aaron hefted his heavy pack onto his back with ease. "I brought you some groceries."

"Good! Good! An old man gets tired of chewing on dried moose everyday." They hiked up to the cabin in silence, saving their breath for the uphill climb.

"Brought your pistol?" Half Ear asked Aaron as they came in sight of the shooting range.

"Yes. I'm looking forward to doing some shooting."

It wasn't long before they were out on the ever-shifting shooting range, ripping through yet two more doomed trees, the woods ringing with the volley of shots.

That night after supper, the two men sat smoking by lantern light. Aaron had also remembered to bring Half Ear a fresh supply of tobacco. For the longest time, neither spoke, then Aaron broke the silence.

"Remember the bitch that bought Trapper Bean's place?"

"Yes,...yes,...why, she's probably high-tailed it out of here by now."

"No, she's still there." Aaron paused before adding, "She and I used to be together."

"You mean you mated with her? When?"

"A year ago, back in Seattle. We lived together for a while."

"Whew!" Half Ear shook his head in curious disapproval. "So what happened? Women can be dangerous creatures."

Aaron's pride still festered from Rahlys' rejection. He tried to be flippant. "Why, I dumped her, of course. A man like myself can't be limited to just one woman, you know. Have to spread it around. How about you, Half Ear, have you ever been seriously involved with a woman?"

"Oh, no, no," he shook his head demurely. "Women are powerful creatures, best shunned; they drain a man of his strength and will."

Aaron looked at his stout, robust friend with doubt, but changed the subject. "Do you believe in magic?"

"I believe in living, and I believe in dying. Are life and death magic?" Smoke from his pipe swirled around them in the lamplight.

Aaron didn't know how to answer, so once again the two men became quiet in contemplative thought. After a while, Aaron broke the silence.

"When I left from here last time, I got off the train at Trapper Bean's trail."

"You did!"

"Yes, I wanted to see her again,…to talk to her."

"And…?" Half Ear leaned forward inquisitively.

"And I found an unusual crystal."

At first Half Ear didn't respond. Aaron had expected him to laugh uproariously, but instead he moved in closer with heightened interest, and whispered as though afraid of being overheard. "Yes, go on."

Aaron told Half Ear about the remarkable crystal that glowed with its own light, and how it had simply vanished out of his hand. He described the paintings, especially the one he had hidden under his bed in town, and told him of his dreams, half expecting Half Ear to interpret them for him.

Half Ear listened to his friend's ravings about a magic crystal, without comment, without interruption. When Aaron ran out of words, the room fell quiet once again.

Finally, Half Ear broke the silence. "What about the girl?"

"To hell with the girl! I'm telling you, this crystal is special. I must find a way to see it again up close." Aaron knew he probably sounded crazy, even to Half Ear, but in the recesses of his mind he was already formulating a plan.

But Half Ear surprised Aaron with, "What do you need from me?"

Aaron smiled, hopeful of a possible alliance. "I'm planning on doing some very secretive, undercover surveillance of the new mistress of Trapper Bean's place, an unusual woman who I believe has recently become even more unusual. I could use some help."

Half Ear snuffed out the short remains of his self-rolled cigarette. "Yes, yes, count me in. Here's what I think we should do."

Leaving Half Ear's cabin the next day geared for a lengthy winter campaign through the woods on foot, Aaron and Half Ear made their way down to the railroad tracks and flagged down the Sunday, southbound train. They hefted up into the baggage car snowshoes and packs laden with food, tent, sleeping bags, guns, ammo, gear, and spotting scopes.

"Going camping a little early this year, I see," the conductor greeted them jovially.

"We thought we would do some Ptarmigan hunting," Half Ear said. "I know a great place for Ptarmigan, just down a ways from here." Not wanting to divulge their true destination, he gave the conductor the milepost of a creek about a mile and a half north of Rahlys' trail. The train ride was saving them about twelve miles of walking. They could hike the last mile or so.

When the train arrived at the small unnamed creek, Aaron and Half Ear stepped off into unpacked snow to let the train go by. Then with snowshoes in hand and packs on their backs, they climbed back up onto the tracks for easiest walking and continued south, hiking the packed snow between the rails with the cold wind to their backs.

A half hour later, they put on snowshoes and Half Ear led them into the woods heading east away from the railroad corridor. "A mile-long swamp stretches out less than a quarter-mile behind Bean's cabin," Half Ear explained. "We'll make our way there by circumventing Vince Bradley's place. A frontal approach is too risky. Our tracks may be noticed."

The two men headed east with the sinking sun to their right, seeking the easiest way up the first rise. Progress was slow at first until finally the landscape leveled out some; then they made better time. But now they had a new concern, approaching nightfall.

When they reached a protected hollow, Half Ear called a halt. "If we camp here, we can have a fire. We're still a safe distance from anyone, so detection is not a concern." The two men made camp, preparing for the night. Shoveling away snow and laying down spruce boughs for insulation against the cold, they set up a low dark green tent with attached floor under a tight band of large trees, and covered it with a waterproof white canopy for camouflage. Then they quickly turned their attention to gathering firewood.

It would take a lot of firewood to make it through even part of the night, and temperatures were already dropping. Pulling off paper birch bark and collecting dead, dry twigs for kindling, they built the fire out in the open, a safe distance from the tent. With the help of a small saw and axe they scavenged deadfall from wind and snow damage, and chopped down a small dead, standing spruce. Pieces too large for the fire, they placed across it, burning out the middle first, then moving the burnt off ends onto the flames.

As darkness descended, temperatures plunged. The panorama of stars overhead offered no protection from the earth's heat loss. Without clouds to blanket in the daytime warmth, it would become steadily colder throughout the night. The men sat together by the campfire, under the Milky Way, their sleeping bags wrapped around them for added warmth.

"Do you think there is intelligent life on other planets?" Aaron said, asking the age old question, as he gazed up at the stars.

"I assume you are using human intelligence on Earth as your yardstick for measuring intelligence." Half Ear shook his head in dismay, "The universe would be in a sad state indeed if Earth were the only source of intelligent life."

Exhaustion and dying embers ushered the men to their tent to try and sleep despite the cold, but before he would retire, Half Ear shoveled snow by the light of the stars over the dying fire, obliterating it. "A campfire pit would be more noticeable from the air, than just a snowshoe trail," he said. Acceptance of a surveillance mission had strangely transformed Half Ear, it seemed to Aaron, from the dull, slow, half-wit he was, to a sharp, quick-witted strategist. He had taken control from the start, working out the details of a plan, and putting them into action.

Morning broke into another clear, sunny day. Radiant solar heat soon brought the air temperature up from its subzero low to a promising double digit high. Aaron had slept fitfully cold through the night, despite the 'good to forty below' sleeping bag, and had begun to wonder if winter camping was such a good idea. Reluctantly, he opened his eyes. Half Ear and his sleeping bag were already gone from the tent. Aaron slipped out of his bag and into his heavy winter coat, putting on hat, boots, and gloves in an effort to get warm, and crawled out the tent into the cold brightness.

Half Ear and his snowshoes were nowhere in sight, but his carefully packed backpack stood ready against a tree. A fresh snowshoe trail headed east out of camp. Figuring he ought to be getting ready, too, before Half Ear returned and chided him for sleeping in, Aaron rolled up his sleeping bag and secured it to the bottom of his backpack frame. Then he rolled up the tarp and dismantled the tent strapping them on to the top of his backpack. Activity and increasing warmth from the sun had finally warmed him some by the time Half Ear showed up, all energy and determination.

"Good morning," Half Ear greeted him quietly, as though in fear of being overheard, "Are you ready?" Aaron nodded, and with that Half Ear donned his pack and headed out again leading the way. Aaron scrambled to put on snowshoes and pack, and struggled to catch up with him.

They hiked through the silent woods over rolling forested hills. Half Ear followed his earlier tracks which led to the rise of a low ridge which they followed, keeping it to their right. Not stopping for breakfast, they gnawed on moose jerky along the way.

Then suddenly Half Ear sniffed the air and changed direction, climbing the slope of the hill they had been following. After a while, Aaron smelled it too; wood smoke. Half Ear motioned for Aaron to follow him quietly as they crested the hill and Vince's cabin came into view through the trees, a wispy tail of smoke drifting out of the stovepipe. Rolling hills of spruce and birch forest stretched out around them in all directions under a clear sapphire blue sky. There was no sign of anyone moving about outside.

Aaron and Half Ear descended back down the north side of the hill, cutting off the view to Vince's cabin and the horizon to the south, and continued east toward the big swamp. Gradually, however, the ridge they had been following bowed gracefully toward the south, and eventually they were heading directly into the noonday sun, the ridge ending in a broad shelf that overlooked a huge expanse of treeless white. It was the large muskeg they had been marching toward. Across the vast frozen swamp, distant forested rolling hills stretched to the horizons. They walked on, facing the sun reaching its zenith, though still low in the sky, to the southern edge of the plateau, overlooking a creek that etched out a narrow ravine. Across the ravine, the forested shelf continued on south and west.

"We will cross on the marsh to reach the ridge on the other side of the creek. Then if we follow the creek going west for about a quarter of a mile, we will be able to spy on Bean's place without being noticed."

Aaron and Half Ear gingerly made their way down the steep slope of the ridge to the big swamp below. Reaching the bottom, they walked across the frozen muskeg, the snowshoes barely marking the crusty, windblown surface. When they crossed over the creek that helped drain the big swamp, gurgling water could be heard under the sturdy snow bridge. Half Ear led the way to the base of the ridge that continued south along the western edge of the swamp until he found a spot sheltered by a contour of cliff from the cold north wind.

"We can set up camp here for the night. It's a safe location; not in danger of being spotted either from Rahlys' place, or George's homestead which is still some distance away, over another rise. We can have a fire." Then in an instant, a glimmer of a luminous curtain shimmered to the horizon, and was gone. The event was so ephemeral, Aaron could not even be certain he had actually seen it.

"Did you see that?" he asked Half Ear in puzzlement.

"That I did. And I've never seen the likes before." Half Ear stood up straighter, a bit mystified, "Maybe it was some of that magic you were talking about."

When Franklin's strength returned, he sent the orb out again. *Seek and follow the use of magic; find the Guardian of Anthya's Oracle*, he commanded. The orb searched repeatedly, but to no avail. Franklin even tried teleporting back to the alder thicket where he had encountered the sorceress, but the location simply could not be found. It was as though the thicket had been removed from the planet.

Focusing his attention to his work laid out on the stone table, Franklin artfully arranged the bones he had collected from the cave on the side of the mountain into an ornamental necklace. Using magic, he bore a hole through each bone, alternating appendages and vertebrae, and strung the bones together with fishing twine scavenged from the beach. Upon finishing the necklace, Franklin placed it around his neck, and turned to face a large, ornate, free-standing mirror, taken from the same furniture store that had provided his bed.

For some time, Franklin stood in front of the mirror, admiring his image, but he wasn't totally pleased. The effect seemed to lack something. A great sorcerer needed a suitable cloak, he concluded. But what should it be made of? He thought of the ravens and eagles that fed on the animal carcasses he left in the woods, and decided to make a cloak of feathers.

Franklin wasted no time. He killed several deer in the coastal forest, magically stripping off the hides for rugs, and leaving the meat in the woods to bait in the ravens and eagles. Several days and bait carcasses later, he had killed enough of the scavengers and collected their feathers to construct his feathered cloak.

Carefully, Franklin wove in his spells as the cloak took shape. When it was finished, he draped the feathery garment over his shoulders, fastening it in place with a bone clasp. The cloak flowed regally around him, making a soft, fluttery sound as he strutted around the cavern. Then he again placed the bone necklace around his neck, and stood before the mirror. This time the image before him met his approval. Gazing at his reflection with admiration, he drew his name in the dust on the glass. Then in a powerful voice, mature beyond his years, Franklin stared back into eyes that were hardly his own, and proclaimed out loud, "I am Droclum, the greatest, most powerful sorcerer that has ever lived!"

Chapter 10
Firewood and Fishing

Rahlys felt a resurgence of energy brought on by brighter, sunnier days and lengthening daylight. In tiny increments, the sun arched higher and wider across the sky, gradually lifting the veil of winter and offering a promise of spring…though somewhat distant still. As winter grew milder, daily chores became a reason for going out into the bright, and somewhat warm, sunshine. Twenty above felt good after twenty below; thirty degrees above zero felt downright balmy.

Maggie's holiday visit ended, and with reluctance she returned to town. After a couple of weeks, she was back for a longer extended stay, a decision backed by Vince. Maggie, who had disdained at first living a rustic lifestyle in the woods, had unexpectedly found everything she had been looking for: contentment, romance…even adventure.

And there was always lots to do. Besides the chores, Vince taught Maggie how to make bread, and Maggie showed Vince how to be creative cooking with canned moose, which worked out great for Rahlys who was invited over often to enjoy the results. Feasting on moose, bread, and wine, they speculated on Droclum's plans and whereabouts.

"I wonder why he hasn't been back around," Rahlys said. There had been no sign of Droclum since Vince had nearly been sucked away.

"Because he can't find us." Maggie had unflagging confidence in Rahlys' protective shield.

"Sooner or later Droclum will find Rahlys again. We must never let down our guard," Vince said, always on high alert.

Vince also laid out strategy for firewood harvesting. The snow on the ground was forming a crust as the surface repeatedly warmed during the day and froze hard again at night. He had the women practice driving the snowmachine on and off established trails, learning the lay of the land, and how to get themselves out when they got the snowmachine stuck in deep snow. They ran the woodlot trails repeatedly packing them down, and Vince groomed them each evening so they would freeze smooth at night.

When the woodlot trails proved firm enough, wood harvest began in earnest. Vince and Maggie headed out with the snowmachine pulling Vince's special firewood sled loaded with snowshoes, axe, and chainsaw, as well as extra gas and oil for the chainsaw. Rahlys, dressed in layers, the crystal secure in its pouch around her neck, stepped out into the cool brightness and summoned Raven. A gentle warmth from the sun touched her face as she gazed skyward. Soon the raven was sending her images, and Rahlys spotted Vince and Maggie on the trail.

As Vince came to a stop, parking the machine a safe distance from the trees he wanted to cut, Rahlys appeared on the trail beside them. "Perfectly coordinated!" Vince said with satisfaction, as the raven came in for a landing in a nearby tree. "We'll take a couple of trees out of that group of five," Vince said, pointing to a stand of trees conveniently close to the trail. He unloaded the sled, setting the gas and oil containers in the snow, then picked up the chainsaw and headed toward the trees he had pointed out. Maggie and Rahlys waited by the sled till further instruction.

The first tree Vince chose was a large, tall, birch tree, its trunk clean and white, the lowest branches at least fifteen feet off the ground. With chainsaw in hand, he stomped the snow down around its base, giving himself room to work. "I'm going to make the tree fall right along the trail there," he indicated like a pool player calling his shot. Putting on headphones and protective eyewear Vince started up the chainsaw, its roar filling the woods, and Raven flew off squawking his displeasure at the noise.

Vince made one deep cut and then another, slicing out a wedge a couple of feet above the ground on one side of the tree. Then stomping down more snow, he moved the chainsaw to the opposite side of the tree trunk and made another cut above and toward the first, until the tree began to buckle and fold on its hinge. As the tree shuddered, cracked, and toppled, Vince stepped back and away with chainsaw in hand. There was a snapping, crunching crash as the tree landed in the snow precisely where he said it would. With a smirk of self-satisfaction, he shut off the chainsaw and set it down on the snow.

"That was incredible!" The women came running up, truly impressed. They looked at the mighty tree with respectful silence. So many long, hard winters it had survived to be sacrificed now to keep them warm.

"I'll remove the branches that are blocking the trail first. Then one of you can go for the snowmachine, getting it turned around in the right direction, while the other clears the trail, piling the branches out of the way."

Vince grabbed the chainsaw, started it with one mighty pull of the rope, and deftly trimmed off the branches. Then he started slicing the trunk up into stove length rounds.

Maggie went for the snowmachine while Rahlys magically lifted the bare, severed branches and tossed them neatly in a pile off to the side. To Maggie's relief the snowmachine started up on the second pull of the rope. Getting the machine started had been her biggest worry. Heading away from the fallen tree, Maggie found the overlap of the first and second loop that served as a turnaround, and was soon heading back toward the group feeling pleased with herself.

Rahlys, spying Maggie's speedy approach, conjured the last tree branch out of the trail and onto the pile with a quick, focused thought, then stepped out of the way as Maggie sped by too fast to stop before the snowmachine and sled passed them.

"Whoa! Whoa!" Vince shook his head, turning the chainsaw off to take a break. There was the flicker of an amused smile before his face went solemn. "Go around again, and this time slow down when approaching so you can line up the sled with the firewood."

While Maggie drove the snowmachine around, Vince struggled to free a large freshly cut round out of the trough the fallen tree had made in the snow. Rahlys teleported the log round out from Vince's grasp to the edge of the trail. The sudden lack of resistance landed Vince on his seat in the snow. Soon she had all the cut sections standing on end along the trail. Vince looked at Rahlys with increasing wonder and deference as Maggie came in for a second landing, braking gently. The sled lined up perfectly with the waiting load.

"Good job!" Rahlys praised her. Vince quickly lifted the first and largest round of firewood just high enough to clear the hitch and shuffled the wood to the back of the sled. Then Rahlys teleported a second round onto the sled, next to the first. Soon he and Rahlys had the sled loaded with the six largest sections from the lower end of the tree, and Vince strapped the wood in.

"I'll take this load," he said. "It will be the heaviest one, and it will have to be unloaded at the woodshed." Rahlys and Maggie readily agreed. Rahlys was already feeling the energy drain from the mental exertion. It was her heaviest use of repetitive magic since her encounter with Droclum, and she frequently peered cautiously about searching for a strange dark cloud of mist, or other threatening phenomenal show of force, but nothing happened. Whether it was because the protective shield was working, or no one was searching, she didn't know.

After watching Vince pull away with the heavy load, Rahlys and Maggie sat on upended rounds of firewood in the warm sun. "We should plan a surprise in the woods for Vince on his way back," Maggie suggested.

"What do you have in mind?"

"Oh, I don't know, maybe you could conjure an obstacle onto the trail…like a dragon or something."

Rahlys chuckled, "Do you really think he is deserving of a dragon?"

Anthya approaches.

"Wouldn't you like to see the expression on his face…" Maggie trailed off as Rahlys stood in surprise over the sudden, unexpected message. "What is it?"

"Anthya is coming."

"When? How?"

And then Anthya was there, standing before them in a long, flowing sky-blue gown that shimmered like her pale silken hair in the late winter sunshine. Maggie fell over backward off her stool into the snow.

"Greetings, Sorceress Rahlys, Guardian of the Light and Warrior Maggie." Maggie slowly righted herself, not taking her eyes off the gleaming apparition. Rahlys smiled at the salutation.

"Greetings, Councilor Anthya, visitor from afar. What can we do for you?"

"Defeat Droclum, for the security of your world as well as the rest of the universe."

"So you have said, and have you come now to tell us how?" Rahlys, surprised by her own audaciousness, recalled her first encounter with the self-assured otherworldly visitor.

"I have come to inform you that the High Council has assigned a highly skilled warrior and talented sorcerer on a mission to Earth, to train you and your warriors in the use of magic so that you may realize the full potential of your abilities."

"A sorcerer is coming here to teach us magic?" Maggie repeated astounded.

"His name is Quaylyn. He is at the beginning of his longevity on our world, but hundreds of years old in Earth-years. This is his First Mission. As Guardian of Anthya's Oracle, your powers are far greater than his, but there is much that he can teach you."

Rahlys sensed that there was much she didn't know about her magical abilities…but an alien visitor? This Quaylyn person could be more trouble than he was worth. So far she had been able to stand off Droclum on her own. Still Rahlys felt it unwise to refuse any help offered. She bowed gratefully to Anthya. "Please thank the High Council for me, for their generosity."

"And where is this sorcerer-warrior named Quaylyn?" Maggie asked.

"He is traveling in permanent physical time, which is slower than *nonpermanent physical time*…as I appear before you now. Expect his arrival in about three Earth days."

"What do I need to do to prepare for him? How long will he be here?" Rahlys asked.

"His needs are modest; a warm dry place to sleep, nourishment, and regional clothing to disguise his origin. The duration of his stay has not been predetermined. His purpose is to serve. Good luck, Sorceress Rahlys, Guardian of the Light."

Before Rahlys or Maggie could ask or say more, Anthya dissolved away. The words "nonpermanent physical time" came to mind.

A fishing boat shimmered on the serene water of the bay not far offshore, while a small skiff languidly hugged the beach. Two people, a man and a girl, were walking on the shore! Franklin was startled by the presence of people and boats. Never before had he encountered boats in his bay, and people on his beach.

Get rid of the boats.

The presence within that haunted his dreams, now found him during wakeful hours as well, but getting rid of the boats was exactly what Franklin had in mind. Hidden from view at the edge of the brush, he focused his concentration on the skiff anchored to the shore, and transported it to the hidden sea, deep beneath the mountains.

The man and girl, probably father and daughter, they had the same brown skin and black hair, didn't notice the skiff's disappearance for they were walking toward Franklin, facing away from where the skiff had been anchored. The girl he saw, as they got closer, was just about his age, maybe a little younger. She would be perfect, he thought.

Franklin stepped deeper into the edge of the brush to let them past. When they were safely beyond him, he focused on the fishing boat anchored out in the bay...and soon it too was gone.

Hidden from view, Franklin waited for a reaction from the beachcombers. He didn't have to wait long. The man came running back up the beach, screaming frantically over the disappearance of his boats, his daughter following close behind him, crying helplessly.

Franklin laughed, his laughter unheard over the cussing and crying. He didn't have any use for the man, but the girl would serve well toward fulfilling his fantasies. Franklin concentrated and mentally grasped the man's heart, squeezing it tightly, cutting off the circulation. The man gripped his chest, slumping quietly to the ground.

"Papa, Papa!" the girl screamed, running to his side, crying all the harder. "Papa, what is happening?"

But Papa didn't answer...he was dead.

Franklin decided to quickly remove Papa from the scene, and teleported the body, right out from under the dead man's grieving daughter, depositing it in the small open cave up the mountainside.

Seal off the cave.

Franklin, under Droclum's tutelage, concentrated power on the mountain around the opening. An isolated tremor rattled the boulders above the tomb, until the side of the mountain shuddered and gave way in a rockslide that effectively sealed off the cave.

The girl's shock at the sudden disappearance of her father from her arms, cauterized the flow of tears. No longer able to comprehend, she looked around bewildered. There were no boats...no father. Where could he have gone? What happened to him? She tried to call out to him, but try as she may, no sound issued forth.

It began to drizzle, the misty grayness enveloping her. Grief turned to terror. At any moment she, too, could vanish into oblivion. Silently she wailed to keep the evil spirits at bay. Perhaps the elders were right, and the new generation was wrong. She had nothing to lose by trying, but would it work without sound?

Franklin stepped out onto the beach and approached the girl unhurriedly. When she spotted him, she squinted her eyes and tightened the muscles in her face in an increased effort to ward him off, his evil aura nearly smothering her as he came closer. She screamed with the terror of a thousand nightmares, a silent scream, too spiritually deep for expression on such a delicate instrument as human vocal cords. Reaching her, Franklin grabbed her arm and teleported her with him to his cavern.

It had happened with the speed of a swallow snapping a fly out of the air. In the blink of an eye, she and the evil spirit were no longer on the beach in the cold drizzle, but in a warm dry cave lit with an eerie orange glow, probably from hell's own internal furnace.

Franklin released his grip on the shuddering girl and walked around her appraisingly, aroused by her tangible fear. She was just what he had been looking for, sweetly young and delicately innocent. He tried to remove her jacket to get a better look at her, but she clung to it with all her might holding it closed with her arms pressed tightly in front of her. A focused thought, and the jacket was magically removed. The girl cried in silent despair at the disappearance of her outer line of defense, tears visibly coursing down her beautifully smooth brown cheeks. Franklin reached out to touch her tears. Startled, the girl recoiled out of reach, bumping into the corner post of a massive bed.

"What's your name?" Franklin demanded.

The girl's lips and mouth moved in an effort to speak, but still she seemed unable to utter a sound.

"I will call you Taku," he decided pulling the word from her mind. "I am Droclum, your master. You belong to me and will do as I say."

Take her.

Franklin's body quivered with desires, the quick fiery desire of impetuous youth, and the burning seething lust of millennia of restraint as Franklin/Droclum moved in for the taking. Taku struggled in silent terror, but inevitably her efforts at resistance were overwhelmed. Finally, unable to bear any more, she went limp in evil's cold embrace.

Taku slowly drifted back into consciousness. A sickly feeling in her heart told her all was not right. She tried to pull together some loose threads of memory. She had a father...she could see him in flashes, but the image wouldn't stay focused...did something happen to him?... she couldn't remember. Her eyelids were still too heavy to lift, but she could feel she was lying on an unfamiliar bed. Where had she seen a strange bed? Or had it been a strange place for a bed? So much thinking soon wore her out, and the soft gurgle of running water lured her back to sleep.

The next time she awoke, her mind drew a blank, offering her no clues to her past. She opened her eyes in alarm and discovered she was in a large cavern, on a strange bed. Slowly, she sat up and looked around, then laid her head back down, trying to remember...trying to remember something...anything, but her memories hid behind a gray curtain, unwilling to reveal themselves. She struggled to recall her name...was it Taku? That didn't seem quite right, but she was certain Taku was the name of something. She sat up again to take a better look at herself and her surroundings. Barefoot and dressed in a pink nightgown she did not recognize, she gazed over the edge of the massive bed, estimating the drop. Spotting the foot stool, she clamored down.

The air in the cavern was warm, warmer than a cave would normally be. Orange light emanated from spots of glowing stone high on the walls, but the stone floor felt cool under her feet. Gingerly, she took a few steps, shaping her feet to the stone, making her way down to the next level.

Here stood a massive stone table littered with bones and feathers, and uneaten fruit in various stages of decay. In a niche along the wall, was a metal supermarket shopping cart filled with bags and boxes of packaged foods. Across the room from the stone table stood a large mirror, framed in carved wood, a cloak of feathers draped over its back. A stranger with disheveled black hair and a tear-stained face stared back at her from the mirror. Not wanting to face the fear in the strange girl's eyes, Taku turned away.

The level below the table and mirror was covered with animal hide rugs, and furnished with a large throne-like chair made of stone. From here she could see where the unceasing sound of gurgling water was coming from. Another level below her, a little stream flowed through the cavern. Carefully, she clamored over the rocks to the level of the water. Reaching the edge of the stream, she cautiously dipped her fingers into the cold water. Then scooping some water up with her hands, she threw it on her face, washing off the crusty salt residue from her tears, and cupped more into her hands to drink, the cold water soothing her dry raw throat. Lifting the pink gown above her knees, she stepped into the shallow, chilled water, the stones slippery under her feet. Soon her feet were icy cold, and she stepped back out onto the heated shore.

Taku looked back toward the higher levels of the cavern, and saw the large four-posted bed on its stone dais. Slowly, she retraced her steps back, thinking hard. The more she thought, the more fearful she became…something about an evil spirit…and it had a name.

Then she saw the name written in the dust on the mirror. Droclum. The spirit who brought her here called himself Droclum! Taku's innards contorted in terror. She needed to find a way to escape before he came back! Where was the door? Looking around, she followed the entire contour of the cavern walls, but there was no door to be found. There had to be an opening somewhere, else how could she have entered? Something nagged at her thoughts, but she just didn't seem to be able to grasp it. Then finally she understood; evil spirits didn't need doors.

Chapter 11
A New Alliance

Vince was stunned by Maggie and Rahlys' news of Anthya's visit, and more than a little concerned about an alien joining them. The prospect was unimaginable. Even his purpose for coming was mystifying. "He's going to train us in magic? All of us?"

"I don't have much magic to train," Maggie said.

"That means you don't know the full extent of your powers," Vince surmised, studying Rahlys.

"He is due to arrive in about three days." Maggie informed him.

"Why didn't he come with her?"

"Because he is traveling in permanent physical time, which is slower," Rahlys said. Vince gave her a puzzled look.

"And what did you say his name is?"

"Quaylyn."

"I wonder what he will be like?" Maggie said.

"Is he supposed to help us defeat Droclum? How long will he be here?"

"The duration of his stay has not been predetermined," Rahlys quoted Anthya. "Since the High Council appointed him, I guess the High Council can take him away. I don't know what say we have in it, if any. I always have the feeling that Anthya knows exactly what is going on here. Maybe the length of his stay will be determined by his effectiveness."

"A noble concept for a governing body," Vince said with skepticism.

"He will need a place to stay," Maggie pushed on.

"He can bunk downstairs on the daybed. I want to keep a close eye

159

on him," Rahlys added quickly. "My magic is supposed to be greater than his, so I should be alright. Anthya said his purpose is to serve."

"If it looks like he is going to be around a while, I'll put him to work building a guest cabin," Vince decided.

Wood harvest continued smoothly from there. Vince cut down several trees and bucked them up, and Maggie and Rahlys loaded the sled, taking turns hauling. Rahlys sped things up considerably by teleporting most of the wood. Soon there was a mound of firewood waiting to be split and stacked in front of both woodsheds. In the evenings, Rahlys painted patterns of snowmachine trails and stacks of firewood. At night she dreamed of voracious chainsaws devouring trees.

Rahlys opened her eyes to a morning glowing with sunlight. This was the day Quaylyn was expected to arrive. By unanimous vote, they had decided to take a break from wood harvesting. While waiting for Quaylyn's arrival, Rahlys planned to concentrate on splitting some of the wood already harvested and stacking it in the woodshed. But there was no hurry, she decided, as she lazed in bed a while longer, lost in thought. *I shouldn't have revealed the existence of the crystal to Maggie and Vince. Now I have put them in grave danger.* An involuntary shudder racked her body as she recalled the evil that had exuded from Droclum when she had wrenched Vince free from his mental grasp. Vince and Maggie were not equipped to handle Droclum. Neither was she, but she put that thought aside. With Quaylyn's help, hopefully she would grow in strength. She would learn how to use the frightful power she felt within. Leisurely, Rahlys rose to start her day.

Sunlight streamed in as she tidied up the kitchen. She smiled, looking out the window at the mound of freshly cut firewood outside her woodshed waiting to be split and stacked. It was a relief to see the mound grow. Her fears during the winter over how she was going to replenish her wood supply were now gratefully resolved, and warmth for yet another winter in the woods was thankfully assured.

Quaylyn approaches.

Rahlys froze in thought. Quickly she telepathed to Maggie, Vince, and Raven. Then Quaylyn appeared in the kitchen beside her. *He's here,* she informed them, intently studying the new arrival. The man standing before her looked more like a superhero from a comic book than an old sorcerer, certainly a far cry from an ancient Merlin, his muscular body admirably displayed in a form-fitting tunic and breeches. His finely sculpted face showed no emotion, but Rahlys saw an unmistakable twinkle in his deep blue eyes. A pouch slung across his shoulder was his only luggage.

"Greetings, Sorceress Rahlys, Guardian of Anthya's Oracle. I am Quaylyn, at your service," he greeted her warmly and bowed.

Rahlys wasn't sure how to address him. Anthya had said he was a sorcerer and a warrior. "Greetings, Warrior Quaylyn," she decided. "Welcome to our world. Should I ask, how was your journey?"

Quaylyn smiled, and his dark blue eyes sparked with friendliness. "It was an incredible trek across the universe. As you can see, I made good time." Quaylyn looked around, feasting his eyes on a strange, new world.

"Welcome to my home. I'm afraid you will have to sleep on the daybed here in the living room."

"And why are you afraid?" Quaylyn asked with concern.

"Oh…what I meant was, you will have to sleep in the living room instead of having a room of your own, which would be preferable."

"I understand. Fear not, Sorceress Rahlys. I thank you for your generous hospitality." His attention turned back to his surroundings. "Your home is made of dead trees." It was more a statement than a question.

"Well, yes. It's a log cabin." And he was to be her teacher. He certainly wasn't what she had expected.

"What did you expect?" Quaylyn asked.

Rahlys blushed, realizing he had read her thoughts.

"My lady, please forgive me, but as pleasant and quaint as your thoughts are, you must learn not to broadcast them for all to hear."

"Aaaark," Raven flew over the cabin, then landed in a tree at the edge of the clearing.

"Come, I will introduce you to one of my warriors," Rahlys said, changing the subject.

Quaylyn gasped audibly upon stepping outdoors, despite his attempt at formality. He gazed around in wonder at the winter landscape glittering in the sunlight, then turned his attention to Raven.

Raven, this is Quaylyn, Rahlys telepathed, but apparently Quaylyn had already spoken for himself, because the raven flew down to him without hesitation. "Raven is an unusually gifted bird," Rahlys said. He has been magically transformed by the Oracle."

"I understand." Quaylyn greeted Raven, *I am honored to serve*, he bowed respectfully.

Klawock, klawock, the raven replied mentally.

I look forward to you showing me the forest, rivers, and mountains, Quaylyn said, sharing his telepathed conversation with Rahlys. How strange that he had gained the raven's confidence so quickly, Rahlys thought wonderingly.

"The others are on their way," Rahlys explained.

"Yes, by a mechanical device. I can hear it. What other wondrous creatures do you have here?" Before she could even answer, a squirrel ran up a nearby tree, twittering loudly. Quaylyn, in hardly concealed awe over the small furry creature, made his way deferentially to the tree, seeking out the squirrel, probably wishing to make its acquaintance, Rahlys thought. But the squirrel didn't have the raven's insightfulness and would have nothing to do with him. Chattering angrily it scampered away over tree branches.

You are being spied upon.

Rahlys quivered, her heart racing. The telepathed message had not come from the Oracle, but from Quaylyn. Who could be spying on her; was it Droclum? She probed the surroundings for a mental presence, and eventually found two hunkered down in the snow on the ridge across the creek. One mental signature actually felt familiar…it was Aaron, she was certain of it. The other one she didn't know. Could it be Half Ear, the local Aaron had mentioned? What was he hoping to achieve by coming here? And how should she deal with this?

"Do you know the two men camped across the creek?"

"I know Aaron. The other, I believe, is his friend Half Ear."

"He is not from Earth."

"What do you mean, he's not from Earth?" Rahlys asked in alarm, stunned by Quaylyn's statement. "How can you tell?"

"He shields his thoughts."

"Well, I'm certain Aaron is from Earth. I've met his folks. And since I can read his thoughts, I'm sure you can."

Rahlys could see Vince and Maggie approaching, the snowmachine accelerating to rush the hill, and then they were there, circling the cabin before coming to a stop. Quickly they were standing beside her.

"Quaylyn, meet Maggie and Vince. Maggie and Vince, Quaylyn."

Quaylyn spoke first. "Greetings Maggie and Vince, warriors of the Guardian of the Light. It is my pleasure to serve." Maggie gave Rahlys a meaningful wink off to the side.

"Greetings, welcome to our little woodsy community," Vince extended his hand. At first Quaylyn didn't seem to understand the meaning of Vince's gesture, then picking up clues from his mind, quickly grasped the concept and took Vince's hand, shaking it dramatically.

"Yes, welcome, Quaylyn, it is a pleasure to have you here," Maggie greeted him warmly, unable to resist extending her hand for an encore handshaking performance.

"Good, now that we are all here, we can begin," Quaylyn said. "Why don't we start by you showing me what magic you've already learned."

"Rahlys is the only one with any real ability," Maggie explained. "But, you've just arrived and we haven't even had a chance to get to know you yet. We thought perhaps you and Rahlys could come over for a barbecue at our place."

"Of course, some socializing first would be in order. I humbly accept your invitation."

"Aaron and Half Ear are spying on us from across the creek, and Quaylyn says Half Ear is not from Earth," Rahlys informed them.

"What?" Vince said in disbelief. "Half Ear! Why, he's practically the village idiot!"

"He must be spying on us and reporting back to Droclum!" Maggie said in dismay. "What are we going to do?"

"Act as naturally as possible, and hope they haven't seen anything unusual. I wonder how long they have been there." I should have been more vigilant Rahlys reprimanded herself silently. At least the crystal has been in its pouch. "Perhaps we should take Quaylyn inside and dress him in more conventional clothing."

The next few hours were indeed interesting as they showed Quaylyn his surroundings. Vince gave him a ride on the snowmachine and even let him drive it around the cabin a couple of times. He was fascinated by their homes, the furnishings, and the way they lived. While they prepared dinner, he asked endless questions about the food they ate and where it came from as Rahlys and Maggie put together some side dishes and Vince fired up the grill and seasoned the steaks.

Then over dinner, Quaylyn told them a little about himself. "I am from the agriculture community of Lyngly. My chosen mother is Mythra, my chosen father, Kyemon, both from Lyngly."

"What do you mean by chosen mother and chosen father?" Maggie asked.

"When the population needs to be replenished, a new person is produced by a chosen mother and a chosen father. Each new person is loved, nurtured, disciplined, and educated by the entire community, with each member contributing instruction based on their knowledge and skills, until the new person's interests and talents emerge. Then he or she is sent to the community of the High Council, where the Academy is located, to hone those talents and interests until ready to be assigned a suitable, challenging First Mission. This is my First Mission. When my assignment has been completed, I will no longer be a new person, but an Accepted One. The outcome of my mission determines my future vocation."

Rahlys realized that in Quaylyn's eyes, he was an explorer to a new world, far more primitive than his own, who had been given a mission to accomplish, a rite-of-self-determination, so to speak.

"Why do you think, you were chosen for this mission?" Rahlys asked.

"I don't know if I'm the best choice for your needs," Quaylyn admitted, having read her thoughts, "I have not questioned the decision. But the Runes of the High Council would not have chosen me, if it were not meant to be. And I can assure you that I will do everything within my power to help you against Droclum." Rahlys wanted to ask what he meant by "Runes of the High Council," but Maggie spoke up first.

"Does your world look much like Earth?" she asked.

"No, not at all. Its colors and texture are very different. Even in the polar regions, we do not have much ice and snow. The sky and water is golden, and the foliage of the trees and plants is mostly blue green and orange. Our mountains are made of crystals and colorful stones of green, pink, and lavender." Quaylyn sent them mental pictures of the landscape as he described it, and a world of vivid colors like fauvist paintings flowed through their minds.

"When Mt. Vatre exploded, much of our world was destroyed. Multitudes died. Many species of life were extinguished entirely. The tainted lands are still uninhabitable, and magic as we know it no longer works there."

When the table was finally cleared, Quaylyn, sitting directly across from Maggie, asked her curiously, "What did you mean when you implied earlier that you have little ability to train?"

"Well, I can communicate telepathically, but I can't move objects like Rahlys."

"Why not?" To find out, Quaylyn reached over for her water glass and set in down in front of him. "Now conjure the glass back to you," he instructed. "Don't even think about the space across the table, just concentrate on where the glass is in front of me, and where you want the glass to be. Then relax and focus, and it will be there. Remember, the crystal has given you the power."

Maggie, obviously feeling ill at ease at being asked to perform, worked at building up the courage to try. All eyes were upon her. She thought of the things Quaylyn had said as she focused on the glass, then tried not to think, but relax. At first nothing happened. Then the glass started to tremble, the water inside jiggled around. Seeing her so close, Quaylyn gave the glass the slightest mental nudge, and the glass vanished, instantly reappearing in front of her. Maggie screeched in excitement. "I did it! Did you see that?"

While Rahlys and Vince congratulated her, Quaylyn teleported the glass back in front of him. "Now, do it again," he instructed her. Maggie would have preferred to soak in success a while longer before risking failure with a second attempt, but dutifully she gave it another shot. Quicker this time, the glass began to move, and just when Quaylyn was about to give it another helping nudge, the glass relocated itself in front of Maggie. It was Maggie's success, but a breakthrough for them all, Rahlys realized. Quaylyn was obviously going to have a tremendous impact on their magical development.

That evening, after her alien guest was settled on the daybed downstairs, Rahlys laid awake in the darkness. Thoughts crowded her mind.

Tomorrow, she would begin her training with Quaylyn in earnest. Hopefully he would help her to embrace her destiny, accept her fate. The tremendous magical force that coursed through her had now become a power to bravely explore, instead of timidly deny.

Clouds moved in overnight, concealing the morning sun. Rahlys had been hoping for another sunny day, but the woods loomed shadow-less and gray outside her bedroom window. She slipped out of bed and into her robe, conjuring the crystal to her hand from the pouch on the nightstand beside her bed, as she approached the window, mentally checking on her spies. They were in the same location. Maybe they were waiting for her to leave, so they could look for the crystal, or maybe they were hoping to witness something inexplicable. How could she drive them away without giving them a chance to do just that? She didn't want to convince Aaron of the existence of magic.

"Good morning," she greeted Quaylyn when she went downstairs.

"Good morning."

Rahlys put on coffee, then looked out at the stack of wood that needed to be split and stacked in the woodshed. Had the spies seen the stack of wood magically grow? I'll just have to work on firewood the old fashion way, she thought to herself.

"We can use magic to split and stack the wood, and not be seen, if we produce an illusion spell," Quaylyn said, reading her thoughts again. "This will be good practice for you in the use of creative magic. And while we do the wood, you can practice shielding your thoughts."

Over breakfast, Quaylyn helped Rahlys formulate the illusion. If the spell worked, day and night, cloudiness and sunshine, rain and snow would transpire naturally in the yard, while their presence and anything they actually did, would remain unseen. Rahlys concentrated, putting the magic screen in place before they stepped outside to start on the task of splitting and stacking wood.

They walked across the yard to the woodshed, in what would be 'in full view' for the spies across the creek, but if the spell was working as it should, and her confidence in her ability was growing, Aaron and his partner were still seeing a vacant yard with nothing happening. Upon reaching the shed, she slipped on the work gloves she had carried out with her, and checked once again on the location of the spies. They had not moved. She could barely make them out in their carefully concealed position, camouflaged like Ptarmigan, in the black and white landscape, under a white tarp.

Pulling the axe out of the chopping block and laying it against the woodpile close at hand, Rahlys picked a round from the pile and set it on end on the chopping block. "Here is the conventional way of splitting wood," she said. Lifting the axe high over her head, she brought it down hard on the log with a sharp smacking thud. The wood cracked loudly under the onslaught. "Does the spell cover sound?" she asked. Because if it didn't, the spies would be apt to wonder what was going on. Quaylyn had Rahlys weave another spell, drawing on the elemental molecular forces around her to block and absorb sound waves. Confident that sound was no longer getting through, she took another mighty whack at the wood, which rewardingly split into two.

Taku studied the forlorn image in the forbidding mirror, trying to identify the reflection in the eerie orange glow of the cavern. She still wore the pink nightgown she had awakened in…how many days ago now? She tried to calculate, but there was nothing meaningful she could use as a measuring stick…no clock, no sun, no stars.

Suddenly, Franklin arrived in the cavern carrying shopping bags. Taku dived under the bed, where to her surprise, she found her lost clothing, and actually recognized them as her own.

"Come out, Taku! You can't hide from me." Then after a pause, "I brought you gifts." Franklin walked over to the stone table and set the bags down. Taku, still under the bed, dressed hastily into her clothes, tucking the gown into her jeans. Crawling around the spacious area underneath the bed, she located her wool socks and boots. By the time Franklin lost his patience and whisked her magically out from under the bed, Taku was lying in a prone position on the stone floor before him fully dressed, including her jacket. The intoxicating aroma of cheeseburgers and fries wafted from one of the bags, gripping her senses. Her empty stomach contracted further, bringing her backbone closer to the floor.

"Get up." Slowly, but obediently, Taku stood. Franklin unwrapped a cheeseburger and handed it to her. Not taking her eyes off him, she took it from him and devoured it hungrily. By the time she finished the burger, he had fries laid out for her on the table. "Have some fries." Taku did not move. With a burger in her gut, she could now resist temptation. Franklin ended up eating all the fries himself as Taku slowly made her way, seemingly unnoticed, toward the bed, and dived back underneath it. Moments later, she was suddenly whisked out again, on the floor before him.

"Get up," he ordered her once more. It was obvious he was becoming irritated. Out of fear, she obeyed. "Don't you want to see what I brought you?" Taku didn't answer. She couldn't have answered if she wanted to.

Franklin pulled something red from a bag and held it up for her to see. A seductive, low-cut, red dress with a tucked bodice and spaghetti-strap shoulders, unfolded before her. Taku gasped soundlessly in horror. This could not be good. "Put it on," Franklin commanded, to her even greater dismay. And when she failed to make a move to comply, Taku found herself suddenly wearing the dress, the sculpt bodice pointing hollowly outward, lacking the breasts to fill it.

Then Franklin handed her another bag. "Go ahead, take it." Taku took the bag and looked inside where she found a long narrow black box with a hinged lid. Pulling out the box, she let the bag drop to the floor. Hesitantly, as though fearful of what she would find inside, she lifted the lid of the mysterious box. Astonishment lit her face.

Diamonds...a whole necklace of diamonds,...breathtakingly beautiful, they sparkled and twinkled at her in the sinister orange light. Slamming the lid shut, Taku reached down for the bag, stuffed the box into it, and handed it back to Franklin. When he didn't reach for it, she threw the bag on the stone table.

"You will wear the necklace," he roared, not at all pleased. Then, in a heartbeat, the necklace appeared around her neck. Its sudden cold weight against her skin startled her, and she yelped soundlessly.

Franklin passed a critical eye over Taku. She needed a hair brush, and maybe some makeup he thought, and with a sweep of his hand transformed her face and hair. Not sure what was happening to her, Taku watched as he reached again into the bag, this time retrieving a pair of slender, red shoes with long, thin spiked heels. Instantly the shoes appeared on her feet, magically made to fit. Taku struggled to maintain her balance on feet, standing on irregular stone, suddenly thrust into high heels.

"Look in the mirror," he ordered, his dark eyes smoldering.

Taku was slow to respond, not sure how to turn around without falling.

"Look in the mirror!" he shouted, his violent anger sending shudders through her body. Taku turned, stumbling awkwardly in the red heels. She fought to keep her balance on the not quite level stone floor as she approached the mirror. A strange girl, this one even more frightened than the one before, stared back at her in desperate despair. Taku trembled uncontrollably, trying to recognize herself.

"Look how beautiful you are," Franklin crooned, coming into the reflected image. Taku shook in terror. Perhaps thinking she was cold, he walked up to the mirror and removed the feather cloak draped over its back. Bringing it to her, he placed it over her shoulders, fastening the bone clasp in front. Taku nearly swooned. An inexplicable tingling coursed through her body and trickled through her brain as the cloak engulfed her.

The cloak, made of wave after wave of flowing feathers, was exceedingly light and airy. The number of birds that must have been sacrificed to make such a cloak, she feared to ponder. With mounting horror, she looked closer at the feathers; they were the feathers of ravens and eagles. Taku's heart pounded, sending her pulse throbbing in her ears. Sickened, she ripped off the cloak, throwing it as far from her as she could. Then she kicked off the red heels, and dashed for cover underneath the bed. To her dismay, her own clothes were not there.

Then suddenly everything was gone, and she was plunged into cold, damp darkness.

———

Heavy, wet spring snow fell for the next couple of days; deliciously miserable weather for the entrenched spies on the ridge across the creek, Rahlys thought, and smiled delightfully over Aaron's certain misery. She knew he wasn't a happy camper even in the best of conditions, surely the cold dampness would drive them away. She checked on their position regularly, but the spies remained glued in place.

Despite the inclement weather, Rahlys and Quaylyn made progress with her wood pile. Moving the chopping block into the shelter of the woodshed, they alternated between splitting the wood with an axe and splitting it with the force of their minds. Both were tiring, each in their own way. "Conditioning of brain waves and body muscles are of equal importance for maximum efficiency," Quaylyn instructed. The muscular tone of Quaylyn's body was proof enough he practiced what he preached.

In the evenings Rahlys painted, her paintings richly expressing the feel and essence of a lifestyle dependent on harvesting firewood. Quaylyn often watched over her shoulders as she worked, saying little. The rest of the time he read books on history, political science, and philosophy that Vince provided.

Then the snow stopped and a new day dawned clear and cold, turning soggy snow to icy snow. When Rahlys reached out mentally to confirm the location of the spies…they were gone. Teleporting over to their fox hole, she traced their tracks out to the railroad corridor.

Rahlys and Quaylyn were finishing up in the woodshed when Maggie and Vince drove up on the snowmachine.

"I see you got all your wood split and stacked during all that snow." Rahlys could tell Vince was impressed.

"It's looking good, huh?" Rahlys grinned proudly.

"Are you sure Aaron and Half Ear are gone?" Maggie asked with concern.

"Yes, I'm sure. Let's go in," Rahlys said. "I'll heat up the coffee." Vince and Quaylyn pulled the wooden table away from the window toward the center of the room so everyone could sit around it, but Vince remained standing, while Rahlys blasted the coffee warm on a small propane burner and filled assorted cups.

"What do you think they saw while they were here?" Maggie asked.

"Nothing, I hope," Rahlys tried to assure them.

"I believe this person you call Half Ear is actually Theon, one of Droclum's followers, and quite intelligent. Without a doubt, Half Ear is just a role he is playing."

"You're telling us that one of Droclum's followers has been living amongst us all these years? Just how many of you *are* there roaming around our planet?" Vince looked toward Quaylyn questioningly.

"As it turns out…three…Droclum, myself, and Theon. When Anthya planted the crystal on Earth," Quaylyn continued, "Theon was in hot pursuit. Anthya managed to elude him long enough to safely hide the crystal and remove herself from it before he could catch up with her again, but that was 12,000 Earth years ago. He was well along in age *then*! Who would have thought he would still be alive today! He must be nearing the end of his longevity."

"Why didn't you tell us about Theon before?" Vince wanted to know.

"When I was chosen for this mission, I was thoroughly briefed on what is known of Droclum's history, but the remote possibility that Theon may still be alive on Earth hadn't been considered possible."

"So Theon has been looking for the crystal for 12,000 years. That's a long time to hold an obsession," Rahlys said. "Surely he must know that Droclum lives. He's probably detected the use of magic. What do you know about the crystal?"

"It is believed that the great Sorceress Anthya wove in several enchantments during the making of the Oracle. I know the Oracle is protected against being used for evil; only one who is noble at heart can draw on its power. Therefore, Theon was seeking the crystal to destroy it, rather than possess it. Another spell makes it possible for the present day Anthya to communicate with the crystal."

"So that is why she always seems to know what is going on!"

"Tell us more about Droclum and the Dark Orb," Vince demanded.

"Well, his early life was pleasant, if not especially noteworthy. He was nurtured in a coastal community that harvested from the sea. By the time Droclum was ready to enter the Academy, he showed incredible magical talent. There is a lot of mystery around what happened next. What is known is that Droclum left the Academy before receiving his First Mission."

"So then what did he do?" Maggie asked.

"He became a renegade. Eventually he had a small band of followers under his command, and they started reeking havoc for power and control. Droclum repeatedly escaped apprehension, and in fact, became increasingly more elusive. After many innocent people were mercilessly killed, the High Council decided that Droclum should be destroyed." Vince took a seat next to Maggie as Quaylyn continued.

"Anthya was a gifted sorceress who attended the Academy during the same time as Droclum. Later the two would become mortal enemies. At least as strong and powerful as he, Anthya sought Droclum out, through ages of time, to destroy him. Finally, Anthya and her league of warriors had him in their grip. But Droclum, smelling defeat and fearing his demise, wrought an evil, sinister spell, drawing on the dark forces. When Anthya struck what should have been a fatal blow, Droclum defied death. His life essence was drawn into the deep recesses of Mt. Vatre and forged into the Dark Orb. When Mt. Vatre exploded, the Dark Orb was catapulted through time and space to Earth, where Droclum would live again through the eventual possession of another soul."

Aaron stared out the window, watching for Rahlys' trail as he rode the southbound train down from Half Ear's place in the woods back into town. Even watching for it, he almost missed spotting her trail as the train sped on by. After two days of camping in heavy wet snow, he and Half Ear had hiked the thirteen long miles back up the tracks from Rahlys' creek to Half Ear's cabin. Spying on Rahlys had been a miserable waste of time, although when he expressed this sentiment to Half Ear, he got a strangely unexpected response. "You were right," Half Ear had said, "there is something mysteriously powerful at work here," but would say no more. What was he talking about, Aaron wondered. They didn't see any magic, they rarely even saw Rahlys the whole time they were there. She must be pissing in canning jars, for as often as she stepped out of the cabin. And who was that other strange fellow with her?

Without making any more stops along the way, the train finally clattered up to the little town's tiny train depot. Passengers got off, mingling on the platform as their baggage was being unloaded, but Aaron would have nothing of pleasantries. He stalked off with his pack, his brooding thoughts blinding him to where he was going. A truck horn blew, alerting him to danger. Jarred back into focus, he stepped out the way to let the truck pass, but now the driver was motioning for him to go ahead and cross. Aaron did so, then stormed the rest of the way to Half Ear's little unpainted plywood town flat, kicking the door open without unlocking it. The flimsy, barely aligned door frame released the door with little resistance. Aaron slammed the door shut behind him, only it swung part way open again, the door no longer connecting with the catch in the door frame.

Chapter 12
The Coming of Spring

"You teleport like a New Person, at the very beginning of his longevity, learning for the first time to mentally project his body forward in time and space," Quaylyn explained. "I'm sure your potential is far greater." Vince had demonstrated limited ability earlier, by actually teleporting himself forward a few feet at a time. This was only after an intense lecture on Quaylyn's part to convince him to even try.

"But how?" Vince asked. The group had gathered in the warm spring sunshine warming Rahlys' front porch, despite the snow still covering the ground.

"I'll try to explain," Quaylyn said. "As you know, no two bits of matter can occupy the same space at the same time, but it does not hold true, that when a bit of matter moves from one space to another, the two spaces have to be adjacent to one another. That is because time and space can be bent, or folded. When you are teleporting the short distances you do, you are not bending time and space. You could run, skip, jump, or hop from your starting point to where you are ending up in the same amount of time it is taking you to focus and concentrate energy, to seemingly make the move instantly. That is because you are not only occupying your starting space and your ending space, but also, all the spaces in between. Eliminate the spaces in between, and you will eliminate your limitations."

"What if you can't teleport yourself at all?" Maggie asked.

"Of course, you can!" Quaylyn came back with such speed and certainly it was difficult to doubt. "Remember the glass you moved across the table? You are creating your own obstacles in your mind. First you must get rid of preconceived notions as to what is possible."

"But how do we do this?" Maggie asked, her interest definitely whetted.

"It's like learning to float." Quaylyn's enthusiasm held a captive audience as he expounded. "The potential is there from the start. The primary step toward accomplishing that goal is to relax and trust that you can. Whether you are moving a cup across the table or yourself across a continent, the principle is the same. First you must relax and trust that you can.

"You have an electrical device, you call a computer," he went on, "that can send audio and visual data instantly to any other computer on your planet. But your brain produces a wave of energy far more sophisticated than your computers use. These energy waves can manipulate the elemental forces and bend time and space making it possible to change the space a bit of matter is occupying instantly, regardless of the distance. By folding time and space, we can place our starting point and our destination, even if it is half a world away, next to each other, making the switch in location happen instantaneously." Quaylyn paused to give them time to catch up.

Rahlys watched and listened with detached amusement as Quaylyn attempted to explain such mind-expanding concepts. Dressed in a cotton plaid shirt and denim jeans, he still looked inexplicably otherworldly. Quaylyn turned to her, as though drawn by her thoughts. "As for Rahlys," he said, looking at her, but not addressing her directly, "the protection spell she created to shield us from Droclum is only a minute example of her potential creative abilities. Anthya's powers were wondrous. While most people can telepath and teleport, the use of creative magic, in which something is not merely moved from one place to another but rather is somehow altered, is dependent on a person's individual talents and strengths."

"You mean, the spell really did work?"

"Yes, but it will only hold Droclum back for a while. You should be able to detect the magic yourself though. The spell is charged with your power." Quaylyn led Rahlys out into the yard away from the porch and together they gazed at the sky. "Gently now, try focusing on your protective shield…reach out to it with your mind."

Rahlys looked up into the brilliant sun-lit sky. She focused thought energy upward, seeking something vaguely tangible. And then…ever so lightly…she touched it. For the blink of an eye, a gossamer dome shimmered overhead and down to the horizons, before it disappeared.

The next day, Vince decided to take Quaylyn with him to the wood-lot to harvest logs for a guest cabin, before the snow gave out. Providing Rahlys with a small guest cabin would give her a needed break from Quaylyn. Rahlys and Maggie's admiration for Vince's tree harvesting abilities was mild compared to Quaylyn's awe when Vince felled the first spruce tree. He was impressed with Vince's skill, the primitive tools he used, and nature's gift itself, the massive tree that came crashing down before them. Vince shut off the chainsaw, and with reverent respect, Quaylyn walked completely around the felled tree, examining it carefully.

Then Vince picked up the chainsaw again, balancing it on the horizontal trunk of the fallen tree before pulling the starter rope. "I'll remove the branches, then you can start peeling the log," he told Quaylyn. Vince started up the chainsaw and set about de-branching the tree. Soon he noticed that not only the branches he had cut, but even those he hadn't reached yet, were cut and the bark peeled away. A bare log stretched out in front of him. Vince looked around to see Quaylyn standing at ease, patiently waiting for whatever was next.

Taking advantage of the situation, Vince moved to the next suitable spruce tree. After cutting all the way through, he took a step back just in time to see the log magically cleaned of branches and bark. Vince shut off the chainsaw.

"How did you do that?" he asked impressed.

"When you peel a log, or an apple, you are severing molecular bonds within the object which require a certain amount of force, depending on the strength of the substance."

It must take a lot of energy to magically de-branch and peel a log, Vince thought, but Quaylyn was still standing, raring to go. It was not until he had cut down their fourth tree, that Vince noticed Quaylyn was looking a bit tired, but he never complained.

"We are making great progress," Vince explained. "We should be able to get a couple of cabin logs out of each tree…but we won't be able to put in a foundation till the ground thaws."

Besides helping Vince in the woodlot, Quaylyn also teleported over to Vince and Maggie's nearly every day to pick out books from Vince's contemporary collection, or to teach them how to tap into the elemental forces. Quaylyn was unwavering in his efforts to teach, however mixed the results. Vince could teleport himself and other objects, but his range proved to be very limited. "It is sort of like sending your computer to page twelve of a ten-page document…nothing happens," he said, when he tried to go further. Maggie, try as she would, still could only move the smallest, lightest objects. Even Raven wasn't exempt from Quaylyn's efforts.

Rahlys made tremendous progress under Quaylyn's tutelage, but she relished the time alone when he was out of the cabin. It was not that he was a *bad* house guest, quite the contrary, it was just that he was a house guest at all. She had moved into the woods to be alone, and coveted that solitude. Plus his constant drilling for her to shield her thoughts, and her constant failure to consistently do so, was driving her crazy. She knew it was an important skill, and Quaylyn was only trying to help, but she just wanted him to go away and leave her alone so she could paint.

Then one night when they gathered once again at Vince's cabin to indulge in Maggie's cooking, Rahlys was startled out of her thoughts by Maggie. "You know, Rahlys, we've been thinking," she looked at Vince who nodded a smile, "when was the last time you've been out the woods?"

"Me? I don't know, why?"

"Yes, you. The last time you were out the woods was Thanksgiving, and here it is already April." It sounded like a reprimand.

Rahlys knew it was true that she had avoided leaving the woods. But with Vince and Maggie picking up supplies and the mail for her, going out hadn't been necessary. She had a stack of paintings that needed framing and marketing, but she was having a hard time reconciling the magical person she had become with the mundane, outside world she had escaped. Avoidance had been the easiest and simplest path. "And you are bringing this up because…?"

"Well, Vince and I need some things, and probably so do you, and

Vince is too busy working against a deadline, so I thought maybe you and I should go out on a supply trip together. If we left this Sunday, we could come back on the first Thursday train. That would give us three full days to get things done."

"Alright, sounds like a plan." Rahlys couldn't believe she had just agreed to leave the woods for four days...departing in just two.

Rahlys and Maggie were cruising down the highway on their way to Wasilla, soaking in the signs of spring. Snow still loomed deep up at the cabins, but here, a hundred miles to the south, snow was replaced by bare ground. Warm sunshine caressed the straw-colored grass, leafless brush, and bare ground, arousing ferns, trees, bushes, and grass back to life. Evergreen spruce trees orchestrated the greening of the forest, offering encouragement by example. Cresting the hills, the highway offered panoramic views of mountains and majestic waves of purple-crowned forest, the plump leaf buds on the birch trees ready to burst. This is what the landscape had looked like when she and Rahlys had first arrived in Alaska a year ago, Maggie recalled.

Ilene was tending the gallery when Rahlys walked in a couple of days later carrying in several matted and framed watercolors. "Oh good, we were hoping you would bring in more of your work. We've sold a couple of your paintings."

"That's good to hear."

"Oh, these are beautiful!" Ilene exclaimed as she looked at Rahlys' latest work. "I see you've been snowmachining, snowshoeing, harvesting firewood, just enjoying winter in general."

"It has been quite a winter," Rahlys agreed. Then in walked the most unlikely person she would ever expect to see in an art gallery.

"Hi, Aaron, I'm almost ready to lock up, as soon as I've finished up here." Then she turned to Rahlys, "Aaron bought one of your paintings."

Rahlys ate up the embarrassed look on Aaron's face. "He did! Which one?" she asked.

"The one of the crystal in the night forest."

Rahlys turned to Aaron, "I didn't know you were into crystals."

"Do you two know each other?" Ilene asked, picking up strange vibes as she issued Rahlys a check for the sale of her paintings.

"We've met," Rahlys said smiling, "but I didn't know he was a patron of the arts." Taking the check Ilene offered her, Rahlys cheerfully exited the gallery.

"You didn't say you knew the artist," Ilene chided him as she locked the doors behind them.

"Does it matter?"

"Well, it seems like something you would say, if it were fact."

"Sorry, I didn't think it was important."

After dinner at the inn, and drinks at the bar, Aaron took Ilene to Half Ear's pad. He had spent the whole day sprucing the place up, including laundering the sheets, and had cleared off one wall in the living room, removing old dusty calendars and yellowing newspaper articles against gun control attached with brittle, yellowed cellophane tape. Then bringing the painting of the crystal out from under his bed, he had hung it where Ilene would be sure to see it as soon as she walked through the door. Otherwise, it would have been hard explaining to her why he kept it hidden under his bed. He had also repaired the front door frame and catch as best he could.

"Oh, the painting looks great there!" Ilene exclaimed upon entering. The crystal seemed to glow in the subdued light of early evening.

"Have you been here before?" Aaron asked, offering her a seat. At first, Ilene did not answer. In the ensuing silence, he lit a couple of scented candles, bought from the gift shop downtown for the occasion, then deciding it was too silent, turned on the radio for some music. Ilene quietly sat down on the sofa.

"Once…the night of my senior prom," she finally said after Aaron no longer expected an answer.

There was a story here; he could sense it. "Ready for a glass of wine?" he asked, heading for the kitchen without waiting for a response.

"Sure," not that it mattered, she already had had so much to drink. She stared at the crystal in the painting. The crystal seemingly drifted out of the painting and into the room as a glowing hologram.

"Here you go." Aaron said passing through the image as he handed her a glass. The crystal returned to the painting.

"Did you see that?" Ilene asked.

"See what?"

It was not the first time Ilene had seen the strange phenomenon. The first time, the painting had been hanging on the gallery wall. "Nothing," she said. There was no point in bringing it up, if he hadn't seen it.

"So, what happened on the night of your senior prom?" Aaron sat on the sofa next to her, a beer in his hand.

"Huh? Oh...well this guy, his name was Drew...he doesn't live around here anymore...I had a real crush on him, and I thought heaven itself had burst wide open when he asked me to the prom." Despite the animation of her dialogue, she stopped, took a long pause, and sipped her wine deep in thought.

"And so what happened?" Aaron coaxed her to continue. She still hadn't gotten to Half Ear's role in the story. "Did you and Drew go to the prom?"

"We did." Slowly, pensively, she told the tale, reliving it in the telling. "He hardly paid any attention to me throughout the dance," she pouted, "then on the way home he pulled off on this little service road to the railroad tracks that ended in a deserted parking area surrounded by trees, and proceeded to try and rape me...only he didn't succeed, because literally, out of nowhere, Half Ear came to my rescue." Again Ilene fell silent, a tear rolling down her cheek.

Aaron moved over, closer to her, to give her a shoulder to cry on. Half Ear, a knight in shining armor, rescuing a damsel in distress. Aaron had to adjust his take on Half Ear; the man seemed to be full of contradictions. His colloquies on woman did not correspond with the champion for women persona.

With relative ease, Aaron eventually lead Ilene to his bed. They were both still snoring in an alcohol induced slumber when the train blew its whistle leaving the depot the next morning, conveying Rahlys and Maggie back north.

Taku found herself suddenly surrounded by cold, damp darkness. Frightened, she reached up to touch the underside of the bed for reassurance, but her hand met cold hard stone instead. The stream that ran through the cavern sounded like it was right beside her ear, but it was so pitch black dark, she couldn't see it. Cautiously, she explored her surroundings with her hands, and discovered she was enclosed in a tiny cave, barely large enough to shift position in, the stream just inches away. The cold dampness on her exposed shoulders and seeping through the thin red dress, quickly chilled her to the bones.

Not bothering to hike up the already damp dress, Taku braved the cold, shallow stream, crawling in under the low ceiling of the cave. Feeling her way around, she blindly searched in the darkness for an exit, but the stream was tightly enclosed, and there was no opening in the stone walls large enough for her to pass through. Unless you were water, there was no way in, and no way out. Drenched, and in total despair, Taku curled back up onto the cold, damp rock shelf, crying and shivering.

It's so cold…and so dark…Please, someone help me.

Minutes turned into hours, and hours turned into days, but there was no means for Taku to denote the passage of time as she laid cramped and cold in the unrelenting darkness. She wiggled down deeper into the dress, which had dried somewhat from her body heat, working her slender bare arms and shoulders into the bodice, seeking even that minimal layer of warmth. Stay awake, she told herself, if you fall asleep you will never wake up. But would that really be so awful, she thought; sleep, especially perpetual sleep, would be an escape from the cold and darkness…and all the emotional pain she couldn't face.

Despite her intentions, Taku fell repeatedly in and out of consciousness. Sometimes she cried deliriously, moaning hopelessly for help; other times she dreamed she was on a fishing boat in the sound, breathing in deeply the fresh smell of the sea, misty rain obscuring the forested mountains in the background.

Over the timeless hours, hunger tormented her. She tried desperately to ignore it, turning her focus on trying to remember her name instead, and her family, for surely she must have one. Then falling asleep again, she was back on a fishing boat, the reassuring fishy smell of nets on the deck filling her nostrils. And there was someone else on board. "Papa!" she cried soundlessly.

⸻

Break-up was finally here. Rahlys felt downright giddy over the longer daylight, warmer temperatures, and melting snow. Each day the sun popped up earlier and earlier, arching higher and wider across the sky, its hot rays turning the dwindling snow pack into mush during the heat of the day. Ever-widening bands of bare ground expanded around trees emitting heat of their own in the flush of spring. Expand-ed circles of exposed ground mottled the landscape white and brown. The snow-free circles grew, creating islands of straw colored grass, old brown leaves, and dark earth in the thinning, retreating snow. Already there were large areas of snow-free ground around the cabin and other out buildings, and grass was turning green up against the sun-warmed wood of the cabin skirting. But at night, as soon as the sun let up its guard and sank below the horizon, the cold quickly stole back in, turning the remaining undefeated snow mush into ice as temperatures dipped below freezing overnight.

Break-up was a time of waiting, waiting for the snow to melt, wait-ing for the ground to warm, waiting for green leaves to sprout. In the mornings, the hard crusted snow was strong enough to walk on. Rahlys took advantage of the morning crust, to hike and explore through the emerging spring forest, hopping across patches of snow from one area of awakening forest to the next. The woods were warm and sunny and alive. Rahlys searched the glaring bright sky to spot swans honking high overhead on their way to their breeding grounds further north and west. Chickadees chirped and flittered about so-much-to-do-and-so-little-time-to-do-it, and the first robin of spring landed on a branch in front of her, posing long enough for her to make a quick sketch. Twice she disturbed squirrels doing their spring cleaning, clearing their underground homes of discarded spruce cone husks, piling them around the base of their tree.

Raven, where are you? Was he off courting, a champion among ravens, driven by instinct and the pulse of renewal?

"Aaaark!" The sudden cry was so close it took her by surprise. Raven landed heavily in a nearby birch tree, the leaf buds on the branch split-ting, ready to burst. "Aaaark! Aaaark!"

Why, Mr. Raven, how have you been? In response, Rahlys picked up a sense of well-being. The raven seemed especially handsome in the vibrating warmth, and she pulled out her sketch pad. *You know what I would like for you to do? I want you to pose for me, if you will, with your wings spread out a little,* Rahlys actually spread out her arms a little in demonstration, *like you were ready for take off, without actually flying away, while I sketch. Do you think you could do that for me?* Of course, she didn't expect the raven to understand, or comply, as she commenced to sketch him sitting on the tree limb. But to her surprise, the raven took on a comically serious stance, unfolded his wings partway from his body, and crouched ready to leap as she made the sketch, at one point losing his balance and catching himself in a flutter of feathers, which sent Rahlys into peals of laughter.

"Aaaark," he squawked in wounded pride.

When the study was complete, she decided to enjoy the day further and pay Vince and Maggie a visit. And she would apologize to Quaylyn if necessary. He hadn't returned last night after she had snapped at him. *You can follow me, if you like, I'm headed to see Vince and Maggie.* The raven took off ahead of her. Rahlys teleported to Vince and Maggie's yard, and as she expected, found them outdoors in the warm sunshine.

"Hey, look who's here!" Maggie said, spotting her first. She held an armload of small branches, blown out of the trees over the winter, that she had picked up from the yard. Vince turned from his raking and nodded in greeting.

"I see you've done some spring cleaning, the yard looks nice." Rahlys watched as Maggie added the branches to a pile by the burn barrel at the edge of the clearing.

"Can't wait till it turns green," Vince said, using her visit for an excuse to take a break.

"Where's Quaylyn? Yesterday I became highly irritated with him," she admitted with some remorse. "He keeps interrupting my thoughts every time he can read them…which is every time I let my mental guard down. Anyway, I ended up so aggravated with him I told him to get lost. I hope he didn't take me literally."

"Quaylyn said he was going exploring for a while, and not to worry about him," Maggie said. Rahlys felt a bit hurt that he hadn't told her what he was doing, yet a bit relieved that he had told someone. Well, she wouldn't worry about him.

Raven flew in, landed in the yard, and waddled over to Vince's leaf pile. He pecked and scratched looking for bugs, until he had scratched through, and spread out, the entire pile of freshly raked leaves. Vince rolled his eyes in quiet resignation.

Relaxed and at ease after her visit with Maggie and Vince, Rahlys laid out her paints and the sketch of Raven posing, ready for flight. She clamped a fresh, clean sheet of watercolor paper to her board; the paper stared back at her, waiting to be transformed. Forcing herself to concentrate, she roughly sketched in the forms of the raven and the tree branch, then brushed on some underlying washes before turning away to let it dry.

Quaylyn still hadn't returned when she went to bed with a book, using light from the crystal to read by. Where had he gone? When was he coming back? Eventually her eyes grew heavy, and she gave in to sleep. Sleep turned to dreaming, and in her dream someone cried for help. The silent mental cries seeped into her brain unceasingly. With the cry for help crept in a feeling of cold darkness. In the dream, Rahlys sought the source of the dark, cold distress, drawing ever closer, the pleas for help becoming clearer…*help me, oh, please, someone help me, please help me*…the distressed soul murmured and shivered. But Rahlys could not locate the source.

Where are you? Rahlys tried to connect mentally, but there was no response, just the continuous moaning plea of the subconscious…*help me, someone please help me*…Finally, by morning, the mental noise ceased, and Rahlys fell into restful sleep.

She recalled vividly the distress calls in her sleep the next morning, and a gnawing feeling in her gut told her it was real. The cry for help nagged at her thoughts all day, even overriding her concern over Quaylyn's disappearance. Who was begging for help, and why?

She stepped out into the warm sunshine with much on her mind. But she needed something to do while she thought. Fetching the rake from the shed, she started raking the yard around the front porch, striking a rhythm as she warmed to the task. The mysterious cries for help haunted her thoughts while bird song filled the forest around her.

Rahlys started a new compost pile with the raked up thatch, leaves, and twigs near where she hoped to have a garden eventually. As the day grew warmer, an occasional large, sluggish mosquito, which she viciously smacked, brushed by her exposed hands and face, looking for a donation of a drop of blood.

Then suddenly Quaylyn returned amidst her leaf piles, offering no explanation as to where he had been. "Come with me. I want to show you something," he said to Rahlys, offering her his hand. Hesitantly, she reached for his hand. Then they were standing at the edge of the river on a huge boulder overlooking the mighty Susitna River. The forested ridges lining the river's graceful banks shimmered green in the sunlight. Rahlys gasped…GREEN! The birch forest was leafing out. Zillions and zillions of tiny green birch leaves, forcing their way out of their nurturing buds, painted a spring green wash over the forest. Spring was finally here.

Quaylyn and Rahlys sat on the great rock, soaking up the sun, and listening to the murmur of the river's wisdom. The gentlest of breezes stirred the sun-warmed air briefly, pushing a lone, unhurried mosquito by Quaylyn's exposed hand. Fascinated by the insect life form, he lifted his hand, palm down, stretching it out for a landing pad. Naturally, the mosquito took advantage of the offer and landed, sinking its extended proboscis into his skin.

"Kill it!" Rahlys exclaimed. She couldn't see letting a mosquito bite, when you had a chance to smack it instead.

"Why? Her intent is not evil, she's just hungry. Surely, I can spare a drop of blood to feed her." Rahlys was so surprised and taken off guard by his sentiment, she didn't know how to respond. The mosquito sucked its fill, then took off, nearly too bloated to fly.

Tired from the restless night before, Rahlys retired before true darkness, which came exceedingly late these days. Nights were becoming fleetingly short. But it was dark indoors, at least too dark to read. Rahlys conjured the crystal out of its pouch as she crawled into bed and settled into position, propped up on pillows. When she reached for her book, the crystal brightened radiantly over the head of her bed. Rahlys read some, but her thoughts were elsewhere. Soon her eyes were closed with the book draped across her chest, and she was sound asleep. The crystal softened its brilliance to a soft glow, and nestled itself back into its pouch.

Rahlys slept for several blissful hours before, once again, she could sense someone sobbing and pleading,…*It's so cold…and so dark…Please, someone help me.* The signature was a little weaker than the night before.

Where are you? Rahlys tried again, stretching her mind in an effort to reach the source. The sobbing paused momentarily. Rahlys actually heard a mental, *huh?*, before the answer.

I don't know.

Who are you?

I don't know, the girl cried in despair. *I'm so cold...*

Where are you? she asked again. *You must give me a clue, so I can find you.*

I'm in a cave; it's so dark and cold. So dark and cold...

Rahlys could feel the girl slipping from her mental grasp. *Hold on*, she encouraged, but all her attempts to conjure the girl to her, ended in empty air. Then in a desperate effort to save the girl from hypothermia, Rahlys projected all her mental strength into transferring warmth. She was sure she could actually feel the girl's violent tremors slowly subside.

Chapter 13
Contact

Taku dreamed that someone heard her pleading cries for help and sought to find her, sending soothing warmth to calm her deathly shivers. She woke with a start, her eyes opening wide despite the lack of light to enter them, and felt decidedly warmer. How could that be, she wondered, as her stomach growled angrily, wishing to be fed. Freeing her arms from the bodice of her dress, she attempted to sit up, bumping her head on the stone ceiling of the cave. Taku moaned silently, rubbing the spot that smarted. Then when the pain subsided some, she took a drink from the stream and patted some cold water on the bump on her head. Was someone looking for her? Would she be found before she starved to death? The air in the cave did seem warmer. Was there magic at work here? Perhaps there were good spirits as well as evil ones, and a good spirit was trying to help her.

Aaron and Ilene paced the railroad platform waiting for the southbound train coming in from up the tracks. Instead of Aaron taking Half Ear supplies, Half Ear was coming back to town. The train was already way late, but Aaron and Ilene made good use of the time moving Ilene's clothing and things back to her apartment above the gallery, and tidying up Half Ear's pad, even putting a casserole in the oven for their dinner as they listened for the train whistle, which would give them enough time to run down to the station and meet it. Aaron wanted to take his painting down and stash it by his sleeping area, but

Ilene talked him into leaving it, for it really did spruce the place up, and such a nice painting should be seen, not hidden, she argued. With reluctance, he gave in.

It was warm and pleasant out, winter already forgotten, with the leafed-out forest sneaking in all around, filling in the spaces between lifeless man-made structures, tastefully obscuring them with living green. The train whistle blew again and again, filling the valley with its persistence. Then they could see the train rolling in slowly around the curve and through the shimmering forest toward the platform where it came to a stop. Half Ear, along with a few tourists, disembarked and headed for the baggage car where bags, boxes, and packs were handed down to the platform for claiming. Aaron and Ilene intercepted him, "Hi, there!"

Half Ear looked curiously at the two of them together and smiled, "Hi!"

"Do you have much baggage?" Aaron asked.

"Two packs, a couple of tents, and some camping gear. I figured now that it's summer, it might be time for us to go on another little camping trip together, don't you think?"

"I wish I could go camping," Ilene said, hoping to be invited along, but no one responded. The three of them carried the camping gear to Half Ear's pad.

"So that is what the crystal looks like!" Half Ear said, pausing in mid-stride, as his gaze fell upon the painting gracing his living room wall. Half Ear dropped his pack down on the floor by the door without taking his eyes off the crystal as he walked toward the painting. The image of the crystal floated softly off the surface of the painting in greeting, glowing and twirling slowly. Then just as quickly it was back in the painting.

"Did you see that?" Ilene asked excitedly. She was sure he had.

"See what?" Half Ear asked, as though nothing had happened. She couldn't believe he was denying it. In a huff Ilene headed for the kitchen to take the casserole out of the oven. Aaron, in fact, hadn't seen a thing with Half Ear and Ilene obstructing his view.

Over dinner Aaron and Half Ear planned their camping trip. "We will camp on the southeast point of the creek's north ridge, overlooking the big swamp. That's still nearly a quarter of a mile from Rahlys' cabin. We can go in the way we did before," Half Ear explained, "or follow the creek, but if we follow the creek, we will have to pass right by her. It's best not to be seen. So we might as well have the train drop us off where we hiked in before, a mile or so north of her trail. The woods will be easy hiking right now with the foliage still low to the ground. And with the nearly continuous daylight, we won't be pushed for time to set up camp."

"Take me camping with you, please," Ilene begged. "I'm strong and a good hiker, and you guys will need a woman along to help out around the campsite."

Aaron looked at Half Ear, "Can she come along?" He didn't think there was a chance in hell that Half Ear would let a woman come along, but it wouldn't hurt for Ilene to hear Half Ear's response herself.

Half Ear considered for a moment, then surprised him by saying, "She will need her own tent."

"But we already have two tents."

"We will need three. I'm not sleeping with you either."

"I can borrow a tent," Ilene declared gleefully. "And I have a sleeping bag and a pack."

Aaron had never seen her so excited about anything before. "What about the gallery?" he asked.

"Momma is coming back tomorrow. She can take care of the gallery for a while. When are we leaving?"

"We should be packed and ready to go by Thursday morning's train," Half Ear said, and then he surprised them both by adding, "We will take the painting of the crystal with us."

"Why?"

"You'll see when the time comes."

Thursday morning the three were packed and ready to go, pacing the railroad platform in front of the little depot. Ilene was more animated than usual, and almost unrecognizable, dressed in jeans, a shirt, and a light jacket for the woods. A baseball cap pressed down her frizzy hair. Aaron thought her more attractive dressed this way than in her usual skirts and blouses.

Their packs were filled to overflowing with food and camping gear. Sleeping bags, tents, and tools were secured to their pack frames. Ilene would carry the lightest pack, but she would also be responsible for carrying the painting which had been carefully wrapped, frame and all, in plastic sheeting, cardboard, and duct tape for its protection. A rope handle had been worked into the packaging for ease of carrying. Half Ear would not explain why he wanted to take it with them, but they figured they would find out eventually.

Finally the train was there and all their stuff was onboard. Ilene found a window seat looking out on the town, and Aaron sat next to her. Then Half Ear sat down on the seat across, facing them. Although Ilene had lived in hearing distance of the train all her life, and had watched it pass and stop at the platform thousands of times, she had never before *ridden* the train. No particular reason why, it just never happened. She could hardly believe that she was actually riding into the wilderness for an extended camping trip with Aaron and Half Ear. Ilene longed for adventure, and she sensed that something very unusual was underfoot. Her excitement mounted as the train wheels finally started turning slowly, moving the car forward.

"Going camping again, I see," the conductor said cheerfully as he collected their tickets, and Half Ear gave him the mile post number. "All three of you?"

"Yes, thanks."

The rest of the ride was in silence. Ilene stared out the window at greening swamps and hills, beaver ponds and forest, and the occasional spectacular vista of Denali and the mighty Susitna River. A couple of times the train stopped to let off passengers with packs and boxes. Before too long, it started to slow down again, and Ilene followed Half Ear to the exit. The train came to a stop, and Ilene and Half Ear descended the steps, hurried over to the baggage car where Aaron handed down their packs and the painting, and then climbed down to join them.

Ever so slowly, the train pulled away leaving them alone with the murmur of the river nearby, and the newly leafed forest whispering in the warm, gentle breeze. The forest beckoned quietly, greening warmly all around them. It was as sweetly inviting as a forest in a fairy tale. "This way," Half Ear said once they were set and ready. Then Half Ear stepped away from the tracks and the river, and headed east into the woods. Aaron and Ilene followed.

Walking did prove to be easy enough. The tall, dense underbrush of mid-summer was not yet in full swing. There were the occasional fallen trees to clamber over, under, or around, and patches of still leafless devil's club stalks covered with sharp spines to be avoided. Everywhere green plants were sprouting and bushes were leafing into a wild spring garden of herbs, flowers, grass, ferns, and berry bushes. Violets bloomed shyly through the sprouting foliage, and Ilene nibbled on the cucumber flavored tips of watermelon berry plants, as they hiked along.

When they came to a moist area abundant with newly emerged fiddlehead ferns, their spiraled heads still unfurled, Ilene and Aaron stopped and harvested some to go with dinner. Of course, by the time they finished Half Ear was out of sight, for he stopped and waited for no one, but they followed Half Ear's track in the moist spring forest until they came to a ridge that ran from east to west. Aaron was sure that if they followed the ridge, keeping it to their right, they would come to the edge of the big swamp.

Although Half Ear was out of sight, Aaron seemed to know where they were going, so Ilene let him lead the way. She thought about the painting she was carrying, certain that Half Ear had seen the crystal move out of the painting and into the room. Why wouldn't he admit it? It was not the first time, or even the second, she had seen it happen, but she hadn't told anyone, because she feared no one would believe her. Now Ilene was certain that something strange was going on. "So that is what the crystal looks like," Half Ear had said when he saw the painting for the first time, referring to the crystal as though he knew of its existence. And then Half Ear decided to take the painting with them! Surely it wasn't just coincidence that they would be camping near the artist who painted it. What did Aaron know about all this that he wasn't telling her? There was definitely something very unusual happening here, and sooner or later, she was going to get to the bottom of it. But she knew it would be to her advantage for now not to appear too inquisitive, so quietly she waited.

Rahlys awoke to bright morning sunshine filled with the promise of another beautiful spring day. She could not recall when she and the girl in the cave fell asleep. *Is it all just a dream, or does someone really need my help? Is there really a girl trapped in a cave somewhere?* The girl seemed to be real, but why couldn't she reach the distressed signature while awake?

She was seeking a girl trapped in a cave, and for some reason she couldn't pinpoint the girl's location. That was all she knew, but Quaylyn had been teaching her a technique called *journeying*. With the help of the crystal, she could travel mentally, without physically leaving home. Droclum was probably journeying when he located her, Quaylyn had explained. That night, Rahlys conjured the softly glowing crystal to her hand. She didn't know if journeying would help or not, but she had to try. Stretched out on her bed, she focused on her target as best she could, seeking in the direction she had mentally gone before. Then holding the crystal, Rahlys invoked her wish. *Help me find the signature of the girl lost in a cave.*

Immediately, the crystal faded from her hand, and Rahlys felt herself being tugged along with it, hurtling at great speed over mountain ranges and ocean, although she was certain she remained physically on her bed.

Where are you, girl in cave? I am here to help you, Rahlys called out. *Why do you haunt my dreams so? Communicate with me now while I'm awake.*

But there was no answer.

Then Rahlys felt the encroachment of unspeakable evil. *Droclum is near,* the Oracle warned.

Rahlys could sense Droclun's foreboding signature as she soared over the coastal range. She had found him after all. The evil aura reached toward her, sucking her in!

Go back! Go back! Rahlys screamed, as her mind began to shudder. With all her will, she pulled back mentally. The crystal had already changed direction, dragging her away, but Droclum was still latched on. Then abruptly, she and the crystal were jerked back, and she found herself on her bed upstairs, with her head spinning, and someone standing over her.

Rahlys! Are you alright? She could hear Quaylyn's thoughts and feel his concern through the pounding in her head.

I think so. As the pain subsided, she opened her eyes, grateful for the brief sub-arctic night; glaring light would have definitely grated on her charred senses. "What are you doing here?" she asked reverting to spoken language.

Quaylyn straightened, his anxiety over her easing, "I felt the invocation of powerful magic," he explained, "and out of concern, called up to you. When there was no response, I came up to check on you, and discovered you were journeying with the crystal. Then I heard your mental stress, and latched on to you, to help pull you back."

So that was the jerk she had felt; she looked at the crystal in her hand and then at Quaylyn. "Thank you!" she said.

"So, what happened? Where did you go? I sensed Droclum's signature."

But Rahlys did not want to discuss it with him now. "I will tell you tomorrow when we are all together working on the guest cabin. For now, it is good night."

Quaylyn knew he had been dismissed. *Good night, Guardian of the Light.* He bowed, and descended the stairs to his bed. After hearing him settled in, Rahlys fell into a deep sleep, undisturbed and restful, until early morning.

Then, as though in a dream, she heard again the mental pleas for help...*It's so dark...please help me...I can't take the darkness any longer,...so hungry...so hungry...please,...someone,...please, help me...*and the girl's heart-rendering sobs, void of hope and steeped in despair, could be felt racking her body and soul.

I am Rahlys; I am here to help you. Can you hear me? The sobs subsided as the signature absorbed the message.

I can hear you in my head, she replied tremulously, *where are you?*

I am far away still, but I may be able to help you. You must tell me all you can about where you are, and how you got there.

Taku could now recall her father since he appeared in her dream. She and her father had been on the fishing boat. They had come ashore in a quiet bay to wait out a storm, and then she had been whisked away by an evil spirit. She couldn't remember what happened to her father, or even her name. But the evil spirit called himself Droclum. Rahlys felt the child shudder; so Droclum did have her! The girl without a name described Droclum's cavern, the stream passing through it, stones that glowed orange giving off a strange light, a large bed, stone table, and the dreadful mirror. She told how her warm clothing had been magically changed to a seductive red dress, but didn't mention the diamonds she had discarded in the little stream that ran through her prison. But how was it possible for the girl to telepath out, when she couldn't reach in, Rahlys wondered. How was she able to telepath at all?

Please, I am so hungry.

How did you learn to telepath?

What's that?

Speaking as we are now.

I don't know. I've never spoken this way with anyone but you.

Hold out your hand, I will try and send you an apple. Rahlys could sense Taku extending her hands in the darkness and hoped she could deliver; she still couldn't get a solid fix on the girl. *Now, I need you to help me. Try to conjure the apple to you as I send it your way. Are you ready?*

Yes.

Concentrating, Rahlys mentally snatched an apple from the bag in the root cellar and tossed it in the signature's general direction. Rahlys felt the girl's startled jerk when the apple landed in her outstretched hands. She sighed with relief at the girl's sudden rush of joy, and her rapturous enjoyment over the first bite.

Then, like a door being slammed shut…the connection was gone.

––––––––

Franklin relished Taku's anguish. Her pain and suffering stimulated him into frenzied excitement, her slow tortuous dying, a thing of beauty. He spent hours tuned in, soaking up her despair. Sometimes his imagination fast forwarded to her last weak breath and conscious thought, then to the slow deterioration of her flesh, along with the red dress, until all that remained was a pile of bones wearing a diamond necklace.

Forget the girl, we have work to do, the part of him that was Droclum demanded, taking over his consciousness. For a time he was distracted, but days later when Franklin again focused on Taku's signature, he found her hungry and in despair…although still very much alive. Then Droclum sensed the presence of the Guardian of Anthya's Oracle journeying toward them, and wrenched Franklin's attention away from the girl once more, directing all focus in pursuit of the sorceress.

He latched on to the Guardian of Light in a mental strong hold, pulling her in, until someone wrenched the sorceress from his grasp. But who? Droclum smoldered in thought. There was something familiar about the signature, but he just couldn't place it. Who else would be capable of such magic? Certainly not Theon, his old crony from the past. Theon's magic had never been that great even in his prime. Besides, Theon would be long dead by now. Once again the Guardian of Anthya's Oracle had gotten away, and the thought enraged him. Then to add insult to injury, he discovered that the Guardian of Light had been in communication with the prisoner, right under his nose, using magic to keep her alive. How was that possible?

"The cloak, you fool; you put it on her," Droclum roared from within. "Your magic is woven into it."

In anger, Droclum conjured Taku to him. She appeared in the cavern at his feet, lying on her side, curled in a fetal position, a partially eaten apple clutched in her hand. The sudden return of light, and hence sight, came as a shock to her senses.

"Get up!" Droclum shouted in anger fueled by his wounded pride. As Taku stood, disoriented by light, her legs wobbly from cramped disuse, he violently knocked the apple out of her hand."

No, Taku cried out silently over her lost treasure, and attempted to dart after the precious fruit, now bashed and bruised on the stone floor, but Droclum conjured her back in front of him.

"Where is the necklace?" he roared. Taku couldn't answer, but moments later she shrieked silently as the diamond necklace, chilled to icy cold in the subterranean stream, appeared heavily around her neck. Then with a whisk of his hand she and the red dress were clean and fresh. Droclum moved in closer.

"What's her name?" he demanded.

Taku shivered in fear, not sure who the question referred to.

"The sorceress who has been helping you, what is her name?" he clarified.

Taku staggered backward. The good spirit who was trying to help her was a sorceress? She had said her name was Rahlys, Taku remembered.

"Rahlys!" Droclum hissed, picking up on Taku's thoughts.

Had he read her mind? How unfortunate, Taku lamented, for she knew that names held great power.

"Where is she?" Droclum pressed on. To Taku's relief, she could not betray her benefactor this time, for she had no clue as to her whereabouts. The girl knows nothing, Droclum quickly ascertained, but she is not without worth. I will use her as bait to bring Sorceress Rahlys to me. She will not escape from me a third time.

"How would you like to go on a little cruise?" he laughed sinisterly out loud. "I know just the cruise ship you should take. Bon voyage!" And with that, the cavern was gone.

Cold damp darkness enveloped her once again. Taku was standing barefooted on what felt like the deck of a fishing boat, with the sound of a waterfall in the background, and the smell of fishing nets in the air.

Rahlys awoke to sunlight streaming in, and the sound of Vince and Maggie chattering excitedly with Quaylyn outside her window. How late is it, she wondered.

"Wake up, Sleepy Head!" Maggie called up to her. "You're two hours late for work."

"I'm coming," Rahlys called out her bedroom window, feeling a great need to be in the light, to be out in the sun. Bright warm sunshine drenched her as she stepped outside, and she thought of the young girl in Droclum's clutches, imprisoned in darkness. The thought weighed on her heavily, while all around her the forest quivered with emerging green leaves and sprouting underbrush in the warm spring sunshine. She summoned Raven and joined the group sitting on the porch in the sun. She wanted Raven there when she shared what she had to tell.

"Good afternoon, Rahlys, Guardian of the Light!" Quaylyn greeted her. If he was upset over her curt dismissal last night, he didn't show it; at least he hadn't taken off again.

"Good afternoon," Rahlys returned, not without some contrition for oversleeping. "How's the work going on the guest cabin?"

"Work? On a beautiful day like this?" Even Vince had been struck with spring fever. Rahlys meditated peacefully in the sunshine, along with the rest. Then Raven circled overhead and landed near the steps. "Klawock, klawock!" he greeted them.

"I have something I want to tell you," Rahlys began right away. It was apparent that Quaylyn had filled them in on some things, for they all stared at her attentively. "A few nights ago I mentally picked up moans and cries of delirium and despair in my sleep, but I couldn't locate the source. The following night it happened again, and I managed to communicate a little telepathically with a young girl trapped in a cave and in danger of dying from hypothermia. I couldn't latch on to her physical location, but strangely enough, I was able to soothe her across the distance with an aura of warmth that restored her dropping body temperature. Three times I have managed to pick up on her subconscious pleas for help, but only when I'm in a dream state. I have consciously searched for her, but I can not find her. So last night I went journeying with the crystal, to use Quaylyn's terminology, in search of her…and I found Droclum instead."

"What?" Vince jumped at Quaylyn, "I thought you were here to help protect her!"

"I was not consulted," Quaylyn spoke up in his own defense. "When I sensed the use of strong magic, I went up to check on her, and helped pull her back."

Vince looked toward Rahlys for confirmation, but did not apologize when he realized he had spoken in haste.

"You found Droclum?" Maggie asked to put things back on track.

"Or rather he found me," Rahlys said, "traipsing in his territory. The crystal gave the warning, and helped me pull back, but it was Quaylyn who finished bringing us in."

"So where is Droclum?" Vince asked.

"In a cavern somewhere deep beneath the coastal mountains of Southeast, Alaska. The young girl I have been in communication with, has described the cavern to me. Droclum is holding her prisoner in a small cave."

"Aaaark!" the raven responded. The rest of the group looked at her in astonishment.

"Oh, how horrible! The poor girl," Maggie said sadly.

"Last night, or rather, early this morning, I picked up the girl's distress cries again. She's starving. I tried repeatedly to grab her mentally and pull her out, but I just can't reach her. I did manage to send her an apple though. Now how that was possible, I do not know."

"Who is this girl?" Vince asked.

"I don't know? The last thing she remembers, before Droclum took her captive, is being on her father's fishing boat, but she can't remember her name, or what happened to her father. She has been raped and imprisoned in total darkness in this tiny cave without food or warm clothing."

"So you have been keeping her alive by cloaking her in warmth and providing her food. What about water?" Maggie asked.

"She describes a small stream that runs through the cave through fissures in the rock, but there is no opening large enough for a person to pass through."

"So why don't you just teleport her out?" Vince asked.

"I've told you, I've tried, but I just can't get a clear enough fix on her, to do so. I was quite surprised when I managed to send her an apple. I haven't been able to sense her at all when I'm awake. That is why I was journeying with the crystal. If I could locate her, I could rescue her."

"Are you sure this captive of Droclum is real, and not just a dream? Or worse yet...a trap?" Vince questioned.

"I am convinced that the signature I've been in contact with, and the despair and anguish attached to it, is real. The worst of it is, as soon as I sent the apple our connection was abruptly cut off, as though our communication had been detected and blocked against our will."

Quaylyn had remained quiet through all this, neither asking questions, nor commenting. Now the rest of the group looked toward him for answers. "When I first arrived here," Quaylyn said, "I sensed the protective shield Rahlys had put in place to prevent Droclum from locating you. That spell is signature specific. For instance, it didn't block me from locating you. It would be safe to assume that Droclum has also thought to put in place spells that prevent Rahlys from surprising him in what he considers his terrain. That is probably what is preventing her from reaching the girl. But apparently there is nothing in place blocking the girl from reaching out, and inadvertently it seems, she has subconsciously sent out mental waves of distress that Rahlys has been able to detect. I'm only assuming here, but the girl must have come into contact with something of magic that has awakened her telepathic abilities in much the same way that the crystal has affected the rest of you, something that Droclum has worked his magic into. When the girl sent out telepathic waves, it opened a channel through which Rahlys could transmit a spell of warmth and even send food, but we can be certain, now that Rahlys has been detected both journeying with the crystal, and tampering with his prisoner...that channel is now closed."

"We can't just let Droclum have his way with this girl," Rahlys pleaded, "we must find a way to rescue her."

"Just what do you expect us to do?" Vince asked.

"I don't know, but we have to think of something."

The group gazed upon the greening forest in silence as they tried to absorb all that had been said, and come up with a suitable plan. When ideas were not rapidly forthcoming, Vince proposed another course of action.

"So where exactly do you want that guest cabin?" Vince asked Rahlys. "We might as well be working on it while we're thinking of a plan to rescue this girl and defeat Droclum."

The group made quick work of clearing an area of ground several yards into the woods east of Rahlys' cabin, where a stack of logs, harvested earlier, were ready to put on the walls. Maggie and Rahlys cleared small brush with a Swede saw, hatchet, and magic, stacking the brush, while Vince and Quaylyn dealt with a couple of larger trees, bucking them up for firewood. Soon the site was cleared and the four of them, each at a corner, were squaring off the foundation with string, wooden stakes, and a tape measure. Then Vince marked off the spots where the foundation posts would go, including those in the center, and started digging.

"How big of a hole are you digging?" Quaylyn asked.

"Oh, about this wide, and about this deep," Vince indicated with his hands, and went back to work scratching at the hard-packed, rocky soil. It was hard work, and slow going. After some time, Vince paused, leaning on his shovel to check on Quaylyn's progress, and was astonished by what he saw. Eight perfectly formed and precisely located holes dotted the site with a pile of excavated dirt and rocks next to each one, and a rather exhausted Quaylyn stretched out on a grassy spot of ground, his arms behind his head. Only the foundation post hole that Vince was working on remained incomplete.

"Aaarrk, Aaarrk! The raven flew over projecting an image of a passenger train weaving through the woods.

"The train!" Quaylyn cried out in delight. Jumping up, he teleported himself to the edge of the woods to watch the Aurora Express breeze by, carrying visitors from around the world between Fairbanks and Anchorage. Quaylyn stepped out from the cover of the woods and waved to the passengers. Many waved back, wondering where he had appeared from out in the middle of nowhere.

By the time Quaylyn returned to the building site, the group had stopped for lunch. Even Raven flew in to join the picnic. Over lunch they brainstormed ideas for a plan to rescue Droclum's captive.

"I'm still unable to make further contact with the girl," Rahlys said.

"Even if you did make contact with her again, you can be certain she is bait in a trap," Vince said.

"Vince is right. Even if you do find her, you can't just go to her knowing Droclum is lying in wait," Maggie agreed. "We need a plan."

"When we face Droclum, we must be prepared to fight. And we still don't know what role Half Ear, or rather Theon, is playing in this. Perhaps I should confront him?" Vince said, his face lined with apprehension.

"We need to penetrate Droclum's protective shield without him knowing it. It would be nice to have the element of surprise on our side," Rahlys said.

"There may be a way," Quaylyn said. "Creative magic has no limit. Or rather, it is limited only by the imagination and ability of its creator, sort of like writing a novel," he said indicating Vince…"or creating a painting…or raising a new person," he said nodding with reverence toward Maggie, for it had become known that Maggie and Vince were expecting a baby. "You must continue to diligently train in drawing increasingly greater force to use against Droclum," Quaylyn said to Rahlys. "You are at least as strong as he is. You didn't really need me to rescue you when you were journeying with the crystal, you were already on your way back, I just speeded up your return. You would have made it back without me. Droclum is also gaining strength though, and it is important that you keep the upper edge."

When Vince announced that he would have to go into town to get spikes, dry cement mix, and other building supplies to continue on the cabin building project, Quaylyn jumped to his feet, asking to go with him. "You should take Quaylyn with you so he can see a bit of the world beyond these woods," Maggie coaxed. "You wouldn't even have to take the train. The two of you could teleport to the house in town, drive the truck into Wasilla, pick up a few groceries and the building supplies we need, drive back, then teleport yourselves and the supplies back up here, all in one day." But Vince wasn't comfortable with the idea.

So far, they were the only humans that Quaylyn had had contact with. "What if he did something strange in public, drawing attention to us," Vince worried. "Think of the consequences?" But Maggie wasn't buying it.

"Ride in a truck! Shop in a store! See people and roads and traffic! Vince, I promise you no one will know that I am not from this world. I will speak only when necessary, say as little as possible, and do as you do."

Seeing Quaylyn's yearning desire to explore and experience their world, Vince knew he would have to give in. "You can come, but... no magic! From the moment we arrive at my place in town to the moment we teleport back here, there is to be absolutely no use of magic. An inexplicable occurrence of any kind, no matter how minimal, will draw attention."

"Agreed!"

"Believe me, our world is not ready for you," Vince added.

"The Runes of the High Council agree with you," Quaylyn replied.

"What are the Runes of the High Council?" Rahlys asked, not willing to let the opportunity to ask slip by again.

Quaylyn hesitated before answering. The books he had read from Vince's library bespoke of a chaotic world. How could he explain so they would understand? "The Runes are the nemesis of Chaos," he said. "Long ago,...that is long ago even to me,...there were three great and powerful masters who foresaw the fall of our society due to rampant greed and corruption. Society had already broken down into social strata. Magic and the arts floundered, and lawlessness abounded. The three great wizards were wise, but despite their great wisdom, they didn't know how to fix what was wrong. As political, social, and economic systems continued to fail, the wizards feared the world would be thrown into darkness, so came up with a plan to turn things around. Pooling their powers, they wrought a great oval table from the purest crystal. With their combined strength, they drew in the wisdom and power of the elemental forces and worked together on a spell to aid the Councilors in making wise, impartial decisions for the greater good of all the people. With the power of the Runes of the elemental forces, they etched into the table the runic symbols for crystal, water, fire, sun, soil, air, moon, and void.

"When the Councilors meet at the Crystal Table, the Runes not only access the ideas Councilors bring to the table, but foresee to some extent the path of consequences that would occur if these ideas were implemented, thus directing them into making the wisest decisions. The position of Councilor is a highly exalted one. Only the most compassionate, wisest, and most selfless are chosen."

"You let some old magic spell run your lives?" Vince asked.

"We tap wisdom for the greater good of all."

The next morning Vince and Quaylyn teleported to Vince's place in town. While Vince puttered around the house, Quaylyn peered out the windows as though he were looking out on forbidden territory. To him, there was much to see. A car passed on the road out front, and a family of four got out of a camper trailer parked down the street, and walked away. A dog came into the yard, then left again. When Vince led Quaylyn out the door, a small plane flew fairly low overhead as they walked to Vince's pick-up truck parked in the driveway.

Looking up at the airplane instead of forward, Quaylyn bumped into the parked truck before focusing on it. But when he did look down, it was love at first sight. Quaylyn caressed the truck with his hands, feeling the contours of its body, noting the intricacies of its parts. He climbed into the seat next to Vince, studying the details of the truck's dashboard and interior, and sighed exquisitely when Vince turned the key in the ignition, bringing the engine to life. Mechanical devices used for transportation were particularly fascinating to Quaylyn.

Quaylyn sat in utter fascination as Vince drove. It was his first glimpse of this world beyond their tiny, woodsy community. Here there were roads, buildings, and vehicles full of people. They passed cars, trucks, buses, campers, and trailers hauling boats and ATVs. When they passed their first semi on the highway, Quaylyn's excitement was uncontrollable. Why would a man with no actual need for mechanical means of transportation, be so infatuated by such, Vince wondered. When they stopped at a gas station to fuel up, Vince wouldn't let Quaylyn out the truck for fear of what he might do out of zealous curiosity, but when they arrived at the building supply center, Vince knew he could not confine Quaylyn to the truck, and fearing the worse, allowed him to follow him into the store. But Vince need not have worried, for Quaylyn looked without touching, spoke not a word, and did nothing to draw attention to himself. He walked casually throughout the store, looking at everything and bothering no one. Fortunately, the store clerks were all too busy to offer him help. He passed by people, eyes downcast, not making any eye contact. When Vince was finished with his purchases, Quaylyn followed him out the door. No one had the faintest idea an alien had walked amongst them.

"How was that?" Quaylyn asked as they got back into the truck and headed for the loading bay to pick up their merchandise.

"That was fine."

The stop at the supermarket was just a little more challenging.

Having come from an agricultural community, Quaylyn raised many questions about food. There were quite a few items down the aisles that didn't seem to meet his criteria as substances to eat. Only the fresh produce, nuts, beans, and grains actually registered. When he wanted to know what was in some of the bags and boxes, Vince pointed out the ingredients listed on the packaging.

Prices and the concept of money for food also puzzled him. "Don't people have to buy food where you come from?' Vince asked.

"No," Quaylyn said. "Enough food is produced to feed everyone, and everyone is fed. There is no money involved."

"What about greed?" Vince asked.

"You mean like Droclum?"

"I take it there aren't a lot of power-hungry tyrants where you come from."

"Droclum did have followers," Quaylyn replied.

When Vince had found all the items on the shopping lists Maggie and Rahlys had provided, and Quaylyn was certainly no help, they headed for the checkout stand. On a whim, Vince added an Anchorage newspaper to the cart. Maybe there would be mention of someone missing that would serve as a clue to the identity of Droclum's prisoner.

"How are you doing today?" the clerk asked rudimentarily.

"Good," Vince and Quaylyn responded as one. They stood around in silence as the groceries were scanned and bagged, then pushed their cart out of the store toward the parking lot.

Coming from the opposite direction, a little boy slipped from his mother's hand and took off running into the traffic lane, headed right in front of an oncoming car. Quaylyn responded instantly, mentally grabbing the tiny tot and relocating him back within range of his mother's grasp. The car passed by harmlessly.

Grabbing up her child in her arms, the mother wept abundant tears of joy. "It's a miracle! It's a miracle!" she cried over and over.

"Sorry," Quaylyn whispered to Vince.

"It's alright. I've seen enough mothers grieving over their dead children to last a life time. Just keep walking."

The woman drew a small crowd in front of the store as she told her story, but no one especially noticed or associated Quaylyn in any way with the incident. They loaded their groceries into the truck and pulled out of the parking lot heading north toward home.

Chapter 14
Spying

Taku cautiously felt around and above her, stretching her arms out in the dark. Her hands touched nothing. But the cold, damp, textured surface under her bare feet felt strangely familiar. Gingerly she stooped down in the blackness and felt for continuation of the surface she was standing on; it extended all around her. Reassured that she would not step into an abyss, she straightened back up and carefully took a step forward with her hands out in front of her, searching for contact with something. With the completion of one step, her groping hands brushed a smooth surface which turned out to be a porthole window in a sturdy door like one would find on a fishing boat. Reaching naturally to the door handle, she opened the door as she had hundreds of times before, and made her way gingerly down the familiar steps into the galley and wheelhouse.

Locating the stove, table, and captain's chair by feel as she made her way, she stepped down into the bow section of the boat where bunks and storage bins lined the walls, and blindly reached over the starboard bunk into a cargo net hanging along the wall. Her heart pounded as her hand searched and found the flashlight she knew would be there. Turning it on, a beam of light confirmed what she already knew, she was home...on the *Taku*!

Images of her life snapped back into her memory, one by one. She saw her long-dead mother lighting four candles on her birthday cake, and there were images from years of living with her father on the fishing boat. She remembered the beach where she and her father walked together for the last time, and her father's anguished rage over the disappearance of his boats. Then his sudden death and disappearance… and Droclum. Tears of unshed grief streamed down her face as she flashed the beam of light around, taking in the familiar surroundings.

And my name is Melinda! *My name is Melinda*, she cried out silently between sobs. Her body shuddered from the release of grief and the pain of memory. Then the shudders turned to shivering as the cold dampness seeped persistently through the thin red dress she still wore.

Melinda dug in the storage bins under her bunk and found warm clothes; a jacket, socks, jeans, even some old tennis shoes. Tears subsided as she changed quickly, tossing aside the red dress and the diamond necklace that hung like an albatross around her neck.

Warmly dressed and carrying the flashlight, she went back out on deck. Inky blackness surrounded her and the boat. Melinda directed the flashlight all around, but there was nothing for the beam of light to reflect off of, except the eerily calm, darkly serene water below. The sound of the waterfall was becoming increasingly distant. Was the boat moving? She reached for the deck bucket, a rope tied to the handle, and dropped the bucket over the side, holding onto the rope. By the time the bucket started to sink, the boat had moved the length of the rope forward. Still managing to hold the flashlight, she hauled up the bucket with some water in it, and set it on the deck. She was on a slow cruise to she did not know where.

Making her way up front on the bow, she checked the anchor. It was out, apparently dangling uselessly; how deep could it possibly be here? She made her way to the stern of the boat, still shining the light onto the water. There was no churning action in the water; the prop was not turning, but she could detect the slight lines of a wake forming a wide V behind the boat. The *Taku* was not just drifting with a current. Even with the anchor out and no engine running, the *Taku* was moving forward, as though with a destination in mind. Was Droclum in control? If so, where was she headed to, and why?

Going back into the cabin, Melinda turned on the fathometer. To her astonishment she read off a depth of over two thousand feet. If she started the motor, she would be able to turn on the running lights up on the mast, and maybe see her surroundings. She knew how to start the engine; papa had taught her how long ago. Many times she had started and stopped the engine at her father's command as he worked down in the bilge. Bracing herself for the harsh noise, Melinda pressed the ignition button. The motor clattered loudly, springing to life. Anxiously she flipped switches flooding the space around her with light.

The sound of the boat engine reverberated through an immense cavern, the mast lights overhead reflecting across an uncharted underground sea. Melinda stepped back out onto the deck and looked around in amazement. The high stone ceiling was barely discernible far above a shore-less watery plain that stretched into darkness, unruffled by wind and waves, undisturbed by fish or mammal.

She was lost, alone on a vast subterranean sea hidden in darkness. Even if someone was looking for the *Taku*, they would not find it. No one would ever find her here. Melinda shed a silent tear, awed by the loneliness of it all. What happened to Rahlys, the sorceress who had sent her an apple? Was she still trying to find her? She tried calling Rahlys repeatedly in her mind, but there was no response. Was Droclum somehow preventing them from communicating?

Melinda went back inside the cabin and switched on the hydraulics. Then making her way up on the bow, she pulled anchor using the hydraulic winch. To her relief, the anchor came up easily. After securing the anchor in its cradle, as she had been drilled, she returned to the wheelhouse to take control of the *Taku*. Pushing the throttle lever forward, she grabbed the steering wheel, turning the boat in the direction of the sound of the waterfall, but the boat didn't respond. Melinda pushed the throttle further and turned the wheel harder, but still there was no response. The motor revved up and the steering wheel turned, but the *Taku* continued slowly straight ahead, unmindful of Melinda's actions. She could not take control. Then spotting the radio, she turned it on and picked up the mike, forgetting momentarily that she had lost the power of speech, but it didn't matter…there was no signal.

If she couldn't steer, she would only need to run the engine enough to keep the batteries up for the cabin lights and fathometer. She knew that she should conserve fuel as much as possible, but she dreaded the utter darkness that lurked so close. Fear clutched at her throat. Without the engine, she could not use the running lights, and therefore, would not see what was ahead.

Her stomach growled angrily; she had to find something to eat. Melinda knew the *Taku* was well provisioned. She turned on the cabin lights. The small table and benches in the galley were built a step up from the main floor, providing space for storage drawers underneath. There was also storage space under the bench seats and in cubbyholes along the wall above the table. She inventoried her food supply, and found lots of peanut butter, which she ate by fingerfuls on the spot, and pilot bread, canned Spam, spaghetti sauce, soup, dried fruit, rice, pasta, boxed milk that didn't require refrigerating till opened, sprouting onions and potatoes, even candy, cookies, and soda pop. And apples. Melinda grabbed an apple, biting into it hungrily. She had enough food to survive for a while. Now she had to work on finding a way out of here.

Eventually weariness overcame Melinda's growing fear of the dark, and she shut down the engine. So as not to run down the boat's batteries, which would be needed to restart the motor, she turned off the cabin lights allowing the darkness to close in on her. With the flashlight clutched in her hand, Melinda crawled into her bunk, burying herself in blankets and sleeping bags. The flashlight she laid next to her like a sword kept close at hand, ready to combat the sudden appearance of the enemy. Twice she practiced drawing the flashlight quickly and turning it on, in case of a sudden emergency. *Rahlys where are you?...Papa help me*, she cried in the darkness. Soon she was fast asleep.

Melinda didn't know how long she slept. Waking up to pitch darkness, she rolled over and went back to sleep. After doing this a couple of times, her brain kicked in, reminding her that she was underground where it is always dark. Groggy from oversleeping, Melinda forced herself to consciousness. She reached up and turned on the light above her bed, squinting her eyes against the brightness.

Then she jumped up in alarm. Where had the *Taku* traveled to while she slept? Quickly she turned on the galley lights and the fathometer, then looked at her father's wristwatch hanging from a hook by the controls. Nine fifteen, but she had no way of knowing if it was morning or night. The fathometer read five hundred feet. Melinda started up the engine, dispelling the silence. When the motor finished revving up, she switch on the running lights, cringing in fear of what she may see.

Melinda gasped in silent wonder at the scene illuminated before her. The *Taku* sailed under massive rock arches that curved gracefully down from the high stone ceiling to the rocky depths below. Many of the arched formations had broken off, leaving thin pinnacles of rock that rose above the surface of the water resembling eerie, gaunt, stone figurines walking on water.

Three hundred feet the fathometer read. Was she finally getting somewhere? But if so, where? She stepped out on deck, gazing around her, as the *Taku* sailed gracefully under a lacey stone arch. The sea and the arches stretched out in all directions. It was like passing through the holes of giant, partially submerged slices of Swiss cheese, that were more holes than cheese, Melinda thought.

Suddenly there was a scraping noise, and the boat lurched violently, throwing Melinda off her feet and smacking her sprawled facedown, flat on the deck. After the jolt, the *Taku* sailed on serenely as though nothing had happened. The boat must have passed over a submerged rock pinnacle, she thought. It probably ripped off part, if not all, of the nonfunctioning prop. She waited for another collision before moving, but the *Taku* floated on smoothly.

Peeling her bruised body off the deck, rubbing her smarting hands and knees, Melinda cautiously peered over the side. There was nothing to see but inky black water. Returning to the cabin, she checked the depth again on the fathometer. Two hundred and eighty feet.

As she continued to watch the fathometer for a while, the readings fluctuated up and down dramatically. From two hundred and eighty feet, the water depth plummeted down to five hundred feet. Then just as quickly the bottom zoomed back up to eighty feet, only to plunge back down to seven hundred.

When the depth climbed from seven hundred feet to a mere fifty in seconds, Melinda braced herself for impact…then breathed a sigh of relief as the *Taku* continued doggedly on its way in seven feet of water that immediately dived back down to a depth of nine hundred feet. As the hours drifted by, Melinda looked about her in despair. *What if there is no way out of this underground world? Will I ever again see the light of day?*

In the newspaper that Vince and Quaylyn brought back from town, Maggie found an article that captured her attention. She read it aloud to them. "A fishing vessel, named the *Taku*, reported missing a month ago, has disappeared without a trace, along with the two people believed to be on board. Pete Poponof, the captain and owner of the boat, and his twelve year old daughter Melinda, were last seen in a region of southeast Alaska that has been sometimes referred to as Alaska's equivalent of the Bermuda Triangle."

"Her name is Melinda," Rahlys sighed. "I wonder if she's still alive." Armed now with an identity, Rahlys tried repeatedly to contact Droclum's prisoner, but Melinda was not to be found. The dilemma over what to do, assuming she was still alive, remained unresolved.

Meanwhile, the foundation for the guest cabin was complete with the sill logs in place, and the walls coming up. Several more logs, cut to length, were ready and waiting to be notched and fitted into place. With Rahlys and Quaylyn's help, progress on the guest cabin was rapid. Cabin building offered an opportunity for Rahlys to work on building her magical strength. "You must pull on the power within you to draw on the elemental forces that abound," Quaylyn instructed Rahlys at the construction site. Vince listened as he chiseled out a notch on the next log to be put into place, while Maggie watched with fascination. "Build up your power, layer upon layer, like a gathering storm. Let's see if you can put the air in motion and make the trees sway."

If it's a storm Quaylyn wants, it's a storm he will get, Rahlys decided irritably. She focused intently, stirring dust and sawdust into the air. Then quickly adding force, she sent the air currents spiraling out and upward. Soon the trees around them were swaying gracefully as spiraling air currents rustled the leaves.

"Surely you can do better than that," Quaylyn taunted her.

Rahlys drew deeper on her power, pulling more sun-warmed air from near the ground higher up, mixing it with the colder air above, creating a powerful convection current. The breeze around them became noticeably cooler as Rahlys drew hard on the elemental forces around her, gathering energy that she continued to direct upward. The sky darkened as dust particles gathered moisture, becoming increasingly darker and denser, until clouds blocked out the sun over the rustling forest. Vince stopped his work to watch the sky as lightning flashed and thunder rumbled, and the turbulent dark clouds columned, sucking up still more warm air into the system. Then suddenly, torrential rain poured down upon them, and hailstones the size of marbles pounded the ground.

Vince, Maggie, and Quaylyn rushed to the edge of the clearing, seeking cover under the trees. But Rahlys stood firmly in place, her arms stretched out. "Melinda, where are you?" she shouted into the storm, releasing her pent up frustration, but she received no answer.

"Very good," Vince shouted back. Now can you make it stop?"

Feeling better from the release, Rahlys complied, and almost instantly the storm was gone, leaving the forest drenched and hailstones covering the ground, glittering in the brilliant sunlight. As the group returned to the clearing to avoid the dripping trees, Rahlys cast a spell drying everyone off. Then she noticed that Quaylyn looked troubled.

"What's the matter?"

"Our spies have returned. They're not far from here, camping on the point overlooking the big swamp," he informed them when things quieted down again.

"Aaarrk! Aaarrk!" Raven flew in, loudly protesting the storm.

Sorry, Rahlys apologized.

"I detect a third signature at the campsite, a woman," Quaylyn added. "Do you know who it might be?"

"Maybe it's Ilene, from the gallery," Rahlys surmised. "In fact, Aaron showed up at the gallery while I was there. Apparently he and Ilene are a couple now."

"Aaaaark!" Raven flew off to investigate. The hailstones were already melting in the sun.

"Why do you think Aaron and Half Ear have come back? If they're really spying for Droclum, their presence could be a sign that something is about to happen," Maggie said.

"We know Aaron and Theon are up to no good. What are we going to do about them?" Vince asked.

"Theon's mind is a closed book, but I can't detect any knowledge of Droclum's existence in the unguarded minds of the other two. They know about the crystal though."

Raven flew over the ridge and the big swamp telepathing images of the campsite on the point back to Rahlys and the rest of the group. "The woman is Ilene," Rahlys said, recognizing the daughter of the gallery owner.

After much discussion and still no plan for action, the group went back to work on the guest cabin. Rahlys was really looking forward to the guest cabin's completion. Then Quaylyn would be out the house, for the most part, and she could have time alone again. But the more pressing issue on her mind was Melinda, Droclum's frightened, young victim. How could she find her, even if it meant facing Droclum in battle? Was she strong enough to defeat Droclum?

That evening, Rahlys decided it was time to do some spying of her own. She cast a spell of invisibility about her, hoping it would be enough to conceal her presence, and teleported herself to the edge of Theon's camp.

The underbrush in the forest grew an inch a day in the nearly continuous daylight. Devil's club unfurled their giant leaves, and the high bush cranberry bushes speckled the woods with white flowers. By the end of the week, the underbrush was knee high. Wild roses, geraniums, mountain ash, spiraea, elder berry, and devil's club bloomed in overlapping rapid succession.

Ilene was enraptured by the campsite; it was so scenic, overlooking the big swamp to the south and east, offering an eye stretch to the forested ridge on the other side. Three tents formed a broad half circle around a communal campfire ring. Their sleeping bags lay on deep, cushiony mounds of spruce boughs, and tarps were strung out over the tents in case of rain. But comfort didn't stop there. Ilene collected stones to place cooking pots on when she fetched water from the creek, hauling them up from the bottom of the ridge, and she collected wood for the evening fire, while Half Ear and Aaron sawed and chopped at a fallen tree until they had two suitable size logs, which they hauled in by rope to serve as benches to sit on. They even flattened out some of the curve of the logs with their axes to make the seats wider and more comfortable. In the evening they built a campfire to cook by, and to gaze at, for with the sun reluctant to set, there were no stars visible in the late spring night sky.

The next day, Half Ear and Aaron took off exploring, or so they said, but she knew they went to spy on Rahlys. Ilene didn't mind being alone at the camp. She liked the quiet solitude of the forest; she liked being alone, but why Aaron and Half Ear wanted to watch Rahlys, she couldn't quite figure out. She was certain it had something to do with the painting she had so carefully carried into the woods with them. The mysterious painting was still protectively wrapped, stashed in the back of her tent. Sometimes she felt as though the crystal in the painting was trying to tell her something.

With little else to do, Ilene lounged complacently in the sun on one of the log benches with a romance novel. She just loved reading romance novels; they made her feel happy. Only an occasional insect interrupted her reading from time to time.

Then suddenly, a strong wind tousled around the trees that had stood so serenely still only moments before, and the sky darkened rapidly overhead. Ilene eyed the dark, rumbling clouds with dismay. She had never seen a storm build up so fast. Lightning crisscrossed the sky, followed by grumbling thunder.

Ilene dashed to her tent for shelter just as the first hailstones rained down. Peeking out of the door of her tent she watched the storm, fascinated by its sudden, violent outburst. The black clouds boiled in anger, the wind whipped the trees, and hail pummeled through the leaves to the ground, bouncing upon landing. Then, like someone had turned off a faucet, the storm was gone, and once again, the day was sunny and bright and still.

Ilene had never seen a storm act quite that way before. The hail covering the ground started to melt in the warm sunshine. Before long, Aaron and Half Ear returned to camp soaking wet.

"Wow, wasn't that a crazy storm. It came up so fast. Ended fast too." Ilene nearly danced around the soaked men.

"Yeah, crazy," Aaron said, disgruntled.

"I'll build a fire to dry things out," Ilene volunteered. She dashed off to her shelter and gathered the dry kindling she had stashed by her tent under the tarp. Despite the warm summer day, a crackling campfire felt good, especially after the brief, but hellacious, storm.

In the cool dusk of evening, now that everything was dry again, Ilene

213

was cheerfully attempting to roast some badly squashed marshmallows over the fire. "It is time to unpack the painting," Half Ear announced unexpectedly. Slipping a roasted glob of marshmallow into her mouth, Ilene quickly leaned her roasting stick against the log bench and rushed off to her tent to retrieve the painting.

Half Ear unpacked the painting with great care, as Aaron and Ilene watched, still wondering why he would bring a painting on a camping trip. When it was finally freed of its wrappings, Half Ear propped it up against a chunk of firewood for all to see. The image of the crystal seemed to glow with a light of its own in the dusky night.

Then Half Ear conjured the image to his hand.

Aaron's jaws dropped open loosely in stunned disbelief over what he was seeing. He glanced dumbfounded from the empty painting to the spectral crystal glowing so softly in ever changing colors as it hovered enticingly over Half Ear's outstretched hand.

Ilene, somewhat less surprised, felt gratification. Her suspicions that something exceedingly unusual was going on were being validated.

The somewhat shy and innocent Half Ear that they knew, seemed to transform before their very eyes from a backwoods oddity into some-one burdened with the knowledge and the sins of the ages as he began to speak. "My name is Theon, and I am not from Earth…I'm from a world I will never see again," he said, his voice weighted with much sadness and regret.

"What kind of hokey crap is that?" Aaron burst out with disdain.

"You're from another world?" Ilene's eyes were wide with wonder.

"Let me tell you a true story,…"

Aaron cut Half Ear off, "Look, I don't know what kind of hocus po-cus is going on here," he pointed to the hologram, or whatever it was still hovering above Theon's outstretched hand, "but you are not from another planet."

Theon paid no heed to Aaron's outburst. "The crystal you seek is also from my world," he said with heavy patience.

Aaron stood in a huff, putting his back to the fire. "So you've known about the crystal all along! It probably wasn't even coincidental that you gave me a ride that day; you were already spying on Rahlys."

Theon said nothing.

"How did Rahlys get the crystal? She's not from your world....Is she?" Aaron asked when Half Ear didn't respond right away.

"A raven found the crystal and brought it to her. Actually, Trapper Bean tamed the bird years ago, but the real crystal enhanced the raven's cognitive abilities and bonded the raven to Rahlys as a familiar. The crystal then chose Rahlys as the Guardian of Light, transferring to her the powers of Anthya's Oracle."

"The crystal has magic?" Ilene gasped.

Aaron glanced fleetingly at Ilene, then back toward the image of the crystal, "Well, Theon, if that's who you really are, you wanted to tell us a true story. Let's hear it." Aaron took his seat again beside Ilene, not at all pleased over being played the fool.

Theon stood, waving off the ghostly crystal. It flew across the intervening space to Ilene, and settled above her knee. "Oh how pretty," she breathed as she reached up to touch it, but her fingers passed right through.

"I have lived on this planet for twelve thousand of your Earth years... it has been my penance," Theon began, poking the fire restlessly, sending up sparks. "I witnessed the New Stone Age, the Bronze Age, and the building of Stonehenge." Ilene and Aaron gazed at him, Ilene with astonishment, Aaron in disbelief. "I've seen holy wars, world wars, famine and plague, and through it all, I have seen how brutally cruel humans can be to one another, all for the acquisition of wealth and power."

"You have room to talk," Aaron broke in, "You want the crystal too, or you wouldn't be here."

"You are wrong, I am here out of curiosity. However, there was a time when I sought the crystal to destroy it....But no longer."

"Why did you want to destroy it?" Ilene asked, the holographic image still twirling above her knee.

"I was a fool, and chose evil over good. Lured by power and greed, and desire for recognition, I became Droclum's most loyal follower and closest confidant. What I did not know at the time, and have learned over the ages since, is that the only real use for power is to do good."

"Who is Droclum?" Aaron asked a bit confused.

"Droclum is a powerfully wicked sorcerer from my world who has defied death. When he was finally defeated by the great sorceress Anthya in battle, Droclum cast a dark spell of abominable evil, and his living essence was drawn from his dying body and sucked deep into the bowels of Mt. Vatre. In the volcano's molten furnace, Droclum's evil powers and signature were encapsulated in a smoky orb. Then like a pill too bitter to swallow, the mountain spewed out the Dark Orb delivering it to Earth by the power unleashed in the cataclysmic eruption and destruction of Mt. Vatre, which left our planet in ruins. Now Droclum has taken on new life here on Earth by taking possession of another's body and consciousness. He is also looking for the crystal, or rather the Guardian of the Oracle's powers."

"Well, that's just great!" Aaron burst out, not knowing what to believe.

"Tell us more about Sorceress Anthya," Ilene said, as though Theon were relating a fairy tale.

"Anthya was the greatest sorceress and warrior that ever lived, but Droclum proved to be her nemesis. Her last great feat of magic was the creation of the Oracle of Light. Having failed, after all, to rid the universe of the scourge that was Droclum, she made the ultimate sacrifice. She created the Oracle of Light by siphoning her own magic into a special crystal, draining her body of her life forces. After her death, the Oracle was brought to Earth by another, younger Anthya, her namesake, in the hope that someone, with the help of the Oracle's powers, would someday destroy Droclum, before Droclum destroys Earth. The young Anthya's First Mission was to deliver the crystal to Earth, hiding it for safekeeping, until it was needed. It was while trying to prevent her from succeeding at that mission, that I lost half of my right ear. In the end, thankfully, she eluded me."

"And you expect us to believe this cock-a-mania story?"

Theon ignored Aaron's rage. "For centuries afterwards, I roamed the continents in search of both the orb and the crystal, but found neither. Eventually I gave up the search, and sought to live out the rest of my longevity in peace. Then less than a year ago, I detected the use of magic."

"So that is why you two have been spying on Rahlys!"

"I must have that crystal," Aaron said emphatically.

"And what would you do with it?" Theon asked philosophically.

"Why, with the crystal's magic I could have anything I wanted."

Theon shook his head, "The crystal is of no use to you. Rahlys is already in possession of its power. Also it is likely protected with enchantments designed to keep it from the not so pure of heart, such as yourself. Heed my warning, my friend, and stay away from it."

"So what are you doing here?" Aaron asked Theon.

"Rahlys' position is not an enviable one. Sooner or later Droclum will seek her out, and try to destroy her. I am now on her side. When the time comes, if there is anything I can do to help her...I will."

"What about *this* crystal?" Ilene asked, pointing to the phantom still hovering near her.

"Probably unwittingly, Rahlys has imbued the painting with a little magic. How much, remains to be determined." Then a startled look crossed Theon's face. Quickly he snapped his fingers and the image of the crystal returned to the painting.

"What did you do that for?" Ilene asked.

"She was here," Theon said, nodding toward the edge of the woods.

"Who was here?" Aaron asked.

"Rahlys. Rahlys was here," Theon chuckled. "Now she's spying on us."

"Are you sure?" Aaron questioned looking around. "I didn't see anything."

"Of course you didn't, she was hidden in an aura of invisibility. Anyway, she's gone now."

"Then she knows we are here, and where you are from, and she saw the crystal leave the painting," Aaron moaned.

"Yes," Theon said, not sounding at all upset about it.

"So what are we going to do?"

"Nothing. We will wait and see what happens."

When they finally turned in, Ilene took the painting with her to her tent, propping it up on her pack where she could watch it from her sleeping bag. She laid on her back in the semidarkness, staring at the glowing image of the crystal nestled snuggly in its spruce branch.

"Come," Ilene whispered softly with vivid imagination, and to her delight, the holographic crystal left the painted spruce bough and floated to her, hovering over her chest. Again she tried to touch it, but there was nothing tangible for her to grasp.

What else can you do? Ilene thought to herself.

As though in response, the crystal started somersaulting around the tent, drawing designs in the air by leaving a light trail behind it that slowly dissipated like the smoke of a jet stream.

Why, that's amazing! Ilene patted her chest, and the crystal returned to her. For the longest, she stared at the glowing image as her eyes grew increasingly heavy. It was not until Ilene fell asleep that it returned to the painting.

Chapter 15
A Rescue Plan

Aaron became increasingly disgruntled as the warm sunny days were replaced by one overcast gray day after another. Then, mere cloudiness turned to rain. The rapidly growing underbrush, now waist deep, broke new records of growth as moisture was added to the formula. Steady rain soaked the forest and filled the bogs with water, hatching a new batch of mosquitoes that attacked with a vengeance.

Aaron didn't notice Raven circling high above the camp as he lazed around on one of the log benches slapping mosquitoes, gazing sullenly into the flames trying to stay warm. The rain had stopped for the moment, but it didn't make him any happier. Ilene added wood to the fire, then sat next to him. For some reason the mosquitoes didn't seem to be so bad as long as she was near, Aaron had observed. It was as though she had an invisible protective shield around her, that repelled the mosquitoes away. Ilene watched the raven as it circled lower, landing in a tree not far from camp.

"So where do you think Theon goes everyday?" Ilene asked Aaron, as she stared placidly at the raven perched in the tree. Theon had been leaving camp early each morning to go they knew not where. The disquieting part was his total unwillingness to tell them anything about his whereabouts.

"I have no idea." Aaron continued to stare into the fire, not turning to look at her.

"Why don't you follow him?"

"I don't know when he leaves, and besides, he doesn't seem to want me around. Do you really believe he is from another planet?"

"Don't you?"

"You saw him conjure the crystal from the painting. I never did believe that story of his about losing half an ear to a bear. But I certainly can't see Rahlys taking out that Droclum dude."

"I can conjure the crystal out of the painting, too." Ilene's statement startled Aaron momentarily, causing him to turn and look at her. Then he smiled slowly, brushing off her claim without considering the possibility that she may be telling the truth.

"You can not," Aaron said, turning back toward the fire.

Ilene didn't bother to retort. Instead she mentally focused on the painting stashed in her tent. *Come!* she called silently, opening her hand before her. The image of the crystal appeared, hovering over Ilene's long slender fingers.

Catching the crystal's glow out of the corner of his eye, Aaron jumped up in shocked surprise. "How did you do that?"

"It's easy. You just call it to you with your mind, while concentrating on it. Try it."

Aaron eyed the mock crystal with hungry desire to possess its counterpart. "Come here!" he commanded, sticking his hand out.

The glowing spectrum didn't leave Ilene.

With angry impatience Aaron took a step forward, but before he could reach it, the image vanished from Ilene's hand. "Look what you did!" she accused. Upset over Aaron's behavior, she ran to her tent to reassure herself the crystal had safely returned to the painting.

Gloomily, Aaron sat back down by the fire and stared into the flames.

"It doesn't like you," Ilene said when she returned to the campfire.

"Well, I don't care," Aaron slapped at mosquitoes that seemed to have closed in on him after Ilene moved away. Then Theon arrived at camp carrying a snowshoe hare, already dressed and ready for the spit. Immediately he skewered it and put it to roast over the fire.

"What's happening?" he asked in good humor, cleansing his hands in the rainwater-laden grasses.

"The rain stopped, so we're sitting out by the fire," Ilene said. She always felt better after Theon had returned safely.

"Where have you been?" Aaron asked, knowing he wouldn't get a straight answer.

"Oh, I've been out hiking around, exploring the countryside, studying the terrain…and shooting dinner," Theon said indicating the hare spitted over the fire as he joined them. "What's cooking in there?" He pointed to a pot nestled on some coals.

"Beans," Ilene said, "I put them to soak last night."

"Smells good."

Theon sat down on the other bench, and the three sat in silence for a while. Theon took his knife and stone from his pouch and began sharpening it, the soft grating sound of stone against blade adding to the twittering of a few birds in the trees and the occasional buzz of an insect flying by close enough to hear. A week had passed without anything unusual or spectacular happening. As far as they knew, Rahlys hadn't returned to the campsite, nor had she confronted them in any way. And there hadn't been any sign of Droclum either.

Restless from inactivity, Aaron stood stretching, and walked around. Not wanting to get soaked by the wet underbrush, he stayed within the perimeter of the well-trodden campsite, then pausing at the edge of the overlook, he spanned his eyes out over the big swamp, soaking in the panoramic view. So much empty, unused country, and what miserable country it is, he thought, while his hands batted at the annoying horde of mosquitoes that clouded around him. Lacking motivation to do anything, he rejoined the others at the fire.

"Tomorrow we will pay Rahlys a visit," Theon announced unexpectedly, "on the way to the train stop."

"What? Are you crazy?" Aaron burst out. "How do you know she won't just blow your head off as soon as you step out of the woods?"

"I have done nothing to Rahlys," Theon said, addressing Aaron's concern, "…except camp in her neighborhood. I believe she will give me a chance to speak before shooting. She is not an irrational hothead like you. The two of you will be taking the southbound train back to town."

"Fine with me," Aaron said bitterly. "I'm ready to get out of this cold, damp, mosquito-infested hellhole."

"What about the painting?" Ilene said.

"Take it with you, it is of no use to me."

"You seem to forget that Rahlys overheard you say you were Droclum's closest and most trusted follower."

"If she overheard me say that, she also overheard me say that I'm on her side. As a turncoat, I may hold valuable information that could help Rahlys in her mission. And furthermore…all conversation during tomorrow's short, friendly visit is to be mannerly and polite. There is to be no mention of magic, lovers, crystals, Droclum, or other planets… then, or ever. It would not be to your advantage. You would only be thought of as loony."

"And will you be saying anything to Rahlys about anything special?" Aaron asked, acidly.

"On the way back, after the two of you are on the train."

"How will she know you can be trusted?" Aaron asked.

"That's a chance she will have to be willing to take."

"I know she doesn't want to see me."

"It doesn't matter, you will be with us. Are you afraid of your former lover?"

"You used to be lovers!" Ilene exclaimed, her eyes smoldering with displeasure. "So that's how you know each other!"

"What did you tell her that for?"

"Perhaps you should have told her yourself."

The campers on the point paid no heed to the raven taking off in the misty evening light. Little more was said for the rest of the night. As they were finishing dinner, the rain returned, driving them to their individual tents. Ilene lay in her sleeping bag staring at the crystal in the painting. It drifted out toward her. *Aaron and Rahlys were lovers*, Ilene confided to the crystal, *Did you know that?* she asked rhetorically, fuming.

Before her eyes the crystal spelled out 'YES' in a stream of light. The word soon faded into the dusk. Ilene sat up in amazement. Incredulously she watched the spectrum twirl slowly on its axis as it hovered before her.

What else do you know?

'LOTS,' the crystal wrote in the air.

Does Aaron love me?

The crystal did not respond. *Why don't you like Aaron?* she asked, and the crystal blazed into action.

The words 'HE IS NOT GOOD AT HEART,' filled the tent as the gossamery crystal zoomed about...then reentered the painting. The ghostly words slowly faded away.

Ilene was disappointed by the reply. She knew Aaron wasn't the nicest of men, but he wasn't really evil either. Perhaps she could sweeten up his personality a little over time, she thought.

Theon, a.k.a. Half Ear, is, or was, Droclum's right hand man, Rahlys pondered as she paced her bedroom floor, the floorboards creaking under her feet....Aaron wants to possess the crystal...she continued in her musing...To what lengths would he go in his effort to do so?... Theon, Aaron, and Ilene; what a strange threesome!...What really surprised her was the presence of her painting at the campsite. And the crystal was outside the painting! Did the magic come from her? She thought back on the night she painted the crystal's portrait, and how she had felt the magic tingling through her. Now Aaron owned the painting. How ironic!

Exhausted, Rahlys sat on the edge of her bed. And poor Melinda, what has happened to her? She forced herself to relax and emptied her mind. *Melinda, where are you?* she called out telepathically. But after some time, without contact, she gave up, and finally laid down, surrendering to sleep.

Quaylyn could hear her pacing and wished he could help, but he knew not to violate her privacy. Often he had picked up on her desire for solitude, despite his teachings on shielding her thoughts. Soon the guest cabin would be complete, and Rahlys would have the solitude she desired. Meanwhile, when he was not cabin building, or instructing, he took off on long hikes, studying the flora and fauna.

Sunny days were replaced by cloudy ones, then rainy ones, as Raven kept watch over the campsite at the point. Aaron and Ilene mostly stayed close to camp except for short excursions for water and firewood. Theon, however, was a lot harder to keep tabs on, disappearing under Raven's watchful eye.

The building materials needed to finish the cabin project arrived by railroad freight down at the foot of Rahlys' trail, including lumber and insulation for the roof, two small windows, a door, and the additional spikes needed to finish the log walls. All the materials were quickly teleported to the building site. Progress was rapid, with the help of magic, despite the cloudy skies, and Rahlys and Quaylyn wove spells to repel the ravenous mosquitoes that swarmed around them. "I notice you don't freely offer your blood to feed the poor, hungry mosquitoes anymore," Rahlys commented.

"There are just too many on them," Quaylyn lamented. "There wouldn't be enough to go around."

Another gray, sunless day dawned, and by mid afternoon Raven was sending Rahlys images of Aaron, Theon, and Ilene hiking through the wet, waist high underbrush toward Rahlys' cabin. Aaron slapped at mosquitoes buzzing around his exposed hands and face as they followed the game trail on the ridge overlooking the creek. A couple of times Ilene and Aaron slipped and nearly fell from stepping on slick wet tree roots, poking out of the cold earth in search of warmth, hidden beneath the tall foliage of summer. They hadn't been hiking long when the group came to a clearing featuring a small, nearly finished, log cabin surrounded by piles of lumber, aluminum sheeting, insulation, and stove pipe covered with blue tarps against the rain. No one was around, and Ilene thought the unfinished cabin looked forlorn in the misty rain. They continued on through a tiny patch of woods to the edge of the clearing that surrounded Rahlys' cabin, and Theon indicated a halt. As though their arrival had been heralded by trumpet blasts, Rahlys and Quaylyn stepped out on the porch to meet them.

"May we approach, my lady?" Theon called out cautiously from the edge of the clearing. There was a weighty moment of silent hesitation.

"Yes, of course," Rahlys said, "welcome."

"Thank you," Theon bowed his head respectfully as they approached the porch, "I am seeing my young friends off on the train, and when Ilene learned you were so close, she insisted on stopping in and saying hello." *I think we should talk*, Theon telepathed tightly to Rahlys on the side.

"I'm glad you stopped by." Rahlys introduced everyone. "This is Aaron, Ilene...and Half Ear," she said pointing them out, "and this is Quaylyn." *When?* she asked Half Ear telepathically.

"You can call me Theon," he said out loud, giving everyone a slight jolt of surprise. *How about, after train?*

"Please, come on in out of the drizzle." *After train would be fine.*

"Quaylyn is an unusual name. Where are you from?" Ilene asked casually.

"Seattle," Quaylyn answered with complete naturalness, "Rahlys and I are distant cousins, from my mother's side of the family."

Then to Rahlys, *You still need to tighten up your telepathy,* Quaylyn scolded his student, *I picked up a one-sided conversation.* Rahlys blushed from the reprimand. She thought of a not very nice reply and hoped, for his sake, she was shielding her thoughts sufficiently.

The hikers peeled off their light rain gear, leaving it with their packs on the porch, and stepped inside. One piece of luggage Rahlys noticed was probably the painting of the crystal. An awkward silence followed as they settled into chairs around the massive birch table. Rahlys could pick up thoughts from Ilene and Aaron that explained why they kept looking between her and each other. She also noticed that she picked up nothing from Theon or Quaylyn who studied each other intently in silence. She wondered what was going through their heads, but there was not a single loose thread adrift for her to latch on to. She had to try harder to shield her thoughts she realized with dismay. Quaylyn had been right in being so relentlessly insistent.

Then everyone's eyes were gazing at the walls. Rahlys had teleported all her matting and framing equipment and supplies to the woods, and over the summer had been covering her cabin walls with paintings of birds, wildflowers, and scenes of cabin building. Mystified by the works, Ilene stood and walked around to get a better look. "These are wonderful," she whispered.

"You do good work," Theon agreed, obviously impressed.

"Thank you," Rahlys said to both.

After some polite discussion on art and the art of cabin building, Theon made a move to go. "Well, we best be moving if these two are going to catch the train."

With grateful, but hopefully not obvious, relief Rahlys followed them out the door and made small talk about the weather while they donned their raingear. Then Aaron, Theon, and Ilene headed down her trail into the drizzly summer forest, headed toward the railroad tracks.

"I'll go visit Vince and Maggie and inform them of what is happening," Quaylyn offered as soon as the others were out of sight. Of course, either one of them could have telepathed a message to Vince and Maggie, but Quaylyn wanted to give Rahlys some time alone to think.

"Thanks," Rahlys said, and Quaylyn was gone.

Rahlys breathed in deeply; relishing the solitude. Returning indoors where it was warm and dry, she sat at the table. What does Theon have to say? She had overheard him tell Aaron and Ilene he was on her side. It would be dangerous to trust him…but he would still be dangerous if she turned him away. Theon would know more about Droclum than anyone.

Calming herself, she thought of Melinda, then of Quaylyn's lecture. 'When you are telepathing a message, it is best to focus as tightly as possible on the signature you are communicating with, thus making the signal stronger and harder for others to intercept. It is like the light of an adjustable-beam flashlight. The tighter the beam, the less spread of light; the tighter the telepathed message, the less spread of receivable information.'

Rahlys focused on tightening and strengthening her projection in search of Melinda's signature. She could almost feel the signal tightening and intensifying as she focused. *Melinda, can you hear me? Where are you?* Rahlys called out. She waited, searching; there was nothing in return. Over and over again, she focused with all her will, strengthening her projection. *Melinda, where are you?*

Rahlys, where are you? Melinda cried silently in the ear-ringing quiet as she sat listlessly at the little table in the galley of the *Taku* with cabin lights on and engine off. Outside the cabin windows, darkness lurked so dense and heavy the feeble light of the cabin was defenseless against it. What was going to happen to her, Melinda wondered, tears welling up and streaming down her face. If not destroyed by Droclum directly, would she die from starvation first…or from the never-ending darkness consuming her soul. Maybe she should start up the engine and take a look around, she thought. But she continued to sit, unmoving… as she had for hours…lacking the will to stir. How many days had she traveled across these dark, hidden waters? She had lost track of time long ago.

Finally she forced herself to move. Her legs were numb beneath her as she scooted down off the bench and stood. Bracing herself, Melinda reached over and pushed the boat engine's starter button. The engine hesitated, but then sprang to life. She waited a minute, shaking. Slowly her fingers reached for the running lights switch…and flipped it on. Melinda screamed silently…then tried to calm her pounding heart as she took a better look.

The *Taku* was traveling through a large tunnel, stalactites reaching down from the low ceiling like pointed shark teeth, the water stretching to the walls on both sides of the long watery passage. At first, it had looked as though she and the *Taku* were floating into the maw of a monstrous sea creature.

She turned on the fathometer; it read fifty feet. Watching it for a while, the depth varied very little. Melinda stepped out on deck. The *Taku's* forward movement was more perceptible now that the mast lights reflected off the walls and ceiling. Detailed features could be seen slowly gliding by. Was she finally reaching her destination? There was no shore. Should she try to drop anchor and see if she could stop the boat's progress? But what advantage would there be if she were successful? Did she really want to stay here?

Melinda, can you hear me? Where are you?

The voiceless message, addressing her by name, startled her. Melinda looked around searching for someone who could have spoken. But she was all alone. She had been alone for so long, she feared she had imagined the voice. But then, there it was again.

Melinda, where are you?

Rahlys, is that you? Melinda asked timidly.

Melinda! Yes. Thank goodness, I've finally found you! Are you okay?

I'm on Papa's fishing boat, the Taku. *Droclum sent me on a cruise, and for days I have sailed across a huge sea completely hidden deep underground.* Rahlys picked up mental pictures as Melinda described a dark sea with stone arches and pinnacles, and stalactites that looked like shark teeth.

Where is your father?

There was a short grief-stricken pause. *He's dead. Droclum killed him.* Melinda described the heart-wrenching scene. *Please, can you take me back to the surface?*

Yes, but I will need your help. Are you in any immediate danger?

No, but I'm really scared, and it's so dark. Melinda bit back the urge to cry.

I know, but it's going to be okay. Rahlys concentrated on mentally soothing Melinda's anguish. *My warriors and I believe that Droclum has set a trap using you as bait. We will have to out-smart him if we are going to be successful.*

What kind of trap? Melinda dried her tears on her sleeves.

I'm not sure. Tell me what happened after we communicated last.

Soon after you sent me the apple, I was back on the floor of Droclum's cave again. He knocked the apple out of my hand, and I tried to go after it, but somehow he stopped me without even touching me. It was like some invisible force was holding me in place.

Then what happened? Rahlys coaxed.

He asked me your name, and I didn't tell him, but then he said it, like I had. Then he asked me where you were, but I didn't know, but he said I still had worth, and he was sending me on a cruise, and suddenly I was on the Taku…Melinda paused. *I guess I am bait in a trap,* she concluded. *Why is Droclum after you?*

Because he is an evil sorcerer, and he knows I wish to destroy his powers. He would like to do the same to me. I can mentally locate you now, unlike before, but I also perceive a spell that surrounds you. I fear that if I just try and whisk you away, Droclum will intercept us, but I have an idea that may work. I need you to tell me exactly where you and your father encountered Droclum for the first time.

Okay, but why?

An enchantment prevents me from locating his hideout, but perhaps I can locate this beach, and draw Droclum out in the open. Then I can confront him without putting you in any further danger.

Melinda focused on remembering the details of the little nameless bay where she and her father had taken shelter so many times when the passage was rough. Most fishermen didn't risk taking their boats through the bay's shallow narrow mouth, even at high tide, but Papa knew the course of the winding channel. While the waves rolled and tumbled out on the sea, the sheltered water of the bay, enclosed by high mountains that captured the clouds and dropped steeply into the water, remained perfectly calm. A small creek, imprisoned by dense alders, cut through the mountains and spilled out onto the rocky beach in braided rivulets that trickled into the bay. Melinda even located it on a chart her father kept in a drawer under the captain's chair. She read off the coordinates.

Good, you have been a big help, Rahlys reassured her.

Don't leave me, Melinda begged.

I am only a thought away. Can you take control of the boat and drop anchor, stopping its forward progress?

Melinda described her failed efforts to gain control of the *Taku* before. She glanced at the fathometer and read thirty-eight feet. There was plenty enough anchor line, but she didn't know if there would be anything along the bottom that the anchor could grab on to, or if the anchor would be sufficient to hold against the force that was propelling the *Taku* forward. *I will try*, she telepathed back.

I will get you out of there, Melinda...I promise. Melinda could feel Rahlys' resolve. It gave her a degree of hope.

I'll drop anchor, she said.

Melinda made her way onto the bow. Even at this rather slow speed, there would be a bit of a jolt if and when the anchor grabbed. Melinda released the anchor from its cradle and dropped it over the bow letting the weight of the anchor and chain feed the line off the drum. She held on tightly to the hand railing along the outside of the cabin as she watched the anchor line feed out. When most of the line was out, she reached down and engaged the drum, stopping it from turning. Placing her foot on the line, she could feel the anchor bouncing on the bottom, as it tugged at the boat. Then all of a sudden the boat halted its forward momentum as the anchor hooked onto something below, spinning the boat around in a 180 degree turn. The anchor was holding, the *Taku* straining against the hook, stern first. *It's holding!* Melinda silently cried out.

Rahlys?

But Rahlys was gone.

Quaylyn teleported back to Rahlys, with Vince in tow, shortly before Theon returned. "Maggie wasn't feeling well, so she stayed at home," Vince said when they appeared.

"I found Melinda!" Rahlys beamed with excitement. "She's okay!"

Rahlys related all the information Melinda had given her. "We must attempt to rescue her as quickly as possible. Perhaps Theon can be of help. I have a plan."

Raven projected images of Theon approaching.

"He's almost here." She gave Vince and Quaylyn stern looks of warning. "There is to be no outward show of unwarranted hostilities. Twelve thousand years can change a person. We will give Theon a chance to speak…and maybe redeem himself." Both men agreed, albeit somewhat reluctantly.

Rahlys opened the front door as Theon reached the porch. He paused and bowed upon seeing her. "Greetings, Sorceress Rahlys, Guardian of the Light. I am Theon from Anthya's world, and I have come to offer you my services to help defeat Droclum."

"Come on in, Theon," Rahlys invited, opening the door wide. She could feel the tension mount among the men as he entered the cabin. "You met Quaylyn earlier. He is also from your world…which I'm sure you have figured out. Again Quaylyn and Theon stared at each other intently, Theon looking decidedly puzzled over Quaylyn's presence.

"And you already know Vince." Vince was reassessing the man he had known before only as Half Ear. It had to be a hard adjustment, Rahlys realized. Vince barely responded to Theon's respectful nod of recognition. He wanted answers, and he wanted them quick.

"Look, Vince, I know I have a lot of explaining to do," Theon said humbly, "And I'm ready to start, here and now."

Why don't we sit around the table," Rahlys suggested before there could be any confrontation. Stiffly, they took their seats, chairs scraping across the floor.

"Have you been in touch with your old friend Droclum lately?" Vince asked with forced calmness once everyone was settled. He expected Theon to flinch at the question, but patience instilled over centuries served Theon well.

With unforced composure, Theon replied firmly. "No, Vince. As far as I know, Droclum hasn't thought of me as being still alive, much less living on Earth."

"You know Droclum lives again, why haven't you contacted him?" Rahlys asked.

"My lady, there is already enough evil in this world. Droclum must be destroyed." Again he gave Quaylyn a strange look, then turned back to Rahlys. "Since I have known Droclum personally, I thought maybe I could be of help."

"Do you know where he's at?" Rahlys asked.

"No, but I may be able to help you locate him."

"And tell us again why you are willing to help us," Vince demanded, his voice still sharply edged. Theon did not answer right away.

"Because you are the good guys," he said firmly, giving Vince a hard look. "Being a military man, I think you can relate. During your long honorable career, you must have seen much pain and suffering, cruelty and death. With your heart and soul saturated with man's brutality to his fellow man, you retired and sought peace in the woods, did you not?" Theon looked directly at Vince, but Vince did not answer.

"Then consider this, I have witnessed all of man's ruthlessness to his fellow man throughout the ages. From the time your kind nestled in caves, humans have cruelly murdered, raped, and plundered the lives of others in selfish greed. Like you, I seek peace. But no one knows better than I, that unless Droclum is destroyed, there can be no peace...for anyone...ever." Again he glanced at Quaylyn, not quite sure what to make of him, which was particularly strange, since up until now, Quaylyn hadn't even spoken.

"Why do you seem so puzzled over my presence?" Quaylyn asked at last, a bit annoyed.

"Because you are Quaylyn. Why are you here?"

"The High Council sent me to help Rahlys and her warriors develop their magical abilities and aid them in destroying Droclum."

"The High Council sent you?" Theon asked in amazement.

"This is my First Mission. Is there some reason you question my placement?" Quaylyn asked offended by Theon's tone of voice.

"Because you are Quaylyn," he said again, dumbfounded.

"I still don't understand," Quaylyn said in protest. "You don't even know me. I wasn't a new person yet when you left for Earth. I'm still at the beginning of my longevity."

When Theon didn't respond, Rahlys took the floor once again. "What did you mean when you said you might be able to help us locate Droclum?"

Before answering, Theon pulled a dark medallion etched with silver runes from the leather pouch he always wore across his shoulder and held it out in his hand for all to see. "Droclum forged this medallion for me. It is enchanted with a spell that enables me, once his closest and most trusted confidant, to locate him, and communicate with him, through all his protective shields. I haven't used it for millennia now... but maybe it will work."

Rahlys looked at the medallion Theon held out toward her, without touching it. Silently she focused her mind on the crystal, hanging around her neck. *Is Theon being truthful?* she asked.

Theon speaks the truth as he sees it, and his intent is honorable, but he withholds a secret about Quaylyn.

"Perhaps we will give you a chance to try it," Rahlys said, eyeing the medallion he still held.

"How do we know he can be trusted?" Vince asked.

"Ask the crystal," Theon suggested.

Rahlys indicated to Vince with a slight movement of her hand, that she already had, and pushed on. "Droclum is holding a young girl captive in a cavern deep underground in Southeast Alaska. We need to rescue her, but a spell surrounds her that will, no doubt, alert Droclum as soon as we try. If what you say is true, and Droclum is not aware of your existence, maybe it is time you paid him a visit. Perhaps your sudden appearance would be enough of a distraction to give me the time I need to whisk Melinda to safety before he can intervene. How would you feel about taking on such a dangerous mission?"

"I am ready and willing, my lady. And from where shall I try to contact him?"

"From a beach down in the panhandle. I have the coordinates; the crystal can take us to it."

"And why this beach, if I may ask?"

"It is where Droclum first encountered Melinda and her father," Rahlys explained. "If you contact him from there, you can tell him you have been looking for him, and detected the use of magic. Offer him your service. I need you to distract him long enough for me to rescue Melinda."

"Then what?" Theon asked.

"I guess that will be up to you, depending on who's side you're on."

"And when do you want to do this?"

"Now."

Chapter 16
Rescue

Ilene and Aaron hardly spoke to one another on the train ride back to town. After they disembarked and collected their baggage, Aaron headed off with his pack. "See you," he mumbled, without so much as a glance.

Ilene glared at his retreating back. "What about the painting?" she shouted out to him, possessively eyeing the carefully packed bundle leaning against the pack at her feet.

"Keep it," he said, and continued walking away without looking back.

Why is he so irritated all the time, Ilene wondered. We're so good together, he should be happy. Aaron couldn't even enjoy the camping trip, always fretting over one thing after another. She collected her pack and the painting and headed for the apartment over the gallery. The painting was hers, but as a precaution, she thought it best that her mother didn't see it. Catching a glimpse of her mother downstairs in the gallery through the glass in the door, Ilene dashed by instead of going in to say hello, and hurried upstairs. Quickly she dropped her pack on the floor in her bedroom and slid the painting under her bed. Then catching a horrified glance at herself in the mirror, she rushed to the bathroom, and washed her hands and face before making her way downstairs.

"Well, there you are! How was the camping trip?" her mother greeted her when she entered the gallery.

"It was great, but the mosquitoes were getting pretty bad at the end. They didn't really bother me, but they nearly ate Aaron alive. How has business been?" she asked, changing the topic.

"Oh, slow, but steady. Are you ready to take a shift tomorrow? I need to go into town for some things."

"Sure," Ilene said agreeably. "Stay overnight if you want."

Her mother gave her a questioning look. "Sounds like the camping trip was a good break."

After a quiet mother-and-daughter evening of dinner at home and a movie, her mother left for town early the next day, leaving Ilene plenty of time to think while she tended the shop. It was easy enough to believe that Half Ear was actually Theon from another world, and Rahlys a powerful sorceress… while in the woods. The woods seemed to exude a magic of their own. It was not so easy to believe in magic under the heavy reality burden of town. Here magic and other worlds existed only in fantasy novels. Then she thought of the painting hidden under her bed, a painting too strangely unusual to leave exposed on the wall. She couldn't risk her mother seeing the crystal leave the painting. It would raise too many questions she couldn't answer.

All day Ilene watched for Aaron, hoping he would stop in at the shop. She was ready to forgive him for not telling her about Rahlys… and for not being liked by the crystal…but Aaron didn't show up.

That evening, alone in the apartment, Ilene pulled out the painting from under her bed and brought it into the living room where she propped it up on a chair. As she stepped back, the crystal floated out into the room. *But I haven't even called you out yet*, Ilene thought. As though reprimanded, it jumped back into two-dimensional space. But when she turned her back to it, the crystal left the painting again, drifting around aimlessly while Ilene settled comfortably on the sofa.

Would you like for me to ask more questions? Ilene asked. She was getting used to the idea of communicating with thought. At least she couldn't be overheard.

'YES,' the crystal blazed in light across the room.

Let's see, can you predict the future? Ilene asked, a little frightened by the thought.

'NO,' the crystal wrote.

That was a bit of a relief. At least she didn't have to worry about receiving bad news before hand. *Is Theon really from another world?*

'YES,' it answered and on a second flyby underscored it.

So Rahlys is a sorceress?

The holographic crystal zoomed up and down, back and forth, blazing words across the room. 'RAHLYS POSSESSES ANTHYA'S POWERS.' Ilene watched pensively as the words faded away.

Theon an alien, Rahlys a sorceress, could it be true, and just how far did the crystal's knowledge go. There was one very important question she wanted to ask, the question that had remained unanswered all her life…but Ilene hesitated. Was she afraid of the answer? How would the crystal know anyway? Yet somehow she sensed it did.

The space on her birth certificate where a father's name should have been written, had been left blank. Her mother told her he was dead, but she suspected he may still be alive. If he were dead she reasoned, her mother wouldn't be so reluctant to reveal his identity. She tried asking about him numerous times, but whenever she brought up the topic, her mother snapped at her for no reason, so she always dropped the subject.

Would the crystal know the answer? It was worth a try. All she wanted was a name. At least she should have that much. Minutes passed while Ilene worked at building up her courage. Finally, staring at the softly twirling light, she took a deep breath. *Who is my father?* she asked, bracing herself for the answer.

Quickly the crystal etched his name in light before her eyes: 'THEON.' The letters blazed across the room, suspended in air, slow to dissipate. Ilene's heart raced as she absorbed the shock. Surely this was a mistake! Theon,…Half Ear…If so, that meant that she…and…had… why it was simply unthinkable!

Is Elaine my real mother then?

'YES,'

Does Mother know Half Ear is Theon? she asked in shock.

'NO.'

A sudden knock on the door jarred the silence, causing her to jump. In the blink of an eye, the crystal was back in the painting. Ilene hurried off with it, slipping it back under the bed. Forcing herself into a calm state, she went to the door. "Who is it?" she called out.

"It's me, Aaron."

Although she had looked for him all day, she wished now he hadn't shown up. Still reeling over the crystal's answer to the unanswerable question of her life, she opened the door.

"What do you want?" she asked rather abruptly.

"Can't I come in?" Aaron looked surprised by the cool reception.

"Come in," she said, trying to sound casual as she moved away from the door.

"Where's your mother?"

"Anchorage."

"And the painting?" he asked looking around.

"Hidden in my room."

"Look, I'm sorry I didn't tell you about Rahlys. There's nothing between us anymore," he said, assuming her coolness was because she was still angry with him over this.

"Apology accepted. Anything else?"

That was easy enough, he thought. "So do you want to watch a movie?"

"No, I'm sorry, not tonight, I promised Mother I would spend some quality time with her."

"But you said she's in Anchorage."

"Well, she is…or was, but I'm expecting her back any minute now. Look, maybe tomorrow night. I have a lot to do right now before Mother gets back, okay?"

"Okay," he said reluctantly and stepped into her, kissing her hungrily on the lips, his tongue probing her mouth. "But think about what you will be missing." Then he turned and left, closing the door softly behind him. A part of her wanted to call him back. Instead, she went into the kitchen and fixed herself a drink.

Why had her mother kept her father's identity a secret? Was it because she was ashamed to admit she had a child by Half Ear? Had he raped her? Her mind flashed back to the night of her high school graduation. Half Ear had come to her rescue when her date had tried to rape her. Had he used magic to watch over her? Perhaps he had been watching over her all her life.

Then a lightning-bolt thought hit her. I am half alien!

Suddenly Ilene felt weak with shock. And where was Theon…her father…now? He was going to offer Rahlys his help in defeating Droclum. He could be in great danger, she realized. It was possible she would never see him again.

Magically shrouded against the misty, cold rain, Theon stood on a deserted beach encircled by mountains, their tops clipped low by clouds. A few feet from him, a creek washed over the rocks on its way to the inlet. Raven, hidden perched in tall alders that strangled the little creek, sent back images. Dusk was closing in on the cloud shrouded bay as Theon pulled the dark medallion out of his pouch, its silvery runes glowing eerily. He shuddered over what he was about to do. Steeling his nerves, he focused upon the cold disc…cold despite its glow. Slowly, the medallion rose from his hand. Suspended in air, it began to turn, the silvery runes etched on its surface shimmering in the fading light. Theon focused on Droclum's signature, seeking contact.

Rahlys, Vince, and Quaylyn watched Theon through the raven's eyes from the safety of Rahlys' front porch. Tightening her projection as wrenching-tight as she could, Rahlys sought Melinda's signature, and found her sleeping soundly in her bunk on the *Taku*. The boat had not moved. Could she snatch Melinda out of there without even waking her? With extreme concentration, she focused on the crystal, waiting for the most opportune moment to make her move.

Then something was beginning to happen. A dark phantom, darker than the approaching night, permeated the air above Theon. He could feel the horror of Droclum's presence, but stood firm in his resolve, as Droclum's foulness swirled around him, stirring the air and rustling the nearby trees.

"So you search for me, Theon." The resonating voice of the phantom filled the air.

"Greetings, Droclum, Master of Darkness! It is indeed I, Theon, your loyal and most trusted follower, Great One," Theon said reverently, and took a little bow, "I am here to serve."

Now! Rahlys commanded the crystal. With wrenching force Rahlys teleported to the *Taku*, defying earth's mass, and breaking through magical barriers. With the aid of the crystal, Quaylyn followed her mentally, to help her pull away, if necessary.

Then Droclum bellowed as though mortally wounded. "Traitor!" he roared, detecting the ruse. Before Theon could react, a stunning blow caused the world to wink out, and he and the medallion dropped to the ground. With hideous speed the dark phantom was gone.

As Rahlys reached the *Taku*, a tremendous force struck her broadside, sending her spiraling down into pain. Bracing for a fall, she landed hard on the deck of the *Taku*, the impact intensifying the agony. Pain, instead of substance, made up her being. *Quaylyn, help me!* Rahlys struggled to remain conscious, struggled to gain control of the pain.

"I've lost contact with her!" Quaylyn cried in sudden anguish. Droclum had already barred shut the trap door.

Leaving the sanctuary of the alders, Raven flew to Theon, lying prone on the beach. Quaylyn, still listening and searching mentally for Rahlys, teleported with Vince to Theon's unmoving form on the drizzly cold beach. Quickly they rolled him over and checked for vitals. "He's still alive," Quaylyn said, and they teleported back to Rahlys' cabin with Theon in tow.

After the others were gone, Raven waddled over to the dark medallion left behind on the deserted beach. The silvery runes etched upon it still held a low phosphorous glow as it lay on the pebbly shore. Raven gave it a perfunctory peck. There was no response. Then he pecked at it again. Still nothing. After staring at the disc for some time, Raven picked up the medallion with his beak…just as Quaylyn teleported him home. Arriving in the tree above the bears' favorite picnic site on Rahlys' creek, Raven dropped the dark disc into the empty nest…for safe keeping.

Vince and Quaylyn settled Theon as comfortably as they could on the daybed downstairs. "Shouldn't we take him to a hospital?" Vince asked.

"No, your doctors wouldn't know what to do for him, and if tested, his genetic makeup could raise serious questions. We must do for him what we can. Regrettably, I am not a healer."

Quaylyn and Vince sat by Theon and waited. The hours passed tortuously slow, without change. There was no sign of Rahlys, and all efforts to reach her telepathically failed. By early morning Theon still had not moved…and Rahlys still had not returned. Exhausted, Vince teleported, with Quaylyn's help, home to Maggie and woke her to give her the bad news. Assuming the worse, Maggie sobbed brokenheartedly overcome with grief.

Quaylyn watched diligently over the unmoving form of Theon, formerly an inhabitant of his own world. Theon had lived during the legendary time of the great Sorceress Anthya and Droclum...before the Dark Devastation...when their world had been greatly populated and held great wonders. What had caused a man like Theon to follow an evil master like Droclum, Quaylyn couldn't help but wonder.

Vince and Maggie arrived by four-wheeler at Rahlys' cabin as another gray day loomed, ragged with grief. "Rahlys is not dead," Quaylyn assured them. When magicians die, their current spells die with them. I can still detect the protective shield that surrounds us; therefore, Rahlys still lives."

"Quaylyn is right,..." They heard a weak, whispery voice from the direction of the daybed. "Rahlys is alive." Theon opened his eyes, turning his head to face them.

"She's still alive!" Clutching Vince's shirtsleeve, joy leapt to Maggie's heart, brightening her sorrowful face. Quaylyn quickly brought Theon water as they gathered around him.

"How are you feeling?" Vince asked.

"Thrashed."

Vince held Theon's head up while Quaylyn brought the cup to his lips so he could drink. "Thank you," Theon said when he laid his head back down.

"How do we find Rahlys?" Vince asked. "Do you have any ideas?"

"Where is my pouch?" Theon asked. Vince reached for it, hanging on a chair, and handed it to him. With feeble hands, Theon reached inside, and pulled out a tiny, thin, plain box, made of an unknown substance, and handed it to Quaylyn. "This belongs to you," he said still clutching his pouch. "I feared I wouldn't live to return it to you."

Decidedly puzzled, Quaylyn took the little box without comment and attempted to open it, his large fingers fumbling with the miniscule latch. Failing that, he held it out in his hand and opened it magically. The tiny lid lifted up on its even tinier hinges and fell open. Quaylyn reached in and pulled out a delicate golden chain, and studied it intently in silence. A tiny silvery rune hung from the chain...glowing ghostly from his touch. "I do not recognize this as mine," he said finally, still obviously confused.

Ignoring Quaylyn's denial of ownership, Theon continued on, his voice becoming stronger with the need to explain. "It was given to you by your mother. You were wearing it when your father stole you away from her."

Quaylyn gasped in horror, "I am certain my chosen father did no such thing!"

"You do not have a chosen father…or a chosen mother. You are the illicit son of Sorceress Anthya and Droclum!"

The gasps that then filled the room were emitted from the throats of Maggie and Vince, Quaylyn stood silent, too stunned to speak. He stared unseeing at the golden chain and rune entwined in his fingers, his head exploding with lack of comprehension. Looking as though he would fall, Maggie eased him into a chair. "How can Droclum and Anthya be Quaylyn's parents?" she asked.

"I can tell you only as much as I know." Theon closed his eyes as though keeping them open required too much effort. "Droclum and Anthya were the most talented magicians the Academy had seen since the creation of the Crystal Table, and entered the Academy around the same time. Droclum was infatuated with Anthya from the start, but she would have little to do with him. Even then she must have sensed that his ambitions were evilly dangerous. But Droclum couldn't handle rejection, and ultimately committed an unthinkable act. You were the result," Theon said, straining to look at Quaylyn, but Quaylyn didn't lift his gaze from the tangle of gold chain. Theon closed his eyes in a strength-gathering pause, then opened them again and continued.

"Of course, Droclum was expelled from the Academy. Actually, he simply walked out; the formal expulsion came later. For her protection probably, Anthya was assigned her First Mission by the High Council to the Temple of Tranquility. It was there that you were eventually born." Theon strained to look at Quaylyn, this time he got a response.

"It's not true," Quaylyn said defiantly. The tiny rune symbol brightened in his hand in protest, causing Quaylyn's voice to quaver. "How would you know this?"

"Because I was there." Theon's voice rasped dryly. Vince reached for the cup and holding Theon up with one arm, helped him drink. Then Theon cleared his throat and continued on.

"I first met Droclum soon after his expulsion from the Academy. Not as talented as he, I became caught up in his quest for power, and we bonded together quickly. I had already become defiant toward current social values because of my own shortcomings, and Droclum promised great things. Having shirked all sense of responsibility, we entertained ourselves by reeking havoc, and stole all that we wanted. Soon there was a band of us, and Droclum being the most talented, became our leader. It was a jolly, adventurous time," Theon reminisced wistfully, "but it didn't last long. Droclum's power was great, and so was his ambition." Theon's eyes looked dreamy and distant...when you could see them at all.

"As Droclum became maliciously more formidable, he sought out Anthya, hoping to impress her with his strength and power...and notoriety. It couldn't have been easy for Droclum to break through the magic that protected the temple, but eventually he did so, and when he finally found her...he also found you." Again Theon struggled to look at Quaylyn. "Of course, Anthya still disdained him totally, but Droclum found a new interest...his son."

"How did Droclum," he couldn't say the words 'my father,' "steal me from my mother?" Quaylyn's curiosity was a first stage of acceptance of facts.

Theon sighed softly. "The Temple of Tranquility should have been impregnable, but inexplicably, Droclum managed to transport us to the side of your crib. It was I who lifted you out of the crib, because of the necklace he dared not touch you." Theon leaned toward Quaylyn, then in exhaustion let his head fall back on the pillow.

"When we arrived back at our hideout, Droclum had me lay you in a strange capsule, padded inside, that he had prepared, and commanded me to remove the rune from around your neck...which I did. But still, he never touched you. Not once did he caress your soft downy head, or brush a finger against your smooth cheeks. He made no attempt to hold you in his arms. Not once." Theon turned toward Quaylyn again. "What happened to you after that, I don't rightly know, for suddenly the capsule sealed shut, and then you and the capsule were gone."

"What about my mother? Didn't she look for me?" Quaylyn asked.

"As the galaxies expand in the universe, your mother searched for you, but you were never found. Failing at that, she turned her focus on destroying your father, making it her life ambition." Theon's eyes caught another glimpse of light from the rune hanging on the chain in Quaylyn's hand.

"Droclum instructed me to get rid of the little chain and rune, but instead of destroying it, I kept it in safe keeping. I was never quite able to part with it." Theon paused. "You can't imagine my surprise when I found you here. You are nowhere near as old as you should be, but your signature is undeniable."

"If Anthya created the magic in the necklace, and she is dead, why does the rune still glow when Quaylyn touches it?" Maggie asked. "Shouldn't her current spells have died with her?"

"Some spells are designed to outlive their creator, or creators, usually with an object involved to hold the magic, in the same way Anthya's magic was transferred to Rahlys via the crystal Oracle." Drained from the prolonged effort, and in need of rest, Theon fell back into his pillow, his eyes shut.

Melinda was awakened by a loud thud as something hit the deck hard. To her surprise, the *Taku* swayed and rocked, tugging violently at its anchor. Surely there were no storms underground! She heard something that sounded like wind, and sensed the cloying evil that was Droclum. Struggling out of the bedding with flashlight in hand, she staggered to the control panel in the wheelhouse, hit the engine start button, and switched on the running lights. Tendrils of wispy blackness swirled away from the *Taku*, fleeing the light's feeble effort to beat back the darkness. The usually tranquil water of the flooded cavern frothed with agitation, and hideous laughter echoed like thunder through the cavern.

Struggling to maintain balance in the pitching boat, her heart pounding madly, Melinda ran to the door of the cabin, flinging it open. Sprawled on the deck lay the unmoving figure of a woman, who she assumed had to be the sorceress Rahlys. Melinda crawled to her, nudging her frantically. *Sorceress Rahlys, wake up! Please!* She didn't know if the honorific was necessary, but didn't want to take the chance of maybe angering the sorceress by not using it.

"I have you now, Sorceress Rahlys, Guardian of the Light!" the voice of evil boomed. Hideous laughter echoed through the chamber, reverberating off the walls of the cavern...and then Droclum was gone. The agitated sea relaxed, the air calmed, and the *Taku* stopped its frantic tossing about, all quietly dark once again, except for the hum of the motor, and the pale illumination from the running lights.

Rahlys tried to focus her mind as pain racked her body. Where was she? It took all her might to deal with the pain as she lay unmoving, no strength left to open her eyes. She could sense someone near by, jabbing the pain. It was Melinda's signature.

Wake up, please! He was here. He'll come back.

Rahlys moaned as she tried to move.

Wake up! Wake up! Melinda cried fervently, shaking Rahlys harder with greater determination to rouse her.

Melinda, I'm awake. Just give me a moment. The painful jabbing and shaking stopped. Then without warning, a great wave of water curled over the stern of the boat, and cascaded frigidly over them. Drenched, Rahlys shivered alert, opening her eyes. With Melinda offering support, Rahlys worked to get her elbows and knees under her. Then gritting her teeth, she stood with Melinda's help, certain she would have been down on the deck again if it were not for Melinda's guiding hands placing her own on convenient handholds. Rahlys held on to the handrail as she fought to gain stability and control of the unceasing pain. The sea became rough again, and the *Taku* bucked in agitation. Tendrils of darkness stirred the air around them and Droclum's hideous essence seeped into their senses.

What are we going to do? Melinda cried, as Droclum's noxious presence choked and gagged them.

"I'm not sure. Maybe you should go inside." Melinda did not move. Droclum's voice rumbled like an angry storm, drowning out the sound of the engine.

"Surrender now, Rahlys, and I'll let your little friend go!" his gruesome laughter chilling their blood to ice water.

No, don't! Melinda cried telepathically. Rahlys realized that Melinda was yet to speak vocally. Was the child mute?

"Listen to the girl. You can not escape. Give me the crystal, and I'll give you the girl."

"Never!" Rahlys bellowed into the wind, grabbing Melinda. She could see the interior of the boat through the porthole window, and gathering her strength, teleported them inside before the next, larger wave broke over the deck. The *Taku* shuddered and reeled, and the anchor line snapped sending the boat spinning undecidedly in unanchored freedom.

We're moving! Melinda shouted mentally as the *Taku* dipped and rose in the maelstrom as it resumed its journey forward. Instinctively, Rahlys grabbed the wheel, but it was a fruitless effort. Then there was a low, foreboding rumble underscoring the sound of the engine, the turbulence, and Droclum's hideous cackle. At first it was difficult to tell where it was coming from, until boulders came crashing down into the water around them.

"It's an earthquake!" Rahlys shouted above the din.

Move back, the oracle warned.

Rahlys pulled Melinda against the door just as a boulder dropped on the bow and front of the wheelhouse, shattering the windows, and smashing through the roof. Boulders dropped like guillotines, piercing the deck behind them.

"Give me the crystal!" the booming voice demanded again as rocks showered around them, their impact adding to the turmoil of the water. Rahlys searched for an avenue of escape, but Droclum's trap enclosed them…except below…where there was only stone and water. Drawing on the molecular power around her, Rahlys deflected falling boulders that threatened to strike them.

We're taking on water, Melinda cried out silently, pointing frantically at the swirling water that could be seen in the bilge through the gash in the cabin floor. Complacently the bilge pump kicked on.

It's not going to matter, Rahlys telepathed back. *Look!* Melinda stared where Rahlys pointed in horror. Ahead of them, as though someone had pulled the plug out of the bathtub, a giant whirlpool filled the cavern, spiraling down…and they were headed right for it.

"Last chance to save the girl," the swirling darkness echoed above them. Melinda stood paralyzed with fear.

Melinda, listen to me, Rahlys clutched the girl's arms. *We're going to be alright. I have a plan*, she telepathed tightly to the terrified child.

What is it? Melinda looked around doubtfully.

We are going to go down the whirlpool.

No!

It's going to be alright.

No, Melinda said again, still not convinced.

Melinda, listen to me. I need you to be brave. Rahlys shook the frightened girl gently, trying to get her focused attention. *I need you to hold on to me tightly, and don't let go, no matter what.*

I'm scared.

So am I, she answered honestly.

The *Taku* reached the fringes of the whirlpool, and started to circle around its huge sucking gullet. There was no beach to escape to, no protrusions to grab on to...nowhere else to go, for Rahlys detected Droclum's spells all around them...except down. As the boat whirled around the outer perimeter of the whirlpool, it listed to starboard, picking up speed. Suddenly, the engine died and the lights went out. All went dark, and quiet, except for the sucking sound of the whirlpool. Droclum's evil presence oozed around them in the darkness, relishing their demise.

In terror, Melinda clung to Rahlys as they made their way through the darkness on what remained of the deck of the *Taku*, hugging close to the cabin while hanging on to the railing, until they reached the starboard side of the boat. By now, the *Taku* was riding low in the water. *Hold on to me*, Rahlys stressed again, although she doubted she could pry the girl loose if she wanted to. *When I say jump, we jump.*

We're going to drown, Melinda whimpered fearfully.

No, we're not, but you have to trust me.

Rahlys focused tightly on the crystal, snug in the pouch she wore around her neck. *Take us safely through the whirlpool, providing us with air*, she said, weaving her spell. *And find us a safe passage out of here*, Rahlys directed the crystal. Then drawing on her strength of will and determination, she hugged Melinda to her and gave the command.

Now! Jump!

They didn't so much jump, as Rahlys teleported them into the water. It was shockingly cold. Quickly Rahlys cast a spell of concealment. If Droclum's trap didn't extend underground beneath the hidden sea, it was possible they could escape through a hole under the fence. Without resurfacing, they sped downward, an aura of breathable air surrounding their faces. Rahlys cast a spell of warmth around them. As the water and the crystal pulled them downward, they no longer felt Droclum's presence, his magic receded in the distance above them.

She could feel Melinda holding on to her for dear life, but after several breaths of air...instead of water, Melinda's panic subsided a little. Rahlys conjured the crystal out of its pouch.

Light, she said, and felt Melinda's gasp as the crystal lit the way in front of them. Magic pulled them rapidly along through a channel of swirling, tumbling water, the river of water weaving its way through rock, branching and bending in its course. Their progress was rapid, and before too long, they landed in a shallow underground river flowing between rocky shores.

Immediately Rahlys cast another protective shield against detection. She and Melinda crawled out of the water onto the rocks, the crystal still hovering over them, providing them with light.

Had they escaped Droclum's trap, Rahlys wondered. Perhaps the cage had only been over them, and not under. Hopefully they had covered enough lateral distance to clear it. Carefully, Rahlys probed for Droclum's magical barriers, but she detected nothing. The crystal continued to hover nearby providing light, as Rahlys magically dried them out. She could read Melinda's astonishment over all that had happened.

Awesome! Melinda smiled, amazed at being warm and dry...and having light...not to mention a companion! It felt good to smile again. For Melinda, Rahlys' presence did as much to dispel the darkness as the light of the crystal. She had been scared and alone for such a long time.

"Are you alright?"

Yes.

Unable to detect anything threatening, Rahlys made up her mind. "Melinda, take my hand. We are going to get out of here," she said standing up. Eagerly Melinda stood and placed her hand in hers. Then Rahlys closed her eyes and drawing on the elemental forces around her, she envisioned home...the porch, the creek, and the summer green of the forest.

The next moment they were there, standing in front of her log cabin in the woods, the crystal hovering nearby. As though in greeting, the rain stopped and the clouds tore asunder, releasing the sun to paint a rainbow across the sky. Abounding with joy, Rahlys turned to Melinda.

Oh, Melinda sighed, her eyes tearing at her first sight of sunlight in over two months. Living green grass, trees, and blooming flowers filled the space surrounding her. A gentle breeze blew fresh air into her tear-stained face as vanishing clouds unveiled more blue sky, and the heat of the sun caressed her face. With wonderment in her eyes, Melinda turned to Rahlys who grabbed her up in her arms.

"Ah haaa!" Rahlys cried jubilantly, swinging Melinda around in triumph. Soon the cabin door opened, and people tumbled out.

"RAHLYS!" Maggie cried running to her. Vince was close behind. They fell upon her, overcome with joy. Melinda stepped back shyly. "Oh, Rahlys, you made it, you're back." Maggie hugged her, laughing through her tears. Quaylyn stepped out on the porch, but he neither spoke nor approached her in greeting.

Then Rahlys reached for her shy young companion, and stood behind her. "Everyone, this is Melinda!"

Chapter 17
Droclum Approaches

Droclum, capable of seeing in darkness, watched with malicious glee as Rahlys and Melinda bravely faced the whirlpool. What did they have in mind? He tried to probe the sorceress' thoughts, but they were tightly closed. According to the girl though, they were going to jump. Droclum laughed uproariously. Then mirth turned to seriousness. He wanted possession of the source of the Oracle's magic; eliminating Rahlys would not be enough. But Rahlys would have to die first, or willingly give him possession, before he could safely touch it. The source was kept in the pouch she wore around her neck, he was sure of it. He could feel its potent magic emanating from the pouch.

Droclum drew on the elemental forces around him and with great mental strength reached for Rahlys' heart…but Rahlys was gone! At first he thought she had escaped to the surface, but the shield enclosing them had not been penetrated. Then he searched for her below, but couldn't detect the presence of her signature…or the girl's either.

"Nooooooo……!"

Droclum conjured the orb before him. *Find Rahlys and the source of the Oracle*, he demanded angrily.

Journeying with the orb, Droclum scanned the watery network beneath the whirlpool, but Rahlys, the girl, or the source of the Oracle could not be found. Were they still alive, but undetectable, protected and concealed by the Oracle? It was not until he sensed the use of magic, when Rahlys teleported them out from the underground world, that furiously, he knew for certain they had escaped. By then it was too late. He had been foiled by his own faulty reasoning. Rahlys had outwitted him, making him look like a fool.

Howling ferociously, Droclum swirled through the caverns of the hidden sea, hurling bolts of flashing energy that toppled rock formations and blasted water into steam. But his rage was immitigable. Zooming to the surface, he uprooted trees, flung boulders, and shook mountains seeking release, but no amount of destruction could soothe his rage.

When finally worn out, Droclum returned to the cavern and conjured the orb to his hand. Red flames licked through black smoke inside the tiny sphere. Flinging it out from him, the orb went into a spin, sparking the air around it. Drawing on the power of the orb, Droclum worked his spell.

"Anthya…I am coming…and finally…you will be mine."

If Melinda had concerns over the reception she would receive, she needn't have worried. For in addition to the joy of reunion with trees, grass, flowers, and sunshine, she was also engulfed in kindness.

"Child, we have been worried about you for so long." Maggie's hug was warm and comforting, and Melinda melted into her embrace.

"Melinda, welcome! It is certainly good to meet you. You have indeed been in our thoughts for a long time," Vince said, shaking her hand and patting her on the shoulder.

Melinda doesn't speak, but she can hear, and she's telepathic, Rahlys quickly informed the others.

"How did you get away?" Maggie still had an arm around Melinda's shoulders.

"Luck."

"What about Droclum?" Vince asked.

"He still lives."

Through all this, Quaylyn still had not joined them in the yard. "Congratulations on your success Sorceress Rahlys and Warrior Melinda," he finally said, with little emotion from the porch.

"What's wrong with him?" Rahlys turned to Vince. "And where's Theon?"

"Theon was struck down by Droclum…he's inside, and very weak. Quaylyn…well, it's sort of a long story."

"I want to see Theon."

"Then, come on in," Maggie said, dragging Melinda along with her as she headed for the door. "I'll look into putting out some refreshments."

Melinda couldn't understand why anyone would want to go indoors and leave all the wonderful bright sunshine, flittering birds, and droning insects behind. But the word 'refreshments' sounded good. Reluctantly, she allowed Maggie to take her inside.

To Melinda's relief, it wasn't nearly as dark indoors as she had feared it would be. Numerous windows, framing in portions of the shimmering forest, let in abundant light, the window scenes blending in with the framed paintings that hung on the log walls.

Maggie led Melinda to a chair at the table. *Why, you must be starving? What would you like? A peanut butter and jelly sandwich maybe?*

Melinda stared at Maggie, a surprised look lighting her face. *You can do it too!*

Everyone in this room is telepathic.

Really?

Really.

I would love a peanut butter and jelly sandwich, please.

Coming right up, Maggie said jovially, and she gave Melinda another little hug. *Would you like to help?*

Yes. Can I take it outside to eat it?

Sure.

Immediately Rahlys walked over to the daybed and placed her hand on Theon's forehead, assuring herself that he was still alive. Vince filled her in on what happened. "When Droclum sensed your jump, he struck Theon a nearly fatal blow...and was gone. Then when you didn't return right away with Melinda..."

Rahlys closed her eyes momentarily, focusing on transferring some of her renewable strength to Theon. Then she told them of her encounter with Droclum, and the *Taku*'s voyage through the flooded cavern... the earthquake...the whirlpool...and finally how they had managed to escape from Droclum's clutches."

While the others stared at Rahlys, absorbed in her tale, Melinda, carrying her sandwich and a can of juice, quietly opened the door and slipped out into the sunshine. A fleeting memory of cold dark caves made her shudder, despite the warmth and light. Sitting on the sun-warmed porch, she gazed about her in wonder.

When she finished her lunch, Melinda made her way to the edge of the sun-dappled forest where alyssum, fireweed, monkshood, and wild geranium bloomed profusely, attracting the attention of myriad little bees. Distracted by her own thoughts, Melinda watched as the busy little bees worked the blossoms. Perhaps she should run away before they tried to send her away. She considered the idea, but didn't even know where she was. She didn't want to go back to her village without her father. Even if she could talk, she couldn't explain what had happened…she didn't want to try.

Melinda stepped into the woods drawn by the play of light and shadow. With her first step under the canopy of the trees, the underbrush went aflutter with wings beating the air. A covey of spruce grouse, a mother hen with several nearly grown chicks, flew up in all directions, disappearing into the surrounding trees. Wrenched from her thoughts, Melinda searched the branches carefully, managing to spot the hen and a couple of the chicks, camouflaged by their determination not to move.

Then coming back into the full sun of the yard, Melinda saw aerial images of herself walking, the images drifting across her mind like a movie on a screen. But how? She looked around her for an explanation, a possible source. Where had the images come from? A raven circled overhead, then flew in and landed on the woodshed. Melinda stared at the raven intently. *Did you do that?* she asked in excited astonishment.

"Caw! Caw!" With that confirmation, Melinda received telepathed pictures of the raven relishing a mound of apple wedges.

Oh, I see, you're a beggar.

"Aaarrrrk," the raven cried in protest.

Meanwhile back inside, Rahlys strived to learn more of what had transpired while she was gone. "Has Theon regained consciousness at all?"

"Yes, once." Vince nodded, twitching his head to one side. Following the direction Vince indicated, Rahlys glanced again at Quaylyn, who had followed them in, stood fixed in place, something clasped tightly in one hand. Something definitely wasn't right here, but the thoughts she picked up from Vince and Maggie didn't seem to make sense. "What's that in your hands?" she asked, seeking to understand his peculiar behavior.

Quaylyn revealed a strange little box, opened it, and pulled out a little golden chain with a glowing silvery rune dangling between his fingers, "Theon said he was returning it to me. It was given to me by my mother." Quaylyn's speech was monotone, void of emotion, his movements stiff as though in shock.

Vince cleared his throat. "Theon regained consciousness for a little while just before you arrived. He said Quaylyn is the son of Droclum and the Sorceress Anthya."

"What?" If this were true, Rahlys could understand why Quaylyn was in such state of shock. "Droclum and Anthya!" She looked back at Quaylyn, trying to absorb it, "Is this possible?"

Quaylyn looked too distressed to answer, so Maggie retold Theon's tale as Rahlys listened…stunned. When Maggie was done, Rahlys approached Quaylyn. "Is there even a remote possibility that you could be Droclum and Anthya's SON?"

"I don't know," Quaylyn answered quietly. After some time he added, "I guess it is possible, but the High Council sent me here…."

"…to destroy your father," Vince finished the sentence for him.

"I have your mother's powers,…" Rahlys realized. A contemplative silence ensued. Then Maggie pointed to the necklace in Quaylyn's hand.

"Does it still have magic? Could it still protect you from Droclum?"

Quaylyn glanced at the glowing rune. "It didn't prevent him from taking me away from my mother."

"Quaylyn has learned of his parentage," Zayla informed Brakatar with grave concern. The two austere councilors met in the beauty and splendor of the garden atrium outside Zayla's living space.

"But how?" Brakatar asked. He had come right away, detecting the urgency of her summons.

Zayla paced the sunny garden path between spectacular blossoms and foliage, "Theon is alive…living on Earth."

"Theon is still alive?"

"Yes, and he has returned to Quaylyn the rune necklace that was suppose to have protected him from his father."

"Spells do not always work the way they were intended," Brakatar reminded her.

Zayla paused and turned to face him, "Do you think we made the right decision back then, when we found the capsule?" The capsule they had found on their expedition into the devastated lands around Mt. Vatre had been a marvelous work of magic, preserving the baby Quaylyn in magical stasis even through the Dark Devastation.

"Would you have preferred that we had destroyed the enfant instead?" he asked her, lifting an eyebrow questioningly.

"No, of course not, but now we have sent him to destroy his father."

"The Runes sent him to destroy his father."

"We did nothing to stop it," Zayla said, accusingly.

"Apparently, the Runes believe that Quaylyn may actually be of help."

"Too often," Zayla lamented, "we shun the responsibility for our actions by hiding behind the decisions of the Runes."

I will find that crystal, no matter what I have to do, Aaron solemnly promised himself. Would he take Ilene with him once he had possession, he mused, as the train made its way north to Rahlys' trail. Probably not, since Ilene wouldn't approve of him exploiting the crystal for his own personal gain. Besides, there would be other women…lots of women…lots of beautiful, sexy women flocking to him once he got some money in his pocket. If Half Ear, or Theon, or whatever the hell his name is, thinks he is going to get the crystal for himself he has another thing coming, Aaron swore vehemently.

The Oracle sensed Aaron's approach even before he got off the train, but it did not alert Rahlys. Arriving at his destination, Aaron disembarked, ignoring the friendly acknowledgment from the conductor. Disgruntled, Aaron watched as the train pull away. Then he donned his pack and started up the trail. Still the Oracle did not warn Rahlys of Aaron's approach, but the protective spells guarding the Oracle had been ignited, and unbeknownst to Rahlys, the power of the Oracle masked the real trail, creating an illusionary one under Aaron's feet, that soon led him far astray.

Aaron fumed as he hiked the magically induced trail. A cool breeze under a partly sunny sky added a nip to the air and loosened the first few golden birch leaves from their branches. Shoulder high underbrush of purple monk's hood and bloomed-out fireweed in sunny meadows of seeded grass, patches of fruit-laden high bush cranberry bushes, and spiny devil's club stalks sporting inverted cones of bright red berries hugged the narrow trim foot trail that wound its way through the forest. Aaron hardly noticed the beauty around him, nor did he appreciate the light breeze that helped with the mosquitoes, keeping him out of range as long as he kept moving.

Eventually it occurred to Aaron that he should be getting somewhere soon. The terrain didn't look particularly familiar, and this began to worry him. Had he unwittingly taken a wrong turn, he wondered. Perhaps the landscape would look more familiar facing the other way. To check, he turned and looked behind him. Aaron yelped in panic, his heart pounding in his ears. There was no evidence of a trail in the dense tangle of woods behind him! Quickly he turned again in the direction he had been going, just in time to see the trail he had been following...fade and disappear before his very eyes. What!? His breathing became labored.

Suddenly Aaron was very much afraid. His heart raced with the shot of adrenalin coursing through his system. A chilly tendril of fear crawled down his spine, and panic clouded his thinking. The breeze stilled, and hordes of mosquitoes, now easily finding their mark, targeted in on his body heat. Panic-stricken, Aaron took off running, crashing through the brush in the direction he hoped would take him back to the railroad tracks. Unable to maintain the crushing pace for long, he slowed, his back wet with sweat, the unceasing whining of the mosquitoes driving him even madder.

When he could go on no more, Aaron dragged to a stop. He peeled off his pack, letting it drop to the ground. Batting mosquitoes and wiping sweat from his eyes, he remembered he had a can of mosquito repellent with him in his pack. Aaron turned around to retrieve the repellent, but when he reached for his pack...the once solid pack dissolved away like a mirage. Aaron gasped in shocking horror. His pack was gone! His gun...his gun was gone!

"What is going on here?...Who's doing this?" he cried out to the wilderness, his level of distress rising by the moment. Frantically, Aaron looked about, rustling through the tall brush, searching for the pack he knew in his heart he would never find.

Then in the near distance, Aaron heard another rustling equal to his own. He paused to listen; the sound was coming straight for him. Something big was barreling through the brush. In panic, he took off running again, stumbling blindly through thorny devil's club and rose bushes as the rustling noise closed in on him.

As powerful as a bulldozer, the bear plowed into him, biting into his arm and shoulder. "Ahhh….!" Aaron cried out in pain. He tried to cover his head with his arms and play dead, but the grizzly tossed his body around, tearing at his flesh with its sharp, mutilating claws. Aaron screamed out in agony. The foul, fishy breath continued to bite him with daggers on his arms, torso, and head, eventually severing a jugular vein in his neck. Silently, Aaron took his last breath.

Where's Aaron, Ilene wondered. Despite the provocative kiss of three days before, she hadn't seen hide or hair of him since. It had been a busy weekend with people from Anchorage and Wasilla out and about enjoying what was left of the short Alaska summer, as well as out-of-state tourists, crowding the little gallery. In addition to the paintings and sculptures by local artists, the shop sold a wide variety of other locally made crafts. Candles, ceramics, soaps, embroidered pillowcases, fur hats and mitts, knitted caps, photo greeting cards, etc., filled the shelves and racks, and the customers' needs kept Ilene and her mother hopping.

As they worked, Ilene pondered over her parentage. She gazed at her lonely, graying mother, when Elaine wasn't looking, and tried to picture her with Theon, a quarter of a century ago. As though sensing her daughter's glances, Elaine looked her way. "Everything alright?"

"Yes, why?"

"Your mind seems to be elsewhere."

Ilene tried to look busy and focused. She longed to ask her mother directly if Theon was her father, but she didn't dare pry open what had always been a closed door. She wouldn't use the name Theon anyway. The crystal said her mother didn't know about that. Had her mother ever bothered to ask Half Ear for his real name? And if she had, what name had he given her? Probably something real common like Bill or John.

"Ilene, the customer is waiting to check out." Her mother's voice jolted her back from her musings.

Later that evening Ilene went to Half Ear's pad looking for Aaron.

She knocked on the weather-beaten door, but there was no answer. The door was unlocked, so she opened it, calling out as she walked in. "Aaron, are you here?" Receiving no answer, she walked in further, searching for clues to Aaron's whereabouts. There was an almost empty beer bottle on the coffee table, dirty dishes in the sink, an empty pizza box on the kitchen counter, his small bed, a crumpled mess of bedding and clothing, didn't look like it had been slept in for quite a while. Where could he be? Not finding any leads at Half Ear's pad, Ilene visited all the eateries and watering holes in town. But no one had seen him for days.

That night, after she was certain her mother was safely down for the night, Ilene pulled out the crystal painting and propped it up on her dresser. Staring intently at the crystalline image, she put out her hand, and mysteriously, the glowing holographic image moved toward her. Ilene couldn't help but smile.

I have a question for you, she said. *Where's Aaron?*

GONE! the crystal wrote, flying up in a blaze of light.

Gone? What kind of answer is that? Gone where?

HE IS GONE, the crystal answered again…then the image returned to the painting as though refusing to say more.

How strange, Ilene thought, in restless confusion. Why was the crystal being so allusive? Stashing the painting back under her bed, she crawled under the covers, and laid awake in the darkness of the short late summer night, unable to sleep. Has Aaron returned to the woods, Ilene wondered. She knew he was still obsessed with wanting to possess the crystal…even though Theon had tried to talk some sense into him.

The next morning, Ilene checked Half Ear's place again; nothing had changed, not a single item had been moved, removed, or added. Aaron had not been back. Ilene formed a plan, and sought out her friend Angela to help her put it into action. A nagging feeling in her gut told her that Aaron had returned to the woods for the crystal. She would take the train to Rahlys' trail, and warn Rahlys of Aaron's intent. Then she would hike to the camp at the point to assure herself that Aaron and Theon were alright, and have Theon confirm…or deny…that she was his daughter.

Knowing that her mother wouldn't like the idea of her going into the woods alone, Ilene arranged for Angela to pick her up for a pretend camping trip to a state park located on the road system. But instead of going to the park, Angela would drop Ilene off at the train station before continuing on to Anchorage.

"Now, are you sure you have enough food?" Elaine asked worriedly, while stuffing even more fruit and cold cuts into the already full ice chest. "And enough warm clothing? You don't want to be cold. There's getting to be a nip of fall in the air already."

"There's a cafe and store nearby, we won't starve. And I have plenty of warm clothes, including my heavy jacket."

Angela arrived, cheerful as always, "Good morning, everyone. Are we ready?" she asked eager to get going.

"Just about," Ilene answered with practiced casualness. Angela was going into Anchorage to meet up with her boyfriend, and would be out of town for the next few days. Therefore, there was little chance that she and her mother would accidentally run into one another while Ilene was up the tracks.

"Now, you girls, be careful," Elaine said.

"Don't worry, Mother. I'll see you in four days." Ilene threw her pack on her back, and her heavy jacket over her arm, then gave her mother a perfunctory peck on the cheek.

"Bye," the young women called out to her with the ice chest between them as they walked out the door.

"Alright, have fun," Elaine said, and closed the door behind them.

———

Maggie took Melinda home with her while Vince and Quaylyn worked on the guest cabin. Having lost the zest for living, Quaylyn worked quietly without humor or feeling. He hadn't been the same since learning that Mythra and Kyemon weren't his real mother and father. How had they been convinced to go along with the cruel deception? Thoughts of them brought only pain...the searing pain of his identity being ripped from his soul.

Rahlys stayed with Theon. Throughout the day she sat by his side, sending healing energy to his body and mind. Theon's breathing was steady now, but he still hadn't regained consciousness.

When Maggie and Melinda returned with a picnic lunch for everyone, they found an exhausted Rahlys by Theon's side. Prying her away, Maggie steered her upstairs to her bed, and tucked her in. While Maggie was upstairs, Melinda curiously approached Theon's bed, when unexpectedly, Theon opened his eyes, "Hello, little one. Who might you be?"

Melinda.

"So…you are Melinda!"

Upon hearing Theon's voice and seeing him awake as she came down the stairs, Maggie telepathed a message to Vince and Quaylyn, *Come quickly! Theon is awake!*

Moments later, Vince and Quaylyn appeared in the room, and to their surprise, Theon sat up with ease. "Where's Rahlys?" he asked.

"I just put her to bed; she was worn out."

"I can imagine," Theon said, looking decidedly better, "she saved my life. She needs to get some rest. There isn't much time left."

"Glad to see you are recovering," Vince said. "Maybe now you could answer some questions for us, beginning with, what do you mean there isn't much time left?"

"I have heard much of what has been said, and it is plainly evident that Droclum's strength is growing fast. Soon he will be capable of penetrating Rahlys' protective barrier. I've seen it happen before. No doubt he is enraged over Rahlys' escape, and such anger will only empower him more. Yes, a confrontation with the Master of Darkness is imminent. Rahlys may have outwitted Droclum this last time, but when he comes challenging her, and he will, she will have to stand up to him and fight…or run like a coward." Maggie gasped over the horror of the inevitable. But Quaylyn's unfocused stare was void of readable emotion. Only Vince noticed as Melinda slipped out the door. He didn't like this news one bit.

"How can I help her in this fight?" he asked. The thought of standing by and watching helplessly, while Rahlys battled with Droclum… was unthinkable.

"I'm not sure that you can."

Then Maggie saw Rahlys coming down the stairs. "Well, you didn't stay down long."

"I'm glad you're feeling better, Theon," Rahlys said, ignoring Maggie's comment.

"Thanks. And how about you?"

"I'm fine. I've been listening to your conversation from up there." She looked around. "Where's Melinda?"

"Outside…and while she's out the room, we should discuss what we are going to do about her." Vince had been pushing, over the last few days, for a decision on Melinda's future. "She must have family that's worried about her."

"Her closest relative, I found out, is a married aunt, her mother's sister, living in Ketchikan," Maggie said. "They have four boys."

"Then they would probably love to have a girl!" Quaylyn said, more like himself than he had been in days.

"And how are we going to explain to authorities how we found her?" Rahlys asked.

Vince thought for a while. "We don't; we place her on a beach where she can be found."

"You can't be serious!" Rahlys exclaimed indignantly.

"Rahlys is right, we can't just dump her and place all the burden of explanation on her shoulders," Maggie said. "Besides, she isn't ready to go back where she came from."

"Maybe you should ask her what she wants?" Theon suggested.

"But she's just a child. A child can't make that kind of decision. And if what Theon says is true, she would be safer somewhere else," Vince argued. Then Melinda walked in, a bouquet of wildflowers in her arms, bringing the conversation to an abrupt halt.

Over the next couple of days Theon and Rahlys regained strength; Rahlys rather rapidly, Theon quite slowly. All seven of them, including Raven, gathered at the nearly finished guest cabin to contribute labor or encouragement, either manually or magically, depending on one's gifts, in an effort to bring the cabin to completion. The plan was for Theon and Quaylyn to move into the cabin immediately, and Melinda would have the daybed downstairs…for the time being. Her eventual destination was still undecided.

Vince and Quaylyn installed the woodstove and chimney, while Theon constructed a rustic table with two rounds of firewood standing on end for chairs. Maggie hung curtains she made herself over the windows, and Rahlys hung a couple of her paintings on the walls. Spare kitchen items and bedding were rounded up from both households, and Melinda picked flowers for the table, using a canning jar for a vase. Theon had his own bedding, also some camping gear and dried food to contribute from the campsite at the point.

"It looks so cozy," Maggie said, when the group declared the job was done.

Ilene is approaching, the Oracle announced.

"Ilene is coming up the trail," Rahlys informed the group.

"What about Aaron?" Maggie asked.

Rahlys scanned for Ilene and Aaron's signatures, but found only Ilene. "She is alone." Raven flew off to take a look. Surprised by the announcement, Theon also scanned for Ilene's signature. She knows, he said to himself when he found her.

Curious as to the meaning of Ilene's unexpected return, Rahlys quietly left the merry gathering at the building site, and strolled down the short stretch of trail to her clearing. Then Rahlys received a second message from the Oracle…this one chilling the blood in her veins. The message that she had dreaded for so long filled her brain.

DROCLUM APPROACHES!

Chapter 18
The Final Battle

DROCLUM APPROACHES!

Rahlys froze to a halt in her front yard. The others, also curious as to why Ilene had returned, were soon right behind her. Rahlys turned toward them, already steeling herself in preparation for battle. "He's coming!"

"Who's coming?" Vince said.

"Droclum." The enormity of the situation silenced them all. "I want everyone out of sight and out of danger," Rahlys said with urgent concern."

"What about you?" Maggie asked.

"I have to face him," she said with decisive, quiet reserve that masked the cauldron of fear simmering deep inside of her.

"I will not just stand by and watch you face Droclum alone," Vince said, holding his ground.

Rahlys knew there was not much time. Quickly she turned to Quaylyn, "Quaylyn, I need you to stay hidden for a while. I don't know why, but I feel you are an important key to the outcome of all this. I'm sure you will find an opportune moment to make an appearance. Until then, I want to keep you in reserve."

Quaylyn neither spoke nor moved, his eyes and face motionless, void of expression, his mind in a quandary over what he should do. Droclum was coming. Droclum, the scourge of the universe…his father… was approaching. Quaylyn removed the miniature box Theon had given him from his shirt pocket, opened it, and removed the little gold chain necklace with the tiny silver rune. "Here, take this," he said, to his own surprise, handing it to Rahlys as though it were a good luck charm. "Perhaps it will work better for you than it did for me."

Perplexed, Rahlys opened her hand, receiving the amulet. Then without further explanation, Quaylyn simply vanished away. Not knowing what else to do with it, Rahlys opened the pouch that hung from around her neck, and dropped the little necklace in with the crystal. Pushed by the need for speed, she turned to Maggie.

"Maggie…please…go and intercept Ilene," Rahlys said after Quaylyn was gone. The day began to darken as ominous blackness boiled in from all directions, consuming the sunny sky. "And stay out of sight."

"Take Ilene with you to the house," Vince called after Maggie as she started to leave. The darkness grew.

Maggie turned toward him in protest, but decided to keep her own counsel. She would intercept Ilene, and they would keep themselves hidden in reserve until an opportunity to help presented itself. With fear gripping her heart, Maggie headed down the trail to meet Ilene. The unnatural, quickening darkness continued to close in overhead, urging her to pick up the pace.

"Where's Melinda?" Rahlys asked looking around.

"She's still back at the guest cabin," a frail looking Theon informed her.

"Go, and watch over her," then she softened the command, "…please."

"I'll go check on her," Theon said, not moving.

"Vince, you must let me confront Droclum alone," Rahlys said, turning toward him. Reading the hard lines in his face, she added, "You could cover me from the edge of the woods." Still Vince and Theon didn't move, their eyes glazing in horror at the darkening sky. "Go!" Rahlys shouted, stomping her foot to jar them into motion. To her relief they both stirred.

Stepping just out of sight into the woods, Vince conjured his gun and ammo from home, and quietly loaded the rifle while keeping a watchful eye out for Droclum. A bullet should kill a sorcerer as easily as any other man, he reasoned, loading the chamber and taking the gun off safety.

Melinda had hung back when the rest of the group left the newly completed guest cabin to join Rahlys and Ilene. She didn't know Ilene, and wished to sit alone in the late summer sun and think, immersed in the clean smell of new wood. Theon found Melinda standing in front of the little cabin, gazing up at the sky as the swirling dark closed off the last spot of blue. In a matter of minutes, the bright sunny day had been transformed to lingering dusk. She turned her gaze toward Theon as he approached. He was from another world, she knew, as was Quaylyn, but she did not fear him. He had tried to help rescue her from Droclum, and had been badly hurt in the effort. When Raven transmitted images of a somewhat worried-looking Ilene coming up the trail, Melinda received the images as well. But she was unaware of the Oracle's second message.

Why has the sky turned dark? Melinda asked him in alarm.

"Droclum is coming," Theon told her. "I think it's best you stay inside." Melinda nodded silently in agreement, her youthful face transformed into an expression of horror. Theon followed her into the cabin and pulled out two pistols from his pack, which he quickly loaded, although he was less certain than Vince of their likely effectiveness against Droclum. "Stay here," he told Melinda as he strapped a gun holster around his waist and walked back out, closing the door behind him. Melinda ran to the window, and looking out, caught a fleeting glimpse in the mounting darkness of Theon's back headed in the direction of Rahlys' cabin. The darkness rumbled and flashed.

As Ilene walked up the trail from the railroad tracks, recognizing some of its features from the week before, a strange darkness started consuming the sky. Her heart raced with foreboding. Quickening her step, she was startled out of her wits, when in a blind curve in the trail she nearly collided with Maggie in the almost dark. They both came to a halt, hearts beating wildly.

"What's happening?" Ilene asked with frightful concern, recognizing Maggie, even in the eerie darkness.

"It's Droclum," Maggie cried. "Oh, you wouldn't know…"

"But I do," Ilene said, her alarm increasing. "Theon told us about him. Where's Aaron?"

"Aaron? We haven't seen him since he left with you. Why? Is he missing?"

"Yes…I thought he was here, trying…," Ilene paused, then decided to finish off her sentence after all. "…trying to steal the crystal." Lightning lit up the sky, punctuated with a rumbling boom of thunder.

"Why, that fool! The crystal can't be stolen, at least not by the likes of him. Well, if he's here, he hasn't shown himself."

"What about Theon?"

"Theon's here, but he's still weak from his last encounter with Droclum. I doubt he will be of much help."

"He had an encounter with Droclum? Why happened?"

"Theon contacted Droclum to give Rahlys time to sneak in and rescue Melinda." Ilene didn't know who Melinda was, but she didn't stop Maggie's dialogue to ask. "When Droclum figured out what they were up to, he dealt Theon a terrible blow. It pretty near killed him, but Rahlys managed to help him recover...somewhat," she added.

"Where is he? I need to see him," Ilene said with urgency.

"Surely, whatever you want to tell him can wait. Droclum is coming!" Maggie explained. "Rahlys wants us to stay out of sight." But Ilene would not be deterred. Determined to reach Theon, she continued on.

"I'll go with you," Maggie said, and the two women headed up the trail together. As they drew near, they slowed their pace, looking out for signs of danger. Cautiously, they skirted the edge of the clearing, weaving their way through the dense underbrush in the thickening darkness.

Hearing rustling in the brush, Vince lifted his rifle to his shoulder, aiming in the direction of the sound. Then Maggie and Ilene dimly came into view. "Don't shoot, it's us," Maggie whispered loudly.

"What are you doing back here?" he said, lowering the rifle. "I told you to take Ilene to the house." Vince did not sound at all pleased.

"I must see Theon," Ilene said, heedless of Vince's rebuke.

"Now?" Vince asked incredulously, as another surreal flash of light preceded another roll of foreboding thunder. Ilene and Maggie didn't answer him, their eyes focused on Rahlys, transfixed in the middle of the clearing, the boiling dark swirling above her.

Unmoving, Rahlys stood in the center of the yard, drawing in power as she watched the sky apprehensively. Then a tremendous flash charged the dome of her protective shield, blowing it asunder. The reverberations from the destruction of her spell, knocked Rahlys a blow that sent her careening to the ground. The protective shield was no more. Regaining her footing, Rahlys willed herself under control, gasping for breath, as the foul stench of iniquitous evil seeped into her being. Despair. Horror. Pain. Sorrow…all infinite…overwhelmed her senses.

Droclum appeared before Rahlys in his true essence;…what he had become. Sorrow…and endless heart-wrenching grief…flooded her psyche. Rahlys staggered under the weight of immeasurable, unquenchable sorrow…a burden of sorrow too deep to ever know gladness. Horrific dread and hopelessness overpowered her mind, robbing her of her will to live. Pain and grief…horrendous, horrifying, unceasing pain and grief…Rahlys shuddered uncontrollably as her soul cried out against the crushing writhing agony that permeated her being… more anguish and suffering than could be eased in all of time. How could she hope to endure?

Rahlys struggled to focus. She had to fight! But how could she fight such insurmountable corruption? *Fight! You must! You can't let this evil consume you…and the others…the whole world.* Clenching her fists with the strain to gain control, she drew on the elemental forces around her.

"Rahlys," evil hissed like a dying breath.

With all her strength Rahlys struggled to repel the debilitating despair, drawing on the power within her. *You must fight! Good must prevail over evil, or all will die.* Pulling in energy from around her, she compressed it into a superheated fireball and flung it hard. *Burn in hell!* With ease, Droclum curved the fireball's trajectory, hurling it back toward her. It missed her only narrowly as she dived and rolled to avoid being struck, the fireball searing a charred path to the fiery combustion of a spruce tree.

Up again and running, Rahlys dodged a volley of flashes. A searing flash streaked through her clothes and across her back as she dived behind the full woodshed for cover. Gritting her teeth against the intense, burning pain, she crouched behind the protection of the woodshed, trying to catch her breath. *Fight! Don't be a coward,* she reprimanded herself. *You must fight or all will be lost.* Taking the offensive, Rahlys teleported herself out in the open within close range, pulling in such tremendous energy, it charged the very air around her, and flung the charged bolt with all the force she had, knocking Droclum back only a step.

Recovering quickly, Droclum struck back, the impact sending her sailing. Landing in a painful fall, she went into a roll, then quickly shifted position, barely avoiding yet another strike. Bruised and battered, pain cruising through her body…Rahlys vanished an instant before Droclum's next hurled bolt of energy exploded, leaving a hole in the ground where Rahlys had been.

Theon, hiding in the strip of woods between the house and the guest cabin, was about to step out and unload his pistols into the abomination Droclum had become…when Rahlys vanished. Now, he couldn't be certain of her location, and he didn't want to take the risk of hitting her. An image of the raven beside him flittered across his mind. Looking down, sure enough, there was raven, the medallion Theon had thought was lost in his beak, the rune's phosphorous glow the only thing discernible in the eerie darkness.

Theon took the disc from Raven's beak as Droclum struck in what he perceived was Rahlys' direction, hitting his mark. Rahlys took part of the force of the blow, barely managing to deflect the blunt of it. Pain wrenched her left arm and shoulder as she went rolling down the slope toward the creek. Taking cover behind a patch of alders, she rematerialized, writhing in pain, barely able to move.

Having located Rahlys, Theon stepped into the clearing as Droclum's dark form headed in pursuit of his victim. Holding up the medallion, he invoked its power. The runes glowed brightly as they sent out their signal, the recipient exceedingly near.

Droclum turned to face Theon, "You dare to summon me again?" he growled.

"You doubt my loyalty?" Theon asked, approaching closer. Then quick drawing, a pistol in each hand, he emptied both rounds, rapid-firing nearly point blank into the gruesome horror that was Droclum. The bullets pierced and the demon roared hideously from the impacts, but remained standing.

"Traitor!" Droclum boomed, drawing on the darkness around him, imploding it into great density, then fired the spear of darkness at Theon…bringing him down.

"No!" Ilene screamed as Theon fell. Without thinking of the danger to herself, she jumped up and headed for him. Vince quickly grabbed on to her, and pulled her back.

"Stay here!" he said, pushing her down. "And stay low." Maggie and

Ilene crouched lower into the concealing brush. Then Vince left to try and rescue Theon, if he was still alive. Ilene wept on Maggie's shoulder while Maggie tried to console her.

Before Droclum could finish Theon off, Vince teleported himself in front of him, and fired his rifle repeatedly point blank into the heinous corruption. Droclum howled in anger, knocking the rifle out of Vince's grasp.

Then Vince felt something clamping down forcefully on his throat. Suddenly, he couldn't breath…the need for air rapidly became agonizingly urgent. He was being straggled, he realized, and frantically groped at his throat with his hands as he gasped for air, but there were no hands there to remove.

Rahlys picked up on Vince's stress, and gathering strength from she knew not where, teleported herself back up the hill. Drawing on unknown reserves of power, she hurled all the force and vigor she could muster toward Droclum, stunning him momentarily, forcing him to release his stranglehold on Vince.

Vince gasped repeatedly, painfully filling his lungs with air as Droclum turned his attention back to Rahlys. Seizing the opportunity, Vince grabbed a hold of a groaning Theon, and teleported with him, not questioning at the moment how he did it, back to Ilene and Maggie in the comparative safety of the forest.

"Father!" Ilene cried softly, bending over him tearfully. *Father!* Vince and Maggie glanced at each other in startled surprise. Ilene cradled Theon's head in her lap, willing him to live, trying to ease his pain.

"Daughter," he moaned in a whisper, unable to say more. But it was enough, for Ilene heard it clearly.

Then Rahlys felt her own throat painfully constricting. "Surrender the Oracle!" Droclum demanded, bringing her down to her knees. She gasped for breath, and the vice grip clamped down harder. While straining with all her might to oppose the crushing pressure at her throat, she clutched the pouch containing the crystal and necklace. Pain coursed through her body, as she struggled to remain conscious, struggled to breathe, and struggled to maintain possession of the pouch and its contents.

Then suddenly Quaylyn appeared beside them. "Father, stop!"

In shocked surprise, Droclum mentally let go of Rahlys, and faced

Quaylyn. With enormous relief, she took in deep gulps of air, refilling her searing lungs.

"My son," the monster said softly, after looking him over, reading his signature, assuring he was real. "…Quaylyn."

"You must stop this, Father. What you are doing is wrong."

"Righteous, like your mother, I see." Droclum crept closer. Quaylyn, his heart numb to any threat, did not step back. "Don't make the same mistake she did, my son. Forget these…creatures," Droclum said, as though casting a forget spell. "Come with me, and I will make you greater and more powerful than you ever dreamed!" Quaylyn began to shake as Droclum moved ever closer. Whether it was in fear, or in rage, Rahlys couldn't tell. She regained her feet, drawing on her draining energy reserves, waiting for Droclum or Quaylyn to make a move. Then Quaylyn broke like water over a dam, burning with hate, burning for answers.

"You destroyed my world!" he shouted in rage. "You destroyed everyone's world! Why? Why did you do it?" Quaylyn paused, his body trembling. "You defiled my mother, and stole me from her!"

"Your mother was a fool. I offered her the universe, but she failed to see our potential together. She wouldn't love me, so I took what she loved most dear…I took you…and placed you in safe keeping. I planned on coming back for you, but now I see that you have conveniently come to me. How unfortunate…for you." Then without warning, Droclum drew on the darkness, flinging out a lance of powerful dark energy.

Quaylyn fell to the ground.

As Quaylyn fell, Rahlys struck. As though drawing the lightning from the sky, she struck Droclum with one bolt after another, driving him back, away from Quaylyn's still, unmoving body. Most of the strikes were blocked, but a couple brought forth, sharp cries of pain. With her surge of energy exhausted, Rahlys prepared to teleport to cover, her sights on a nearby tree at the edge of the clearing. But before she could make the jump, Droclum struck her with full force, sending tortuous pain radiating throughout her body. Writhing in agony, Rahlys fell to the ground, losing awareness of the things around her, her entire being consisting only of pain.

"Give me the pouch!" Droclum roared.

"No!" she managed through gritted teeth, her trembling hands grasping the pouch, clasping it to her heart in an effort to protect it. She had to prevent Droclum from getting the crystal.

"Give me the pouch!" Droclum roared again.

"No…," Rahlys groaned, weak and hurting, clutching the pouch to her. Droclum stretched mentally toward her, magically drawing on the pouch, beckoning it to him. She could feel the pull, and strained to maintain possession.

"Give me the pouch…or all of your little warriors will die."

"Why don't you just kill me instead?" Rahlys gritted through clenched teeth.

"My pleasure." Instantly, the pull ceased, and Droclum flung a blazing ball of energy in her direction. But Rahlys was just as quick, launching a similar shot in return. The two blazing spheres met in mid-space, bursting into brilliant fireworks that momentarily lit up the arena.

"Give me the pouch!" Droclum demanded again as the fire and light show ended, advancing on her quickly.

Give him the pouch.

What? To Rahlys' astonishment, the message had come from the Oracle. But why would the Oracle want her to surrender the crystal? "No!" she cried out, clutching it to her all the harder.

GIVE HIM THE POUCH, the Oracle repeated, even more emphatically. She felt an overwhelming compulsion to trust the Oracle and relinquish the pouch. Reluctantly…Rahlys relinquished the crystal.

"Here, take it," she said, and she let go of the strain to maintain possession.

Instantly, Droclum had the pouch in his possession.

"Finally, Anthya, you are under my control," he said fondling the soft leather, with relish. Then he emptied the contents of the pouch into his open hand.

Droclum's roared with unbelieving horror as the little gold chain with the silver rune fell out of the pouch. Upon contact, the necklace stiffened into glowing life in the shape of a small, but deadly, serpent, the silver rune forming the snake's head, and the golden chain defining its body and tail. The screams of countless nightmares ripped through the air as the little glowing silver and gold serpent circled Droclum's form, around and around, leaving a smoking trail wherever it passed. Droclum screeched and bellowed, bringing forth blood-curdling cries that sent chills down Rahlys' spine. Frantically, Droclum struggled to rid himself of the deadly omen, howling in terror as Anthya's spell unfolded. In time frozen, Droclum smoldered, screaming, crumbling before her eyes, until in one last defeated howl…what had been Droclum…crumbled into a pile of dust, and was no more.

The rune necklace fell lifelessly to the ground.

Trembling, Rahlys stared at where Droclum had been in astonished disbelief. The swirling darkness dissipated rapidly, letting through increasingly more light. Soon Vince and Maggie were by her side. "Kaw! Kaw!" Raven flew in to inspect the dust pile. Then Ilene and a very weak Theon joined them in the clearing as the sun's rays began to filter through.

As the sky brightened, they gazed down at what remained of Droclum, a non-threatening pile of dust.

"Great job, Sorceress Rahlys," Vince congratulated her.

"You did it. You destroyed Droclum," Maggie said.

"It wasn't me, it was Anthya's magic that destroyed Droclum."

It was true. Droclum was gone, and in the end, it was Anthya who had finally destroyed him. The protection charm she had created to secure the life of her son as an enfant, united with the crystal she had empowered with her magic, had produced magic of their own.

"Quaylyn," Rahlys said, and they rushed to where he lay unmoving in the summer grass. Gently they rolled him over, checking for signs of life. He was still alive, but barely. Grasping his hand and forehead Rahlys sought for healing strength to share with him. To her surprise, Ilene joined her.

"I can help."

"Let her," Theon said, "My daughter is a healer."

"Daughter," she murmured in shocked surprise. It was evident by their demeanor that Vince and Maggie had already heard the news.

"As you can see, I'm standing," Theon offered as proof.

Just barely, Rahlys thought, but she gladly bowed in agreement. In her drained, exhausted state, she had little strength to spare. Poor Quaylyn, she thought sadly. His life had been shattered. Rahlys wobbled in an effort to stand, and Vince stepped up to offer her support.

What happened to the crystal, Rahlys wondered. Had it been destroyed along with Droclum and the pouch? Involuntarily, she reached for the pouch she had grown so used to wearing, but it was no longer there. She tried summoning the crystal to her. Instantly it appeared, hovering before her, its soft light glowing.

So that's the crystal Aaron covets, Ilene gasped silently. It looked exactly like the one in the painting, only more solid.

As the sky lightened, Melinda opened the door to the guest cabin, and peaked out. Sunshine winked back at her, beckoning to her. Cautiously she stepped out. Raven flew over sending her images indicating for her to follow him. *Where's Droclum?* she asked the raven, as they reached the clearing. Raven flew to a pile of dust not far from the rest of the group, and landed beside it. The sun came out in full force, shining brightly in a crystal blue sky.

Walking up beside the raven, Melinda stared at the innocuous little hill of ash. Then she reached down and picked up the little necklace that lay hidden in the grass, and walked over to where Ilene was administering healing energy to Quaylyn. *Is he going to be okay?* Melinda asked.

Ilene looked up at Melinda in surprise. A young girl she had never seen before was standing beside her, and she had spoken telepathically. Could she speak to the girl like she did the image of the crystal, Ilene wondered, and gave it a try. *I hope he will be alright. I'll do all that I can to help him*, she said.

Are you from another world, too?

I am Theon's daughter.

Satisfied with that answer, Melinda knelt down in the grass beside Quaylyn and placed the chain and amulet in his unmoving hand. The tiny silver rune glowed softly.

Anthya approaches.

"Anthya is coming," Rahlys announced.

The air was charged with anticipation. Except for Maggie and Theon, the others had never actually seen the Councilor before. Maybe she will be able to help Quaylyn she hoped.

And then Anthya was there amongst them, gleaming in the sunlight. All eyes were riveted on her; Ilene and Melinda stood in greeting. The crystal flew over to Anthya, circling her excitedly, before returning to hover near Rahlys.

"Congratulations, Sorceress Rahlys, Guardian of the Light! You have completed your First Mission," Anthya said, bowing to her respectfully.

"Councilor Anthya, greetings," Rahlys said. "Please, can you help Quaylyn?"

"I have come to take him home." Anthya went to Quaylyn, and levitating him up to her, touched him tenderly, placing a patch of light on his forehead. "Quaylyn has suffered much heartache and sorrow, in addition to the blow from Droclum. We will do for him all that we can."

"Will he be alright?" Maggie asked still concerned. She thought about how different it was going to be without him around. He had been so changed these last few days, she felt that she missed him already.

"He will be fine, over time," she assured them gently. "I would also like to take Droclum's ashes, if I may."

"Sure, of course," Rahlys said. No one objected.

Anthya pointed a pale, slender finger at the pile of ash that had been Droclum, and it disappeared as though sucked by a vacuum. Then she turned toward Theon.

"Greetings, Warrior Theon."

"Councilor Anthya," he replied politely, bowing his head in respectful greeting.

"I can also assist you in returning home, if you so desire."

"Thanks, Councilor," Theon said, "I appreciate the offer, I really do...but I want to stay near my daughter."

"As you wish," Anthya bowed in return, and turned again toward Rahlys. "Sorceress Rahlys, you have fulfilled your destiny; Droclum has been destroyed."

"It was Anthya who defeated Droclum, not I?"

"She couldn't have done it without you. The powers of the Oracle and the crystal are yours to keep. Their power will endure through your lifespan only. Remember to always use them wisely."

"Thanks...I think."

Anthya smiled warmly, "I see you do understand. Before I leave you, do you have any requests, Sorceress Rahlys, Guardian of the Oracle?"

"Would you let us know how Quaylyn fares, and..." Rahlys choked on a sudden rush of emotion. "And thank him, for us, for all his help," Rahlys said recovering.

"Yes, of course."...and then Anthya and Quaylyn were gone.

Chapter 19
Order of the Oracle

Franklin sat up suddenly in his great bed, awakening from a nightmare...or so it seemed. The cavern was thickly dark and clammy cold. What had happened to the light and warmth? What could have extinguished the heated rock walls that bathed his home in a comforting warm glow and kept the damp chill at bay? Franklin pointed forcefully at the cavern wall that he could not see, but knew had to be there.

Light, he commanded.

Nothing happened.

Something was wrong, he reasoned, as he started to shiver in the encroaching cold.

Warmth, he commanded, a little less self-assured.

Again, nothing happened.

With more than a little apprehension, Franklin felt for the orb through his jeans. To his great relief, it was still there; at least he still had that. Reaching into his pocket, he pulled it out. But to his utter shock...the orb did not glow. He couldn't see it at all in the total darkness, only feel its smooth, round surface in his hand. Fear prickled through him, tying his innards into knots.

Light! he demanded urgently.

The orb remained dark.

With mounting fear, Franklin climbed out of the great bed, and stood barefooted on the cold, stone floor.

Light! he shouted frantically in the dark...but darkness prevailed.

Groping in the heavy blackness, Franklin searched for shoes and socks, found one shoe and one sock, and put them on, the shoe on one foot and the sock on the other. Tendrils of cold crept in, tightening around him, the darkness weighing down on him heavily. He reached out into the black void, searching for the mirror, which reflected no light, and inching forward, eventually came into contact with its smooth surface. Franklin located the feathered cloak, draped over the back of the mirror, and wrapped it around him, imagining himself standing in front of the mirror he could not see.

"I am Droclum, a great and powerful sorcerer," Franklin shouted into the blackness. His voice sounded weak and vulnerable; the other presence was gone. Franklin held up the Dark Orb in his hand.

"Light!" he commanded again, fruitlessly.

Unrelenting darkness prevailed.

In anger, Franklin threw the orb as hard as he could. In stunned silence, he listened to it bounce a couple of times, then roll and drop on its way to the little underground stream. There was even a barely audible 'plunk' as the orb plunged into the softly whispering water.

I will just teleport myself out of here, Franklin decided, and closed his eyes to the darkness, focusing on the feel of the hot, sultry, late summer heat of the deep south, the salivating aroma of deep fried seafood and gumbo, and the compelling rhythms of New Orleans jazz…but Franklin remained in the cold, dark cavern.

Eventually, in failure, he gave up the effort. Climbing back up into his great bed, wearing one shoe and one sock and clutching his feather cape around him, Franklin sat quietly in the unending darkness.

Pounding rain drummed unnoticed on the roof, its loud pelting unheard as Vince and Maggie slept soundly exhausted, nestled together cozy and warm in their bed, snoring. Surely the little bones in their ears picked up the vibrations, but their brains would have nothing of it.

The driving rain on the roof of the little guest cabin woke Theon from a deep sleep, leaving him wondering where he was momentarily. Then scenes from the day before flittered rapidly across his brain, beginning with the battle against Droclum and his daughter calling him Father, and ending with him spending the night in the little guest cabin, orienting him to the present and pounding rain. There is likely to be snow a few hundred feet higher up the mountains he thought after getting his bearings.

Raven, perched deep in the sheltering branches of a spruce tree, envisioned the approaching winter. It was raining now, but he instinctively knew that soon the winter snow would arrive.

The deafening pounding of the rain startled Melinda into wakefulness. For an instant she feared Droclum had returned, but once she reassured herself that it was only heavy rain, she relaxed under the warm covers on her pallet on the floor. She thought of the paintings she and Rahlys had started the night before, and wanted to get up and go look at them on the table where they had been left to dry, but it was barely light yet and chilly and damp in the room. Ilene, asleep on the daybed, and Rahlys, sleeping upstairs even closer to the pounding on the roof, did not stir, so Melinda closed her eyes instead. When she opened them again, it was bright and sunny outside, a fire in the stove had taken the chill out of the room, and Ilene and Rahlys were nowhere to be seen.

Melinda jumped out from under the covers, quickly pulled on her jeans and sweatshirt, and rushed out the door into the sunshine as Raven flew in from the northeast squawking urgently.

"Aaaark! Aaarrk!" he cried, landing on the woodshed roof.

Rahlys stepped out of the outhouse, the crystal following her. Melinda thought the crystal looked like a fairy as it floated around sparkling in the sun. Since Droclum's demise, along with the pouch, the crystal had been given free range, but generally remained near Rahlys. "Good morning," Rahlys said as she came up to Melinda, giving her a hug.

"Aaarrk!" Raven squawked again.

What's the matter? she asked him, including Melinda in the telepathed inquiry. Theon and Ilene entered the clearing coming from the guest cabin in time to receive Raven's projected images of fresh, new, glistening snow on the mountain peaks.

"Termination dust," Theon grumbled. "Winter is coming; it is the end of summer."

Then Raven telepathed images far more gruesome, from lower down in the rain soaked valley, images of a torn and mangled partially eaten corpse on the forest floor.

"It's Aaron," Ilene cried out loud.

It would have been impossible to identify anyone with the images Raven sent, Theon thought, but Ilene seemed certain.

"How did he get way out there?" Theon asked with uncertainty. "Where did he think he was going? There's some mighty rugged country between here and those mountains."

Rahlys telepathed a message to Vince and Maggie, and they arrived almost immediately. Raven shared with them what he had seen.

"Should we see if we can make a positive ID before calling in the authorities?" Vince suggested. Everyone agreed, and taking a tarp, some rope, and surveyor's tape, Vince and Theon, with Raven helping them to pinpoint the location, teleported to what appeared to be a bear mauling.

"Bear scat," Theon pointed out as they followed the tracks to and from the kill. Torn up brush and the torn and mangled body were also clues. There was no pack or gun to be found. "It's hard to tell who it is without a face."

Vince gagged as he searched for some form of identification, and found a wallet in the victim's back pocket with an expired Washington state driver's license. It was indeed Aaron.

"What could have possibly gotten into his fool head to bring him way out here without a gun?" Theon shook his head mystified. "It doesn't make sense. Getting here on foot across this kind of terrain would be quite a trek. I suspect magic was at work here."

"Magic!" Vince gasped in alarm. "Who's magic?"

Theon shrugged, "Maybe the Oracle's."

Vince was startled by the implication. Did the Oracle have something to do with Aaron's death? Both Theon and Ilene claimed that Aaron sought the crystal with visions of power and wealth in his head. Had the crystal taken action against him because of his intent? Vince cringed; it was a scary thought.

After wrapping the remains in a tarp and tying it securely, they threw a rope over a tree limb, and hoisted the body up off the ground out of reach of predators. Then they marked the spot clearly with long stretches of bright orange ribbon to facilitate spotting it from the air. Returning to the group, Vince and Theon described to the others what they had found. Ilene broke down and cried, and Rahlys and Maggie couldn't help but shed a few tears themselves as they offered Ilene solace. Working together, Vince and Theon fabricated a story for the police about how they were scouting out the area to set up a hunting camp when they came across the body. Moose hunting season was about to open.

Teleporting to the top of a nearby hill where he could pick up a signal on Ilene's cell phone, Vince phoned authorities and reported the find. Yes, he and his friend could help troopers locate the body by helicopter. Yes, they would come into town tomorrow by train.

The troopers were waiting for Vince and Theon when the train pulled into the station. After answering some initial questions, they boarded a state trooper helicopter, and took off following the railroad corridor at first then veered more northeast toward the mountains at Theon's direction. The hilly landscape was carpeted with gold, green, and red forest, the mountains sugar-coated with glistening fresh snow. Theon's intimate knowledge of the landscape led the pilot right to the spot, and a nearby muskeg provided a place for the helicopter to touch down.

"It's the strangest thing," the train conductor told investigators later, after the body had been removed, "I could have sworn I handed that guy down his pack when he got off the train; after all, a man doesn't take off into the woods without a pack, and not notice it....Yes, he got off at the foot of the trail...Yes, I'm sure...but you know it's the strangest thing...," the conductor said getting back to the pack, "I can remember the space where his pack had been being empty when the train pulled away, and for some time afterwards...but it's the strangest thing," the conductor repeated shaking his head, "I know you're not going to believe this...but when the train pulled into the station that evening, that guy's pack was back in the baggage car, in exactly the same spot....Yes, the pack is still at the train station...no one has claimed it."

After going with Troopers to airlift the body, Vince and Theon teleported back to the woods from Vince's place in town. The day had warmed up nicely, and the group of friends took up comfortable positions in the sun on Rahlys' front porch. Tomorrow Ilene and Theon were returning to town. Ilene's four-day camping trip and Theon's millennia long wait to confront Droclum were over. Father and daughter enjoyed the warmth of the weakening sun, both in deep contemplative thought, quietly absorbing the peace of the woods.

Maggie and Vince sat with their backs against the warm cabin wall, their faces glowing softly with contentment. By Thanksgiving, they would be parents…but for now they were lovers without a care in the world, lazing in the sunshine.

Melinda and Raven played at the foot of the steps. Rahlys had provided Melinda with two apples, one for her, and one for their feathered friend. Melinda couldn't resist taunting the raven for a bit with her control of the treat before giving it to him.

The oncoming fall colors glowed cheerfully around them in the warm late summer sun. Golden patches of leaves triggered by cool nights gave the birch trees a mottled look. Beneath the trembling green and gold canopy, the blushing red underbrush spilled out to the edge of the forest. Ripe red rose hips beckoned where, seemingly so recently, rose blossoms had unfurled. Plump reddish-purple wine-filled watermelon berries dangled from fragile pale stems with yellow leaves, and the leaves of the seeded-out fireweed formed a hardy mosaic of brown, yellow, red, and green. But the most brilliant splashes of color were the high bush cranberry bushes dominating the underbrush with dazzling red leaves as red as the berries themselves that weighed down their heavily laden branches.

"I would like to call a meeting of the Order of the Oracle while we are all gathered together," Rahlys said breaking the silence. The assembled group nodded in agreement at the designation. The crystal, which had been hovering stationary, zoomed around, anointing them with sparkle.

"The Order of the Oracle!" Ilene said mystified.

"It will be an honor to serve," Theon approved, and bowed respectfully.

"And for the first item on the agenda," Rahlys continued, "I propose that we discuss Melinda's education." There were looks of pleasant surprise, but no objections.

"That's a wonderful idea," Maggie seconded. Vince nodded his head in agreement, and Raven squawked his approval. Melinda was for anything that supported the concept of her remaining in the woods with

Rahlys and the rest of the group. School would be starting in the out-side world, but they couldn't register Melinda, even for home school-ing, without providing records.

"The education of a new person is a community responsibility, and the Order of the Oracle is Melinda's community. Each of us should participate in nurturing and teaching her based on our interests and abilities," Rahlys explained. There were no protests.

"I could teach her language arts," Vince volunteered, "since I'm a writer."

"I'll take home economics." Maggie had been actively pursuing the homemaker's arts, from canning fish to making blueberry jam, since arriving in Alaska. "Classes can start tomorrow. We will be making high bush cranberry ketchup."

"I'll take social studies," Theon offered. "I know a lot about Earth's history and geography."

Raven projected images of him and Melinda playing outdoors through the seasons. "Raven will take physical education," Rahlys filled in for him, and I'll take art."

"I'm good at math," Ilene finally spoke up when she was the last one left.

Super! Melinda smiled radiantly over the idea of going to school in the woods and having the members of the Order as her teachers.

"Very good. Then all we are lacking is science and music, but we have enough subjects to get started." Rahlys summed up. Then Theon spoke up again.

"I'm pretty sure I could teach some basic science, too. After all, I'm not that busy." Everyone looked at Theon in surprise. Quaylyn was not present, but they felt certain he would approve.

"And I played the flute in high school," Ilene volunteered.

"We could set up the guest cabin as a school room, providing an area to lay out school projects, and a quiet place to do homework and study," Maggie suggested.

Rahlys conjured paper and pencil to the porch, and the members of the Order of the Oracle worked out a schedule together. Rahlys watched them, smiling contentedly to herself as they laughed and joked together, excited about their new project. She had come to the woods, longing for isolation, she mused.

She had found an extended family instead.